The Burnchester Dome and the Sacred Cell

The Burnchester Dome and the Sacred Cell
is the second part of an evolving story and the sequel to
The Mysterious Burnchester Hall

The Burnchester Dome and the Sacred Cell

Dominic Miéville

D
M

DM
Productions

Published by DM PRODUCTIONS
PO Box 218 IP22 1QY United Kingdom

Copyright © 2005 Dominic Miéville

First impression March 2005

The right of Dominic Miéville to be recognised as the author
of this work has been asserted in accordance with the Copyright, Designs and
Patents Act 1988

British Library Cataloguing in Publication Data
A Catalogue record of this book is available from
The British Library

ISBN 0 953 6161 4 2
ISBN 0 953 6161 5 0 (Adult cover version)

Cover design and typesetting by Luke Florio
Set in Palatino

Printed in Great Britain by
The St Edmundsbury Press Limited
Bury St Edmunds, Suffolk IP33 3TZ

To Pamela and Sophie

and to all seekers
Deo concedente

I

"What was that all about?" shouted Tyro, as she burst out of class for break.

"Don't you remember?" said Jess, hurrying alongside.

"Of course I remember! How could I forget? Taking precautions is one thing, but this is ridiculous," she added. "Fancy cancelling Bonfire night."

Tyro had lost none of her impatience, but was not going to give in to those feelings that had come back to her.

"It's a long way off. They'll probably change their minds," said Jess, ever the diplomat. She had been there too.

"We're not allowed to do anything any more! They'll be cancelling holidays and Christmas soon!" shouted Tyro, as she stormed off. Tyro had changed. They all had. The innocence had gone.

Occasionally Tyro would have a nightmare about the figures and the underground tunnels. The face of the injured Mr Gruff would appear to her out of nowhere and haunt her dreams. There were odd times when the three of them would talk over events, but these were intermittent. They were wary of too much getting out. They were the subject of enough scepticism and scorn already. It is surprising how popularity can soon turn sour, especially when jealousy is in the mix. Especially when the power you thought you had seemed no longer yours.

The list of restrictions was growing. There were guards at

the main school gate. Once inside, it was impossible to leave school without a parent or a teacher. More places were out of bounds. The old boathouse on the river; the river itself. The woods by the river were like another country. The school grounds had been marked with red markers. Anyone who went beyond this line would be suspended or kept within the main area of school buildings for the rest of term. Nobody could go cross-country running over the bridge to Folly Ridge. As for boarders going out at night, that was out of the question. Worst of all were the journalists who sometimes stalked the school, pretending to be lost, hoping to get some inside information about the stories which had now become part of local myth.

Julia, Tyro's enemy, made things worse.

"Where are you going?" Julia snarled. "It's you who caused the problem in the first place!"

Julia was the Headmaster's daughter, and had been fuelling rumours that Tyro had been the cause of all the restrictions. The fact that others - Jess, Rick, not to mention Tom, Mr Gruff (the caretaker) and her parents - had been intimately involved in "events" meant nothing to her. Julia was good at exacting revenge, for no good reason. In fact she was good at pre-empting revenge, for no good reason.

"I warn you, Julia! Stay off my back!" Tyro shouted.

The school yard buzzed. Small groups gathered in corners under the shelter of the large yew beside the main drive, against the wind, in secret cabals. Who was in with/going out with who? Fashion, music, boys/girls, had, for many, replaced play and TV. School gossip reigned. The myths were becoming embedded and would become glorified in new language.

Boys kicked a football across the yard, satchels were strewn on the ground. The laughter and running made things seem normal. But they could no longer be. Beyond them were the security gates, now operated throughout the day. The beautiful Elizabethan mansion that formed the main building of the school, Burnchester Hall, had become more like a prison.

Its majestic grounds and outbuildings and the whole expanse of fields that led to the river, where the old boathouse was hidden, were nothing but an alien backdrop.

Above them, high on the tower, like an electronic eye, a camera swayed mechanically.

The yews also seemed to keep watch, like huge guards beside the church of St Mary Magdalen, the school chapel. Like centurions guarding the forbidden king.

*

Tyro and Jess made towards the changing room.

Jess wished that it had never happened. She did her best to erase it from her mind. She did not seek adventure. She did not feel compelled in the way that Tyro did. She wondered where it would lead. Tyro's compulsive behaviour frightened her.

Yet now "events" were becoming remote. If it hadn't been for the others, and the practical changes in the school - the outside effects - she might have forgotten about what she had seen. For her there were no nightmares. And yet she too had been in the presence of Darkness, she too had experienced the Other Side. And she had experienced flying, which was beyond her ability to understand, so she denied it to herself.

Tyro and Jess entered the changing room.

"I hate Julia. She blames me for everything," said Tyro, half angry, half in despair. She was looking in her sports bag for the homework that she hadn't been able to find. The changing rooms were a safe place to talk.

"I feel like running away. I hate all this. What have we done to make us so hated, yet so envied? I tell you, Jess, I'm going to disappear. Will you come?"

Some eerie premonition caught Jess off guard. There was a moment's pause.

"Ignore Julia. She's just jealous. All we can do is stay alert.

Stick to the rules but stay alert."

"Why stick to the rules? If we'd stuck to the rules we would never have found out."

"Are you expecting something to happen to us?"

"You didn't answer my question!" said Tyro.

"About what?"

"About coming with me if I decide to disappear."

Tyro hated being pushy with her best friend, yet it was part of her character. The wilfulness that made her shout back at her mother, who was trying her best in difficult circumstances; that made her stand up to teachers, when she should be quiet; that made her get caught up in things.

"I think something is bound to happen. Even with all the precautions. In fact I think the precautions might make it more likely," Tyro said.

"My father says that you can never be sure - however careful you are. You can only do so much," said Jess. "Of course I'd come with you."

The mention of Jess's father made Tyro feel inadequate. Her father was dead. However much she tried to get used to it, she couldn't, and it caused her terrible pain. It haunted her.

"Thanks, Jess. We must meet up with Rick and Tom. I need a plan, something. We can't go on carrying this burden on our backs forever, without action or sharing. Come on, let's go to class."

Tyro felt primed. Meeting the others would help. They had been virtually banned from doing so, as it might create suspicion. But they couldn't stop them, could they? It would have to be in secret.

Mr Rummage had indicated to them that they would have a special role. He hadn't said anything more. Perhaps he had forgotten. He had said he would tell them more when the moment was right.

"I can't find my prep. Mr Roberts is going to throw a wobbly."

Tyro and Jess made their way back to the main teaching block.

Mr Rummage, the Headmaster, stood watching as the girls and boys hurried in. He watched Tyro and Jess appear, then disappear into the building. He was standing with Mr Baxter, the English teacher, and Ms Peverell, who taught Art. Mr Roberts had gone in a few minutes before and was already in class.

"How's Tyro's drawing?" Mr Rummage asked.

Ms Peverell took her time to answer. When she did, it was in a playful and slightly understated tone. Mr Rummage listened and watched at the same time. One of the guards at the gate, over and above to the left, seemed to be having an animated discussion with a visitor. A journalist, he thought. Would that all visitors entered by the main gate, and in daylight. He thought of the the subterranean world not far below. Silent, unexplored. Alive. Some of the secrets he was aware of; others were to be discovered. The world below seemed endless.

"A little erratic. Unusual though."

Mr Rummage looked at Ms Peverell, his mind elsewhere, though his question had not been entirely perfunctory. He glanced at Mr Baxter, who remained impassive.

Mr Rummage looked about him. Even now he could see them, in his mind's eye, the figures that had come from nowhere and had gone as quickly. He was doing his best to hide a deep and growing anxiety. The "virus" was there, but invisible. It would come back, stronger, more virulent, and spread. When, how and where he could not know.

The once smooth skin of a benign young face (as his wife had described him) was cracking. And yet, week five and the pressure of the new year had begun to subside. The changes that had been put in place had gone quite smoothly. Security is normally welcome in times of trouble. He had introduced new rules and new staff with relative calm. He had managed

5

so far to reassure parents, even though his main task was still to come. He was planning a meeting. He was also planning for eventualities. Especially for Tyro, Jess and Rick. Tom had disappeared.

The Ministry had warned him. The signs were potent. The moment was approaching.

Mr Rummage often wondered if he'd got the balance right between freedom and security. He had a duty to both, but he was never happy with the balance. He believed freedom to be a vital component in any child's upbringing, as it was to the democratic life. More and more these days it was difficult to develop. More and more children were no longer children. They needed myth and fantasy. They needed play. Not the manic bombardment of the mediocre and profane, which swamped them nightly on their television screens, in the guise of a suspect reality, claiming to be cautionary if not reassuring. With the events of last term, and the actions he had been forced to take - by the governors, the police, and even the military - he had become more fatalistic. This was the price of the school's history, which was still unravelling. His responsibility was growing. More and more he needed answers to unsolved mysteries, the first clues to which had tantalised him out of despondency.

His basic instincts were positive. The team that he was forming made him confident. Nothing would allow him to abandon his mission. The underground stream could never run dry. He would never give in.

"Do you think we should offer something in return?" Mr Rummage asked Mr Baxter.

"A trip somewhere. To Stratford."

"How about the National Gallery?" said Ms Peverell.

"I don't think Stratford is quite the same thing as Bonfire Night. Nor is the National Gallery."

"I don't know," said Mr Baxter as he moved towards the classrooms. "Might fit in well with Macbeth. 'There's no Art to find the mind's construction in the face.' 'The play's the thing' after all."

With that Mr Baxter, who always carried a mask with him, left, briefcase in hand.

Mr Rummage turned to the young Art teacher. He was aware of the friendship between herself and Mr Baxter.

"I don't suppose he's referring to the triptych," Mr Rummage said.

These were some of Mr Baxter's favourite expressions. Sometimes when there was an opportunity to comment on the discrepancies between image and behaviour - which wasn't rare - he would quote them. It was as if he wanted to remind his audience of what it already knew, but hadn't found the words. Most people took it as one of his calling cards, and accepted it lightly. Some didn't understand it at all, or misconstrued it, or thought it didn't apply to them. Not unlike the seed in the parable of the sower.

Even the Biology teacher, Mrs Limpet, had agreed, especially in recent months. Mrs Limpet had gone a bit funny. She, the exemplary professional of many years, reliable if not popular, had begun to lose control some months before and had to take temporary leave on her doctor's advice, though the doctor's diagnosis was equivocal. She had apparently taken to drink following her divorce and then the death of her husband, which itself had not been without ambiguity. Some suggested she had begun to drink long before his death. Certainly her nerves had worsened; she had become irritable, manic, occasionally cruel. One might have said haunted. She had been tempted by the devil, one had said. Tyro and Jess, who were perhaps in the best position to comment, having found her that summer evening at the back of the Biology lab, with rat's teeth deep in her flesh, said nothing. Mrs Limpet's piercing eyes were not forgotten by Tyro. Her haunted face made her shiver, and angry. It was the haunting of unfulfilled dreams as much as fear.

Mr Baxter never used such phrases about the children. He was an adept at judging character and, interested in the benign arts, would sometimes bear down heavily on bad behaviour, but never used that phrase about them. Was it because children were somehow more honest, despite being no less capable of lying and manipulation? Or was this the willed fiction of adulthood, the old projection of the corrupted onto the innocent? Perhaps the masks of the Gods had not been sufficiently formed in the young or taken up residence as surely as they would in time. Mr Baxter watched the dance between the Gods within, and the face without. The moral arbiter, where present, would try to orchestrate the struggle, often in vain. Who would win? The game was evolving as man entered a new era, and would take different mythological forms. The new rules had not been forged.

Ms Peverell enjoyed the vicarious pleasure of hearing the Headmaster repeat the phrases.

"No, but painting, like literature, contains truths, which have the capacity to illuminate, as we have found with Burnchester's own immaculate church painting," she said. Ms Peverell was thinking of the immaculate conception, something she didn't think was likely to happen to her.

The pre-Reformation painting in the Church of St Mary Magdalen was reputed to be one of the most important medieval paintings in England.

Mr Rummage was silent.

"Has the fragment been analysed yet?" she asked.

Mr Rummage looked at her blankly, as if to imply that certain subjects should not be spoken about aloud. It wasn't so much that "walls have ears", he felt, more that the entire place, inside and out, might be "bugged", which might have been nearer the truth than he realised. Security can have the reverse effect, and tempt treachery more than openness. Then he smiled. He knew how close she was to Mr Baxter.

"It is being examined by experts at the moment. Curious

8

that it should be found by a farmer whilst ploughing a field, don't you think? In a way, I wish we hadn't found it, though its authenticity is still to be proven."

"And if it is authentic. Will it lead to . . . ?" Ms Peverell's voice faded. She could not mention the Spearhead of Destiny, the object of great power, whose location might cryptically be revealed in the symbolism depicted on the lost fragment of the rim of the painting. The fragment now possibly found.

Mr Rummage didn't answer. He wasn't certain of the exact nature of the Spearhead, whether it was a literal object or a complex symbol, or both. That there was likely to be a physical thing he felt sure, just like the Holy Grail was by some supposed, amongst other deeper things, to be the Cup. One of its uses was that it forced seekers into the open, even enemies who wanted it for their own ends. The Priory was perhaps most keen. Somewhere in the equation he felt sure of the presence of the Order of the Magdalene.

Mr Rummage looked about him, at the guards by the main gate, at the tower in the main school building which was being used as a lookout by security. Hidden cameras scanned the school's domain. Searching for movement: for the appearance of the figures, for the return of the Stranger. Day and Night. The tower had once been used as a watch tower by Isaac Newton. Mr Rummage thought of Bonfire Night. Was he mad to cancel it? It could be policed, after all.

"Do you think that some knowledge brings more trouble than it's worth?" asked Ms Peverell, returning to the fragment.

Mr Rummage looked at her.

Ms Peverell walked across to the Art building, which offered a sanctity of sorts from the depravities of the intellect. It was covered in pupils' work. The walls, the cupboard, the notice board, even part of the ceiling and the back of the door were covered in pictures. Ms Peverell made a point of seeking expression through colour as well as design; technique as well as flair. Discipline wasn't enough, but was essential. Children used art as a release. In it they could play, experiment, let go, fail and still be complimented. She kept Tyro's most recent work in a drawer. It was excellent if confused. Ms Peverell sometimes wondered whether the whole school couldn't become one big Art Room.

Mr Rummage walked over to the school entrance. Built in the Elizabethan era, on the site of an older building. Moved into by Sir Cheesepeake in 1597. 1547 was also a critical year. The date was never far from his mind. Somehow it was crucial, but the clues were scattered, the insights incomplete. Stay alert. It was only that way that he could begin to see the whole. He stood back from himself and examined the school motto: "Deo Concedente" ("According to the Will of God").

*

The Maths lesson was boring. Tyro liked the idea of Maths, but lessons were different. She looked out of the classroom window and saw an empty sky. A couple of weeks before the telephone line had been filled with swallows. Now they were no longer there. Maths, lunch, Biology, then English. Tyro thought of France. They hadn't met their new Biology teacher yet. Mrs Limpet's replacement had only recently arrived. They were behind. Mrs Limpet had locked Tyro up in the cupboard at the back of the Biology room. She had gone mad. Serves her right. It was always good to round off the day with English. It had only been recently that she had begun to read.

Mr Baxter made her laugh. He was an actor. To her surprise Tyro found poetry particularly absorbing. This she kept to herself, just as she did her diary. Not for the consumption of her friends. It might give Julia fuel, as she read so much. It doesn't do to like poetry.

She thought of home. More and more she looked forward to home. Yet she dreamed of other places too, of journeys. The new rules made her want to escape more. She could cope with the security, not the restriction. Flying. Father, Aunt Jane. Her mother. She imagined getting a detention. Why was she always getting into trouble? What this time? Or was that before? She became confused. She would be late. Should she phone home, or just make her own way back? She knew the roads well. Forget the new rules. No, stupid. Her mother would come early and then wait! No need to phone at all.

Mr Roberts droned on in front of the blackboard. He was doing some geometry on the board. He was alright.

Tyro tried to make the triangle into the mammoth that Jess had drawn when she and Jess had visited the school during the summer holidays. That had been the beginning. They had come into the classroom. Jess had pretended to be Mrs Rachel and drawn the great hairy beast with huge curvaceous tusks on the blackboard, signifying a test. If she looked carefully she imagined she might see the traces of the mammoth still (even though it was a different room). The thing she remembered most about flying was not the flight itself, but the ability to see things close up from afar, things that might not be visible on the ground. She remembered the knock at the door while Jess was doing her impersonation, and the panic that ensued only to find that it was Rick, who wasn't supposed to be there either. Rick, Tom, Jess and herself.

They had gone into the Biology lab and found Mrs Limpet. She had stared at Tyro from some distant evil place. How could she forget? Why should she forget? Why was she drawn?

Rick was scribbling a note to pass to Tyro.

"What are you smiling at, Tyro? If it's that funny, we'd all like to hear." Mr Roberts's voice spilled across the room.

Mr Roberts had become edgy.

"Sorry Mr Roberts, I wasn't with it."

"She's never with it," came a familiar voice.

There was laughter. Tyro turned and stared.

"Shut up, Julia!"

"Tyro! Come and see me after the lesson! I won't have that

sort of attitude!"

"But, Mr Roberts! It wasn't me who . . . "

Tyro looked at Mr Roberts as she said this. Something made her recoil. Something about Mr Roberts's stare made her shiver. It was as if she was looking at somebody else.

Mr Roberts was not going to let this one go.

"Have you done your homework, Tyro?

"No, Sir. At least . . . well . . . "

"That's not acceptable, Tyro. I shall inform the Headmaster and your parents. Answer the question on the board!"

Tyro tried to focus. She fought against her drifting mind. Help me, someone! She turned to Jess and glared. She caught sight of Julia. It was the relish in her face which gave her the strength.

"It's a golden mean, Sir."

"Ummm!" mumbled Mr Roberts grudgingly. "If you can answer that without paying attention, think what you would do if you did."

"If she'd paid attention she wouldn't have got it right, Sir!"

"That's enough! If anybody answers that, the whole class comes in after school!"

Tyro had a premonition.

Mr Roberts's head turned as he looked around the class until he reached Rick. Then Mr Roberts stopped. Rick was still scribbling. He might as well not have been in the class at all. He stopped and tried to hide the piece of paper. The class could see it.

The class waited nervously.

"I'll have that, Rick, thank you!" Mr Roberts bawled as he moved over to where Rick was sitting.

"What, Sir? I haven't got anything, Sir!"

"Then you won't mind showing me your hand then. Give it here!"

"But it's private, Sir. You shouldn't look at what's private, Sir."

"Don't you dare tell me what I don't have a right to see, Rick! Never speak to me like that again! It is you who are in the wrong. You who have something in your hand when you shouldn't. You who are holding the class up!"

"All right, Sir. All right!"

Mr Roberts turned and looked at the class. The normally gentle face of Mr Roberts was red with fury. He glared in uncontrolled rage. Rage that had come out of nowhere. Over the top. How come teachers were allowed to do this, when they weren't? It wasn't right.

"It is time you people learnt some manners. Yes, manners. Manners and discipline. Give me that piece of paper!"

Rick held out his hand. The teacher took it and began to unfold it.

"Please don't, Sir. It's private!"

Mr Roberts held the piece of paper up and unfolded it carefully. Without glancing at the writing, he held the piece against his teeth, both hands at the top edge. Then with a dramatic downward swing he ripped the page in two.

"The whole class will stay in after school. I expect all of you here at 4.15. No questions!"

Tyro knew this was going to happen.

"But, Sir!" It was David, Mr Roberts's favourite.

"I can't, Sir! I've got a dentist's appointment at 4.30 and my parents are coming early to pick me up."

David sat in the front row, and had never uttered a word of defiance in his life.

The teacher walked to the back of the class. He was enjoying this.

Tyro caught a glimpse of Jess's face, and then the furious accusing stare from Julia. She, and now Rick, were in trouble again. The note was surely for her. And the term so young. She tried to look concerned, but felt the anger rise up, to counter her tears. She looked at the board.

Things were beginning to go badly wrong. Mr Roberts had

definitely lost it. Why was it always her? She would fight this, as she fought everything else.

*

At lunch, everyone surrounded Rick and Tyro. Julia led the attack. They were waiting in the noisy dining room queue, where the rattle of cutlery, the sound of talking, laughing and shouting rose and fell, checked by the occasional admonition of a teacher. Tyro and Jess were in front. A lady was trying to serve Tyro. She ignored Julia.

Another friend, Sabia, stood behind them, and then David, the quiet one who everyone ignored, but secretly admired, because he was too innocent to know when he was being teased, and who was very generous in lending everyone his prep. As he was normally top of the class, this meant that the class itself did rather better than the teachers, who had seen them develop over the years, expected, as they were lazy, if bright. "They're not lazy for me," Mr Rafferty, the Classics teacher, said confidently.

Mr Rafferty was of the old school and ruled with an iron fist. He didn't allow the slightest murmur in his lessons. He lined the pupils outside the door, in military fashion, before going in. He was tiny, like many dictators. He loved rote learning. His results were mixed.

Parents who were a little unimaginative in their assessment thought Mr Rafferty was an example of traditional teaching at its best. Mr Rafferty had discipline problems of his own, though nobody knew about these, certainly not the parents. The pupils were too afraid to speak and he hid them from himself. The problem for Mr Rummage was that Mr Rafferty was an expert in his subject, and beneath the surface was a vulnerable colleague, who needed help.

Mr Baxter's style was more relaxed. One or two exploited his easy style, but generally he was a master of control.

Discipline problems tended to be self-defeating, exposing the perpetrators to his verbal scalpel. Parents were prepared to allow that English was a little different, though none would have enjoyed the word subversive. Yet who could read Blake seriously and think otherwise? For that matter, who could read the New Testament and not think so?

Julia sat on the same table as Tyro, along from her. Tyro was next to Jess, another girl called Lori, and Rick opposite. Rick was next to a boy called Harry, who was a great sportsman, and didn't like girls much. Underneath he was shy, but to most of the class his sporting talent gave him the veneer of confidence.

"Don't worry about it," said Rick to Tyro. "Roberts is losing it, like Limpet did. We'll have to keep an eye on him!"

"It's fine for you to say that, Rick, but it's just as much your fault as that girl's," hissed Julia along and across the table.

Lori, normally implacable, turned to Julia.

"Stop whinging, Julia. One day it may be you."

"Cut it out, Lori! She's too good to be true," said a voice in an undertone, loud enough for Julia to hear. She thought it was Tyro.

"You would say that, you of no name. You who never do your own prep, and are always in trouble. Next time they'll expel you! I'll see to it."

Tyro turned to look at Julia, and was about to speak, when someone interrupted her.

"I said it, not Tyro. It's true, Julia. Why are you so bloody perfect? I'm surprised you're not Head Girl already. In fact, I'm surprised you're not Headmaster. Why not ask your father?" said Sabia, sitting nearby.

Rick laughed.

"I can't help it that I'm . . . " Julia paused, lost for the right words. "I am who I am."

"So am I," Tyro said.

The truth was that Julia was thought to be the ideal

15

candidate, even by many of the girls and boys, which put her father in a difficult position.

Rick was still chuckling. He was imagining Julia as Headmaster.

He was thinking of Hallowe'en. And Bonfire Night.

"Julia's quite right," said Jane, Julia's friend who sat between her and Rick, "we're all suffering because you two got us into trouble. It's you two who should be punished, not the whole class."

Tyro looked at Rick, Rick at Julia. No amount of anger could prevent her from fancying him a little. Tyro was quite aware of it, but was not jealous, not yet anyway. She had other things on her mind. Not least Tom, who had not returned to school this term. Where had he gone? It was important they find him. He had been there too, was one of the four. She liked Tom, though it was not a fancying kind of like. She decided to find out more about him. She needed him to be part of the plan.

"Call this spaghetti, do they? Dead snakes, more like." David said.

There was a sudden commotion. Everyone went quiet. Heads turned towards the door, knives and forks slowed. Teachers at the heads of tables leant forward.

Mr Rummage had entered. Though popular, he was also at times feared. He had that rare ability to let the children know where boundaries were and when they could or could not be crossed. There were those who no doubt hated him, but they didn't dare show their faces, watching carefully for their chance.

The Headmaster walked into the room. He stood at the head of the top table, nearest the older pupils, and some of the teachers. A new History teacher, Mr Vespers, seemed preoccupied. After a word with Mrs Rachel he turned to face the school. It was very rare for Mr Rummage to interrupt lunch, as there were plenty of opportunities for giving out notices in daily assembly. He tapped the table with a spoon and waited.

"I won't keep you long," he began. "I have a couple of important notices. Then you can carry on with your gourmet lunch."

This raised a murmur, half in outrage, half in appreciation, though not all the pupils knew what gourmet meant.

The chef, who was looking on, seemed pleased.

"You 'ave ze best food of any school I 'ave ever been to," he confirmed, as if to himself, doing as little dance on the spot by the kitchen door.

The murmuring subsided into a ripple of approval.

"First. As you all know, we have changed the way day boys and girls are collected from school. The driveway was getting too blocked and the whole business was taking up too much time. But it is no good your parents remembering if you forget. Please remember the changes. Check with your teachers, check with the notice board. Details are also in each classroom. They are important. In fact they are very important. Is that understood?"

The Headmaster looked around the room.

"With the evenings drawing in, and the weather worsening, it is essential that these rules are followed. I would remind you of the reason for this: it is not, as rumours tell you, a matter only of security. We are very concerned with that of course. But we also want to make the process more efficient. We do not have the space for all parents to arrive at the same time, and the school buses have been increased which adds to the congestion."

"Two. Biology lessons start today. Therefore class 8B will go to the Biology class, as normal. Mrs Moffat is taking over from Mrs Limpet while Mrs Limpet is away. She is very good. We are lucky to have her. You will learn a great deal from her."

The children were getting a bit bored. Some were beginning to scrape plates and rattle knifes. A few began to cough. The Headmaster was aware of it.

"And lastly the good news." The rattling ceased. Total

silence. The Headmaster waited. He looked around.

"Is the pudding ready, chef?"

M Le Petit, late of the Burnchester Arms, for it was he, nodded.

"As you know, we have banned the celebration of Hallowe'en in school this year. I have explained my reasons. We have banned all costumes. No masks, cloaks, witches' costumes, nothing that could frighten or annoy. Some of the younger children are especially vulnerable. Nor will there be any "trick-or-treating". I would rather we recognised the ancient significance of All Souls. If you don't know about All Souls, ask your teacher.

"What you do at home is of course up to you, though it was parents who asked us to ban it in school, so I guess there won't be much "trick-or-treating" at home this year either."

There were the beginnings of a murmur. Mr Rummage raised his hands.

"However, I have some good news."

The murmur stopped.

"I have changed my mind about the other ritual celebration."

All eyes on the Headmaster.

Mr Rummage waited.

He looked around the room.

"Bonfire Night will take place as usual," he said, very quietly.

He was about to add, "With one or two extra details . . . " but he could not be heard.

The Headmaster's voice was drowned in cheers and shouting. Harry stood up and cheered. Others stamped their feet. Knives clattered. Teachers at the heads of tables did their best to preserve the peace. The Headmaster rode it well, but seeing the dismay creep over the faces of his staff, who continued to try to settle them, he held up his hand.

More cheering.

He spread his hands horizontally. The shouting began to

stop. The Headmaster looked as if he was going to speak again. Silence.

He looked at the chef and walked towards the door to the kitchens.

He cast an eye towards his daughter Julia (but without singling her out) and his son Simon (who sat at another table) and at others, including Tyro, Jess and Rick.

He sometimes wondered whether his presence could have been the cause of Tyro's dislike of his daughter, as her father was no longer alive. A father he had known well, though Tyro did not know this.

He had meant to remind pupils to ignore anyone, especially journalists, who asked questions about the school.

*

Everywhere uncertainty grew, just as the waters of the river Dean were rising. Papers were full of stories . . . it was not just within or near the confines of the school, though the stakes here might be higher. The school could no longer remain an isolated bastion, as he would see it, of civilisation against the growing barbarism. Hidden in the depth of the countryside, a world without the world, the keeper at the gate of another wisdom, couched in what others might call rural exclusion. There were very many other schools and other institutions working with the same purpose, though here their resources were unique.

He was deeply aware of the risks in Bonfire Night, but had been assured by others that with the right planning and precautions it could be controlled. He had his doubts, though on the face of it Hallowe'en posed a greater threat. There were other reasons for allowing Guy Fawkes Night to go ahead.

He would ask Mr Granger, the new gardener, to build the fire up high. He wanted the flames to reach the sky, and the fireworks to be better than ever. There was something in the timing of the event, the correspondences in play and the energies he had been monitoring, that made him anxious, yet primed too. It might offer hope through potential uncertainty. He felt the pain of the children's destiny. He could use Bonfire Night as a run up to the Great Celebration that was to take place next year, for which he had long been planning. He only hoped that events would not take over and cause havoc, just at the very point when the flames were at their highest.

2

Class 8B were everything that Mrs Moffat had expected: excitable and a little too hasty to show what they knew. For this reason, after introducing herself and getting each pupil to give out his or her name, she gave them a little test, just to "get an idea of what you know." The class settled into the quietest twenty minutes that they had had for most of the year.

Mrs Moffat was tall and slim. Her hair was blonde and short. She wore glasses which gave her a distant look, adding to a sense of reserved austerity which made Tyro feel that she was older than she was. Yes, she could work with Mrs Moffat. She could sense that she was very different from Mrs Limpet. She would do her best to get on with her, despite her earlier defiant mood.

Tyro opened Rick's note beneath the desktop. "Meet after school, gym. With Jess. Rick."

Tyro looked up towards Rick, who had turned to catch her eye, and mouthed the word "detention".

"Anything the matter, er, you there in the back row? Tyro, isn't it?"

"No, Mrs Moffat. Nothing."

Mrs Moffat returned to her desk and continued working on her notes. She looked at her watch.

She could always skip detention.

Mrs Moffat got up and went to the front of the class, towards the door which led into the preparation room, where Mrs Limpet had locked Tyro.

When she reached the door, she opened it wide.

As she walked round the class again, she cast her eyes at the answer papers. The usual array of the neat and the scrawling. She smiled inwardly. Her own writing was, like other academics', pretty bad. She cast her mind back a moment to her students at Cambridge. What was she letting herself in for, coming to a school like this? To a school at all? Mr Rummage had been persuasive. The opportunity that he was offering her was unique, so she decided to accept, though only for the rest of the school year - up to the celebration. The school was, after all, rather more than a school.

Mrs Moffat looked more closely at some answer papers, pointing to where there were mistakes or omissions, blotches, crossings-out, with the eye of an unbiased observer, as much as a teacher. She bent down and whispered suggestions when necessary. Mrs Moffat managed to calm the class simply by walking around.

When she reached the back of the class she stood next to the door. To her left the window overlooked the school yard. Across the way was the main teaching block.

Other classes were in progress. In one classroom, hands were held high as a teacher - Mr Vespers, the new History teacher - was standing behind the desk, obviously asking questions. A young class. So much enthusiasm. Everywhere enthusiasm, energy, sometimes misdirected, normally benign, and essentially creative. She looked away. When she looked back, the class was quiet and the teacher was standing over them. He suddenly looked rather malign. It was like watching a film. The children were frightened. Children can be so difficult.

Mr Rummage had hinted that there had been change. What was going wrong, she wondered? Mrs Limpet, she had learned, had broken down.

In the next room along, another class was writing, another test perhaps. She could not see the teacher's face.

Round the corner came a group of pupils in sports gear.

Her class looked up and someone gave a subdued whistle. They watched some of their friends struggling towards the changing rooms after PE, with Mr Bellevue.

Mrs Moffat looked again at her watch. She looked round the room.

Another whistle went up, this time more aggressive. Perhaps it was more of a sigh. Next to the window stood Mr Gruff with his new assistant, Mr Grudge, bigger than Mr Gruff, and nastier looking. He carried a stick. There was no Titan, Mr Gruff's loyal dog. Mr Gruff had lost Titan in the holidays in a tragic accident, the pupils had been told. Most of the children thought he deserved it for being so nasty.

"Stop writing," Mrs Moffat said.

Some of the boys had already stopped and tried not to look bored. Some of the girls continued to write, including Tyro and Julia. Jess had finished minutes ago, and was checking everything through.

"While John is collecting your papers," Mrs Moffat said, "I want to draw your attention to the open door - the door that leads into the preparation room. I don't want anyone going in there. Not without my permission."

John gets up with a shuffle. John is big and brawny, and no fool. He is the class fall-guy. Harry can't resist a "nice one John!" Even Mrs Moffat smiles - yes, the class is going to get on with her. She has noticed everything. The preparation room door opens onto a patch of dark. One or two are uncomfortable, so Mrs Moffat switches on the light.

"Thank you, John," she says. "On the desk please. I have three things to say. Mrs Limpet was a very good biologist. She has been unwell and is taking time off. In case any of you had other ideas, ask yourself if you have ever had time off for being unwell."

"It's called bunking off!"

"That will do, Harry. I want you to remember that. I am here to teach you Biology, and to encourage you to enjoy it. We've got some catching up to do, but with your support we'll make up the lost time. If you try hard you will be rewarded. But if you break the rules, my rules, I will come down hard on you. Is that understood?"

"But Miss!" It is Rick.

"Another time, Rick. Please. If you forget your books, you will not be marked, and that will count in the end of term results. Your parents will of course also be told. Don't forget your books."

The gloss is already beginning to wear off. It's always the same, thinks Tyro. Why can't teachers ever chill out?

"I repeat. The preparation room is strictly out of bounds. One or two of you have been in there recently" (she does not look at anybody in particular) "without permission, and this led to unfortunate consequences."

"Tell us, Miss. Is there a mystery?" asks Harry.

"There's no mystery. At the back of the prep room there is another door - which most of you will not know about - a door which leads below ground into the school . . . tunnels. They form an important part of the history of the school. You might ask your History teacher about them. Otherwise I will tell you myself if we have time. It is important that you learn about them. It will soon be time for secrecy to be over."

Mrs Moffat looks around the room. Tyro and Jess are looking at her.

"In time I will take you down there myself. For the moment the doors are locked and alarmed. If you try to go in and are caught, you will be severely punished. However, before you leave the class you may look into the room at the sealed door, if you wish."

"Miss?"

"Yes, Jane?"

"Why are you telling us this, Miss?"

Mrs Moffat didn't answer.

"You may come forward. One row at a time. If you do not wish to, you may leave. Quietly!"

There was a scramble. Chairs scraping, one or two falling over, pupils being shoved into the sides of the desk. A few went to look into the prep room. Several pupils, including John, left without bothering. What had the preparation room to do with him? It was where they killed frogs and rats. Smelly chemicals lined the walls. An unmentionable odour of death. No way! He wanted nothing to do with it.

Tyro, Jess and Rick stood in the doorway. They could feel the force. It was a force that all the children felt, though in different degrees. It was this that Mrs Moffat had meant them to experience. She wondered why not all the children were drawn to it. Julia was there, behind the others.

Before leaving class, Tyro wanted to thank Mrs Moffat, but couldn't bring herself to. It wouldn't do to be seen to be thanking a teacher. She was getting too old for that. Yet at the bottom of the briefcase she still carried a small metal cross-sword. It was something her father had given her as a young child. It had been plastic then. It had mysteriously become metal. She hadn't believed in magic, and still found it difficult, though she had experienced a new reality. Much of it came back in dreams, "noughtmares" as she called them. She couldn't even admit to the strangest and most impossible experience of her holiday. She had discovered a new power. If people knew, they would think she was mad.

She thought about Rick's note as she walked along the corridor into the yard. She thought of Tom. She must go in search of him. Where was he?

"What do you think, Jess?" Tyro asked.

"I think she's great."

"I hope it lasts."

Mr Gruff and Mr Grudge watched as the class made its way

across the yard to the main teaching block. Mr Gruff had a blank look about him. Not quite of fear, rather as if he was haunted by it. Perhaps even its servant. He was never out of the company of Duke Grudge.

From the tower the camera followed the children. Every movement was recorded and sometimes monitored by a person in uniform. It wasn't the children of course that they were interested in. It was the possibility of something else.

*

Mr Baxter had been teaching one of the junior classes. He took it in his stride, moving into mechanical mode, cracking the occasional joke, awing them with the mask of Anger, which he would bring out from the cupboard, then turn to confront them. It was a sort of pantomime. He played the eccentric as a device. The children seemed to prefer the mask. He had much else on his mind. These lessons allowed him to think, despite the particular form of attention that they required.

Intimately connected with the mysteries of the school, and one of Mr Rummage's closest allies, Mr Baxter was more involved than anyone. A trip to France over the summer had taught him something important which helped build the jigsaw. He had visited Toulouse with Ms Peverell. They had toured the countryside, visited retreats, obscure gorges, ruins. They had made progress. They had researched the Priory, who had been active there for centuries, and were followers of the Templars. Of the Order of the Magdalene they heard only rumours. But the most important thing was devastating, if it could be proved.

The next class was his favourite. He could spend more time on the subjects closest to his heart. There was a conscious mutual expectation which gave the lessons an edge.

Theirs was an important year. Difficult exams were on the horizon, offering a kind of transition into adolescent complexity, in which the first precepts of genuine insight could become articulated, an expression of a consciousness of dark material, as well, occasionally, of the sublime. These, fortunately, weren't the ritual exams that formed part of the burden imposed by government, but specific to the school.

Mr Baxter had started the year with poetry. Poetry cut corners, went straight to the heart, like the sea. Once you got it, it was difficult to remain untouched. Those who claimed indifference, or even fear (often through laughter and boredom) had cast aside a potential inner guide, which they would need in later life, like Parcival, to undertake a journey. Play and intensity, anger and confusion, added to the volcanic mix in which the Goddess of feeling danced.

Poetry and myth, the flesh and the backbone, was a way into Shakespeare. Shakespeare was inevitable, and he had recently read some. The legend that Shakespeare's father had visited Burnchester Hall, perhaps with his young magus son, helped.

Wherever he journeyed, in whatever role, Mr Baxter always returned to the masters. He hoped to share this with others. For this reason he carried masks. They were aspects of the greater unity which bound all into One, and of which the masters alone were the greatest examples. A bit like God in humanity, and the humanity in God.

"Shakespeare," he told the students, "would have been the lead singer of his own band, and would have played every instrument in any orchestra, every position on the football field, had he been alive today. He would have been the master of make-up, of the catwalk, lover, loved, slayer and slain. Everyone and no-one, hidden yet visible everywhere. Incomparable. In us all."

Sometimes he said that Shakespeare was actually alive today. It didn't always work. Some just didn't buy it. Just a dead poet.

Mr Baxter didn't just feel that he was swimming against the

tide - but that the sea was on the ebb, and he didn't know which way it would go. The River Dean had never been so high.

The class had done some composition, which gave motion to the bones and flesh.

*

Last week they had written a story (Mr Baxter didn't follow the idea of themes. He followed the intrinsic patterns, interests, books as they emerged).

The stories were an unusual mix, as were the patterns of thought and creativity, partners in the scheme of which he was temporary surveyor.

The subject he had given them was "Heroes". They had been talking about them.

He had read them some Greek Myths and the legends of King Arthur. He had talked about how people were heroes in different ways, in all walks of life. They referred to TV stories, newspaper reports, soaps of course, films, books, families. There had been some amazing stories.

Harry's story was about a centre forward who had stolen the World Cup. The boy had taken the object to a pawnbroker and got enough money to buy sweets for a year. He never saw the cup again, though he enjoyed the sweets.

David had written about a mad scientist who had invented a computer capable of doing homework. This took into account age, personality, sex, subject, handwriting, and teacher, he said. He called it Compuhome. This went down well with the class, until he told them how much it cost.

Jane had written about a pony who had fallen in love with a girl. The girl had then fallen in love with a boy who then became a pony. The symbolism was devastating. Everyone knew that Jane fancied John, though John couldn't grasp the idea of becoming a pony.

Jacqui wrote about the love between two pupils at school. Yes, Jane and John, disguising themselves as herself and Ben - another boy who passed his time in not being visible very much. The setting was based on a television series called Handsome High.

Whistles sounded as Jacqui's story reached a conclusion.

Tyro had written a strange piece about a dream. Her dead father had given her an important message ("Did he speak it or write it down?" Mr Baxter had asked. She could not remember), that she must transmit to the world without telling anyone the source. The problem was, although she knew it was important (it had to be if she was to transmit it to the world), she could not understand the message. Nor, for that matter, could the class. This made Tyro embarrassed. She had already been loath to read it, but had been persuaded to do so. Mr Baxter felt a little guilty, and sorry for Tyro. But he complimented her by saying that dreams were difficult. "Why don't you write them down?" Mr Baxter suggested.

This led to a general discussion about dreams. The class was engaged for the rest of the lesson, even more so than for any of the stories. Everyone had dreams. If not, they could make them up. Nobody could disprove anything.

Julia had dreamt of killing her sister. The fact that she didn't have a sister meant, to the class, that she must be thinking of Tyro. This led to denial.

Harry had been chased by a tiger, across a dark moonlit landscape (looking rather like a football pitch). The tiger, in this case, was the opposition centre back.

Jane had tried to climb a staircase which had no end but a few broken steps which, if not avoided, would lead to descent into an abyss.

Every form of anxiety image, from death by drowning to ritual slaughter (even one crucifixion), emerged from the depths of the class. Most of it, Mr Baxter presumed, had been made up, but that was OK. Tyro had even mentioned getting messages in her dreams. Not just her father's. Mr Baxter let that pass.

"Where do dreams come from?" he asked.

"Perhaps outside beings invade our minds to frighten us," someone suggested. The class laughed.

"Where did these horrible images come from then?"

"TV, books, our own experience or minds," Jess said.

"Yours maybe! I've never seen a dragon before," said one of the quiet girls of the class.

Nobody mentioned the figures. There had been rumours, but nobody really knew, apart from those who had been there, though Julia suspected.

There were some funny dreams too, delightmares. Not all could be repeated.

Ben dreamt of eating a plate of chips the size of a football pitch. This made him feel sick so he rushed out of class holding his tummy.

John had once dreamt of flying, which was great. Everytime his parents asked him to do something, he just rose into the air. Others had dreamt of flight. Most had dreamt of flying.

Jess looked at Tyro, Tyro at Rick. They so wanted to stand up and talk about their experiences. How could they? Nobody would believe them. Perhaps nobody should. What was it that had given them the power? The potion? Only Tyro had drunk it.

"There is sometimes not much difference between a dream and reality," said Mr Baxter.

This led to a further discussion, though one or two turned off. "Dreams predict the future!"

"Rubbish!"

"Dreams come from another world!" David repeated.

"Like you!" said a voice.

*

The next lesson Mr Baxter went back to Shakespeare. The sonnets.

"Yes Sir, we know Shakespeare was the Master of Murder Mysteries, and that he was thought to have played centre forward for Stratford-upon-Avon as a young man."

"Don't be cheeky!"

Harry jotted something down on his hand.

"He definitely stole a deer and yes, Shakespeare's father did visit Burnchester. We even know which room he stayed in. The one next to the observatory," Mr Baxter said.

"How do we know, Sir?" asked Jess.

"Documents, Jess. Records, here in the school archive. Old man Shakes signed the visitors' book of the family who then owned the Hall - the Cheesepeake Lumsdens - and left an account of his journey. Pretty wild it was. He even refers to his son, though not by name. However, there was more then one son. There are lots of important documents in the school archive. You should ask your History teacher."

"Including about spying in the Second World War, Sir?"

Mr Baxter said that there had been a lot of places in East Anglia doing secret work, and no doubt there still were.

Tyro wanted to act some of the scenes from Macbeth (which Mr Baxter had talked about), not do more poetry. She loved drama. Mr Baxter was still thinking about the school play for later in the year, which would coincide with the 600th anniversary of the building of Burnchester Hall. That would be in the summer. There was still Bonfire Night to get over.

Mr Baxter read them a sonnet. The one that begins,

"Shall I compare thee to a summer's day . . . "

Most of them got something from it, though some said it was pathetic.

"Why a summer's day, Sir? In summer, it normally rains."

"Don't be cheeky, David. Summer is *supposed* to be beautiful, isn't it? We're not talking about reality here. He's trying to conjure up an idea."

"Like in a dream," said Rick.

"You mean like it doesn't snow at Christmas, but we like to think it does."

"Exactly. Well done, whoever that was."

John was imagining the Bard writing a sonnet to his dearly beloved over the Christmas Turkey, "Shall I compare thee to a Christmas Roast."

Mr Baxter had got them to write a sonnet. The only two conditions were that they had to make a comparison between something (preferably someone) they liked with something apt or interesting. And that they had to get the metre right. A sonnet must have the right metre. It took a long time to remind the class what syllables were - he had explained often enough - and it seemed difficult for some people to count to ten (Harry got to nine). The results were variable, and subject to improvement, but indubitably original. The launch was more successful than the continuing flight.

Here are some examples:

Shall I compare thee to a hairy frog . . .
(Harry: first effort)

"Since when were frogs hairy, Harry?"

Shall I compare thee to a centre forward . . .
(Harry: second effort)

"Try something a little more appropriate for your girlfriend, Harry."

"He hasn't got a girlfriend, Sir"

"He's unlikely to get one if his poem goes on like that, is he Sir?"

Shall I compare thee to the light at morn . . .
(Tyro)
"Why not dawn, Tyro? Anyone?"
"Dawn's too ordinary."

Shall I compare thee to a living dream . . .
(Jess)

"Excellent, Jess."

Shall I compare thee to a lover's kiss
Which touches not but seems to capture bliss . . .
(Julia)

Mr Baxter was struck by some of the results. The only person who didn't write anything was Rick, though Mr Baxter thought he was listening. Rick was busy drawing what looked like maps on a scrap of paper. His dreams were real. Feelings weren't for him.

The metre was difficult, but far harder was to write a whole poem around a single central idea. After the laughter, most had taken it seriously. Many were proud of their achievement, one or two blushing at the thought that their passions might be revealed. Mr Baxter tried to explain how important revision was. How a poem was more like sculpting out of words. Most of them didn't believe this. Inspiration was the driving force. Not revision.

*

The next lesson came Macbeth. They had already done one or two scenes from other plays, including Hamlet and A Midsummer Night's Dream, but this was their first taste of blood-red tragedy.

Mr Baxter brought out the mask of Tragedy from the

33

cupboard, and wore it intermittently to make his point. He explained the story briefly. He emphasised the language, he dwelt on the supernatural. He knew that blood and murder would hook them.

"Who believes in witches?" he had asked. Hands shot up around the room.

"I want you to imagine what it would be like to meet a group of strange and decrepit beings - let us call them witches - in the darkness of a winter storm, in some wild place, that you didn't know."

"Like meeting the second eleven after losing 9-1 in the rain, Sir."

"More like Tyro, Jess and Julia," said John.

They read the first three scenes, and were now going to act them out. Mr Baxter put them into groups.

He got the class to clear the desks and place them around the walls of the room. The floor in the centre became the "blasted heath". The class sat around it. They performed being witches in groups of three, while the others watched, helping or hindering in a chaos of half-controlled anxiety that always preludes involvement - even short ones such as these. They put on weird accents, and screeched with high-pitched voices (the boys were good at this), with others adding the special effects of wind, rain and thunder. With the curtains drawn and Mr Baxter's cunning orchestration, their imaginations filled in for every missing prop.

Best of all were the three girls, Tyro, Jess and Julia. At first they had run around the stage, holding their hands high, carrying imagined capes. Then they settled around the cauldron (the waste-paper basket put in an admirable performance; the rotten banana skin adding realism and effect).

The mistrust of Julia for Tyro and the reverse hatred might have made it impossible. But with Jess's mediation, and Mr Baxter's interventions, they managed to capture the essence of the community more than they realised, not to say the conflict of darkness which the witches represent. Little did they know who, in some other sphere, was listening, who watching. When it came to the words, "Fair is foul, and foul is fair. Hover through the fog and filthy air," the class was spellbound. Even Harry was transfixed. Mr Baxter felt sure it had been right to cancel Hallowe'en.

By the time the class finished scene three, everyone was tired. Mr Baxter was slightly worried that some other energy had crept into the proceedings, as if the pupils had no longer been themselves.

"Next time we'll dress up so as to make it more fun, and realistic." The class had been genuinely moved, and wanted more. One or two had felt a glimpse of unnerving fear.

Things relaxed when the boys acted out part of the battle scenes that are reported in scene two. These scenes show Macbeth as the raging hero, overcoming the enemy against all the odds. Harry did himself proud when he danced around the stage in mortal combat with Rick, swirling his sword (a broomstick from the cleaning cupboard) shouting the words, "'till he unseamed him from the nave to the chops", though it was in fact Rick who was playing Macbeth and did the unseaming, with a wonderful flourish: "Just like my dad (who is a butcher) with a dead cow," said the prostrate Harry, with considerable empathy for the language and the victory of his adversary.

*

Everyone enjoyed the acting and discussion about witches. Some had got very little from the language, others a great deal, in that strange process of intuitive recognition that apt words can achieve in striking a chord with the heart of any age.

Tyro had been curiously withdrawn and silent. One quote particularly struck her.

"But 'tis strange;
And oftentimes, to win us to our harm,
The instruments of Darkness tell us truths."

She had leant over to Jess while they were preparing to perform the witches, and asked her what it meant.

Jess understood the meaning very well but found it difficult to put into other words, perhaps also because she knew Tyro so well, or because Julia was sitting next to her. She tried her best but said that she would talk about it later. Mr Baxter had heard her request. He explained with clear reference to Macbeth's character. He saw Tyro's look and sensed danger.

Tyro thought of her cross-sword, thought of the events of the summer, thought of the figures which had followed them in the tunnels, and which they had later followed to the sea. She could not shake from her mind the words "The instruments of Darkness tell us truths". She was more than ever determined to pursue her quest for some answers, and her search for Tom.

When the bell rang the class was animated, and as soon as they left they threw bags down, dug out sweets from pockets, raced to the changing rooms to get footballs, swapped notes, and ran to the shop.

Julia came up to Jess and Tyro.

"I enjoyed the acting. Typecasting I should say."

She walked off.

"She means, you being a witch, I think," explained Jess.

"What a cow!"

"She might have been referring to herself," said Jess.

"Rick wants us to meet up, but I've got to go and see Roberts. Do you want to come?"

Jess reminded Tyro that they all had to go to his class.

*

Mr Roberts dismissed the class as soon as they drifted into

his room (some twenty minutes after the bell, with a variety of excuses), except for Tyro and Rick. He might have got angry at the limp excuses and the lateness, but at least all of them had turned up, even the boy with the dentist's appointment, which showed a certain respect. Mr Roberts was tired and didn't want the trouble of looking after a class who had, after all, not been in the wrong. He had had a difficult day.

Mr Roberts had to put on a show for Tyro and Rick.

"I will not have disruption in my class, Tyro. Don't try to answer back. You were laughing and distracting the class and you hadn't done your prep. What have you got to say for yourself?"

Rick was about to interrupt.

"I'm not talking to you, Rick! Well, Tyro. You do have a reputation, you know."

Tyro was a little distracted. She was angry and tearful. She wanted to fight back, to explain how unfair it was, but she didn't, for once, know how to. She expected to be victimised, and couldn't gather the energy to defend herself. Had Mr Roberts been stricter she would probably have fought hard. But she could sense his own discomfort, as he could hers.

She managed to say that it was always the same. She seemed to get the blame when others had been involved. Rick pointed to himself.

For his part, Rick couldn't deny that he was about to pass the piece of paper around class, and was keen to defend Tyro because she hadn't really been in the wrong. Equally, Tyro would not let Rick take it all on himself.

"It's true, Mr Roberts, I haven't been myself recently. I'm sorry I didn't do my prep. I'll do it for tomorrow."

She knew she wouldn't but it just came out.

"Is anything the matter, Tyro? Anything troubling you?"

Tyro paused. Clearly there was. A great deal. But she wasn't quite sure what. Tom's absence. The experiences in the holidays. A desire to run away, a creeping unhappiness. A yearning for adventure. And of course her father. She missed her father. Who was going to help her with that?

"I'm always getting into trouble, but I don't know why," she said. "I don't mean to. Then I think the anger builds up, and it happens again. I don't know, Sir. I promise I'll do the prep for tomorrow."

"Can I help? Is it Tom?" enquired Mr Roberts.

Tyro hated being found out, especially by teachers, but she was so worried that she answered, "Partly."

Mr Roberts waited a moment, and then turned to Rick. To Rick's surprise, Mr Roberts brought out the piece of paper he had been about to pass to Tyro.

"I thought it had been ripped, Sir! It's unfair. You shouldn't have kept it, Sir. That's worse."

Mr Roberts's silence forced Rick onto the defensive, but gradually he explained that the note had been intended for Tyro. When pushed he said that the note showed a map of (here he lied) a place where they sometimes met up. He wanted to meet up after school.

Rick did not apologise, only said that, yes, it had been wrong. Mr Roberts would not give him the paper back. He said he would keep it. He also said that if he had any more trouble from him he would be in detention for a week. Rick said nothing. He wanted to go. Mr Roberts knew Rick's circumstances were not easy, but was not going to back down.

Then he added, "I know that this map, Rick, and what Tyro is feeling, is to do with what happened in the holidays. You have got to realise that we have been told the story, even if your friends haven't. We have been asked to make allowances, but not too many. I understand it was difficult, but you have got to get over it, and forget it. I've heard from other teachers - ("What other teachers, Sir?") - that you have both been a little distracted this term and this is having a bad influence on others. It has to stop. Next time, I shall take a heavy hand. Now get going."

Mr Roberts didn't like speech-making, but felt he had no option.

He was worried enough, and not a little concerned about the re-instigation of Bonfire Night, which he felt was a bad idea, in view of security. There wasn't much he could do. Perhaps he would share it with Mrs Moffat, his new colleague.

*

The playground was emptying, school buses were lined up just inside the gates, parents' cars on the drive adjacent to them.

"I want to explain the map," said Rick. "But it'll have to wait. We're late for your mum."

"What's prep?" asked Tyro.

"History," said Jess. "We've got to read that chapter on the Reformation and the burning of heretics and witches. You really hate Julia, don't you?"

Before Tyro could answer, she saw a figure standing by the school gates in the usual place. Security guards beyond. Above, the eye, following everything. She did not know that the tower led right down to the deepest recesses of the school, into the marbled interior she had not explored.

There was the mother she loved, to whom she wasn't always very kind. Though she normally loved school, she was happy to get home. In the back was her dog, Rompy, who was wagging his tail. She loved Rompy. He followed his nose. She wondered if there were instruments of darkness for him. He was like an overgrown rabbit, except that he would never have considered eating himself.

"Mum," she said, as she and Rick got into the car. Abby, Tyro's mother, regularly dropped Rick home.

"Yes, dear?" said Abby, who was still in uniform. Abby waved at another mother as she passed in the car, as it was checked by the security guard.

"These guards are over the top!" Abby said under her breath. "They'd better not stop and delay me! Evening officer," she said.

The guard nodded.

"Bonfire Night is on again. Can we go and get some fireworks?"

Rompy wagged his tail.

"The school normally provides them, doesn't it?"

"For us, Mum. Please! Dennis will, if you won't."

Dennis, Abby's brother, had been staying with them for a while, in their large house in the village of Haydon a few miles away.

"Did you have a good day at school today?" Abby asked.

As Abby drove up to the gates, she slowed. Mr Gruff peered into the car. "Ridiculous," thought Abby, "as if Gruff is going to catch anyone!"

Tyro explained why they were late. She told her mother most things. It was the best thing about her mother. She was a good friend. She noticed Mr Gruff's face. She hadn't seen it so close to since the attack. It didn't seem quite right.

"Go on, Mum!"

Abby had not said no to the fireworks, which may have been why they were heading for Wyemarket.

This meant that they might have to return home in the dark.

Like the instruments of Darkness, whose agents were stirring.

3

The firework shop in Wyemarket stocked everything from carpets to candelabra, magic lanterns to kettles and, like all good retailers, went with the season. So, being October, the picnic baskets had been removed and the coal scuttles had returned; garden chairs became kitchen stools, and barbecues, seasonal table mats, on which stood candles presaging Christmas.

In the corner by the entrance door Mr Bloodstone the manager stood like a Chinese wizard, with a long beard, beside the huge firework case, with rockets projecting nobly upwards, showing teeth through a smile that seemed to echo the impulse of the sun, and would soon be extinguished. Perhaps the sun itself was some huge firework, God's sparkler, after all. Perhaps people were little rockets, needing to be lit, in order to begin their journey, only to run out of fuel or be melted by the heat.

Abby and Tyro bought a few fireworks for the house, and then made their way home. Rick dreamt of buying the largest banger in the world and placing it under his aunt's bed.

Aunt Patrolia was waiting for Rick by the gate when Abby's car pulled up. Uncle John was leaf-raking.

"Good evening, Mrs Grumble," said Abby, window down.

"Good evening," Abby repeated, a little intimidated. "Sorry we're late. I've been buying fireworks. It's not Rick's fault."

Abby smiled as only a nurse can when dealing with the unconsciously disabled, and turned to Rick as he slammed the car door.

"See you in the morning, Rick. Don't be late."

"I won't!" said Rick. "I'll ring you later, Tyro, about . . . er . . . homework."

"You will not!" screamed his aunt. "If you don't know how to do your homework, you shouldn't be at school in the first place. Plenty of work to do here. Some of us never went to school at all, and it never did us any harm."

Uncle John continued to rake leaves. He had unusual imaginings as to who this year's Guy Fawkes might be and was ready to light the bonfire himself.

Rick went inside. He had had so much of Aunt Patrolia. Her generous welcome meant no more to him than the evening news on the telly, except that, for once, his attention was caught by an item as he passed. It mentioned that a diver from Dunemoor had discovered the site of an ancient ruin at the bottom of the sea.

The diver was curiously reticent. When pushed, he said that he had discovered something else but had been asked by "the authorities" not to say anything. It was as if the man was speaking under threat. The face seemed familiar. Rick ran upstairs.

Uncle John stood by the small pile of leaves by the hedge. There was not a stray leaf anywhere. He looked up. Rick was at his desk. Uncle John made a sign as the match lit the leaf litter. It seemed to be the sign of the cross.

Upstairs, Rick was thoughtful. He was in an unusual mood. He could not get some of the words from the English lesson out of his mind. He could see himself very easily unseaming Aunt Patrolia from the nave to the chops. Maybe there was something in this Shakespeare after all. He wasn't there to do his homework, he was there to devise a plan. He had mapped as many of the tunnels as he could. He had told no-one. Soon he would have to. What would happen to his map if he was taken? Mr Rummage had hinted at something when he'd spoken to them all at the beginning of the term. He had said that they might be required to go on a journey. Perhaps Bonfire Night would be the occasion. Rick missed Tom. Tom had helped him all summer, and acted as a guide through thick and thin.

It was Tom who drove him on. Tom had confided in him, things he hadn't even told Tyro. Why should he? Rick was set to explore further that night, and began to prepare.

"Come down and help your uncle, you ungrateful child!" Aunt Patrolia bawled.

"Yes, Aunty Patrolia, coming! What about my homework?" He liked Aunty!

Hallowe'en may have been cancelled, but Rick had other ideas. He went to his cupboard and pulled out an old robe that he had made from sacks and dyed black. No reason why a little bit of trick-or-treating couldn't add flavour to the occasion. He'd copied the robe from a discarded cloak which Tyro had in the garden shed at the Hall. Dennis had picked it up off the road and put it in the back of the car. It was the day they had come back from crabbing at Warblersbay.

Rick threw the robe on his bed and went downstairs. There was a man being interviewed on the beach at Dunemoor. It was Mr Greenshank. Rick paused and waited until the item had finished. He went through the kitchen. He was more alert than usual.

"I've come to help with the bonfire, Uncle John."

Uncle John worked with an unusual energy.

Aunt Patrolia stood by the door. Rick carried sticks from the pile to throw on to the fire. Meanwhile he was thinking that the time was drawing closer when he would let Uncle John into a few secrets. Uncle John was never allowed to do anything, certainly not under Aunt Patrolia's reign of terror, and needed encouragement. Besides, he could keep secrets as he had no-one else to tell them to. Not having a father himself, Rick felt a bit fatherly towards his uncle. He was beginning to love him too, however slow or stupid he was, however weak in front of his wife. Perhaps Uncle John would come with him.

*

The hedges and the fields flew past the window in the short drive home. Occasionally, last summer term, Tyro and Jess (who lived in the next village of Stimple) would cycle to school, just as they had over the holidays, though they had recently been forbidden to.

Nowhere, not even home, was entirely safe now. Rompy had become more excitable. The break-in at the Church of All Saints, next to their house, had shaken them, and they were on alert.

Special alarms had been put into the church, the cottage next door, and in their house. They had been asked to be vigilant. The police had been advised to make special provision for the family, now that they had been singled out, it seemed, by the Priory. Tyro's powers had not gone unnoticed, nor had Rick's knowledge.

Dennis had checked the alarm systems, and had spent quite a long time in the church, as the break-in had involved a very unusual feature: the church tower had been climbed, and in the outside wall had been placed what looked like climbing-irons, invisible almost to the naked eye, but clear in the right light. These irons had been examined. The metal was highly unusual. No-one had yet identified it.

Irons had also been reported at other sites of ancient power.

Nobody had come up with a convincing explanation.

Dennis had been closely involved in the events at Burnchester Hall. Not only was he wary and concerned - but he put great energy into researching what might have been the cause, and who could have been responsible. He would go away for days, sometimes abroad, and would come back with fresh theories and more bits of information. Though generally discreet he was very open with his family. Break-ins at two churches; the known presence of the Priory in East Anglia; the search, and recent discovery of the missing piece from the painting at the church of St Mary Magdalen; the theft of cloaks; further break-ins at the school; dark figures, who were at once, it seemed, human and apparently something else as well; a chase across the East Anglian countryside at dawn with helicopters and naval vessels out to sea - were enough to make anyone inspired.

Dennis encouraged Tyro to talk about these things at home, as she was not allowed to do so at school. The blanket clamp-down on the whole story within school added to the speculation, it is true, but was a necessary condition to maintaining a degree of stability (young people's imaginations are quick to make something out of nothing - just as adults' are inclined to ignore possibilities). The journalists didn't let go. Abby's friend Jane, who had stayed when the family had gone to France, had warned them. There had been phone calls, visits to the door. It was not possible to know who these people really were. That some of them were not journalists, there was little doubt.

Dennis had added his own security measures. These included a sophisticated listening and recording device between the Church of All Saints and the house. The kind used by those engaged in psychical and other forms of energy research. He called it his "night-stalker reporter". He also placed "mirrors" in locations around the perimeter of the grounds.

Dennis was convinced that some of the activities were connected to the top secret research that had been carried out in the area during and since World War Two.

As the car swung into the drive Bill was wheeling a barrow in the direction of a bonfire, the smell of which drifted into the car. Bill was relaxed about most things, not least what he didn't see. Biscuit was sitting on the paving by the side door and began to stroll forward as Abby pulled up to a halt. Everything seemed its old self. It was still light.

"I'm going to chill out first and then do my homework, Mum!" shouted Tyro as she got out of the car, bending to stroke Biscuit. Rompy leapt out and chased Biscuit away whereupon Tyro tried to chase Rompy. It made Rompy more excited. He thought Tyro was playing.

"How about taking some stuff out of the car, Tyro? Unlike you, it doesn't fly, you know."

The words just came out. Tyro did her best to ignore them, but the damage was done. Tyro hated being treated differently or as if she were special in any way, even though she had to acknowledge that what had happened to her was very special indeed.

Abby was afraid for her daughter.

Tyro said nothing and took the fireworks out of the boot of the car. Rompy had now run off in the direction of Bill.

Within an hour, Tyro was doing her homework on the kitchen table, and Abby was preparing supper.

Dennis's presence gave Abby a more secure feeling, which gave her more energy. She had begun to wonder what had happened to his girlfriend. She knew from experience the pain of being alone for long. With a daughter, of course, that aloneness was very different.

Tyro had begun to tell Abby what had happened in Mr Roberts's lesson, but wanted to wait until Dennis was there. He had asked her to report anything unusual in the behaviour of any of the teachers. She also wanted to see his reaction to the news about Bonfire Night. But she did say something about the new Biology teacher which reassured Abby: "Quite cool," she said, which for her meant brilliant.

Abby was becoming increasingly concerned about Tyro's variable moods, from bullish to manic to excessively quiet. They were closer, but the relationship was more complex, not least because there was less hidden between them. At the same time, Abby felt that she was beginning to lose Tyro, as if, she dreaded to admit to herself, Tyro was just beginning to sense the journey which she had been destined for. Jack had always said that she was destined in some way.

When she had finished her homework, Tyro cleared her things away and began to lay the table. She appreciated more what her mother did for her, working and looking after her and the house, without much help from anyone. She was beginning to feel a little more how privileged she was, and that by most people's standards she was very, very, lucky. Perhaps this contributed to the feeling that she must pursue the quest she had set herself, and be afraid of nothing.

Of course, the feeling sometimes passed, especially when enemies were concerned. And it didn't reduce her anger.

Dennis came in after dark.

Soon they were at supper. Tyro told Abby and Dennis about Bonfire Night. She imitated Mr Rummage's entry during lunch. They could see the actress in her. Tyro said nothing about the near detention, though she did tell them about the Maths lesson. Dennis asked her for the details of Mr Roberts's behaviour. Was there a pattern to Mr Roberts's new aggression? Tyro didn't know, except that she felt that Mr Roberts knew he wasn't on his best form, and felt a little sorry for him. Nevertheless, her outrage at being singled out again, unjustly, made up for any sympathy she might have had.

Regarding Bonfire Night, Dennis looked at Abby and said that he was sure it would be a great evening. Nevertheless, the mental image of the whole school being out in the vast grounds of Burnchester Hall, in the dark, with parents and teachers dotted around drinking mulled wine whilst watching flames and fireworks, filled him with anxiety. Especially with news of increased Priory activity.

During supper the phone rang. Tyro got up and answered, then ran into the drawing room where there was an extension, telling her mother to put down the receiver.

"What time's he coming over?" asked Abby.

"Quite soon, I think," Dennis replied. "He said he'd try to get here by about eight-thirty. He was very apologetic for giving so little notice. Must be important."

"A bit strange, isn't it? I wonder if it's about Tyro? I hope not."

"It won't be about Tyro. Not directly anyway."

Tyro was at the door.

"Who?" she asked.

"Who was that?"

Tyro walked over to the receiver in the kitchen and put it down.

"You haven't been listening, have you?"

"Of course not!"

"Who's coming over?"

"Mr Rummage. And one or two others, I believe."

"Rummage! What's he doing here? That means he'll bring Julia! If she comes, I'm going!"

"I don't know why you hate her so much, Tyro. She's very polite, and clever with it. Someone you ought to be friends with. You might like each other if you tried."

Tyro was not taking any of this from her mother. She got up, threw her knife and fork down on the table and stormed out.

Dennis followed.

There was shouting on the stairs, and what seemed like tears. Biscuit came running along the corridor, flew through the kitchen, and out of the cat flap into the night.

Tyro came in again, her eyes red, and walked over to her mum.

"I'm sorry, Mum, but I hate her and there's nothing you can do about it, I'm afraid."

Abby gave Tyro a hug.

"You can help clear the table. You're getting good at that."

"Good old Mum," thought Tyro through her fading anger. The idea that one day she would not have one haunted her.

There followed the sound of clattering kitchen things. Abby asked Dennis if he would put the fireworks away. You could still see Bill through the window. Rompy was asleep in his basket.

*

Dennis went out into the cool autumn air and walked down towards the fire. At first he thought Bonfire Night a silly idea, not to say madness. Never expose people to unnecessary danger. But perhaps the threat was receding. And then he remembered the news item which declared that cells of the Priory were active in Britain and one was known to be operating in East Anglia. This was not news to him, but it was public for the first time. Their presumed aim - to blackmail the church - was dependant on information believed to be hidden within the grounds of Burnchester Hall. Perhaps they had heard rumours that the fragment had been found. The fragment that contained or might contain clues to the whereabouts of the Spearhead. The overwhelming power that they had seen begin to be incarnated in the Domed Chamber under the school, with the emergence of the Dark Master, and which, Mr Rummage later explained, had been nullified, partly through the counter measures generated by the power of the mind with its impact on the physical domain. Suppose the fragment was not authentic but the Priory believed it was?

The fragment was now being analysed in Cambridge, under strict security. The Priory seemed to have the capacity to break security. The evidence showed that there were other groups involved, connected perhaps to the Priory, who might have their own agendas. This meant that any analysis of the threat needed to be considered on multiple levels simultaneously, yet acted upon with enough focus, when the time came, to make action possible at all. There remained the mystery of the climbing-irons. What were they doing, attached to two local churches, and recently found at other sites? What were they made of? No-one had found any trace of a similar substance.

*

Tyro went upstairs and tried to do her history project, but she was soon bored, and took out her diary instead. Heresy? As far as she was concerned both sides were as bad as each other. She was suspicious of organised religion. Why couldn't we believe what we wanted as long as we didn't hurt others?

She couldn't concentrate. School work was nothing compared to the world out there, and the mysteries that beckoned. She phoned Jess, and told her to meet her in break tomorrow. Jess was about to go to bed and couldn't talk for long anyway. Tyro then got to thinking of Rick's plan and of Tom. Then she picked up the book that lay beside her bed and began to read. She had read The City Beneath the Sea. She had been intrigued by the idea of a once thriving city, now lost under the waves. What happened to the secrets of that city once it became submerged? Once that city had been a dream, now it was gone. Who chooses which dreams become fulfilled, and which others don't? She was reading a book on space. Maybe soon people would travel to planets. Somebody's dream becoming a reality. She thought of Mr Baxter. She was beginning to enjoy English, though reading novels was too much to ask. It was almost as if words were too powerful and frightening, as they seemed to draw something else from people.

Tyro thought about the Headmaster arriving with Julia.

How she hated Julia. She could not explain the reason. She didn't care about the reason. It was just there. She would have to disinfect the kitchen as soon as they'd gone. In order to avoid her, even the possibility of her coming, she decided to go to bed. She was soon asleep.

*

Tyro was woken by voices coming from below. Not the familiar sounds of her mother and Dennis, but different sounds. In the dull light that came from the hall she sat up, eyes blurry. She could see the picture on the wall, her latest attempt. It was one her mother had tried to persuade her to take down. A figure in a landscape. The figure, a teenage girl, wore a cloak and had long hair. She seemed to carry something in her hand. Perhaps it was a cross, or a dagger. There was a blood-red sky above her, focused on the setting sun. There was blood-red dripping along strands of the girl's flowing hair. In the foreground, on the edges of the picture, animals stood at the edge of a forest and watched. The figure, perhaps it was her, was looking at them, but could not stop for the animals. There was no knowing what was at the end of the field. Perhaps it was the sea. But it was not visible, and gave the impression of being an eternal horizon. One that the figure must pursue.

She recognised herself and not herself. She was proud of her work and yet she knew it was also the hand of someone else, some unknown guide who watched over her, as she drew. She felt the guide's presence in other circumstances as well. The guide that helped her but perhaps also deceived her into believing that she was always protected. Tom came to mind. Then Tom's words, "There are many ways to fly."

"That's strange", Tyro thought. Perhaps it was the light. It seemed for a moment as if a shadow passed across the room, and left it a little darker than before. Almost as if a shadow had passed on the landing outside, which was the source of the half-light through the crack in the door.

There was a figure out in the hall, watching her.

Tyro was now fully alert. She tried to listen, but could only hear muffled sounds. No high-pitched squeals - Julia could not be there unless she was silent, and that was an impossibility. She looked at her picture again and saw, not herself, but Julia's smile, this time with her head turned towards her. Tyro turned away, unable for the moment to look, and fell back onto the pillow, with her head turned up to the ceiling. Now she could distinctly make out the words of someone speaking. Now, she heard everything.

The figure continued to watch.

*

Mr Rummage sat at the table, his hands moving as he spoke. There was no humour in his voice. Those present were Inspector Relish, Dr Vale, the expert on religious sects, and Dr Bartok, who had treated both Mrs Limpet and Mr Gruff.

Mr Rummage was telling the story of what had happened at the school. There would be a chance later to hear of other developments.

It was early evening and Mr Bellevue had taken a group of boarders - with his permission - to help with the preparation of the bonfire. Mr Rummage's sudden late decision to allow Bonfire Night to go ahead had put Mr Granger, the head groundsman, under pressure; and Mr Bellevue had asked, on behalf of himself and Mr Grudge, Mr Gruff's assistant, if the children might help carry sticks to the fire so that the two of them could carry the heavier items to the pile, which was rather smaller than would normally be the case at this stage.

All the parents would be there, as well as all the children, watching the great annual show. Mr Rummage wanted a real spectacle, the best ever. The effigy of Guy Fawkes was the domain of Mrs McCleod, the church warden, who chose the best of the effigies made by the younger classes. Mrs Rummage had composed music, and Mr Baxter was preparing his own surprise.

When the young children from class 6R went down to help, they were under strict supervision. The excitement was palpable as they ran down to the river's edge close to the bonfire site. It was always exciting to be roaming around the grounds, especially to make the fire. Especially now. And they had got off homework.

"Was this wise?"

"In retrospect, perhaps not," Mr Rummage said. "However, we could not possibly have anticipated what would happen."

Mr Grudge, now joined by Mr Gruff - who seemed to be particularly agitated - had gone off to get some of the larger items for the fire. There was always an old desk or two, if not a mattress, that could be burned. These were kept in one of the sheds with the larger logs, boxes and other items which were stored for burning.

This left Mr Granger with Mr Bellevue and class 6R to continue to pile up the fire.

It was beginning to get dark and the weather was deteriorating. The stack was now really beginning to take shape. In fact, Mr Granger had cracked a joke about it.

"Who's to be the Guy?" Mr Granger had asked. The children did their best to offer up the names of their most hated teachers but were drowned by the wind which made hearing difficult.

Suddenly they all turned and pointed at Mr Bellevue, and then broke into laughter. Mr Bellevue was not amused. Then, in one voice, they called out a name that most had only heard of, "Mr Vespers."

During this episode Mark and Ali, two of the younger children, had decided they would do some exploring. They broke free from the others, saying that there were better logs beneath the trees inside the wood itself. So they went off into the wood adjacent to the bonfire plot. The other children had looked at each other, both jealous and afraid. Lotty wanted to tell the teacher but was too scared of him. So they all said nothing and carried on with their work, until the two boys were out of sight, when they started to get really worried.

Mr Bellevue, meanwhile, was bending down at the bonfire trying to shove leaf litter under the smaller sticks at the base, so as to create a proper core.

"There's nothing worse than a bonfire without a core!" he said.

The wind increased. The chatter of the children was drowned, as were Mr Granger's and Mr Bellevue's instructions. It all became background noise, intermingled with the sounds of the emerging night.

Mr Bellevue stood up again, satisfied, having made the centre strong. He looked at his watch, and then around him at the fading light.

It was time to go back in. The fire had grown substantially, thanks to all their work, so he decided to call it a day.

He called the children. Getting no immediate response, he shouted loudly, ordering them to gather round.

"Come on, class 6R. It's time for supper! You've done a good job but it's getting dark."

As the children approached, he could tell that something was wrong. The children were huddled together and less than enthusiastic, as if the fire had already started and they were seeking warmth. He was about to tell them off for being slow when one of them came forward.

"S . . . sssir . . . " the boy began.

Before he could continue, there were two piercing cries from inside the wood.

Everyone froze.

Mr Bellevue moved faster than he had ever done in his life. The cries came as if from another world. He pushed the children aside, and ran into the trees, shouting at the children to stay behind with Mr Granger.

Mr Granger gathered the children to him. They were terrified. Mr Granger could not phone security - though the tower far off could have seen him easily - as the phone was dead. But he could not let Mr Bellevue go into the wood alone. He looked around in vain for Mr Grudge and Mr Gruff. He would have to take the children into the wood with him.

He told the children to line up behind him, in two rows. He told them to do nothing but follow his instructions. He broke through the undergrowth at the edge of the trees, but soon stopped dead in his tracks.

A little way ahead, through the next thicket, he could see Mr Bellevue standing. Mr Bellevue was not standing still of his own accord.

Mr Granger turned and pointed to the children and put a finger to his mouth and raised a hand. The children stopped. Mr Granger moved forward. He was not afraid of anything for himself. He must protect the children at all costs, yet help Mr Bellevue. He went forward, alone, to the gap in the trees and walked straight through. He was now almost alongside Mr Bellevue.

Mr Bellevue's face, only moments ago, had been fresh and active. His face and body were now like iron. He stared into oblivion, paralysed from head to foot.

What lay ahead made Mr Granger turn, yet some shield guarded him from looking straight at what he saw. He did not want the children to see. Out of the corner of his eye the two boys, Mark and Ali, lying on the ground, their faces upright, staring blankly into the dark above. They looked lifeless.

Beyond them some yards ahead were two cloaked figures, taller than he by many inches, standing like priests over an open grave. They looked at Mr Granger. Although he could not see their faces, nor indeed their hands, he could sense their irritation, as if they had been interrupted from a ritual. Their arms were crossed, as they moved towards the children on the ground.

In that momentary pause, the figures looked up and tried to catch Mr Granger's attention, but he would not look. He held up his hand and arm as if to shield himself from a nauseous energy. He caught sight of the figures reflected on the face of his watch.

He moved sideways, blocking the sight from the other children behind him, blocking the figures' line of sight.

For a moment the figures stalled, uncertain whether or not they had Mr Granger in their power. Then they moved forward and began to close in on him.

As they did Mr Granger screamed at the children behind,

"Run, children, run! Get help. Run back to school. Run for your lives!"

Seeing the children turn, the figures delayed momentarily again, caught between Mr Granger and their wish to follow. This failure gave the children time. Time to run as fast as they could over the growing dusk and meadow, like night swallows.

They knocked into Mr Grudge and Mr Gruff coming down the hill. The children reached the door of the Hall, panting in fear and exhaustion. They bumped into Mr Rummage, who had been warned by security of the crisis and had alerted a unit along the river towards Shelter Field. The rest of the school was so far undisturbed.

Mr Rummage told the children to go at once to their houses. He instructed security to go to the area, went outside and ran down to the bonfire site.

The two figures were by now in pursuit of Mr Granger, who had decided to go on into the wood and lead them away from the school. They did not see Mr Grudge and Mr Gruff, soon followed by Mr Rummage, come into the wood.

The three men had seen the figures and Mr Granger. They went past the still figure of Mr Bellevue, and went on into the wood - Mr Grudge shouting down the line (which was working again) to security for more help as he went. Seeing a changed look in Mr Gruff's face, and remembering the ordeal he had suffered, Mr Rummage ordered him back to get help for Mr Bellevue. But Mr Gruff could not stop.

It was as if he was now out of control. At this Mr Rummage ordered Mr Grudge to help Mr Gruff carry Mr Bellevue and the two boys back to the school and get an ambulance immediately. It was only the two men together that could persuade Mr Gruff to move and he turned back from where he had come.

The boundary of the school was soon covered by security units, one of which Mr Granger could see ahead.

If Mr Granger went on, he would be safe. However, Mr Granger decided to move across the river and deeper into the wood that led towards the Iron Age Fort on Mr Strangelblood's land.

The figures tried to follow but were not quick enough. Though not apparently mortal, they were substantial in their present form, and could not avoid the broken trunks and divots in the ground. Mr Granger ran on, turning from time to time to keep them in view. He shouted at Mr Rummage to keep them out of his direct sight. He began to increase the gap between them. And then he fell. Back over a branch that crossed his path, hitting his head hard on a stone.

The figures slowed and approached like spiders onto a trapped fly. Mr Granger, dazed, tried to rise, with his arm in front of his face, as they raised theirs to strike him down. But Mr Granger, dazed though he was, ignored his fear, and drew from the depth of his soul reserves of unknown power. He thrust his arm forward, holding a knife, slicing into the cloth that protected their bony hands.

He stood up straight and thrust at them again. The figures were angry, and started to close.

But as they did they were forced to stop. It was their turn to be frozen into stillness. The power in them was drained, they became inert.

Close by them stood another figure. Between them and Mr Rummage, who was following, a young innocent-looking boy stood above them all. It was Tom. He seemed to have an open wound on his side.

In a moment Tom and the two cloaked figures were gone. Mr Granger and Mr Rummage were left bemused and uncertain, looking for clues on the ground, making their way back, too stunned to talk.

*

Mr Rummage finished his story with a wipe of his brow. Dr Vale, Dr Bartok and Inspector Relish waited for their hosts to respond first.

Dennis had been patient. Now he wanted to get up and go. He wanted to be there searching. He didn't care who these figures were, or why they had returned, he knew that he wanted to confront them. Abby was dumbstruck. She was thinking that it might have been Tyro. She wanted to know that the boys were OK.

In that pause they heard steps. Dennis jumped up, Abby sat upright, rigid with fear, then relaxed. It was only Tyro, upstairs, going to the bathroom. They listened and yes, it was the sound of familiar feet on the corridor above.

"Perhaps we could have a brief pause, before we have questions," Mr Rummage said.

*

Tyro had heard everything from her room, as if her heightened senses had been able to penetrate walls, feel the subtle echoes of voices through the house. She also heard another voice. At first it was no more than a distant and indistinct cry. Then it became clearer. It was calling her. She got up off the bed and went to the door of her room. Turning she saw the cat, Biscuit, asleep on the carpet outside her door. The watching figure had gone.

"Biscuit!" she cried. "Was that you?"

She walked a little down the corridor to the stairs. She rubbed her eyes, and looked out of the window on the landing. She could hear the sound of voices and then she heard them suddenly stop. A cold reality broke through into her half-sleep and she leant forward, trying to remember what they had just been saying below. The kitchen door must be open. Had the new voice that she had heard, she was quite sure that she had, also been someone downstairs? Before the conversation resumed, and before she could answer herself, she heard the voice again say, "Follow me!"

She turned her head. The hall behind her was empty. The light gave it a curious glow. Biscuit was still asleep.

She checked herself and turned to go downstairs. Now she was awake. She must go down and find out more. She was being watched. Then she noticed something out of the window.

Below and far ahead in the darkness outside, she saw a light. At first she thought it was the light of one of the neighbour's houses, through the trees. Then the light moved. She could not normally see the neighbours' lights from up here.

She had often checked for reassurance, as a small child, which lights belonged to which house, and from where they could be seen. She knew very clearly that it was none of these. Besides, the light was moving, or wavering. She looked again. There were too many trees, like haunted giants cloaked in leaf, hung about with an autumn mist. It was not possible to see anyone.

She was sure that the light came from the churchyard.

Tyro was not afraid, though she should have been. She was drawn.

There were the familiar voices of her mother and Dennis, even her Headmaster ("How embarrassing!" she thought).

This was the perfect opportunity to go alone. She had heard a voice which was as real as any of her dreams, and it was not threatening.

She went back to her room on tiptoe. Below there was even what seemed like a burst of laughter.

She went to her clothes cupboard, threw on an old pair of jeans and a jersey. She took the small cross-sword from her bedside table and hung it about her neck. Its use was limited no doubt, but it made her feel better. It had stalled the figures, once, it seemed. There was no place for a wishing key and magic potion now. She blushed in embarrassment.

She would go down the back stairs. She didn't want to disturb anyone. Jess was not here to hold her back. Yet she missed her. Rick would be proud of her.

"Tyro!" came a voice from below. It was subdued but sharp. "Are you alright?"

"Yes," Tyro said, as if from under the bedclothes (actually through the sleeve of her jersey), followed by a diminishing "Mum". She didn't want anyone to come upstairs to check. It seemed to work.

The conversation below was dominated by a voice she did not know. It was that of Dr Vale, briefing the group on recent Priory activities. Not only was it their intention, apparently, to blackmail the church, but also to establish a new one, under their guidance.

This was followed by Dr Bartok, who spoke about the Dream Notation Chamber. He seemed to be having some success in making people's dreams visual. The most interesting point however was that he was receiving signals - unknown images - from an unidentified source, certainly not from any of his patients. He had no explanation. Mr Rummage listened with intense interest.

Tyro crept downstairs, unlocked the door with the key still

in the lock, pulled on her boots, took an old coat off the rack and went out into the night.

Rompy decided he needed some night air too. She tried to shove him back, but he would not budge. She felt in her pockets and found his lead. She would tie him up further along the drive, and go on alone. Rompy was wagging his tail.

Tyro hadn't seen the figure who watched her leave.

4

Tyro's feet made a crunching sound over the gravel, so she edged to the side of the drive where the grass would muffle her steps. Rompy was jumping up at her. She tried to push him down, firmly but quietly, irritated that she was losing concentration. Rompy eventually got the message and was soon walking in front of Tyro, out of the exit onto the road.

The figure who had stood sentinel outside her room had followed and was now standing amongst the trees.

Tyro turned right, losing sight of Rompy. She opened a gate into the churchyard, all the time keeping an eye on the light that seemed to come and go. It seemed to appear when she was about to lose sight of it, and then, just as she was getting complacent, it vanished.

Tyro glanced back at the house now visible through the trees, with several windows lit. At first she didn't notice the stones around her, mostly gravestones, though one was the remnant of an ancient stone circle. She didn't notice the dark fall of shadow that bled from the yews dotted here and there. She had lost the light, but remembered its direction. She looked at the church as she walked more slowly, trying not to disturb the resting places of the dead, nor to knock over the flowers and decorations which even at night seemed to give a glow of life.

She began to think of the empty shell of the church. The

spirits that it contained in its still, cold interior, flanked by echoes from the centuries, struggling to put justice above faith. It was this more than anything that made her frightened.

There was no movement. The figure had become part of those shadows. Everything was frozen momentarily - the trees, the headstones, the flowers of remembrance, the plaques of the young who had died in infancy, lost in the grass, but reflecting the stars. The mist hung heavy now. She still could see lights from her house beyond. The neighbour's house just the other side of the church became blurred.

She heard the sound of a broken branch. The click of a snapped twig.

"Is somebody there?"

She turned, listening to her own breathing, and felt the touch of a cloak graze her hand.

Tyro leapt back, trying to catch a glimpse of the face which glared at her, a face lit up by a torch, the face of someone she knew.

"Rick!" She muffled a scream, wrapping her arms around him. She stood back again, and saw his homemade cloak beneath the crude hat that made him look like a sacred scarecrow.

"Rick! What in Heaven's name are you doing . . . ?"

"Shh! I think I may have been followed."

"Who by? But what are you . . . ?"

"Shhhh! Does anyone know you're here?"

"Of course not. What are you doing here?"

"I thought I heard a noise. I'm checking out a theory," he said. "I didn't mean to bring you out. I didn't know I could be seen."

"You mean you weren't signalling to me? You weren't going to call me? I heard a noise too."

"I . . . "

Rather than explain, Rick led Tyro to the south of the churchyard to an old yew.

They could now hear voices from the house. Rick stopped a moment to listen. He could clearly make out Abby.

"Who are they all?"

"Mr Rummage has been over with others. I heard something I must tell you about. They're very worried. Something happened at the school, which they have kept very quiet about."

"Later, Tyro. Look here!"

Rick helped Tyro closer to the yew.

"Down there."

Tyro saw a tunnel entrance in the torchlight.

"It goes all the way to Burnchester, I think. There are other tunnels leading off it, and rooms. Some of them contain old radio equipment. Transmitters, I think. It also goes to Stimple. What's more, I found metal strips attached at intervals to the walls. One of them was loose so I took it."

Rick showed Tyro a rectangular piece of metal a few centimetres long, which seemed to glow in the dark.

"What is it?"

"Tyro! Tyro, come here!" It was Dennis.

"Have you got Rompy, Tyro? Where are you? What are you doing?"

Abby had seen the light and was hurrying over to the ditch which separated her garden from the churchyard. Rick extinguished it.

"I don't know. I've got to go. Take this! Look after it! Say nothing! Be on your guard!"

"Be careful, Rick."

Rick leapt into the dark centre of the old tree.

Tyro wanted to follow. She had lots of questions, not least about who he thought was following him. She put the piece of metal in her pocket.

Tyro felt numbed. It was too late to follow. She moved instinctively away from the old tree.

Abby would never let her out again.

"Rompy!" Tyro called innocently. "Come here, Rompy!"

"Tyro? Are you mad? What are you doing out at this time? Come in at once!"

"I'm looking for Rompy," said Tyro, close to the churchyard gate.

"He's here!" said her mother. "What do you think you're doing, going out alone at night, and out of the garden? Never, never, never do that again! You've given us all a terrible shock!"

Tyro was on the drive, standing next to Abby, whose face she could see by the outside house light was full of tears. She was feeling guilty as well as angry.

"Two shocks for one night is too much! Come in at once."

Tyro didn't react. Abby led her back down the drive.

Dennis had gone on. He suspected that Tyro would have another reason for going out, than to find Rompy. He was angry too. She was in danger of becoming a liability to herself. Yet he knew her role would lead her into danger. He would tell her Mr Rummage's story. That might restrain her.

Dennis went on with a torch to check one of the perimeter trip-beams which he had set up to detect intruders. The automatic monitor which he wore on his belt had registered an unusual note a little earlier, but it was not a full alarm. Something had triggered it. Yet the beam seemed OK. He also checked one of the "mirrors", which was able to take the imprint of energy from a person, even at some distance. It had left no mark, though the ground beside it had been disturbed.

"Has Mr Rummage gone? I don't want to see him."

"You don't have to," said Abby as they entered the side door. "Go upstairs to bed! Never, ever do anything like that again!"

Tyro could see the fear and anger in her mother's face.

Abby followed Tyro up the stairs.

"Go away!" Tyro shouted. "I can get back into bed alone. I don't like being lied to!"

Tyro was confused. Not being able to follow Rick, conscious that something may have followed her, she felt anxious.

"What were you doing, Tyro?" Abby asked quietly, holding her daughter tightly. "You never know what might be out there."

Could she follow Rick? Would she find the right tree? Would Rick be safe? What was he up to?

Abby tried to smile.

"I promise, Mum," said Tyro. "I'm sorry, Mum. I'll go to sleep now. Is Rompy alright? What did Mr Rummage want?"

"I'll tell you in the morning. What did you mean about 'lying'?"

"I heard what was said in your meeting. Will the children be alright? The figures are back, then."

"Yes, I think so. Shocked, but they will survive. Go to sleep now. We are strong too, you know. Stronger than they know. Good night."

Abby went downstairs. Tyro lay down and tried to calm a beating heart and to control a desire to get up again, and go into the night. Far from being frightened, she was animated. The picture on her wall seemed to glow. The horizon, and the journey. Perhaps her dreams would show her the way out. She lay awake, then tossed and turned. She pictured Rick, in a dark tunnel, amidst the damp and the roots of trees. She wished to be there too. She knew that for the moment they would be safe. Until the figures had what they wanted. If they found anything, the hardest task would be to keep it secret. And away from *them.*

In her dreams, Jess stood beside her. She heard the voice of Rick calling from a distant place. The words from her English lesson seemed to come at her, following the rhythm of her heart: "And oftentimes, to win us to our harm, the instruments of darkness tell us truths." Was there some battle raging that made her nothing but a trophy for the Gods? In her half-sleep she got up and put some music on. It was this other enchantment that stole her heart.

Mr Rummage, Dr Vale and Dr Bartok left an hour later. Inspector Relish decided to walk, something he did from time to time. The darkness had always been his ally. Dr Vale would stay at Burnchester overnight, as a guest of the Rummages, before going on to visit the Bishop of Dunemoor the following morning. He was to brief him on the latest activities of the Priory and other matters. The Church establishment, here and in Rome, was increasingly worried about its activities. It felt vulnerable enough without further external threats. Dr Vale wanted to look at the painting again. He knew the painting very well, yet he was sure it held more secret clues to the meaning and whereabouts of the Spearhead. Was it a matter of *how* you looked?

Dr Bartok would return to Cambridge. He had patients to see in the morning.

Abby and Dennis sat down at the kitchen table.

Abby spoke first. She didn't broach the subject of why Mr Rummage had come. It was enough to know that he had, and that what they had heard sent shock waves into her soul. She presumed that Dr Vale and Dr Bartok were there as part of a pre-arranged meeting.

Clearly there were advantages in not meeting at Burnchester, in view of the threats there.

"Are we safe?" she asked. "Is Tyro safe, is what I really mean? I don't believe she went out looking for Rompy. She went out looking for something else. She overheard some of what we said. I am not sure if that is good or bad."

"There's not much she doesn't know, too much for her years. It is a kind of Fate."

"I'm worried for her childhood. She doesn't have much left and it's being torn apart. In ways that she may not know, and which she cannot share with us. I'm worried for the little children, for Mr Bellevue, everybody."

Dennis said nothing. As far as he was concerned Tyro had been chosen, for all that that might mean. Abby continued.

"What will happen now? Two children in a state of shock and Mr Bellevue in hospital. Many children terrified. The figures have returned. The Priory in the news again. We still don't know quite who or what they are, and what their aim is. All parents will know by tomorrow, and the press have caught on again, and will not stop until they know what's going on. Which is fine, but none of us do, and they won't believe that."

"We have to be practical. I will go to the school tomorrow and look around. Mr Rummage has asked Mr Granger, Mr Gruff and Mr Grudge for a full report. He wants to downplay things. The school must go on as normal. Even Bonfire Night must be allowed to continue. I will also put in some further security, at Mr Rummage's suggestion. I think there may have been someone or something near the house tonight. I do not think they will attack us while they think we can be of use. The Spearhead and power is their goal, and they need our help."

"Allowing Bonfire Night to go ahead is asking for trouble."

"What would you do? Close the school down, change your mind again. That would give out worse signals. Safety will not be compromised. In fact, it might offer us an opportunity."

"What do you mean?" Abby asked.

Dennis paused. The telephone began to ring.

Abby let it ring until the answer system kicked in.

"Please call Andrew Veech urgently. We have information that might be of use to you. Someone has reported dark figures attacking children. A community in terror. Could you comment?"

Abby pulled out the plug and sat down again.

"What did you mean by an opportunity, Dennis?"

Abby looked round and saw a figure in the doorway. It was Tyro. She appeared to be asleep. She had always sleepwalked. Abby got up and went over to her.

"Think about it. The whole school: teachers, children and

parents around a bonfire watching fireworks. What better time to strike? What better time to be prepared. What better time to ensnare them. I think I shall encourage Mr Rummage to continue."

Abby was only half-listening as she led Tyro through the hall.

Dennis took this as the cue to check the doors. He was disturbed that something might be in the house. If it were, it hadn't caused any trouble yet. Yes, someone or something had been through the side entrance.

He was armed, but that might not be a protection against this force. Despite the Stranger's injury over the summer, something else was needed. Some other countermeasure.

Rompy was still asleep. He rarely barked at strangers. Dennis listened silently. He heard Abby above. Were there other footsteps as well?

*

Mr Rummage turned his car into the drive that led down to Burnchester Hall. The three men had remained silent for most of the journey, looking out into the countryside shrouded in dark.

The Hall looked magnificent, like a great ship at mooring below in the valley. The Church, its rudder. Mr Rummage glanced up at the observation tower, high on the roof of the school. The security guard at the gate stood up as the car approached.

The Guard looked in at the two passengers.

"No trouble at all, Sir, apart from that gentleman over there."

Mr Rummage looked at a car on the other side of the drive. A man was asleep in the driver's seat.

"Wouldn't go. Threatened him with the police, until I realised that Inspector Relish was with you, Sir."

"Nothing else?"

"Nothing at all, Sir. Quiet as the grave. Security are all over the grounds."

Mr Rummage thanked him and drove on.

Mr Rummage and Dr Vale said goodbye to Dr Bartok as he got into his car. Soon he was on his way.

In the vast grounds, in the still night, somewhere amidst the ruins of time and place, in the scarred landscape of Burnchester's complex past, close to the ruin of an Iron Age fort, in the crypt of a medieval church, or the Dome below the school, unknown powers were at work, figures were lying in wait. Or did they come from outside? Or both? Was one connected to or a creation of the other?

"Could I go and look at the painting now? It would be interesting to see it at night," Dr Vale asked.

Dr Vale was used to the darkest corners of the church. Dr Vale was not afraid, retiring though he was.

"Of course. Here's the key. You know how the lighting works. I would join you but I must go and see Jenny, and wake up Mr Veech. We'll be up when you come in."

Mr Rummage watched Dr Vale go towards the Church of St Mary Magdalen. He decided to leave Veech.

Mr Rummage wanted to outwit the Priory and defend the school as best he could. He wanted to flush them out. He wanted confrontation. He wanted to find a way of pre-empting them, but the power that he had, with others, could only be used defensively, as his training had told him. This was a precondition for training. He had to be patient.

Whilst the children were there, he would take all precautions.

Without the children, there would be no purpose, no purpose at all. They were a part of the future, here and in every place on earth. It was they who needed to be protected. He was still not clear who the enemy was, though he had an idea.

It would soon be time for another call to Doonwreath. Mr Rummage chuckled. He wanted to believe. It was not his job to judge but to bear witness.

Jenny was still up when he went in. She told him that security had completely searched the school grounds. They had found nothing, though would continue in the morning. Had he seen Mr Veech?

As the children had not been allowed to phone home, contact with the press had to have come from someone else. She had no idea who, but staff - those who lived on site - had been on alert, and most were up and helping security. Mr Gruff had, understandably, taken the incident badly though he was being comforted by Mr Grudge. She was worried about a relapse. Mr Baxter had called. So had a Mrs McCleod.

"Our church warden?"

"No, from Scotland."

Mrs McCleod was the Rummages' neighbour on the Island that the family had visited in the summer.

"That's unusual. Did she say what she wanted?"

"She wanted to let us know that a man had been on the island collecting stones. The person had not yet found any of the sort that you had found. He asked many questions."

Mr Rummage went over to Jenny and hugged her. She was his ally in every way. Together, and only together, could they generate the power that was needed. Others were trained and there would be more. But there were not many adepts.

They sat down and waited for Dr Vale. Together, in that curious period which seemed outside time, they devised a plan. One that would involve the children - the three children that is - in a journey of great danger, if the circumstances required it. Jenny knew better than he of Tyro's power. She knew it was unique, but that a team was required, one that had already it seemed been chosen.

By the time the children arrived at school the next day, Mr Rummage had been up most of the night. He had contacted two governors who were not used to late calls, to ensure support for the continuation of Bonfire Night. In his mind this was essential. He had contacted the Ministry in London to brief them, and asked for their further assistance, both in supplying extra security and in order to request that he be informed of their activities beneath ground. The level below the Domed Chamber had been operated for some time.

They were not keen on supplying more personnel. It wasn't their top priority at the moment. They had too many other commitments. Mr Rummage said that it should become one. They would gladly keep him informed of activities beneath ground, but could he not find a local team to extend the search of the network of tunnels which still posed a potential security risk? Mr Rummage would think about it.

Mr Rummage had been briefed by the security teams already in place and by his own staff, including Mr Gruff, about the search last night, and about what exactly had happened. He particularly wanted to know if there had been reports of any similar events elsewhere. He knew from experience that these things rarely happened in isolation. He noticed Mr Gruff's inability to remember certain details, which seemed to have been erased from his mind. He had returned to the bonfire and entered the wood. He must protect Mr Gruff. He asked to be informed of any unusual activities. There was an informant. There was inside complicity. Perhaps there was a member of the Priory in the school.

Mr Rummage had arranged for a detailed forensic search of the stretch of the woodland adjacent to the bonfire, and through the whole area that they had walked. The perimeter also needed checking. The river, the boathouse, all the out-buildings. Figures do not simply appear and disappear without trace, yet the silent figure of Tom haunted him and reminded him that they did. Tom was a puzzle. Desperate to help him, he suspected that Tom was in fact capable of looking after himself. Mr Rummage had relived, some weeks after the events, how Tom had been essential in the suppression of the Dark Master.

Most pressing of all, Mr Rummage had to think how best to tackle Mr Strangelblood. After his return from the church the previous night, Dr Vale had told him something which he felt he could not have shared at their earlier meeting. According to Dr Vale, Mr Strangelblood was involved in financing the Priory. Mr Rummage asked him how he knew, given the extent and complexity of Mr Strangelblood's empire. Dr Vale had said nothing, simply that his connections were extensive. He had mentioned one more thing which was of more importance to him. Inside the church - no, he had not been tricked by the night light - the figure of the Madonna and Child had undergone a transformation. Whereas the Madonna had been a traditional white and blue, she was now cloaked black.

Mr Rummage decided to arrange a meeting with Mr Strangelblood. His cover would be to seek permission to search the entire strip of land between the school and Strangelblood Hall, which included the site of the Iron Age fort and the area behind Folly Ridge, including the woods that led to the Burnchester Arms. If necessary he would have the river dredged. This would be sanctioned by the police, in view of the emergence of what he would call "criminal elements". He needed more information, but he must meet with him first.

Mr Rummage considered how best to handle the media, what to tell them, what to tell the parents. Jenny had been fantastic, offering shrewd and sensitive advice, taking the mother's view, horrified at the slightest suggestion that any child should be at risk.

"Only if you can guarantee the safety of all the children, should you even begin to consider continuing with Bonfire Night," she had said calmly.

Inspector Relish had arrived at seven to offer Mr Rummage his advice. The first contingency would have to be put in place. Other officers were to be detailed to help him, and would be arriving later that morning.

Mr Veech had been invited in for breakfast, to keep him out of the way at this sensitive moment, to keep him, in vain, from asking questions.

*

A great deal had been accomplished by the time the cars rolled down the drive to deposit the children.

Parents and children - those who arrived by car - were greeted at the bottom of the drive by the notice board which normally told of events: concerts, parents' evenings, trips and sports activities.

Abby and Dennis read the words carefully as Tyro jumped out, not even saying goodbye. She ran off shouting, "Jess, Jess, wait for me! I've got some news." She didn't see the notice. Jess, who was just getting out of her car, met Tyro as they entered the hall together for morning assembly. Julia was behind them, with Jane.

Tyro told Jess that she was angry because Rick had not been waiting for them. Aunt Patrolia had said that he was unwell and would not be going to school today - besides, there was too much for him to do at home. This was quite unlike Aunt Patrolia, for whilst she was jealous of Rick's time at school, and did her very best to remind him of his good fortune, making him do more not fewer jobs at home and in the garden in compensation, she nevertheless retained a curious susceptibility to its importance. Jess was not overly impressed.

However, when it came to Tyro's story of the night before, about her encounter with Rick, about the light in the churchyard, and what she had overheard, Jess's interest grew. Julia heard every word.

The notice read:

"All parents are requested to attend a meeting this morning at 11 o'clock (in hall). If you cannot come, please telephone the office. Thank you. It is important. Signed Mr Rummage, the Headmaster."

"I think we know what that's going to be about," said Abby as she drove round along to the changing rooms to leave Tyro's games kit.

"Will you be able to get off work?" Dennis asked as he got out of the car and looked back through the passenger window.

"I'll try. I'd better rush."

Dennis went into the changing rooms to deposit Tyro's kit bag, and came back out. He had permission from Mr Rummage to go anywhere in the school, and look at security. As he looked across the drive he noticed that the usual bottle-neck of cars trying to get out of the drive was considerably worse than usual. In fact it looked pretty much like chaos. There were cars parked everywhere.

Part of the problem was that mothers and fathers were holding everybody up. It didn't take much for him to realise what they might be talking about. Especially as amongst them was a man taking notes.

Dennis thought it was Mr Veech. Within a few minutes, one of the guards from the gate came hurriedly down and asked the man to leave. For all their faults, journalists needed managing. Dennis decided to cut back up the drive, and speak to him.

Tyro and Jess threw their bags on their desks. History first lesson. Tyro was continuing the story of her adventures of the evening before. She was too absorbed to hear the teacher calling for silence, as he began the register.

"Shhhh!" called a voice nearby. "Stop talking!" It was Julia, trying to draw the teacher's attention.

Mr Vesper's manner was crisp and functional. He did not seem to have any affinity with his students. There was something mechanical in his actions, as if he lacked humanity.

"David . . . "

"Yes, Sir."

"John . . . "

"Shhh . . . !" came the voice again. The teacher looked up.

"Present, Sir."

"Rick . . . "

The teacher had said nothing about the whispers, hoping that they would die down, but they did not. He had, thanks to Julia, caught sight of Tyro in conversation with Jess in the back row. Mr Vespers bided his time. Everyone sat still, expecting the worst.

"Rick . . . ?" repeated the teacher. There was a further pause. "Has anyone seen Rick?"

"No, Sir," said John.

"Rick, absent." The teacher paused again. Tyro's voice was now louder.

"Tyro . . . "

For once Jess was too absorbed to notice the loaded silence.

"Tyro! . . . " called the teacher again, more loudly.

There was another brief pause, then Jess, now sensing trouble, nudged Tyro and looked up, smiling innocently. Tyro, catching the drift, but too proud to show it, stopped and bent down to the floor to pick up a pencil which had rolled off the desk a little earlier.

The teacher crossed the class to where the two girls sat. He held his arm high above the point where Tyro's head would have been, holding a hardback book as if ready to strike. The class was dumbstruck. Tyro, who sensed a presence above her, decided to act. So did the teacher, who turned to the class, and asked, with a quivering smile on his face, "Shall I?"

Just as Julia and others, then joined by most of the class, shouted out a resounding, "Yes, Sir!" very loudly, so that it could be heard in the hall outside the class; just at the moment that Mr Vesper's arm swung onto what he had thought would be an elevating head, so Tyro fell to the floor with a crash. In the process, the chair fell over and the teacher's swing just missed the pupil the other side of Tyro, which was Jess.

There was a burst of laughter. Mr Vespers collected himself.

He was not amused. He had been humiliated. His attack had backfired.

"Tyro! Get up at once! Come and see me at the end of the lesson! You've been talking all through the register and now this! Your behaviour is intolerable." Then he added as if to check himself, "Have you seen Rick?"

"No, Sir." Tyro was back in her chair looking defiant. "I think he's gone somewhere, Sir."

She wished she had kept quiet. Without knowing why, Tyro wished that this information should remain secret. She didn't trust Mr Vespers.

"Gone somewhere? What are you talking about, Tyro?" He looked around the class as if to say Tyro has lost it.

"She's talking rubbish," put in Julia, "she always does, Sir."

"OK, wonder brain," spouted John.

"Quiet, both of you! What do you mean, gone somewhere?"

Tyro could not help herself. She hated betraying secrets, especially to teachers, but it just came out.

"He was not at home when we went round this morning. We bring him to school, normally, Sir."

Mr Vespers knew that time was limited. He knew about

Tyro, Jess, Rick and Tom. He needed them. He also hated them. He knew of the dangers that his cover might be blown. Mr Rummage was not yet onto him. As far as he knew.

"How do you know he was not at home?"

"Well, his aunt said he was ill, but I know that isn't true because I saw him the night before" (whistles from the boys), "and he was alright then. His aunt was lying, Sir. I know Rick isn't at home."

"Be careful what you say about Rick's aunt, Tyro. You don't know that she was lying. He may well be ill, though I agree it's not common for Rick to be away."

Mr Vespers was, of course, aware of Aunt Patrolia's reputation. He knew her well, and she was dispensable.

"I know she was lying, Sir, I know it."

Mr Vespers paused, as if his suspicions were confirmed.

"Well, Tyro. I can't comment on that."

The teacher went on with the register. When he finished, he asked Tyro to come to the front of the class. As she stood there, the teacher told the class to get out their books and turn to chapter 10, on page 176. "Heresy and witchcraft in Tudor England: reasons to be condemned." He said he would test them on it in twenty minutes.

"But that's unfair, Sir! You were going to tell us the story of Guy Fawkes, Sir," said John.

Mr Vespers smiled as if his upturned lips were the flames themselves.

"If you're not careful, John, I'll burn you at the stake!"

"Good riddance!" shouted Julia.

"Can I light it?" said Harry.

At this point all hell might have been let loose, had not the teacher brought the class under control by a ferocious whack on the desk with a book, which made everybody jump.

"Get on with it. Or I'll roast you all alive. Guy Fawkes's cause should be celebrated." He'd said too much. "If you're not careful, I'll bring you all in for detention, with Tyro."

Though Tyro was popular with many of the class, it was not enough to encourage them to come to her defence at this moment, and it thoroughly motivated Julia and Jane.

If they were good, he said, after a pause, he would leave them for a few minutes as he had to go to the library.

The thought of the teacher being away, even for a few minutes, made every boy and girl bend his/her head hard against his/her desk in the pose of studying with real interest.

Once the class had settled, Mr Vespers gave Tyro the register and told her to take it to the office and to explain to the secretary what she had told him. Tyro was thinking how she might delay her return, when an idea struck her.

"Could I get the thing from the library that you wanted, Sir? It's on my way back."

Mr Vespers looked at Tyro, as if assessing her motive. Tyro avoided his eyes, and flinched. There was an intense collective sigh from the class, which Tyro heard but ignored.

Mr Vespers paused a moment, saw the boys fidgeting in the back row.

He walked Tyro to the back of the class, in order to keep out of earshot and handed her a note. Heads seemed to move with him, but they heard nothing. Even Jess seemed put out.

Mr Vespers kept his voice low.

"I trust you won't delay, Tyro. There'll be trouble if you do. Go to Mr Blakemore, the librarian, and tell him that you have come on my behalf. He will give you a document that I have asked for. He will know. He helps me a great deal. It is a manuscript from the archive that I wanted to show the class. Hurry."

He was lying.

Tyro left immediately, casting a glance at Jess as she went.

Julia was about to speak.

"Don't interrupt!" Mr Vespers said.

Julia felt afraid. Never had she felt more threatened by a teacher. She so desperately wanted to reveal what she had heard about Mr Vespers. She had overheard her father and mother talking.

There was, for a moment, the semblance of concentration, and the possibility that they were all - or mostly - doing what the teacher had asked. Mr Vespers was enjoying himself.

*

Once Tyro was out of the class, she ran. Ran like the wind. It was almost as if she was flying again. Something about Mr Vespers made her shake to the core. Nothing tangible. An insight that didn't need explanation. She knew that the document was nothing to do with lessons. She was determined to find out what it was.

Within a few moments she had taken the register to Mrs Clicket, the secretary, and told her the story about Rick. She noticed the group of parents outside, waiting for the meeting. There were even one or two policemen near the car park and the changing rooms.

Mrs Clicket thanked her, not before Tyro had told her which lesson she was from and where she was going next. The secretary understood.

Tyro then raced up the stairs to the library, paused, changed pace and pushed the door open.

How was she going to get access to the back room and open the door into the tunnels? The room at the back of the Biology class was locked, and this was the only other entrance. She was sure that Rick was down there. He had got lost, or he had found something important. Perhaps he had been captured. She wanted to be with him, and carry on the search for Tom, though she wasn't going to leave Jess behind. If only she could find him.

She walked into the library with an air of calm, yet watchful.

She told the librarian, the monk-like Mr Blakemore, that Mr Vespers had sent her, and handed him the note.

The librarian turned and asked her to follow.

She wanted to ask him something, but the smell of the library, the dark still scent of leather, mixed with dust and polish, made her pause. She saw the library in a new way.

They went into the archive room, where old stacks stood with books and manuscripts from every age, some behind glass, others behind locked metal grills, from the ceiling to the floor. She could see some of the names, Paracelsus, Ficino, Newton. There were desks and files and shelves, with documents of every size and shape, some papers lying on the tops, a few old cards, scattered in a festival of jottings.

There was a clock on the mantelshelf.

Tyro wanted to retreat. The pictures on the wall were looking at her as if to warn her off. She touched the cross-sword about her neck.

She knew that the library contained many secrets. About the school's past, spy training, not to mention the dark days of the Reformation (Mr Vespers had drummed it into them). He went on about the true Church. The need to return to the right path.

Mr Baxter, for his part, said the library contained books about alchemy and things she didn't understand. He told them to imagine Shakespeare's visit. It was only now that she had thought of Shakespeare as human at all. The library was less threatening than it had been. She began to think of the books too as living, though she preferred the modern ones, about science and practical things. Shakespeare was spooky. "The instruments of darkness" might apply to science too. Newton had been there.

All the while, Mr Blakemore chattered to himself, murmuring what sounded like incantations.

Tyro saw the locked door at the back; the door that led down to the tunnels. The door through which PC Relish had passed and had fought with one of the figures. Close to the place where Dennis had torn a piece of cloth from its cloak. The door which was normally hidden.

The door which led, she knew, into a kind of hell, where she had encountered figures and forces that frightened and yet drew her, half in and half out of her conscious thoughts, somewhere in the battle for her mind. Where did the lift go? Why was it so new, while everything else was so old and decayed? Who went there?

These images mingled with her memories of France.

The librarian returned with a small book. Tucked inside there was some sort of manuscript. It was then that he saw the cross-sword about her neck.

Mr Blakemore went to the desk and put the book inside a plastic bag, and asked Tyro to sign for it. This made her feel rather grand, though she put Mr Vesper's name in the withdrawal column.

As she took the bag under her arm, she looked up at the librarian, who evidently wanted to get rid of her.

"Look after it - go straight to the classroom. You mustn't lose it on any account."

"Yes, Mr Blakemore," Tyro said with unusual deference. Then, in her most innocent voice, she looked him in the eyes and added, "Would you mind telling me what's behind that door, Mr Blakemore?"

The librarian was surprised.

"Books," he said, "and more books. Enough to give you homework for the rest of your life. And thereafter."

"Doesn't it lead to the tunnels? Wasn't it part of the secret missions and work during the Second World War? Aren't they still being used?" Tyro asked.

Mr Blakemore looked Tyro in the eye, and walked back into the main reading room, Tyro following.

Mr Blakemore turned, having thought about his answer.

"Tunnels? Oh, those. They were blocked years ago."

She knew he was lying, and he suspected she knew it too.

The librarian walked to the door and opened it.

"Now hurry back to the classroom. On no account show the

book to anybody but Mr Vespers. Make sure you bring it back straight after the lesson."

And then, as if in afterthought.

"What is your name, child?"

"Tyro."

"I thought so. Your powers are unusual, I'm told."

Tyro turned and left the room. She felt angry and wanted to say, "No, of course not, it was all a mistake." But it hadn't been a mistake. She couldn't deny the truth. For his part Mr Blakemore had seen her father's cross-sword. The Father they must dethrone.

As soon as she was at the top of the stairs, she raced down them - she only had a minute or two before Mr Vespers would start agitating - slowed outside Mr Rummage's office, then turned right out of the back door, which overlooked the playing fields and took her round the main building the other way.

Tyro raced along the wall breathing rapidly all the time. Mr Blakemore was not to be trusted, neither was Mr Vespers. She ducked under windows, where classes were in progress, and hurried to the line of yews where Rick and Tom had hidden their tunnel entrance. She didn't care whether she could be seen. This was too important for her. She must find Rick.

She dropped the book which, fortunately, was protected by its plastic cover, which now showed a ridge of sandy dirt.

As she picked it up, she decided to take a closer look. She unfolded the plastic and took out the book. She opened the page and took out the folded manuscript. She only had a moment to read the top line: "The Lost Secret: the Valley of the King."

She wanted to take the manuscript to Mr Rummage immediately. Although she didn't understand the meaning of the words, she was certain they were important. She wanted to hide the book and run.

She searched each yew to find the tunnel, but found nothing

but a blocked up entrance. She hurried on, back round the school, where parents were still talking, at which point she slowed, and walked back to the teaching block and to her classroom.

She entered, tired and shaking. Mr Vespers had been watching from the window. He had seen her open the book. Jess was trying to signal to Tyro, but Tyro was not focusing.

Mr Vesper's cruel stare was from another age.

"What took you so long, Tyro?" Mr Vespers asked, watching the lies formulate.

"I had to see my mother, Sir," she said. She handed Mr Vespers the book and sat down.

"Writing books out!" Mr Vespers ordered. "Now that Tyro's back, we can have our test. Tyro will have to do what she can."

There was a general noise of pens being searched for, books dragged from desks and from school bags, in the usual attempt to delay the proceedings, during which Jess turned to Tyro.

"Where've you been? Vipers saw you drop the book and look at it."

"Looking for Rick. We were supposed to meet him later, remember. I think he's in the tunnels."

Mr Vespers was standing above Tyro, appearing ready to strike. He was no longer acting. He was genuinely angry. The class sensed it and remained absolutely still.

Tyro looked at her book. Mr Vespers walked on round the class, revelling in the control, the silence. He slowed and began to talk at the same time. The class's despair was in perfect tune with Mr Vespers's pleasure. Despite appearances, most hadn't read a word for the last twenty minutes.

A sense of panic was fed by helplessness. Pen tops were taken off, writing books opened.

"Text books closed. You have ten minutes to write and ten minutes only. If anybody so much as breathes I'll bring you back after school and make you do a two hour detention. I've had enough of your cheek. I've had enough of being lied to."

He looked at Tyro, who now bore the brunt of the class's anger, even though it was unjustified.

He held the book that Tyro had brought to him. Then he added, "I will write my instructions on the board. I want no questions at all. No interruptions of any kind until I say so."

He went to the blackboard. With his back turned one or two quickly opened their text books, hoping to get a clue from the pages they hadn't read.

Mr Vespers took a piece of chalk from the tray. He wrote in large letters on the board, "What was the justification for burning heretics in the Reformation?"

The class was dumbfounded.

Mr Vespers turned and faced the class.

Without a flicker or a hint of humour, he held his finger up to his lips as if to confirm that if they spoke they would be signing their own death warrants. Tyro looked at Jess, Julia at Jane, David at his book and John at the floor.

There was a slow release of breath and the writing began. The panic turned to a kind of manic displacement. Few knew what the Reformation was. Most ended up writing about Guy Fawkes. Several wrote nothing.

*

After the lesson, they left in a state of fear. "I'd like to burn Tyro," said Julia.

Tyro and Jess went back to the library to return the book, on their way to their Art class. Art, then break, then English, then Biology. Lunch. Tyro was in deep thought.

When they finally reached Ms Peverell's class, she was in a state of anxiety.

"But Jess," she was saying, "don't you realise what this means? It means Mr Vespers and Mr Blakemore belong to the Priory. Why else would he be doing that? In the middle of classes, when they see each other in break? Don't they? It's the perfect cover."

"In other words they're traitors! We must watch them carefully," said Jess. "I want to know what the parents are going to be told in break. According to a boy in class 6 the army are going to take over the whole school after last night."

Tyro entered Ms Peverell's class, only to find a policeman in uniform talking with her.

Most of the class were already at their desks. Jess looked at Tyro as if to say, "I told you so."

5

"What can we do?" Jess asked, during break.

"Go in search of him," Tyro replied.

"There are plenty of places to look. The old boathouse. The woods that lead to Strangelblood's. It's harder with the added security."

"We could ask again at Rick's house. Uncle John would tell us."

The difficulty was getting past Aunt Patrolia.

"If we went out of school, judging by what happened last night, we would probably be expelled."

"If there's still a school to be expelled from."

"What are you suggesting?"

"Don't you see, Jess? If there are other attacks, the school will close."

"I never thought I would be against school closing."

The bell rang and they went towards the classrooms. Julia was nearby, talking to John.

"Mr Blakemore and Mr Vespers are definitely up to something," said Tyro to Jess in a low voice. "I will try to get into the library and enter the tunnels to the Domed Chamber."

They passed crowds of people entering the assembly hall, mostly parents but also teachers who were not in class. There was a policeman at the door. Mr Rummage was standing outside. No children were allowed in.

"I'll see if I can find out anything from Julia."

Jess moved up to her as they reached the classroom for their English lesson.

Mr Baxter was ushering them in to class. He had moved the desks and chairs around the sides of the room and got the class to sit in a circle around the central stage, some on desks. An empty space needs filling even in imagination.

As they sat down, the class chatter subsided.

John was taking the remaining desks to the back. Jess was now whispering something to Tyro, and Julia was talking to Jane.

Julia looked at Jess but directed her words to Tyro.

" 'When the hurly-burly's done, when the battle's lost and won'. Are you ready, witch? Or are you afraid?" she snarled.

Tyro stared at Julia.

"There are three witches, remember."

"Stop it, you two!" Mr Baxter said.

He told the class that they were going to act out scene three again (the one where Macbeth is told that he will be King).

"Where's Rick?"

David had his hand up.

"Sir?" David said. "Excuse me, Sir, but what's going on, Sir?"

"What do you mean, David? You know the scene I'm talking about. Where's Rick?"

"I mean here, Sir, in school, Sir." David spoke with conviction and quiet clarity. He was a lively child.

"Explain what you mean, David, I'm sure we're all longing to know."

"First there was last night when the juniors were terrified. They've been forbidden from speaking. There's talk of figures in the wood. Now there is a meeting of parents with policemen everywhere. And Rick is absent, which isn't normal."

"*One* policeman as far as I'm aware, David. Where *is* Rick?" asked Mr Baxter, losing patience.

The class was silent. David had expressed something that

they all felt strongly about. Tyro felt it best to keep quiet in view of the agreement she had made. But she was listening.

Mr Baxter went to the cupboard where he kept some of his masks.

"Nobody knows," said Jess. "He's not where he's supposed to be."

Mr Baxter showed no sign of emotion or a further desire to ask questions. He knew of the power of suggestion and collective anxiety.

When he returned to the centre of the class he repeated his intention to act out scene three. He also carried a mask. It was completely blank - without any expression or colour. It was pure white, and capable of becoming anything. Like a ghost without a personality.

Mr Baxter explained that he wanted to explore some of the themes in the scene, and asked them all to try to work out what was taking place in Macbeth's mind during it. He also asked them to pay special attention to Banquo.

"Most of all, you must follow the witches and ask yourselves," he said, "what role do they have?"

"It's pretty obvious, isn't it, Sir?" said John.

"What's obvious about it, John?"

"He's impatient to become King, and dreaming how to do it. They fire him up. He'll do anything to get what he wants."

"So what sort of a man does that make him, John?" asked Mr Baxter.

"A winner, Sir. We could do with a few more people like that at Wyemarket Wanderers, Sir."

"A bastard," said Julia.

"What does that mean, exactly, Julia, leaving aside the colourful language?"

Before Julia could answer, another voice stepped in.

"It means that he's being taken over by the instruments of darkness, and could be a loser as well as a winner, depending on how you look at it," Tyro said.

Julia looked at Tyro.

"That's ridiculous! How can you be a loser and a winner at the same time?" she said.

Mr Baxter divided the class into different groups so that each pupil could have a role.

He asked them to imagine that they believed in witches and to think of anyone who might, in today's world, remind them of Macbeth.

He asked them to look carefully at the blank mask which he had pinned to the wall behind him.

He decided to play the lead role as it needed a certain weight. Later he would let others have a go.

The class was ready to engage. The cauldron of their minds would perhaps ignite into a ferment of ideas and responses later. If you stopped every time something was capable of further exploration you would never proceed.

Then he said something which made them all sit up. Without any change of tone, and a gentle smile, he added that if they watched carefully and paid attention, what they saw might tell them something about what was going on in the school.

When David asked Mr Baxter to explain, he said that he would do so after they had acted the scene.

As in the previous lesson, the best group of witches was Tyro, Jess and Julia. John did a very honourable Macbeth; David an over-quiet Banquo (John persisted in calling him Bango), but well enough for that same sense of dark energy to emerge as the scene progressed. Despite these shortcomings, the class was spellbound. This was enhanced by a few sound effects, not all intentional, provided by the more imaginative members of the class. The blasted heath was evoked by a symphony of whistles and noises of wind, the thunder coming from the boys in the back row pretending to shoot missiles at enemy aircraft overhead.

The unearthly energy seemed to fill the room, particularly at certain lines. Mr Baxter made the most of his love of performance. He did his best to show Macbeth in the first stages of being taken over, by his own shadow, as well as the witches' timely authority. Whose power it was he did not say. He wanted to see how much the class could tell where the source of this energy lay, before the arrival of Lady Macbeth.

After the scene, and when the special effects had subsided, Mr Baxter stressed the upbeat ending, how it could be interpreted as positive, like winning the lottery, and hopeful, exciting, rather than dark and doom-laden.

Mr Baxter then got them to talk a bit about Macbeth's character, and how he had changed from being the noble hero, to one haunted by a sense of foreboding ambition. He went on to discuss the relationship between the witches and Macbeth and between Macbeth and Banquo.

Later in the lesson Mr Baxter asked them to look at the mask and asked them what they saw. Instead of a blank faceless image, something sinister had appeared on the pale surface; had crept up from under the desks and invaded the face, at least that is how it seemed to many. Suddenly the face was fused with evil intent, and watched each person in the class like a guilty counterpart, which none could evade.

Nobody had any problem with recognising the fear of suspecting your own ambition, or the desire to see a prophecy, however darkly drawn, become fulfilled. One or two of the more honest thought they could imagine reacting in the same way.

When Mr Baxter asked the class to imagine a modern day Macbeth, a person who might behave the way he did at the news he had been given, their minds were full to overbrimming. The list of wounded megalomaniacs (he had outlined what happened later in the play) was extensive, liberally drawn from characters from politics, TV, books, with plenty of relatives (a few parents) and teachers thrown in. Tyro said that Macbeth reminded her of Mr Vespers, at least when

Mr Vespers was talking about his disapproval of Henry's break with Rome. Mr Baxter pretended to not to hear her.

"What has the mask to do with what's happening in the school?" David asked as the end of the lesson neared.

"Think about it, all of you," Mr Baxter replied.

The bell went. Mr Baxter quietened everything down, and promised to tell them something about what was happening in the school next lesson, though he didn't know much more than they did. He told them not to worry, and that there really was a big difference between a play and reality, even though the play could tell us certain things.

"About the power of darkness," David said, looking at his book, in a matter-of-fact way.

*

Tyro's excuse was plainly invented, but Mrs Moffat was as interested as she was disbelieving. She allowed Tyro to leave class for ten minutes to see her mother, on a matter of urgency. She had explained that she wanted her mother to call at Rick's house on her way to work to see if she could find out more about his "illness".

Rick never took time off, and everyone was worried. Last night's episode, about which all the teachers had been briefed, had compounded the situation. Ten minutes of class was worth every bit of help it might achieve.

Tyro found herself standing in the hallway before the main hall.

She could hear the voice of a stranger speak in a serious tone. Her mind was so full that she felt on the point of screaming. Thoughts of the figures in the wood, of the powerful, obscure, distant, but penetrating events of the holidays, mingled with her school work, and the documents and messages being sent between Mr Vespers and Mr Blakemore. The librarian, the guards and the policemen, and the imminence of Bonfire Night were all thrown into the cauldron of her mind.

She put her eye to the door and looked through the gap. There was a uniformed man on the stage next to Mr Rummage, speaking in short, firm phrases. She caught the tone and the rhythms, but not the words. Behind him was a row of people she thought might be the governors.

She could see her mother sitting one row from the back, next to Jess's parents, Clare and John. She looked about her. Lavatories to the left, a cloakroom to the right. She had been given ten minutes.

She went into the cloakroom, took a coat and put it on. She took a scarf and wrapped it round her, and pushed the door. She had taken her mother's, unwittingly. She slipped through the door, hurried to the back row and sat down behind her mother. The policeman by the door had begun to move forward to try to stop her, but was persuaded Tyro must be a mother and let her pass.

Tyro looked for Dennis, but he was not to be seen. She tapped her mother's shoulder. Her mother looked round. At first Abby looked blank, but then caught her daughter's anxious eyes, beneath her own coat! Tyro had taken off the scarf.

"What are you doing here?" hissed Abby, mollified by a natural delight. "Wearing my coat, no less! You're not supposed to be here. Children are not allowed."

"Just to give you this, Mum." It was a note for Rick. "Mum, please call in on Aunt Patrolia and find out about Rick, I don't believe he's ill. I think something has happened to him. Promise? Something important is happening, Mum, and Rick's involved. He's not ill, I know it."

The man on the stage was describing something about the need for caution and vigilance, and the need to avoid panic and continue as normally as possible. There was a sea of heads before Tyro.

He was telling the parents that just as their responsibility was to their children, so was his. He wanted their help and involvement, and part of the reason for the meeting now was to get views about what to do about the school, if the situation should get any worse. Did they want it closed? His view was that it was not necessary at this stage - that would only be giving in to the enemy - but he would understand if some took the opposite view. He needed their understanding and support. There was not much time. Hence they needed, he hoped, to reach a decision now.

Events outside the school were moving very rapidly.

All this sounded confusing to Tyro, but perhaps it was what she made of what she heard. She remembered clearly what she saw on the face of the mask in the lesson. It was her own, with tears in her eyes.

As soon as the man had finished there was a dismal silence, then a buzz of anxiety, followed by a desire to speak.

Abby looked at her daughter.

"I can't, dear. I've got to go to work. We can do it later on our way back home."

Tyro stared into her mother's eyes. Something of her growing confidence and understanding shone from Tyro's eyes, a mixture of love and anger, a desire to dominate as well as to remain the child. That fearful mix of vulnerability and strength, love and hate, passion and will.

"Otherwise, Mum, I'm going up on stage now and telling everybody!"

"Don't you dare, Tyro!"

One or two people looked round.

For a moment the mother and daughter looked at each other, locked in a battle that brooked no outside interference. Some deeper recognition of her daughter's purpose at this critical moment was enough to persuade her to agree.

"Thanks, Mum. I love you!" said Tyro.

With that she turned and walked back out of the hall.

Outside the door, Tyro took the coat and scarf back into the cloakroom and turned to exit when a hand caught her shoulders. It was the policeman. His look was friendly but firm.

"Anything the matter, love?" he said. "Can I help?"

Tyro looked at the policeman.

"It's alright thanks, I had to get a message to my Mum."

"Wearing that coat, I thought you were a mother!" he said, smiling. Tyro saw a chance.

"What's happening, Sir? To the school I mean?" She was at her most innocent and vulnerable.

"Nothing, love. We're onto them. Nothing we can't handle."

"Why is there talk of closing the school then?"

"You'd better get back to your lesson. Go on, off with you."

Dealing with such innocent directness was worse than dealing with the press, which required training and normally failed. Better to ignore, and let Tyro take her chances. The policeman re-entered the hall.

Tyro ran off, but not in the direction of her Biology class. She was going to the library. An idea struck her. Suppose the policeman was not a policeman at all? Why should he have changed so suddenly?

Tyro entered the main building and hurried up the stairs as quietly as she could. At the top she turned.

The empty building seemed to contain shadows, as if it were coming alive. She could in that moment imagine voices: the voices of Mr Rummage, of parents waiting in the hall downstairs, waiting to see him, of the teachers striding in and out to get books, make reports, visit the school secretary.

There were other voices she could not recognise. It was as if they were talking to her. She thought of the figures she had seen from the top of the field last summer, of the school's past. For the first time, the past struck her as not the past. There on the walls were inscribed the names of illustrious old pupils, illustrious old Headteachers. She thought she saw, below in the hall, a play being acted in front of an Elizabethan audience. She shook her head. She liked facts, and tried to dispel her imaginings, which she also admired, but they threatened her. It reminded her of her dreams. Rick, she thought, where is Rick? She called out his name, and then Tom's.

The library was empty, the ticking of the clock on the mantelshelf over the fireplace gave colour to the portraits that hung on either side, the rest of the wall space being taken up with bookshelves. Tyro hadn't taken in the portraits before, had merely glanced at them as if they were part of the furniture. Now she saw them close to. The musty portraits came to life. One was of a middle-aged man with a beard, in Elizabethan costume. In the background was a fool-like figure dancing in a field. The other showed a priest carrying a cross, behind him a church. She looked more closely. Yes, she recognised it. The Church of St Mary Magdalen. In the background, flames consumed the building. Could the past foretell the future, she wondered, in another guise?

Tyro didn't quite know what she was looking for, except that she wanted to see if the door to the back room was open, and to find clues as to what else was being passed between Mr Blakemore, and Mr Vespers.

When she was well inside, she saw that the back room door was open slightly. She thought she heard voices and crept forward. She reached the door and peered through the crack. Mr Blakemore was alone with his head over a desk, reading. He was in deep concentration, as if he was praying. He was murmuring something to himself, like a chant. It reminded her of the witches in Macbeth.

Mr Blakemore turned over the pages of a book between these strange bursts of refrain, and he took up a pen by his side and wrote something down. Tyro was determined to find out what he was reading, and if possible what he was writing.

She tried to study the shelves to see if she could find a space where the book might have come from. She found a gap, and memorised exactly where it was. Three shelves up from the floor. One, two, three, fourteen, sixteen, twenty-one books in from the left. She could not read the library section writing above the shelves in question but she could read the first letter. It was the letter S.

Was she dreaming or did the door that led down to the tunnels appear to move? Mr Blakemore looked up in surprise. He got up from his desk and went over to the door. As he did, Tyro took her chance. She ran into the room on tiptoe. She was terrified that Mr Blakemore might look round or that she might trip and fall and make a noise. She lifted the book.

"Hidden Universe: Secret Power." The notebook at its side was covered in scribbles and diagrams, some of which she tried to memorise. Then, just as Mr Blakemore reached the door, she ran back as swiftly as she had come.

Mr Blakemore made his way to his desk and sat down. Tyro saw him settle and waited for her chance to go.

Mr Blakemore had lost concentration. He put down his pen and closed the book. He went to the bookshelf and returned the book very carefully, making sure that it was flush with the other books on either side. He closed his own notebook, opened a drawer in the desk, and put the book inside. He went over again to the bookshelf and took out the first book on one of the shelves. He opened it and, to Tyro's amazement, drew out a key. A small key, which reminded Tyro of something. He went over to the desk, put the key in the lock and turned it. He returned to the bookshelf and replaced the key and the book. He then made his way towards the door, now murmuring as if memorising what he had been reading. In a strange moment of self-consciousness he turned to a mirror which hung on the wall beside the door. He looked into it. Tyro caught the reflection and saw, instead of Mr Blakemore, what appeared to be a monk, in a habit, though she could not see a face.

Afraid and confused, Tyro ran out of the library. A voice called to her.

"It's Tyro, isn't it?" said the Reverend Sandals, the school chaplain. With him was Mr Vespers. They were on the landing above her.

"Just returning a book to the library for Mrs Moffat."

This was the first thing she could think of. Apart from school services and assemblies she hadn't seen the Reverend Sandals for a long time. She continued down the stairs.

Her mind was spinning with the image she had seen in the mirror. How can a mirror not reflect the person who was outside it! And what was Mr Vespers doing there with the Reverend Sandals? Shouldn't they both be in hall? She ran on down the stairs. She could hear her name being called. Whatever might happen to her, she was not going to stop now. Explanations could wait. The Reverend Sandals would have to accept it, though her mother was a friend of his and helped in the church. She didn't care about Mr Vespers. She knew it was rude but she was not going to stop.

"I shall have a word with her, do not worry, Reverend. Tyro is getting too big for her boots. She'll have her wings clipped, and that's for sure!" Mr Vespers's smile was like a coiled snake.

Tyro's heart beat fast as she ran across the yard towards the Biology labs.

Then she had another idea.

She entered the lab and slowed. She remembered some of the words and images in Mr Blakemore's notebook. "Level one: Initiation. Level two: Activation." She remembered a curious diagram, like a cross above a mountain range, linking certain peaks, which looked like stars.

The noise behind the door made her wonder if Rick was locked inside! That was it! She felt sure, and gasped. Rick was a prisoner. For whatever reason, he had been captured and was being held. How could she get back and help him, how could she get into the tunnels and go in search? She must find a way! She must act now! She must tell Jess and Mrs Moffat. Without Mrs Moffat knowing, if she raised the alarm, everything would be thrown into confusion. She wanted to go back to the library. But that would have to wait.

She looked in at one of the windows at the side of the door and saw Mrs Moffat writing on the board with her back to the class.

Fortunately she and Jess sat at the back.

She wrote a note, gave a gentle tap on the window and dropped it through the window which was open at the top.

Jess picked it up immediately.

Unfortunately, Julia had spotted this and turned to Jane and coughed. Mrs Moffat looked round, and noticed Tyro. Jess looked down guiltily and Tyro walked on back into the building, to the door of the class. She was about to knock when the door opened.

"Come in Tyro, just in time for a little test. I hope you got to see your mother."

Tyro, however, didn't enter the class. She looked up at Mrs Moffat and stared imploringly at her.

"Has something happened, Tyro?" Mrs Moffat asked, in an anxious voice, her head half-turned to the class.

Everyone was listening.

"May I have a word with you, Mrs Moffat?" said Tyro, hesitating, but finding enough strength despite her nervousness.

Mrs Moffat looked surprised.

"Now, Tyro? What's the matter? I hope something terrible hasn't happened?"

"I think something terrible is happening, but I'm not sure what, and I must find Rick, Mrs Moffat. I must find him now! I think I know where he is!" And then she added, "I think he's in danger."

Tyro was shaking with anxiety, because she knew that telling the truth in this situation was probably more risky than a lie. She could easily have said she wanted to go to Matron, because she was feeling unwell, but something told her that

Mrs Moffat had to be told the truth. She had that authority which meant plain dealing.

"Would you mind . . . ?" Tyro began, but she was not allowed to finish.

Mrs Moffat bent her head forward a little, thinking very quickly. The idea of letting her go without finding out more was impossible. It was perhaps impossible anyway, but she recognised the intensity of Tyro's plea and was thinking of ways through the situation. If the situation hadn't been abnormal she wouldn't even have considered it. It was going to get worse.

"Go back to your desk quietly, Tyro," said Mrs Moffat firmly. She looked at Tyro.

Tyro was about to react, when Mrs Moffat added in a low voice, "I've got to think of a way that won't get both of us into trouble."

This was the first time Tyro had been spoken to by a teacher as an equal and in a trusting tone. It made an astonishing difference. Tyro walked into the classroom and sat down. She was still shaking. Jess gave her a pat on the shoulder, holding the note in one hand under the desk.

"Are you OK?"

"I'm not sure, but I've just seen something strange and I want to find Rick. I think Rick's locked in the library. I'm trying to get Mrs Mof . . . "

"Quiet!" said Mrs Moffat.

Tyro was quiet. The rest of class could sense that something was wrong, but most got back to work. It wasn't easy as the tone of the lesson had changed.

Mrs Moffat wrote something on a piece of paper. In a few moments she got up, and asked Julia to come to the front. Julia was unused to being singled out, except for school work, and was a little taken aback. She felt exposed. Mrs Moffat said a few words to her and handed her the note. Julia dutifully walked to the back of the class, now making as much show of it as she could, casting an eye at Jane and Tyro as she did. Meanwhile, Jess was scribbling something on a piece of paper.

"Be quick, Julia, I want an answer as soon as possible. You know where the Headmaster is, don't you?"

Julia said yes, and left.

Tyro was surprised that it wasn't her going out, but trusted Mrs Moffat to be true to her word. Jess passed her the note she had been writing, which Tyro read. "How are you going to find Rick?" it said. Tyro leaned over and spoke in the quietest of whispers, "First, by going to his house, then by trying to find the tunnel. If I can't find him there, I'm going to search the library."

Jess looked a little put out, and then asked, "Can I come?"

Tyro raised her eyebrows and smiled. "Of course, but I can't make excuses for you, if it's during class."

"But what about school, and if we're caught? Where will you be if I can't?" she continued, confused and sensing separation, not unmixed with a certain relief, but still determined to be there. "We might be expelled."

Tyro didn't have time to answer.

Mrs Moffat told the class to stop writing, so that she could go through the answers, and for everyone to be attentive. This woke John up. He looked helplessly at the empty sheet of paper in front of him.

"Can we visit the Chamber, Mrs Moffat?" he blurted out, suddenly.

Mrs Moffat pretended not to hear.

"What do you make of number one?" she asked, "John?"

Fortunately for John the classroom door opened again, and Julia walked in followed by her father, the Headmaster.

Everybody stood up, even though Mr Rummage did not encourage this. Mrs Moffat came forward to meet him, pointing Julia to her chair. They exchanged words. After a moment's silence, Mrs Moffat turned to Tyro and asked her to come forward.

Mrs Moffat asked Tyro to wait outside the class a minute, then went to the front of the class again with Mr Rummage.

For a minute or two Mrs Moffat continued with her questions.

Whilst the class was absorbed, Mr Rummage, to everyone's surprise, walked into the preparation room, leaving the door slightly open. Shortly he re-emerged. He looked at Mrs Moffat and nodded, saying, in a low voice: "All OK."

The class was watching.

Mr Rummage began to speak.

"I know one or two of you are keen to look at the tunnels under the school, which can be reached via the door in the preparation room. You will get your chance, but you will have to wait a little more time yet. Meanwhile, would Jess please come outside a minute - do not worry Jess, you haven't done anything wrong. I need your help. I'm sorry to have disturbed things - you were all excellent."

He walked forward as Mrs Moffat continued.

Jess was shaking a little as she tried to tidy her things. The Headmaster had never singled her out before, except to give her a prize on speech day. She hated being the centre of attention.

Jess was feeling guilty already, for no reason. Nothing could stop Jess from feeling guilty, even, especially, when it was not her fault.

Outside the class Tyro stood shaking. She had not been spoken to by the Headmaster since she had been sent to him last term by Mrs Limpet, even though she had been in his presence on many occasions during the holiday events, and later during the various debriefings.

"Please come with me. Both of you."

Mr Rummage was followed, to Tyro's amazement, by Jess. Jess said nothing. Mr Rummage led them towards the hall where the meeting had just finished.

As they walked, Tyro plucked up courage and told Mr

Rummage that she had seen something important. In fact several things. Mr Rummage thanked her and asked her to tell him later. But she couldn't stop. She told him as much as she could in the few moments they had.

They were led into the hall and taken to the front of the room where Mr Rummage asked them to sit down a minute. Jess was shaking more nervously than ever, but she was excited too, as Tyro was next to her. The policeman at the door was a little more courteous than before, now that she was with Mr Rummage. He looked more like a real policeman.

Abby came forward to meet them. Parents everywhere were getting up to leave.

Mr Rummage went back on stage and thanked everyone for coming. Then he went over to his colleagues on stage and had a few words with them. Most of the audience began to file out.

Abby came up to Tyro and Jess.

"What are you doing back here?" she asked.

"I don't know yet, Mum," said Tyro, "I'm not sure if I'm in trouble or not."

"I doubt it," said Abby. "Mr Rummage has asked me to take you over to Rick's house, just to see if he's there. But you're not to go in. Then I'm to bring you back."

Tyro, though confused with all the things going on in her head, and wanting everything at the same time, nevertheless felt better. She would now be looking for Rick, even if it was not quite in the way that she had planned. And she would soon be back to pursue her search in the library. She was sure he was somewhere close by. She was sure he would not be at home.

6

Leaving school during lessons made Tyro and Jess feel like runaways.

Abby was in a hurry to get back to work, but had been persuaded by Mr Rummage of the importance of visiting Aunt Patrolia's house.

The possibility of the school closing had sent shivers down Abby's spine. In the interim, Mr Rummage had offered boarding facilities for day pupils, to increase his commitment to community, and to help those with far to travel. The idea of boarding, which Abby explained on the road to Rick's house, made Tyro excited, so they decided to take up the offer.

The autumn countryside seemed to pass unnoticed before Abby pulled up outside Aunt Patrolia's cottage, as she had done most mornings and evenings this term, though it was mid-morning now. She told the girls to stay in the car while she went up to the house.

It looked deserted as she walked along the short path. She knocked softly at first. Having no answer, she knocked again, more loudly this time, and pressed the bell firmly. She could hear the ring inside, giving a slightly eerie echo. She bent low and peered through the letter-box, but saw nothing.

Abby looked in at the front room window. She almost expected to see Aunt Patrolia slumped on the floor, but to her relief there was nothing. Perhaps she was upstairs. If Rick was really ill she would not have left him alone in the house, would she?

Abby looked up at the window of Rick's room and called. She picked up a small pebble and threw it onto the window-pane. There was a slight tap and the stone fell to the ground. She walked on round the house, concerned that Aunt Patrolia might see her.

Abby heard bangings and what sounded like voices coming from the shed.

"Mrs Grumble! Mrs Grumble! Is that you?"

She called out again.

"Mr Grumble! Mr Grumble!"

As she approached the door the sounds stopped.

"Rick!" she called.

Abby entered the shed. To her surprise she found the girls inside.

"What do you think you're doing here?"

"Where do you think they can be?" Tyro asked.

The girls had slipped out of the car and run along the path. Abby calmed. Rick's disappearance was too important.

There was one bicycle in the shed.

"That's Rick's," said Jess. "But there's normally another one. The one Uncle John rides, when he goes to the village."

All three of them peered in at the window by the back door, which showed into the kitchen. Everything was tidy. Slippers placed neatly to one side. Plates and cups stacked, surfaces clean and orderly.

"Can't we break in? If Rick's not in there, at least we could find a clue. See if his clothes have gone, something," said Tyro.

A pair of boots had been left outside.

"It's not our business to act like policemen," Abby said. "There'll be a sensible solution, I'm sure. I'm late, you've got lessons. As for breaking in, you'll end up in prison if you go on like that. It's ridiculous. Come on!"

Tyro and Jess looked at each other, then Tyro looked at her

mother. They had by now walked back to the front of the house.

"Mum, can we walk back to school? It's not far."

"No way!" said Abby. She looked at her watch. "I've got to go. I'm very late! Come on!"

"We'll take the bike and cycle, Mum!"

Abby was in turmoil. The meeting at school had put huge doubts into her mind. She was late for work. She was anxious about Aunt Patrolia and Uncle John, to say nothing of Rick. The girls were out of school on some wild goose chase sanctioned by the Headmaster, in which she was complicit. She was angry, and she was trapped. Yet she wanted to find out more.

Tyro seized her chance.

"We're staying, Mum. We have no choice. We've got to find Rick. I think Mr Rummage would like us to look, even if he can't say so. Just think, he might have been captured."

"But I can't leave you two alone! You've got to come now. I'm very late. What do you mean 'captured'?"

Abby was almost in tears. Jess pulled Tyro's arm, but she wouldn't budge. Tyro felt guilty but she had to continue.

It wasn't so much a battle of wills as an acceptance of inevitabilities. Yet she couldn't let her mother down without a hint.

"Mum, I saw Rick last night! He came to the village. You know, when I went for a walk. He's somewhere in those tunnels. He needs us, and we need him."

Tyro hadn't meant to say tunnels - but this was not Abby's main concern. The situation was dangerous. To leave the girls alone could not be justified, but Abby was no longer strong enough just to grab her daughter and force her into the car. She was getting very panicky. She tried, in vain, to look calm.

"I'm going to phone Mr Rummage now and tell him what has happened. Tell him you're here. If he doesn't send someone out immediately to get you, I'll phone Dennis. If he can't come and get you, I'll phone the police. I hope you get properly punished, you spoilt girl. Getting your own way all the time will lead to your own downfall! You mark my words."

Abby sounded like a fussy aunt and hated herself for it. She knew full well that the girls cycled regularly alone along the local lanes in summer, and were known to many people round and about. Things were quiet in this part of the countryside. At least they used to be. She looked Tyro in the eye.

"Stay here until someone comes to get you. Don't break into the house, don't do anything stupid, and remain visible. Someone will be here in ten minutes. OK?"

Tyro was grateful that her mother had not asked her to promise.

"Thanks, Mum." Tyro gave her mum a kiss. "I won't let you down."

Abby went off. She couldn't believe what she was doing, but it was an impossible situation. How she wished Jack was there with her. He had managed to control Tyro who even from an early age displayed a terrible will. She was on the phone immediately to the school, as she drove off.

Tyro ran after her mother, shouting,

"I'm sorry, Mum!"

It was too late. The car raced off along the village street, past Greenfield Church. Tyro was tearful. She knew that her mum had been right. Jess was angry with Tyro. She had let Jess down, and now the Headmaster would know. She had pushed her luck to the limits.

"How could you, Tyro? To your own mother! That was mean, not to say stupid. Really stupid."

"I don't know why I did it, Jess. It just comes over me and I can't control myself. I must do what I want to do. It's like I'm taken over."

"By the instruments of Darkness?"

Tyro didn't react. As some sort of justification for her own confusion, Tyro grabbed Jess and told her what she had seen in

107

the library, about the words and symbols she had read and about wanting to follow Rick last night.

"What a mess you've got us into," said Jess. It had begun to rain. "Now we're here we'd better make the most of it. But we mustn't be long. We've got ten minutes. Now, let me think. How do we break in?"

"We can get through the kitchen window at the back, or climb up the pipe here that leads to that window, just by Rick's room."

"Let's try the back way, otherwise we might be seen."

They ran again to the back of the house. Jess went into the shed and brought out an old oil can, and together they rolled it to the window where the top pane had been left open.

"You jump, I'll hold," Jess commanded. "Isn't it strange?"

"What's strange?" said Tyro, climbing onto the can, holding on to Jess's shoulders. The can wobbled a bit, then steadied.

Tyro held the window with one hand as she tried to balance with the other.

"I've never been inside Rick's house, all the years I've known him."

"There's nothing strange about that. Nor have I!" said Tyro as she stood on tiptoe and put her hand through the open window and felt for the catch. She imagined some horrific beast leaping from beneath the basin and biting it off.

"She's probably put a spell on it!"

"You think she's a witch?"

"Yes. She's probably got a cauldron in the cellar full of newts and eyes of frogs."

The catch was loose and she was able to lift it up with ease. As she did, Jess pushed the pane gently and the whole thing opened wide.

Tyro returned her hand and looked at her friend. Then she bent down and put a foot gingerly on the window-ledge, afraid that the running board inside might not hold. She moved both hands to the sides of the window-frame looking ahead of her for a place to fix her feet. Jess was holding her steady.

With her head inside the window, Tyro balanced herself. Then she chose a spot on the floor and jumped.

She landed without slipping - trust Aunt Patrolia to have a grease-free floor - stood up and turned. She went back towards the window and took Jess's hands. Jess jumped.

"Welcome to my coven," said Jess in an Aunt Patrolia voice. "I would offer you one of my special concoctions - but we seem to have run out," she added, in the same tones, while scanning the shelves. "I could offer you some tap water, but that costs money."

"Come on," said Tyro, "we've no time to waste. First we must find Rick's room."

Tyro led the way through the kitchen and into the hall. The stairs led back up ahead of them. They could follow the banisters upwards, and imagine a cold hand clutching them. The drawing room lay to the left, the little dining room to the right. Both looked out onto the front garden.

"Shall we have a quick look?" Jess said as they passed the two downstairs rooms.

"Later," said Tyro. "Rick comes first. Besides, they might come looking for us soon and we don't want to be caught trespassing."

Tyro was now on the landing making her way to a little door, which was closed, and which she guessed was Rick's room. It was above the dining room, and corresponded to the position they had seen from the garden. Jess caught up with her, and together they knocked. There was no reply. They looked at each other nervously. And then they opened it.

The room was empty and tidy. This was a surprise. They didn't expect to find that Aunt Patrolia's rules would include Rick's room. He had always said she never came into it. They were suspicious, especially as on the door he had written, "Uncle welcome: Arnts keep out!"

There was a small bed in one corner, the head against the far wall, just to the right of the window. On the other side of the room were a desk and chair. There were a couple of drawers in the desk. One was a fraction open. On this side of the desk was a wardrobe. A curious gown, more like a sack, hung from a peg. To the right of the door was a small bookshelf, a few magazines (football and metal detecting) scattered on the shelves. Beside these was a rabbit skull, and stones. A wrinkled conker seemed stuck to the end of a very worn piece of string. There was a small photograph, of a young woman. Tyro and Jess didn't recognise her.

"I wonder who this is?" Jess said.

Tyro didn't know. There were three other doors on the landing, all open slightly. Tyro thought she heard a noise, but it could have been someone working on the farm opposite, so she ignored it and had a quick look in the other rooms. One was a bathroom, another Aunt Patrolia's room (judging by the list of jobs for Rick to do scrawled on a piece of paper by the door). The third, the smallest and humblest by far, she guessed was Uncle John's. Whereas Aunt Patrolia's was full of ornate furniture, black dresses and strange clothes, Uncle John's contained nothing but a small chest of drawers, a tiny bed and a crucifix on the wall.

"Take a look at this," said Jess when Tyro returned. They peered at a notice board over Rick's desk.

"A local map," said Tyro, reading the names of the villages she knew well. "But what are these?" She pointed to a series of lines, some continuous, others dotted, one or two broken, like the roads and paths on an Ordnance Survey map. These had been pencilled by hand onto the map (not very neatly), which was obviously a copy of a real map of the area. Close to the lines were cross marks of some kind, not of buildings, but of something else. What's more the map was old, it had old airfields on it and what looked like military installations, where there shouldn't be any.

"And what are these crosses?" asked Jess.

"Secretive Rick! He never told us about this!"

"I wonder where he got it?"

Tyro pulled the open drawer of the desk wide. In it was an array of odd items. A penknife, a whistle, a water bottle - the sort you use for camping - and a little book, which had a pencil attached to it. At the back was a torch. She picked up the book and flicked through it. It seemed like a diary. The first few pages had lists of places in them, the rest were blank. Against some of the place names a tick had been marked. The book had no title. The names were unusual. Some were of villages she knew, others she had never heard of. There was also an old stone at the back of the drawer, in the shape of a moon. The sort of thing you pick up because you like the shape. It seemed to be made of a funny metal. There was also an old army training manual. The torch was in good working order and splattered with recently dried earth.

Without thinking, Tyro took the stone and put it in her pocket.

"Have a look in the wardrobe for clues," said Jess. But Tyro was looking at the map again.

"Here," she said, pointing, "this is our house, and here is the Church of All Saints. Two parallel lines lead off from the churchyard, in the direction of Greenfield."

Tyro traced her hand along the map. The lines stopped in the middle of a field but by continuing over the ground in the same direction, they joined up with another set, just by the church at Greenfield. Another set, this time broken, led on from the church in the direction of Burnchester.

Jess looked inside the wardrobe.

"His school uniform's not here. He can't be ill, unless they've taken him to hospital for some reason, though I don't think that's very likely. Aunt Patrolia would do anything to make Rick suffer at home. For that matter, where are Aunt Patrolia and Uncle John? Tyro?"

She said this as if in surprise, as if she suddenly realised that something was seriously wrong. It wasn't just Rick's absence. Aunt Patrolia occasionally went away, but never both Aunt Patrolia and Uncle John together.

There was always somebody at his home.

Before Tyro could answer, they heard a noise. They both held their breath.

There was a clumping across the floor downstairs. Jess looked at Tyro, who was pointing at the map.

"I think I know what it is!" she whispered excitedly.

She took the map from the notice board, folded it and stuffed it under her jersey.

"Quick!"

Footsteps, sounding like a man's, could now be heard coming up the stairs. Tyro grabbed Jess and shoved her in the wardrobe, closing the door behind her. She threw herself to the floor and got under the bed.

The door of the room opened wide, just as she pulled the valance over her face.

"Get up, boy! Get up, you lazy ungrateful child, and help me downstairs! That wretched school has been phoning and asking questions!"

Aunt Patrolia's face stared into the empty room. When the face saw it was empty, it turned livid with rage.

"I knew you were lying, you evil child. If you ever come back to this house again, you will get what you deserve, and there'll be no-one to defend you!"

Aunt Patrolia let out a hideous laugh. Tyro, whose eyes peered unseen from under the bed, was reminded of someone - or something. She froze in momentary terror, unable to move. She prayed that Jess wouldn't give them away. She touched the cross-sword about her neck.

Aunt Patrolia's eyes scanned the room, like a snake about to snatch at prey. Her eyes stopped. Tyro could sense that they were looking in her direction. She held her breath ready to burst. For a moment it looked as if Aunt Patrolia would come right in, but she turned and went out. Angry footsteps could be heard across the landing. A door slammed.

Tyro's head appeared. She let out a huge sigh. The door of the wardrobe opened, and Jess's head emerged.

"You look as if you've seen a ghost!"

"Let's get out of here! Through the window!" said Tyro, helping Jess out of the wardrobe.

"Did you see what I saw?" she added, as she tried to undo the catch which held the window fast. Try as she might, the catch would not budge. It seemed to have been tampered with.

"How could I? I heard a door slam. She must be in her room. We'll have to go down the stairs. She's evil!"

Tyro stood for a moment by the door, moved quickly out onto the landing and began to descend the stairs. Jess followed.

They leapt to the bottom, making a thump as they landed.

They ran to the kitchen.

The upstairs door burst open, and footsteps crossed the landing.

"Quick! Hurry!"

Tyro leapt up onto the running board, and jumped out of the window. She landed hard on the ground. Jess was only a few yards behind her. Tyro turned to help her down, when she saw a face come into the kitchen.

The face ran forward and tried to make a grab at Jess, but just as Aunt Patrolia's hands grabbed at her, Tyro pulled her down, and she fell to the ground.

Tyro slammed the window hard on the hands. She heard a cry, as the hands were drawn back. They were dripping with blood.

Aunt Patrolia stood staring at Tyro through the window, with a look of cold fury, one hand shaking in pain, the other moving up to her face.

Jess was staring upwards as she tried to get up.

The hand rubbed its cheek, and seemed to rip its own skin, pulling hard. The other bloody hand now joined the first, and together pulled harder. The two girls backed off in fear. But before they could turn, the hands drew off a mask - the mask of Aunt Patrolia's face - and revealed another face beneath.

Tyro and Jess managed to avoid the eyes of the person they now saw. They turned and ran as they had never done before.

The face was a face they had seen in the summer. The face of the Stranger. They raced across the lawn at the front of the house and fled down the street.

"Stick together whatever happens. He can't harm both of us!" screamed Tyro.

"He's taken Rick!"

They ran as fast as they could though neither was a great sprinter. The Stranger was catching up.

"Head for the churchyard!"

The road curved to the right as they approached Greenfield Church. For a brief moment the Stranger could not see them. Tyro saw a gap in the hedge beside the churchyard gate and dived through it, followed by Jess. She followed Tyro over the graves, through the long grass. Even now Tyro could not help but think of the old bones lying there, and even of their spirits.

The Stranger entered the churchyard. For a moment he paused, as if he was working out what to do. He decided to head for the far side of the church, which would take him along a short avenue of old yews, which would give him cover, and perhaps surprise. The girls might be clever, or lucky, but they were trapped. Now that they were in his sight he could bide his time.

A car passed in front of the open gate beyond the Stranger.

The car screeched to a halt and backed up.

A face bent low over the passenger seat and peered through the open window. The driver got out of the car and stood for a moment. He looked from left to right. He caught sight of a figure bending over a grave, a mourner, no doubt. The driver at the gate turned, got back in the car, and drove on. The two girls were at the far side of the church.

Dennis drove on a short distance and pulled up outside Aunt Patrolia's house. He got out of the car, walked up to the front door, and knocked. He stood back and looked up.

"Tyro! Tyro! Jess! Where are you?"

He waited a moment. Seeing the door open, he went in.

Tyro and Jess crouched behind a large headstone, and looked back over the churchyard. The Stranger moved in their direction like a hunting snake.

Tyro whispered to Jess. She then went one way, Jess the other, spreading out over the open ground, leaving the Stranger ahead.

The Stranger watched one, then the other. Then he began to retreat.

The girls' plan, he could see, was to make for the exit gate.

There was no other way, as there was a wall on one side of the churchyard, and thick hedging on the others.

He would cut them off.

"You cannot escape," he called. "It is information that I want. You will come to no harm."

Tyro and Jess had made up ground.

The Stranger began to retreat again, turning from time to time to check his step. He would not let them go, this time.

The girls worked in silent unison.

He was confident.

Jess and Tyro looked at each other, trusting their plan. He could not get both of them, whilst they were apart. He would have to choose.

The Stranger approached the area most densely covered with graves. He had to put his hand out behind him, to feel his way. He did not want to lose sight of them.

The girls had increased the distance between them. He would have to strike soon.

The girls ran along the outer path, and began to overtake.

They had to make a choice. Double their efforts, and both head for the gate, hoping not to get caught, or find the thing that Tyro was looking for. Both carried risks. The first was no guarantee of escape, as he would be very close behind, and for the second she needed a clue, something to guide her.

The Stranger turned.

By the gate entrance were two large yews. Yew avenues led off on either side for a brief distance before opening onto the very paths that the girls were now on. Another avenue led towards the west door of the church, the one that the Stranger had reached.

Their best chance was to head for the large yews. As they began to converge, they had a stroke of luck.

The Stranger, seeing that he was in danger of losing them, had begun to run forward hoping to cut them off before they could reach the gate. As he did so, he tripped on an unseen footstone in the long grass. There was a Templar cross on the grave.

When he got up, the girls were no longer visible.

Tyro and Jess, now hidden by the trees, made for the churchyard gate.

The Stranger rose like a ghost from the dormant stones, and set off in pursuit, still unable to see them. He seemed to make unearthly strides.

Something caught Tyro's eye.

The largest yew closest to the gate seemed familiar. It reminded her of the yew into which Rick had disappeared only a night ago. It had a similar shape. It seemed similarly inviting.

Tyro jumped onto the branch that seemed to bow low beside her, grabbing Jess as she did so. She made her way along the branch holding onto another above her, towards the main trunk.

There below them, inside the enormous trunk of the old tree, was a gap. They both jumped, falling some feet below ground level, and landed on earth. The only light was the daylight above them. They were surrounded by darkness, a damp and earthy darkness, though from one direction came a slight flow of air.

Above the Stranger looked about him. The girls had disappeared.

"Come out or I will come and get you!"

Tyro and Jess heard his muffled voice.

"Come on," Tyro whispered.

She grabbed Jess's hand.

The Stranger looked back down the avenues of trees that led off in three directions. He stepped out into the road, and looked both left and right.

He swore revenge.

A car came down the other side of the road travelling at speed. Almost simultaneously a tractor could be heard coming the other way, though it was not yet in sight.

Dennis pulled into the middle of the road. The Stranger bent low to the ground.

Dennis pulled up.

"Have you seen two girls?" Dennis asked through the open window.

The man stood up. A cold icy stare met Dennis's gaze. He recognised him immediately. Dennis gazed into the man's eyes, conjuring the energy which he had been trained to project. Both men reacted instinctively.

The Stranger lunged towards Dennis in an attempt to drag him out of the car.

Dennis slammed his foot on the accelerator, rammed the car door outwards and drove it into the Stranger's side. He gave a pitiful yell.

He was hurled to the ground.

The car door swung back and slammed Dennis in the knees, but he kicked it open again and leapt out, twisting the steering wheel to avoid the churchyard wall.

117

He pulled a gun from his shoulder pad and with it smashed the Stranger down as he tried to get up, and hurt though he was himself, turned him over to see blood running down the Stranger's head, as if he were human.

Dennis knelt on the Stranger so that he could not move. The Stranger lay, a grimace of fury on his blood-covered face, incandescent, vowing revenge. He had been pre-empted. The energy that he possessed needed longer to transmute. Dennis had been too quick, too ruthless. His training did not allow for errors. The Stranger was prisoner, at least for now.

Holding the Stranger's arms, Dennis pulled a mobile from his jacket pocket, and put through a call.

He knew the importance of his prisoner. He was not going to let him go. This Stranger was the leader of the Priory. Nothing would induce him to let him go now, no earthly power would force him to give him up.

The Stranger relaxed. He was now at his most dangerous. He would wait. There were other means.

*

Tyro and Jess were dazed, but too anxious to stop, afraid that they might be followed. In the soft light that fell through the cracked roots and mossy leaf-riddled sides of the ancient tree, they could see the tunnel led off in opposite directions.

"That way leads to All Saints and this," said Tyro pointing the other way, "to Burnchester Hall. It was on Rick's map. If we go that way we should reach the school. I think the Stranger was looking for the map."

"Couldn't we wait until dark and then make our escape? He would surely have gone by then," said Jess.

"He might follow us, or wait. We've no choice."

Assuming the tunnel was straight and clear all the way, Tyro didn't think it would take more than about twenty minutes to reach Burnchester. The tunnel cut across country, and would be almost as quick as going by road. Exactly where it would come out they could not be sure, but it was bound to be connected to the tunnel system under the school, and from it they would be able to find a way out. And, with luck, find Rick somewhere along the way.

"It might lead us into the caves beneath school," said Jess. "Who knows what might be waiting for us there. Don't you remember?"

Tyro chose to ignore her, though she had strong memories of that terrifying ordeal. Images of what happened appeared to her in dreams, occasionally by day, obscure hints at a world between worlds, suspended in time, over an abyss. Yet intermingled were glorious moments of light, of fields and cycle rides, and Rompy chasing rabbits.

Tyro picked up a fallen branch and led the way in the direction of Burnchester, the dim light soon fading to total darkness. Moments later they were walking in pitch black feeling their way against the tunnel walls.

At first the walls felt of earth, but shortly they could feel the damp hard rough edge of brick, like an inner crust. The tunnel was just too wide to feel both walls with outstretched arms.

"What do you think the tunnel is for?" asked Jess.

"An escape route, a hiding place, a secret route for communication. Remember what our History teacher said about persecution?"

"Could be a catacomb."

"I hope not!"

Tyro felt in her pocket for the piece of metal that Rick had found in the tunnel near to the Church of All Saints. She took it out, but on this occasion it did not glow.

They were quiet for a few minutes as they crept along. It was now so dark that you could almost touch it.

"Careful, Tyro," said Jess. She had tied her school tie between her belt and Tyro's so as not to lose her. "Careful where you tread."

"The ground seems firm enough."

The early musty smell was soon replaced with the scent of damp mixed with earth and stale air. Yet they could still feel the gentle brush of air against their skin which gave them hope. There must be an exit somewhere near. At the same time, the dark made them afraid.

The tunnel walls were smooth in places, though there were patches where the brick had worn or had fallen into disrepair. Occasionally they felt a piece of smooth stone which had indentations on it, like carvings. Sometimes they could reach the roof above, at others they were forced to bend low. There were no sounds, at first, at all.

They had to concentrate hard, even though the tunnel, it seemed, went straight ahead.

Tyro walked on, the damp now making her shake, and the darkness straining her eyes. And yet in this dark place a strange sensation arose in her. It was as if she could see where she was going, with another sense. Ahead of her, in her mind's eye, were images, leading her on. It was as if a door had been opened in her mind, and she could see the light flowing, and showing her the way. Was this part of the training? She said nothing about this. It felt a bit like flying.

After some time, walking became harder. They became dispirited, as if, far from being a simple tunnel leading in one direction to a place they knew, other passages seemed to tempt them off it, leading into the unknown, the undiscovered country. The images were now blurred.

Tyro's hand felt a gap into one of these byways, then rejoined the wall again.

"How do we know we're going in the right direction?" asked Jess.

"The map showed a straight line to Burnchester, I think," replied Tyro. "I hope."

"But the map won't be complete. Rick can't have finished it. Nobody seems to know the full extent of this underground world. Remember Rumbags's report."

Tyro had forgotten the report on events in the summer. She wished she had taken more notice.

"And what about the other side, on the wall that's just out of reach?" Jess went on, bumping into Tyro who had paused at another byway.

Jess imagined a complex web of interconnected tunnels under the earth. She imagined walking for an eternity in the dark, forever seeking the light, but finding neither light nor air.

"Ty? Suppose we never get out?"

Tyro stopped.

"Who really knows about the tunnels?" Jess went on. "They might take us to places we don't want to go to. Off the map. Suppose all the theories are smokescreens for something else. Like a deliberate cover for a darker purpose. One that very few know about, or are brave enough to explore."

Tyro was listening not only to Jess, but to what seemed like another sound ahead. She focused her mind again.

"Rick, certainly. None of us knows very much."

"The enemy," said Jess.

"Shh! Do you hear what I hear, Jess? Listen!"

"Even Dennis and Mr Rummage have always said there are many more tunnels than they know about. I'm sure the Reverend Sandals would, as it joins his church in Burnchester to Greenfield and to other churches as well. According to the map."

"Churchyards, Jess, not churches. These tunnels are connected to the churchyard, not the church itself. In other words they are older than the churches. Can you hear what I can?"

They stood silently in the total dark.

"Water!" said Jess. "Not far away. We must be extra careful. If we fall in, we will never get out."

"But water? Give me your hand, Jess."

She felt for Jess's hand and held it firm. Jess now came alongside her.

They went on hand in hand, taking one dark step at a time.

The sound increased into a clear gentle lapping sound. Intoxicating, disturbing, it offered hope, but also danger. Tyro's branch suddenly touched nothing and she stepped back. They had reached the edge of what was clearly some kind of underground stream, which crossed the path ahead of them.

Though they did not realise it at first, the wall had fallen back out of reach. The water echoed, suggesting an empty chamber. With it too came something that moving water always brings, a semblance of shimmering light, from the few rays that had penetrated the exit not far off.

Tyro and Jess stood staring, almost feeling the water flow from right to left in the darkness, on a journey towards the far-off sea. The ravine was no more than ten feet across, and about the same depth. They could probably jump to the other side, but it wasn't necessary. There was just enough light to reveal the outline of steps leading down to the water's edge where a small boat lay tied to simple moorings, an iron ring fixed in the solid wall. On the far side of the water, which rippled and eddied here and there, was another set of steps, carved out of the rock, up to the path which continued on, rising slightly.

It was evident that the place was some sort of landing stage, though, apart from the boat, there was no sign of activity. It was too dark to see whether there were any marks on the ground.

"Lucky you heard it," said Jess. "We might have fallen in."

"We'll have to cross," said Tyro, looking in the direction of the light, and bending low, to see where the stream was going. She could not see how deep the water was.

"Over here!" Jess said.

To the right, upstream, the ground sloped upwards and then swung across in an arch over the gorge. Someone had built a bridge at the far end of what they could now see was a cave. It was not possible to go on upstream.

"We can use the bridge if we bend low. I'd like to find out where the stream leads to. A landing stage, but who or what for?" asked Tyro.

It reminded Jess of the river Styx, but she didn't tell Tyro.

Tyro was reminded of the boat they had stolen over the summer, to make their way to the Burnchester Arms following their discovery of Mr Gruff's blood.

She wondered if the boat was being used by the Stranger, and if he had reached the cemetery by the same route that they had taken.

"But surely he can't know about it?" Jess said. "Otherwise he would have followed us now."

"Which means we must hurry! Come on!"

On the other side the dark enveloped them again as they re-entered the tunnel.

"We should have taken the boat to wherever it leads," said Jess. "It can only have joined the river Dean, which means the school grounds and fresh air!"

"I'm not so sure," said Tyro.

It was Jess's turn to trace the wall with her hand.

They began to walk on something harder than earth, their footsteps sounding in the emerging light. Gone was the musty wall of damp earth. A sheen reflected off the clean and newly painted walls. Ahead of them steps rose up to a landing, from which many tunnels led. Beyond, between columns of white marble, was the door to a lift.

Both girls recognised it at once.

Tyro pressed the button. The doors opened and they entered. The lift was brilliantly lit.

They looked at the buttons to the various floors. Upper level; Domed Chamber; Lower level 1; Lower level 2.

Tyro pressed the top button and the door closed. The lift went upwards without a sound.

"Shall we go to the Domed Chamber and take a look?" said Tyro.

Something in Tyro had made her wish to retrace the journey that they had made in summer, half-nightmare, half-reality. She needed to find out the identity of the figures.

She pressed the button saying Domed Chamber.

Within moments they were walking along the corridor that led to the Dome where they had been captured, where they had lost consciousness, where they had had terrible dreams.

As they entered the huge Dome, they could imagine the cloaked figures standing beside the huge stones which stood at the back of the wooden seats where they had sat, enchanted, below the brilliantly coloured roofing, covered with mythological figures and knights, which they now could see in exotic colours. It was as if their dreams had been imprinted there.

They stared at the huge monolith which rose in the centre of the Chamber.

Something caught their eye.

On top of the monolith where the Dark Master had emerged, still vivid in their memories, an object had been placed. It looked like a small casket secured to the top of the plinth, nearly touching the cable, which fell from the apex of the Dome.

Moving around it they saw on one side the casket was made of glass. Through the glass they could make out a shape. They had to move out of the reflected light. They could see what looked like an arrowhead made of stone.

"It can't be!" Jess called to Tyro, clutching her friend.

Before Tyro could answer, a powerful energy seemed to surge from the stones, a tremulous shaking within their stillness.

The room vibrated. The two girls shook in fear. The face of the Stranger came at them from the dark tunnels that led off from the base of the Chamber. Monk-like shapes moved towards them, chanting. Yet these were only imaginings, shadows in the uncertain light.

Tyro struggled.

"The object cannot be original! We would have heard!" she said. "It must be a decoy, some kind of substitute."

They ran from the Chamber along the corridor to the lift, and took it to the next level. They found the door leading to the tunnel which led to Mrs Moffat's room. Tyro said that they should break into Mrs Moffat's classroom.

They thought of Rick and of the figures that the children had seen only two nights ago; of the school closing; of the warnings, the police, the security, the stories, the rumours. The Stranger wearing Aunt Patrolia's mask. It was their task to turn fear into something positive and find what was driving the demons in their search for power. Besides finding Rick, Tyro wanted to find the books in the library that Mr Blakemore had been studying, and the key to unlock the secret archives.

"If we go this way," said Tyro, "we'll reach the library door. I'm sure of it."

They ran up the stairs, now excited. It would be lunch-time. They felt they'd been away for ages, and were famished. And if the library door was closed?

"We'll run back to the boat," said Jess.

They stood in front of the old wooden door. The beautiful white marble had become Elizabethan timber, darkened by time, as they climbed the stairs. The library door was locked.

They heard footsteps.

They could not escape, only go down. It was from there that the footsteps were coming. They knocked on the door, but got no response. Either they could not be heard or the library was empty.

The steps were closer now. The girls huddled flat against the walls of the staircase doing their best to become invisible, but it was useless. The steps were nearly upon them.

They heard a creaking sound. Behind them the door of the

library opened slowly. Then it swung wide.

All three stared at each another in amazement.

The girls fell through it, followed by Rick.

The door shut.

The library was empty. Someone or something had let them in.

7

Mr Rummage was sitting with two of the governors of the school and a parents' representative.

He did not want to downplay the significance of the dangers in the current situation, nor did he want to exaggerate them. He was torn by private concerns and the need for public confidence, not least because he was, unknown to most observers, deliberately drawing the Priory into the open.

Only he and a handful of others knew quite how extraordinary their activities and capabilities were, and even this information was incomplete. Only he and a few others knew that there were other, darker forces involved in the background. The situation offered a rare, possibly unique opportunity, to tackle the powers of darkness, vital at this moment in time, with another major project emerging, which remained "above top secret". Other signs, including the rising level of the sea, synchronised with a historical moment and a conjunction of global importance.

The two governors supported Mr Rummage, though they knew whose heads would roll should the situation deteriorate. The sole fact which gave them a measure of confidence was that despite the severity of the shock that many had suffered, no child had actually been physically hurt.

Mr Rummage did not disclose details of the activities of two of his colleagues, Mr Vespers and Mr Blakemore. Tyro had given him a brief report about what she had observed in the library.

Other agencies, from their HQ in London and elsewhere, were monitoring the situation at Burnchester. This included other intelligence agencies.

Mr Rummage's phone rang.

Dennis spoke hurriedly.

Aware of the faces around the table Mr Rummage appeared calm, and listened without revealing anything. He put down the receiver and, making his apologies, went into his secretary's office. Here he made a couple of calls, before returning with some coffee. He made no reference to the calls.

"There has just been an important development," was all that Mr Rummage said.

The capture of the Stranger was a surprise. He remembered the Stranger's ability to appear and disappear, almost at will.

Mr Rummage despatched Mr Gruff to Dennis's assistance and alerted Inspector Relish. To save time, Inspector Relish, who was in Southwold, called the duty officer at the school to go immediately to Greenfield Church and help make the arrest. Though neither the Inspector nor Dennis knew of his break-in at Aunt Patrolia's, he must be brought in for questioning over events over the summer, and about the missing girls.

Mr Rummage wanted confirmation of the man's identity. This was a problem in itself. Though he had been recognised, and there were several witnesses to his activities, tracing them might be very difficult, as ongoing investigations were proving. Nobody had been able to identify him for sure. Besides, he was bait, perhaps for a larger catch. Inspector Relish, with the help of Mr Greenshank, and the man who had been on the beach that day at Warblersbay, was beginning to piece together anecdotes about his activities in and around Southwold and Dunemoor, but they didn't add up to a picture. All he knew for sure was that he had been involved in a number of nocturnal dives since his last disappearance. The information was sketchy though Mr Greenshank felt sure that they were connected to the ancient City whose remains lay scattered over the sea bed, and whose treasures (so the stories went) had never been found, about which rumours abounded.

*

A police car carrying Mr Gruff and the duty officer arrived at Greenfield Church to find Mr Granger - the same Mr Luke who had given the girls a lift in his tractor over the summer, and now the head groundsman - assisting Dennis with his enquiries.

Mr Granger had the unfortunate Stranger tied to the front of his tractor with the added protection of a crowbar which he held not far above his head, on clear instruction to the said gentleman not to move unless he wanted to feel its subtle effects. The crowbar wasn't quite the Tickler, but no doubt could administer more permanent damage, when wielded.

The Stranger was oddly reticent about using what powers he might have had, unless he was biding his time. For some reason, he was neither exercising nor showing any signs of abnormal strength. This may have been because he was outnumbered or because he was planning his escape. The police officer arrested the Stranger on a count of causing actual bodily harm to Mr Gruff, during the summer.

Dennis had gone into the churchyard in search of Tyro and Jess and had returned alone.

The Stranger sat handcuffed in the back of the police car between Mr Gruff and Mr Granger. The Stranger looked impassively as Dennis grilled him about the girls, knowing that they had been at Aunt Patrolia's house only minutes before. It crossed Dennis's mind that he may have harmed them, but he felt sure that there were good reasons why he would not - not at this stage anyway. They were too useful to him and his cause whilst they still searched for the missing fragment and the Spearhead. They did not know the fragment might have been found. He made it clear to the Stranger that he held him personally responsible for the girls' safety. The Stranger remained impassive. Dennis was reminded of the time he had seen him in the Laughing Mariner at Southwold, with that cold distant look and of the blank reflection in the mirror behind the bar. His confidence subsided.

The police officer was to take the Stranger to Ipswich Police Station in the company of Mr Gruff and Mr Granger, where he should be held for questioning, under the strongest security. The policeman turned the key in the engine and drove off.

Mr Gruff appeared less than easy. He was putting on a brave face, but it was empty and vulnerable. He should not have left his new companion Grudge's side. Dennis was too absorbed at the thought of the missing girls, fully to take this in. The Stranger wore perhaps the very slightest hint of a smile.

As soon as they left, Dennis put through a call to Mr Rummage to explain what had happened and to let him know that he was still searching for the girls. Any hint of pleasure or pride was soon assuaged by the thought that Tyro and Jess were somewhere nearby, unknown to him, and might at this very moment be harmed - or worse.

It was a fate that he could not contemplate, but one which gave him immediate zest to continue, should he have needed any other reason than that he loved them both, and of course his sister too. The church, the churchyard, the houses and fields around it would be turned over and over again, until he found them. He was optimistic. Surely the girls would have escaped, or the Stranger would have been caught with them. He asked Mr Rummage to delay sending extra help, in the expectation and hope that they would be somewhere nearby.

Inside the library Rick, Tyro and Jess were talking.

"Where an earth have you been, Rick?" Tyro asked. She had even planted a firm kiss on his cheek, to his surprise, and embarrassment, as well as to Jess's, who looked a little put out, until she had done the same, with no less enthusiasm.

"We thought you'd been captured," Jess said.

"I had no choice," Rick whispered. "The figures are abroad again. I had to keep a low profile. I've been followed. I just hope they haven't broken into my house."

Rick was less cool than usual. For once he spoke without being pushed.

"I've been exploring," he added. "Mapping, mapping tunnels, making connections, trying to find Tom. I've also been trying to avoid school - and Aunt Patrolia."

Tyro and Jess didn't know where to begin.

"But where is she? She told the school you were ill, but she's not at your house."

Rick looked at Jess. "What do you mean, not at my house? How do you know? She never leaves the house."

"We came looking for you and the house was empty. I was worried and told Mr Rummage. He gave us permission. We found your room," said Tyro, "and your map on the wall. But no Aunt Patrolia. I've got the map here."

Tyro pulled out the now creased map from under her jumper and gave it to Rick. Rick took it and unfolded it. He looked grateful.

"We didn't see your Uncle John either. Only an unwelcome visitor. You won't believe this, Rick. The Stranger who attacked the school in the summer was at your house. Worse. He came in and chased us. He must have been either after you or something you have. We managed to get away, just, along the tunnel from Greenfield churchyard to here, crossing an underground stream. Without your map he would have caught us."

"He was after the map," Rick said. "They must know less than we thought. I'll have to be more careful in future."

"The weird thing is, Rick, that he - the Stranger that is - came into your room and then left, without taking anything. I was hiding under your bed. When he heard us leave he followed us. That's when we saw."

"Saw what?"

"The Stranger wasn't the Stranger at first. At first he looked like your Aunt. He even sounded like her."

"Then, he pulled off a mask and revealed his face underneath."

"Do you remember the mask that we found in the churchyard?

Jess shivered.

"And what about you being ill?"

Rick was trying to take in what he had heard, and explained as best he could.

Aunt Patrolia had been anxious - more so than usual in the previous few days (from before he had visited Tyro that night) - which revealed itself in wild mood swings, worse than usual, when she would fly at Uncle John and Rick for no reason, and then, equally unusually, appear disconcerted, guilty even, at her own outburst, when she would seem, by her reaction, not her words, to apologise. She was not herself.

The situation had become so bad that Uncle John and Rick had confronted her two nights ago (it must have been exceptional for Uncle John to have had the courage to stand up to her, Jess said) and asked if there was anything the matter. She went on as if nothing had happened, and then became aggressive again, swearing at Rick for not helping her more, which she needed now, though she wouldn't explain why. She got mad at Uncle John, who eventually walked out of the house. He had not been seen since.

Rick offered to help her (even though he didn't know what it was she wanted and she didn't deserve it), but she would have to tell the school that he was ill, which is what she did. But when the following day (today) came, she became aggressive again, saying that someone was out to get her, now shouting and screaming at Rick, so much so that he slammed the door, telling her that he was going to school after all. But he didn't. He decided to continue his exploring, and went to the churchyard at Greenfield, where he took a short cut to the school.

"And here I am," he said.

"Did your aunt say who was out to get her?"

Rick didn't answer. He was more worried than he realised.

"Soon I won't have a home at all," he said. "I'm worried about Uncle John. He didn't even say goodbye. That would have hurt him. I'm sure he would want to help. He'd been talking about things changing and his worries about Aunt Patrolia, but wouldn't reveal very much. Now he's gone, there isn't a chance. We've got to find him."

"You can always stay with us, Rick, you know that," said Tyro.

"But where are Aunt Patrolia and Uncle John?" asked Jess.

"I don't know. What you've told me makes me wonder if the Stranger and Aunt Patrolia aren't working together in some way, and she has gone with him, or been taken by him. I don't understand the mask. As for Uncle John, I have no idea - he loves home, despite Aunt Patrolia - and that really scares me. Uncle John is the kindest man in the world, but he's not strong. He reminds me a bit of Tom."

There was a pause. Then Rick added, "We are still just ahead of them, I think."

"What do you mean?"

"Tom and I, all of us, together we know more about the tunnels under the school than they do. Though they know quite a lot - like the power of the Domed Chamber - I think we know more, if only because we are resident here and they're not, or were not. I'm sure they think we or they - the tunnels -

will lead them to what they want - the source of information, the secret, the knowledge that will give them power and control over everything and everyone they want."

"The Spearhead," said Tyro in a low voice, touching the pendant about her neck.

"We must continue to give the impression that we know more than we do. That may save us. They also know we're friends of Mr Rummage - at least he's on our side. Mr Rummage is a powerful man. Remember, it was he and his wife who destroyed them before. Perhaps they think we can help them to discover more about Mr Rummage."

"Or that Mr Rummage has chosen to tell us secrets, even train us in the techniques."

"The problem is," said Jess pointedly, "none of us knows quite what we are looking for."

Rick paused a moment. Then he said,

"We know they want the fragment, but they are not likely to be given sight of it by Mr Rummage under any circumstances. The Chamber is also guarded, I think."

"What makes you think that?" asked Jess.

"Something is preventing them from entering it again. It is empty, and yet they have not tried to go in again, it seems."

"Perhaps the power that they need is only accessible at certain times - at others it is unavailable to them, and the search becomes useless," said Jess.

"Yes, or it is available under certain circumstances, using other special powers. Maybe we have powers too," said Tyro, not intentionally referring to flying. "We've just been to the Domed Chamber and had no trouble getting in."

"Remember how the doors' locks opened and shut as if they had a life of their own," said Jess, reminding her of their terrifying visit when they had been chased by Titan.

Tyro led Rick and Jess to a particular part of the library, the place where she had seen Mr Blakemore at his studies, only a short time before. The horror of the apparition which had appeared in the reflection. The book, the key. The figures came at her, in her mind.

"And what about school? Tell me what's been happening and where they think I am, and about what you have been doing?"

"Later, Rick," Tyro said, "we'll explain everything, but later. We have very little time, the library reopens after lunch. We've got to find the key."

Rick's eyes opened. It was pleasing to hear Tyro and Jess had made progress. Normally it was he and Tom who made important discoveries.

Tyro told him to shut up and then told them to stand and watch, especially the door.

She went to the shelves where Mr Blakemore had taken the book. She counted three shelves from the floor, and twenty-one books from the left. There it was. The book marked S. She pulled it out and held it under her arm. Then she moved back to the end of the stack and took out the first book on the shelf above. She brought it back to the desk and opened it. From it she took a key and opened the drawer.

Jess looked startled.

"Tyro, it's the key that was dropped in the boathouse, the key that was lost which we picked up. How did it get back here?"

Tyro pulled out a notebook - the very same that she had seen not long before, in which Mr Blakemore had written notes - and placed it and the first book on the desk. As she did so she retold the story of what she had seen and heard. She told of the murmuring and the incantation and the notes that Mr Blakemore made from the book.

Rick and Jess moved closer. The book was inscribed in longhand with a name and message that she could not read. She remembered the title which was simple and provocative: "Hidden Universe: Secret Power."

All three of them looked down as Tyro turned to the next

page, which showed the contents, beginning with the Levels. The letters were in Elizabethan script. "Level one: Initiation. Level two: Activation. Level three: Control."

In brackets beneath "Control" somebody had written - it was the same hand as the inscription - the words "light/dark". Tyro turned the pages over, while she continued the story. She paused at one of the sections which read: "Advanced training: The Work."

They looked closely at the text beneath it. They saw figures and symbols, some astronomical, others alchemical, others still geometric. They saw the curious diagram like a cross above a mountain range, linking certain peaks, which looked like stars.

Under the figures and symbols were explanations, and then further instructions with exercises, but the wording was difficult, too difficult to understand. There were also musical notations often placed alongside instructions, as if the music and the words accompanied each other and were mutually dependant. There were strange mythological figures, some like the figures on the ceiling of the Domed Chamber below, so Jess thought. Were they Gods, or Knights?

"It's like Shakespeare," said Tyro, "Whoever's going to understand this?"

Jess pointed to lines which read:

"Only in combination can these powers be used effectively. Alone they are nothing. Long training is required, and struggle and dark journeys. They will only function in combination with the energy from other sources. They who have mastery of these things, will have mastery of much more. The timing must be right. For these reasons, this wisdom, ('these mysteries' had been written in the same longhand) must be treated with great ('great' had been underlined) caution. In the wrong hands, the consequences will be untold, perhaps unredeemable. The powers must only be used for the light. Misuse or wrong motivation will lead to untold consequences for the individuals and those around them. Remember the

Dark. Remember it is always Deo concedente."

"That's the school motto!" Jess observed.

"What does unredeemable mean?" asked Rick.

"It means that you cannot go back," said Jess. "Once it has been used by the wrong people, for their own ends, if they succeed, nothing can be done to stop them. They will have power and the control. Probably forever."

"This confirms that Mr Blakemore and Vipers must be working for the Priory. I knew they were not to be trusted. What do we do?"

Rick was looking through the notebook.

Neither he nor the girls heard the library door unlock in the room beyond.

"Look!" Rick said. "Read this."

"Initiation" had a tick beside it. "Activation" also had a tick beside it. Beside "Control" someone had written "imminent".

"It means they will try something very soon! Bonfire Night!"

"Well done, Jess! Remember they need the energy from other sources. We don't know where from. But do they? Does anybody? Maybe the time will be right then."

"It doesn't seem so," said Tyro. "It feels tentative. Yet it must be connected to the Domed Chamber, and the fragment, and what else, we can only guess at."

"And the climbing-irons!" said Rick. "Nobody knows where they came from, let alone why they are there, though according to Mr Baxter they are of a similar metal to the metal strip I found in the tunnels."

There was a noise. The three of them suddenly looked up. All three of them saw on the wall in front of them, as if for the first time, the old pictures that had hung there for hundreds of years. They saw the picture of the middle-aged man, in Elizabethan costume. They saw the Fool in the background dancing in a field. They saw the other picture of a priest with a cross with the church behind him, and flames consuming the building.

The clock ticked loudly, only broken by the soft tread of feet, which stopped in the door behind them.

A voice spoke. The tone was familiar, but deceptive.

"And oftentimes, to win us to our harm,

the instruments of Darkness tell us truths."

The three of them turned round.

"Doing some revision, you three?" said Mr Baxter. "Lucky for you it was me that found you. If I were you, I'd put all that back as quickly as possible and follow me. Time is running out."

His eyes indicated that someone would be following very shortly.

Tyro hurriedly closed the book and notebook, put the notebook back in the drawer, locked it, placed the key in the second book, and replaced it and the third book onto the shelves, all within seconds. She then joined the others on the other side of the room, where Mr Baxter took out a more recent book, marked, "Countryside rambles - nature walks for the novice".

Before Mr Baxter could explain, Mr Blakemore had entered the room.

"I thought this part of the library was out of bounds to pupils, Mr Baxter," Mr Blakemore said testily.

"Not if they're accompanied," said Mr Baxter, coming over and giving Mr Blakemore a slap on the back. Mr Baxter was not a small man.

"A little research, Mr Blakemore. Preparing them for our nature walk. Making good use of old maps. Great to have a librarian again." Mr Baxter spoke with unintentional irony. "Thank you for your help," he added.

"But . . . " Mr Blakemore began.

Mr Baxter led the three children towards the door. Mr Blakemore may have seen the state of their clothes, or he may not. But whatever power he may have learned, he was no match for Mr Baxter.

"Right, you three," said Mr Baxter, "Come with me!"

Outside on the landing, he gave them a wink.

Mr Blakemore went over to his desk. Teachers had their own keys, and were entitled to bring pupils in at any time of course. Soon the library would be open again throughout lunch, once he'd got the hang of things. He would have to continue his work at night, he reflected.

Mr Baxter led the children downstairs.

"Say nothing about what you have been doing in the library to anybody. Anybody at all. You may be witnessing forces greater than you can imagine. Do not go back there. Ever."

"But, Sir!" said Tyro. She was shocked by the force of his remark. She was longing to tell him what had happened, and she was anxious to follow up their discoveries. But he brushed her interruptions aside, with a "Later, Tyro, later!"

At the bottom of the stairs, he walked them towards the Headmaster's office. The three of them looked at each other, and Rick tried to pull Tyro and Jess aside, as if to make a quick escape. Tyro and Jess wouldn't budge.

"We can tell Mr Rummage what we've just found," Jess whispered, "as Mr Baxter seems in such a hurry. I wonder why?"

As it was lunch break, other pupils were milling around, walking in and out of the hall and along the corridors. Teachers made their way to and from the common room.

John came up.

"Rick! Where've you been? Even old Rumbags has been worried about you."

"Doing some homework," Rick said.

"Sure, just like I'm going to be Head Boy next year. What have we got next lesson? How come you two get to miss lessons?" he said looking at the girls.

"Art," said Jess.

Mr Baxter had knocked on Mr Rummage's door and waited a few moments, before entering.

"Oh, no!" whispered Tyro.

"Shut up, Ty! We had permission and we have to report to Mr Rummage."

"Permission?" said John. "If you had permission, it can't be interesting. By the way, there's a new notice up on the board. Nobody is allowed to go anywhere in the school on their own. Must go in pairs."

With that John left, not wanting to get dragged into the Headmaster's office for any reason, for Mr Baxter was calling them in. Rick tried to run but Mr Baxter grabbed his jacket and pulled him through the door. The girls were standing dutifully in front of Mr Rummage's desk.

Rick's mood changed a little, seeing that he had no choice. Mr Rummage wasn't a bad guy, and he might be able to explain some things.

Mr Rummage sat at his desk. He put the phone down. He was looking more serious than usual. It was the seriousness of reflection, not anger. When the children came in and stood in front of him, he asked them all to wait quietly a minute whilst he finished what he was doing. He jotted something down in a notebook in front of him, then he passed a bundle of papers over to Mr Baxter.

"Have a look at these . . . you've probably seen today's papers, and I'm told the Sundays are doing a piece. The report only came this morning. You'll find it interesting reading."

Tyro couldn't read the title, but she could read the name under it, or one of them, as there was more than one - "Dr Bartok". The rest was a blur. She had a memory of being able to zoom her vision.

Mr Baxter took the papers.

"At least they're back safe," Mr Baxter said. "Any developments?"

Mr Rummage looked at him, and then at the children.

"Things are moving quickly. Our captive is under guard."

Mr Baxter turned.

Rick was fidgety, Tyro was yawning. Only Jess stood upright and still.

"Welcome back, all of you. You didn't hear what I just said by the way." Mr Rummage said.

Rick was wondering how much Mr Baxter knew and how much he shared with Mr Rummage. Tyro was hoping that they could explain everything about their morning.

But in this she was disappointed.

"I want a full report on where you've been, Rick, but I haven't got time now. I'm glad you've been found." He said this in a friendly but concerned voice. He turned to the two girls.

"Well done, you two. I can now fully justify both of you missing a lesson, which wasn't making you or me popular, though Mrs Moffat quite understood. I can't imagine what the consequences might have been if any of you had gone missing. I was getting very worried."

Once again Tyro tried to interrupt, but Jess pulled her arm down. Mr Rummage went on.

"I've spoken to your mothers, and told them you are safe and sound. You can give them a call in a minute from my secretary's office. Wait a moment, Tyro, I want to hear your story. But that and questions, later."

Mr Rummage paused again and looked at them.

"You'll be pleased to know that the man who broke into the school over the summer has been caught. The man who was after you. He's being questioned - under the strictest security. I think we can sleep more safely now."

For a moment, Mr Rummage's desire to sound confident overtook him, perhaps because of the worries he had about reassuring parents. More likely, he felt truly happy to see them as a man whose life, or much of it, had been devoted to the safety and education (and happiness) of the children in his care. At the same time, he needed to be serious.

So when he smiled at them all, with a slightly bowed head, in implicit recognition of the agreement that had been made about the events of the summer, he did so in earnest.

"You have done well to keep the story of the summer secret. Please do so still. All I can tell you is that I will need your help again soon. But say nothing yet. Also as I mentioned to you, I have a plan that involves you three."

This, thought Tyro, was her cue. She and Jess and Rick all wondered if Mr Rummage had forgotten about the agreement they had made. He had not mentioned it again until now. Mr Rummage, however, put up his hand, again.

"Later, Tyro. I will call you when I have the time. I won't forget."

He paused and got up. Tyro was desperate, and burst out.

"But Mr Rummage, we've seen something very strange! In the library! It's important. Like a ghost. And Mr Blakemore . . . we think he's working for the Priory!"

Mr Rummage stood still. He showed no sign of surprise, no reaction at all, except that he was, for that single moment, quite still. Tyro had never used that word before. He looked Tyro in the eye.

Tyro could sense the power behind his kindly stare, the power of resolution which she sensed in herself, but she was powerless, as a young person, to do anything, yet. It was perhaps this that drove her to make sure that she would complete the task, whatever it was, however angry she became. Mr Rummage had mentioned a plan.

Mr Rummage went back to his desk. He asked all three of them to sit down in the chairs in front of him. He then sat down himself. Quietly and without fuss he asked each of them to tell him what had happened in the morning, and anything else of importance. He didn't mention the Priory, though listened intently to every aspect of their adventures, separate though they were, yet interlinked. He asked Tyro to repeat in the minutest detail what she had seen in the library, especially the contents of Mr Blakemore's notebook and the books he'd been researching.

When they had finished there was a brief pause before Mr Rummage stood up.

"You haven't had lunch, I think! I have arranged for the chef to feed you, and explained the exceptional circumstances. I wouldn't normally put him to so much trouble. He has enough to do as it is. Go and eat now, and then go to lessons. I have let Ms Peverell know that you may be a little late. We must keep things normal for as long as we can. You can go now. And thank you."

The thought of food overcame any other concerns.

The three of them said, "Thank you, Sir," and were about to leave when Mr Rummage called Rick back.

"Rick. I want a further word. Tyro and Jess, I will call for you again soon."

Having phoned their mums, the girls went to the dining hall where M Le Petit had laid a special place for them in the corner of the room nearest the fire. They ate their meal hurriedly, trying to forget about their ordeal of the morning.

Nevertheless, Tyro did say to Jess, "When are we ever going to get to tell him everything?"

Jess said she didn't know, but thought it was difficult ever to tell anybody everything, which Tyro thought was Jess being too clever, so she let it drop. Tyro was beginning to need to share more, and felt a bit angry, but was also feeling grateful to Jess for her presence and loyalty, despite her irritating ways. For Jess's part, she was grateful to Tyro for helping her get more confidence but angry at her stupidity too. An equation she couldn't resolve so she continued with lunch. She thought of what she had seen in the library. M Le Petit watched them approvingly from the wings.

*

Rick stood in Mr Rummage's study. He hated being questioned. He hated being alone with adults, let alone the Headmaster.

Mr Rummage sensed this and began by congratulating him on his work. Rick was surprised and couldn't help being pleased, even if he was unclear as to what he was referring to. It certainly wasn't schoolwork. Then Mr Rummage continued. His tone became more serious.

"Rick," Mr Rummage began, "have you any idea where your aunt and uncle are?"

Rick, relieved at not having to tell Mr Rummage where he had been, said "No."

"Please explain when you last saw them, and what sort of mood they were in. It is important. Something may have happened to them, Rick. I know your aunt and uncle - your aunt at least - hasn't always been as kind to you as she might have been, but you owe it to both to tell me everything. Especially to your Uncle John. You know what work I'm congratulating you about, don't you?"

It was this that did it. Aunt Patrolia, she could go and take a running jump, he didn't care about her. But Uncle John, that was different.

Rick hesitated and then began. Against his will, the story began to come out, half in anger, half in relief. Soon, it poured forth, not without a few tears. Rick didn't know what was happening to him. Some of the pent-up feelings that he had held back for so long, or that had been forced into a corner, were given freedom. They were a jumble, but they made up a picture, like broken images. This told Mr Rummage as much as the details of the events themselves. Rick recounted the story that he had heard from Tyro and Jess, forgetting that Mr Rummage had heard much of it already. He knew that Mr Rummage would be interested, especially about the Stranger.

The outcome was that his aunt and uncle were both missing, and he did not know where they had gone.

Mr Rummage watched Rick's face. It was the face of an adult trapped in the face of a child. The child was hidden behind the face of a struggle with life that had made him older than his years. He had no father, and no mother. His aunt was a monster, his uncle weak. Yet Rick's face looked innocent. And the pent-up stress was washed away with the tears about which he felt guilty, brushing them away. Yet in a strange way he was proud of them too. And he smiled through them, at the Headmaster. Mr Rummage was handing him a handkerchief.

"Thank you, Sir," said Rick.

"Thank you, Rick, for mapping the tunnels."

The words had a mellowing effect. "Thank you" revealed love, and he hadn't had much of that either. He found himself saying, "Thanks, Mr Rummage." And then he added, "Please don't tell anybody."

Mr Rummage looked at him and took back the handkerchief.

"There's nothing more, is there Rick?" His voice was firm and confident. Mr Rummage went on. Mr Rummage had grown more concerned as Rick's story progressed, but would not show it.

"You are to stay in the school as a boarder from now until further notice, Rick. I have asked Mrs Wander to collect some things from your house, and bring them over. Would you mind?"

"But, Sir, I can't! It'll be like prison! At least at home, I have my freedom, of a sort. Going to bed at nine will be impossible, Sir. Besides, I like to be outside."

Rick was back to his old self. The defensiveness, the anger, the fear.

"Don't you think I know that, Rick? I know you a little better than you may realise. I said I wanted your help. There is more to do. Besides Tyro and Jess, and one or two others, nobody will know. Now go and have some lunch."

Rick was taken aback. Then Mr Rummage added.

"As for freedom, Rick. When you know what plans I have for you, Rick - don't ask me now - I think you'll find life here is not as bad as you think. Now get going!"

With that Rick moved towards the door.

"And tell Tyro and Jess that I would like to see them as soon as lessons are over, for a brief word. I have something I wish to tell them."

Rick stood for a minute unable to move. His feelings were mixed. Before he could say "thank you" again he ran out of the room, unable to control his jumbled emotions, part excitement, part guilt, part joy. He was already planning how he would be able to continue exploring, and perhaps he could get Tyro and Jess to do that too.

Rick became cautious when he entered the dining room, wanting to make them guess.

But when it came to it, he couldn't. He was too hungry and now too tired to control himself any more, and he told them everything.

Tyro looked at Jess in surprise. She was pleased, just as Jess was.

*

After lunch the three of them made their way to Ms Peverell's Art room. As they entered, they were greeted with cheers (there were hisses from predictable quarters). Very quickly they were back at work, drawing yet able to chat quietly, in that curious world of two worlds, talk and play, even it seemed with the teacher's permission. Ms Peverell did not give them any more attention than the others, merely welcomed them and told them to start their work. She would come and see them in a minute. She was scrupulous in giving each student equal time, as best she could, though it was never quite possible. Classmates kept coming up to ask Rick where he'd been, and to Tyro and Jess to ask how they had found him.

Ms Peverell was deliberately trying to keep things as normal as possible.

*

Mr Rummage sat back in his chair and looked out of the window. The winter landscape was dull, a light mist hung over the playing fields and meadows that lay between the river and the Hall. In the mist, Mr Rummage could imagine shadows walking, and wondered if they bore the shapes of Mr Blakemore and Mr Vespers.

Mr Rummage turned to his desk and looked at his diary. Only a few days to Bonfire Night. The timing was almost right. Would there be an attack? He had been told to cancel it, but he wouldn't. He wanted to draw them out, if they were there. It was a perfect time. The captivity of the Stranger might hold them back. But at least he would learn if other forces were at work. By chance, helped by design, he had decided to hold Bonfire Night on Hallowe'en. The 31st was a Saturday, and the following weekend the school was hosting a sports weekend for schools in the area. He had arranged for extra, but still discreet, security.

Mrs Clicket entered the room.

"Here are the three letters, Mr Rummage."

He scanned the letters. The first was to be sent to all day-parents offering boarding accommodation to any pupil who might wish to do so up to Christmas. The second confirmed plans for Bonfire Night, and hoped that as many "of you as possible will attend". The evening was normally a great success, (the letter read) and gave parents and teachers their last opportunity of the year to enjoy the open air, though, as was normal, winter wear was recommended. The third was to remind parents of the upcoming sixth centenary celebrations the following summer, giving some preliminary details, and asking everyone to make a note in their diaries. There was to be a ball, preceded by the school annual theatre production. There would be lots of speeches, and a dinner, with one or two special surprises.

Mr Rummage enjoyed the festive energy that radiated from two of the letters.

"Thank you, Mrs Clicket," he said.

"There've been three phone calls. One from Ipswich Police Station, asking if you would be able to go down tonight. It seems there have been difficulties, though the situation, I am told, is now under control. It seems the captive may be transferred to London tomorrow. The second from Inspector Relish, who is back in Southwold. He will call back. I believe he has some information regarding the disappearance of the people in the boat in the summer. The third from Mr Brock at the Ministry."

Mr Rummage thanked her and she left the room.

Mr Rummage got up and walked towards the window. He wondered how much further he should involve Tyro, Jess and Rick. He wondered that there had been nothing from Doonwreath.

The water level of the river Dean seemed to be dangerously high. There was a possibility of flooding. There was a knock at the door.

His wife of many years stood before him.

"Jenny!" he said as she came into the room. He walked over to her and gave her a hug.

"What's the matter with you?" she asked.

"Just the person I needed to see. Things are getting difficult. More difficult, despite the good news about the arrest. But what are you doing here? It's unlike you to have time off work."

"This is work," she said. "I've had a call from Dr Bartok. He's had a report of Aunt Patrolia. It seems she's been seriously injured. She was taken by ambulance to the hospital an hour ago. An anonymous caller phoned for an ambulance and gave instructions about where to go. The police were also informed. He does not think she will pull through."

Mr Rummage slumped back into his chair.

Whatever his views were about Aunt Patrolia personally, this was appalling news. He needed to know everything. But the first thing he wanted to establish was whether anybody else knew about it.

"Not yet," said Jenny, as she put her arm around his shoulder.

"But they will have by tomorrow. Two journalists were at the hospital asking questions. No doubt we will read about it in the papers in the morning. They know her nephew goes to Burnchester Hall. They know about the events of the summer. It seems the world is about to hear everything."

8

Mr Rummage set off with Jenny for Ipswich Police Station.

The attack on Aunt Patrolia was a most disturbing addition to recent events, though they could not definitively be linked. There seemed similarities in behaviour between Mrs Limpet and Aunt Patrolia, before each had "succumbed", but once again fuller details were needed, and there were differences also. Nevertheless it was necessary to see both incidents in relation to the attacks on Mr Gruff, Mr Pinchet, and the recent incursions into the school.

Mr Rummage was seeking further information on the backgrounds of all victims, in case there were connections that they had missed. It seemed that Mr Gruff's behaviour had recently begun to cause worry again, though not enough to involve medical help.

The identity of Jane Fellows, whose disappearance had shocked her colleagues, was an added element. Professor Southgate (alias Mr Baxter) was well versed in the psychology of multiple identities and Dr Bartok's achievements in the field of dream notation and interpretation offered intriguing insights, but as yet there were no answers to these mysteries.

Perhaps they were dealing at a depth that went beyond history and to primal forces themselves.

The inevitable concern was who would be next. The press's intrusion would probably destroy Mr Rummage's attempts to reassure parents, but he was determined to continue on his path.

Jenny took a call from Dr Bartok who confirmed that Aunt Patrolia was unlikely to survive. There was nothing more he or they could do.

Mr Rummage reflected on his reasons for wanting to be present at an interview with the Stranger. It was Inspector Relish's intention to take the Stranger under guard to the coast at Dunemoor that same evening as part of his preliminary questioning, before senior officers from London took over. The Inspector's researches had revealed information which might be of interest to the Stranger. He would later be taken to a safe house near the capital.

*

Tyro and Jess relaxed during the Art lesson, even though Rick, with new-found confidence, irritated them by making a great show of his attempts at drawing. However, under the surface there was simmering anxiety.

Ms Peverell looked carefully at their work and made suggestions.

This was always difficult for a teacher who took care to find what was not visible, as well as what was visible, in the work of her pupils.

She asked Tyro and Jess how they had got on in the morning, but didn't engage in any further conversation, except to report that she had been sent a message from the Headmaster to ask whether they would like to board for a few days. Pupils were needed to help arrange and plan supervision for the Bonfire Night. It was normally a magical event. The fireworks were lit in the meadow in front of the wood.

Tyro and Jess greeted this news with pleasure, not least because Rick had already told them on one of his many walks around the classroom in search of paint, that he would be boarding too. "I'm going to search for Tom," he added, "with the Headmaster's permission of course." This news was greeted with interest by others who overheard the conversation, and asked if they could come. Tom was becoming like a mythological figure, an elemental but enduringly necessary condition for the quest.

The only thorn in the side of a tranquil lesson was Julia's continued attempts to dampen down the attention which Tyro and Jess were getting (several classmates had come up to them to "borrow a rubber" with the real intention of finding out more). This tended to backfire and only fuelled her jealousy. Julia's only recourse was to plot and think of ways of getting the interest back on her. This exasperation would eventually lead to Julia deciding to "make enquiries", so that she too could wield some power over the class and her enemies. Her father would have to be the source.

The last lesson of the afternoon was PE. Under strict instructions about where they could and could not go, Mr Bellevue - who had recovered - decided that it was time for their weekly run. Mr Bellevue's response to the events of a couple of evenings ago was curious. Normally an outgoing person, he did not know how to cope with events which seemed to have no explanation. After all, the intruders were not just thieves. His own unconsciousness had also impaired his memory, which led him to deny what would otherwise have been a source of great concern. He couldn't deny the fact that the young pupils had been frightened on his watch (he didn't believe their stories about what they had seen), and tried to ride roughshod over their anxiety. This made him more outgoing than usual, a tactic not exclusive to teachers of sport. He was not going to be restricted by a one-off incident, nor would he let it interfere with PE.

He led the class down to the river's edge, past the bonfire, into the woods, and along the river bank.

The air was fresh (it had rained earlier in the afternoon), and the light still good. The class were unusually co-operative though David lagged behind (as usual, panting and out of breath) while John went ahead with Rick, who was tempted to go off on his own into the woods. They paused by the bonfire, where Mr Bellevue explained, whilst running on the spot, some of the plans for Bonfire Night.

The wind felt colder when they stopped, and their feet were getting soaked through on the rain-drenched grass. The school looked curiously foreboding in the background through the water as it ran down weary faces, whilst the wood seemed oddly alluring, at least to some of them. They had known the wood for many years, and were less afraid than might be imagined. True it was out of bounds, and held its own mystery, but it was part of the landscape. They took it for granted, only a few like Rick and Tyro ever really being tempted to explore it.

It was only when David, in his innocence, who had lumbered up behind the rest, and was catching his breath, asked Mr Bellevue what had happened the other night with class 6R, that the tingling of the dangerous unknown crept into most souls, not least because of Mr Bellevue's transparent attempt to lie. He made light of the whole incident. Nobody had mentioned seeing Tom that night, even the young pupils seemed to be confused about what had really happened, largely because of the explanation given to them by Mr Bellevue (under instructions from Mr Rummage) to make events seem explicable. Woodcutters (the figures) seeking stakes for the fire had taken on strange shapes in their imaginations, a momentary excess of which had added to their fear, which the dark had increased into a form of panic. Any child who might have remembered seeing the temporarily petrified Mr Bellevue or the unconscious Mark and Ali seemed to have forgotten, in a form of amnesia, just as the two boys themselves could not recall details of their ordeal.

"I don't believe a word of it," Rick said.

"Some of you will have to stand guard near the bonfire to keep other children away," Mr Bellevue said. "There will, as usual, be a rope to keep people from getting too close anyway, though there are always one or two who try to climb over."

Mr Bellevue ran on, leading them along the twilight path.

It was as they ran along the river bank, approaching the old boathouse, that memories of the summer began to enter Tyro's thoughts: rowing the boat along the river after their discovery of Mr Gruff's blood; Mr Pinchet shouting at them across the river; the Folly where Tyro had seen shapes that day from afar, on the bike ride home. Perhaps they had been the spirits of agents, who had not returned, who had trained in this very place in the arts which had saved them in the war. She thought of Mr Blakemore's incantations.

"What do you think Mr Baxter meant?" asked Jess as they ran.

Tyro was enjoying the run, the air made her feel like spring again (as did the rain), even like flying, and she turned to her friend.

"What are you referring to, Jess?"

"Insisting we don't go back into the library. If I've got to board I'm going to want to use it more, for homework."

They passed the old boathouse.

"Oh, that!" interrupted Rick, who had run up to them, and was about to overtake and take a tour over the roof (which was sunk into the bank).

They did not stop to look closely at the now barred doorway. Mr Bellevue had been given very strict instructions not to let any student near it. Had they done so, they would have seen that it had recently been tampered with.

"He only meant that room! You won't catch me in there anyway! I've got more important things to do." He raced on.

"I'll come with you, Jess," said Tyro. "We need to find out more. As for the mirror . . . "

It was so easy to say this with the winter sun low over the western horizon, its glow reflected in the windows of the old Hall, and the wind through your hair.

Like the gently flowing stream beside them, given body by the pattering of mud-splashed shoes, their excitement grew as they ran on.

The class was now beginning to straggle a bit, as they reached the end of the field. They began the ascent back up towards the main school buildings, along the track that passed Mr Gruff's house, and then the church. Mr Bellevue tried to make them sprint the last bit, but the wind made it useless, and they were now approaching "home" anyway. He began to relax.

They approached the church of St Mary Magdalen. Rick, who had gone ahead in a race with John, hid behind one of the yews that crossed the path. As Tyro and Jess passed, they leapt out, holding their arms high in a semicircular arc, in would-be cloaks.

The girls were unimpressed, and told them not to be so childish. Mr Bellevue, who now came up to them, gave the boys a telling-off. The rest of the class passed them by. However, the girls were a little intimidated, even though they would not show it.

High on the church tower, a figure watched unseen.

"We'll have the last laugh yet!" said Rick to John.

Mr Bellevue told the two boys to run to the front again, which they did at breakneck speed, pushing the smaller ones aside, doing their utmost to win by any means. There was a furious energy about them. They reached the girls as they were passing in front of the church.

In the winter twilight the Church of St Mary Magdalen looked gaunt and cold. The stones that jutted from the manicured lawns reminded them of monumental soldiers. Tyro imagined the figures from the summer, and whispered something to Jess, who gave a nervous laugh. They moved on.

Now Rick and John were far ahead, though Rick suddenly stopped and allowed John to head off alone for the changing rooms.

Mr Grudge stood watching as if he were counting them off a list.

Tyro and Jess drew close to Rick. Julia was close behind them.

"Did you realise something, you two?" Rick breathed.

The three ran on, now passing the main building of the school.

"What now?" said Jess.

"About Bonfire Night," Rick went on.

"We're not thinking about that now, Rick, we're thinking about food. I'm hungry and frozen."

"Well it's time you thought about it!" said Rick, a little impatiently. "I've found some cloaks," he added mysteriously.

The girls were tired and not very interested in cloaks, and they didn't know what these had to do with Bonfire Night. The sky was still bright. Their stomachs and a shower beckoned. They had a lot else on their minds. Tyro and Jess had to contact their mums about getting stuff for boarding. Perhaps they would go back home for one night, and then start boarding the next week.

The line of students stretched towards the changing rooms, the boys to one end and the girls to the other.

"Last one out gets to clean the showers!" shouted Mr Bellevue.

There was immediate panic.

Rick shouted over to Tyro.

"You know that Hallowe'en has been cancelled this year?"

Tyro looked up at him with a mouthed "So?" as she went on towards the girls' changing rooms.

"Did you realise," he added, struggling to make himself heard, "that Bonfire Night is being held on the night of Hallowe'en?"

Tyro turned. Yes, that was a coincidence. It seemed unnatural even. She really was thinking about tea. She hurried towards the showers, intending to be out before Julia, if nobody else.

Jess was drenched in warm water, as Tyro made her entrance, other girls around her talking excitedly. The information that Rick had given Tyro had little effect on the group, who were enjoying the warmth of the shower after such an exhilarating run. One or two told jokes, and Julia took on the role of chief witch, and made the others laugh. Even Tyro laughed, against her better judgement, though she was unnerved a little, though not as deeply as Jess who, whilst rationalising her feelings, felt quite afraid. The three of them had, after all, been witches in class, why not outside it? The word "hallowe'en", like certain other words, echoed with other meanings. Nevertheless, they had been banned from celebrating it or from doing any hallowe'en-type things. So the echo didn't last long, though the meanings remained, including that of All Souls.

*

Things moved more quickly than expected after school. Abby was waiting for Tyro by the main entrance, with John and Clare.

"Mum, you've forgotten my blue top!" said Tyro, rifling through the holdall which Abby handed over. "And what about my slippers?"

"Give me a ring later or tomorrow, and I'll bring whatever else you need," Abby said.

Tyro shrugged her shoulders, and asked Abby for some change to phone with, which Abby gave her. Did she get the feeling that her mother was actually glad to see her board for a while? The thought made her angry. But even if it were true, she knew that her mum was under great pressure, not just from work, but from her knowledge of the existence of a tunnel near their house, which would have worried her, as well as general security. The Reverend Sandals had asked Abby if she would kindly keep an extra eye on the church, which had been given new alarms. Luckily, Dennis would be at home for at least another month. Added to which she was excited about staying at school too, except for the fact of waking up in a strange bed, and that she would be close to Julia. She was already hatching a plot to visit the library the very next day. She was ready to go off, and gave her mother a kiss and a hug.

Jess had also checked her mother's packing, and was content except that her mother had forgotten the book that she was reading.

"Never mind, Mum," Jess said, giving her a kiss, before giving her father one too. "Could you bring it tomorrow, Dad?"

Tyro watched.

"Yes, dear," said her father, in his slightly patronising way, "of course we will. Are you going to be alright boarding?" he added.

He knew Jess was very sensitive - too sensitive - under her clever exterior.

The thought of Tyro's own father crept closer to her. It was always there in the background, and occasionally came forward. She knew that when this happened, there was normally a special reason, though she didn't always understand what it was. It was normally the sign for a message. Perhaps he would contact her again, and tell her what it was. He would if it was important. Her father's presence linked in some way to the secrets that they had discovered. He would not let her down. In that moment she thought of Aunt Jane too, and the letter she had not opened.

"Bye, girls!" said the three parents as Tyro and Jess turned to enter the Hall. With the dark almost upon them, it seemed for a moment that they were entering a different world, where enchantment could lead to paradise or to hell. That was the nature of mystery and its impact on the mind. Like temptation.

Most parents collected their children as normal, though some had decided to take up the offer of letting their children board the following week, the week of the bonfire.

Tyro, Jess and Rick were the only new boarders apart from David, who had started a few days earlier. They guarded their special status with a certain superiority, though day pupils felt that it should be the other way round. Who would wish to be sent to bed at some ridiculous hour, and not be at home, in their own beds, eating their mother's food, and doing homework in their own time?

On the other hand, teachers often took a kindlier view of boarders, perhaps because they knew them better, out of school, not just as temporary residents on day release. You could not oversee them at teatime, or during the lonely hours of prep in winter, or on the playing fields of late summer, through the seasons, during illnesses, times of trouble and joy, writing letters in the library, without feeling more akin to them as individuals. Besides, you knew the school better than anybody (if you were curious), having access to rooms that were out of bounds during the day. It was indeed a different world. Not just dormitories and washrooms, but special study areas, even a common room (for the older children), and access to the kitchens and time to roam, not available to others. Now of course, the freedoms had been curtailed, but still there was a sense that boarders were the keepers of the school's true identity.

So a kind of mystery surrounded those who lived at the school, and a sort of distance attached to them, just as day pupils, who were more streetwise, fashion conscious and free, seemed a little unapproachable to most of those students for whom school was "home".

It is essential for schools with this responsibility to give the children the best they can, though many, it seems, fall short of the ideal. For some, boarding school is a nightmare, where secret bullying takes place; where cabals of inclusion and solitary exclusion often mock the idyll in a pretence of care. Where tears for absent mothers and fathers, and the touch of pets, and the smells of home, humble or privileged (for Burnchester provided sanctuary for both) underlie the mask of survival, as it does elsewhere.

Tyro, Jess and Rick were for a few days caught in this intermediary world of wanting to belong, yet not quite belonging, though were welcomed enthusiastically by most boarders like initiates to a new order.

Rick was led off by David, whom Rick normally ignored, to the boys' dormitory area, "to dump his things". Rick was in a hurry to get going on his explorations, and to do what he wanted. He was not thinking of doing much in the way of homework. David was a bit of a pain. However, as he was taken round, and saw long since disused rooms, which were being hastily prepared, and beds made up, with opened windows and damp unused sheets from long forgotten cupboards, he became enthralled.

As he was led through the old Hall, a new world opened up to him, just as it does when you visit the underworld of a big ship, and experience the huge operations that keep it afloat, and those who struggle day and night to keep it going, often in darkness and excessive heat. Rick, for the first time in his life, was beholden to David's superior knowledge and experience, and - also for the first time in his life - listened attentively while David explained about dormitory life: where to put his things, where to wash, who was in charge. Rick, taller than David by several inches, was particularly interested to learn whether any teachers came round the dormitories and at what time. Rick found himself liking David, who had always admired Rick.

Once they had returned downstairs, Rick went outside for the half hour or so before prep (David went to the library) to play football with a few other boarders under the light that illuminated the side of the school, watched by Mr Grudge. Something was holding Rick back. Something that Mr Rummage had said made him wait. It was as if he was waiting for guidance or his instructions. Even Rick knew that you don't get two chances. He was prepared to see if Mr Rummage really had wanted him to search for Tom. But he was also thinking of Bonfire Night, and that supply of cloaks. He had decided that he would invite a select few to wear them during the evening, for a bit of fun. If the girls could play witches in class with false cloaks, why couldn't he provide a few side-effects on the real day, without any harm done? He thought of the sacklike cloak that he had made and tried to remember to ask Tyro to ask her mother if she would bring it for him. And he thought of Uncle John. Where was he? He barely thought of his aunt now that he had heard the news.

Tyro and Jess meanwhile were settling in too. Julia had been appointed guide, but seemingly forgot to turn up, much to Tyro's delight, so Jess had to take them round from memory, for there was a time when she was to have boarded - when her father and mother were abroad for a few months - and she had been shown round then.

Though a bit shaky (one door that she thought led to a bathroom in fact led to a cupboard) her memory was good enough, and soon they found their dormitories, and met with Jane, who was showing round the parents of one of their class.

Stowing their things in the personal spaces allocated to them, Tyro and Jess then went down to the table tennis room in the basement, one of the rooms which was for the use of boarders only. These were adjacent to the old kitchens, so the smell of cooked cabbage lingered in the air as they watched a game. It was not far from the very place they had crossed at night into the mysterious tunnel where Tom's carriage had waited for them.

"We're having prep in the library," Jess said. "There isn't the space in the usual room."

Tyro was doing an impersonation of Vipers when the bell rang for tea. The girls playing table tennis laughed guiltily.

Tea was swift and eaten with relish. It was supervised by Mr Vespers who was on duty the whole week. The students normally sat at tables in ascending order of seniority, but as there were far fewer from each class than at lunch, each table had more of a mixture of ages.

Several tables were empty. This made tea more subdued and besides, everyone was more tired, not least at the thought of prep. There was more of an echo to the conversation and the clinking of cutlery was more audible. The relative emptiness gave them more of an opportunity to study the room which was prouder and grander than they realised. Here indeed had been a grand dining room, with a dais at the far end, where many of the teachers ate. Tonight Mr Vespers sat alone with another person, a man, with his back to them.

There had been a time when tea was taken after prep, but hunger led to underperformance, whereas now a full stomach led to sleepiness, proving the rule of consultancy that there is not a better way, only a less bad one. There were fewer rules governing eating status for tea, and it was not uncommon for juniors to be sitting opposite older pupils. This happened to be the case tonight. Rick found Tyro and Jess sitting opposite two girls from a junior class. Normally the older pupils would play down to the juniors in a kind of teasing paternalism (or maternalism), though occasionally real friendships developed, just as many had older brothers and sisters with whom they got on (if they were lucky). Just as often however, there was a latent adulation from the juniors, who looked up to the older pupils. Many of the seniors of course played up to this and exploited their age to the full. This phenomenon sometimes occurs in later life, when you will find that the age gap of only a couple of years between former pupils of the same school carries over in a not quite equal sense of shared heritage.

Tyro was going on about the food - tonight it was soup, bread, cheese and a yoghurt (rather more than some children have in a week). The little ones told her proudly that it was often as bad as this (not wanting to show any of the hurt that they might have felt), except on rare occasions, like celebrations, they said. One girl named Lotty seemed rather gentle, though she seemed to shake from time to time. She watched Tyro and Jess closely, Tyro especially, for rumours had circulated about their heroism, just as they did about everything, real or unreal, about which they were not yet fully equipped to discriminate. Jess noticed the shaking, and asked her if she was alright. Lotty said yes, unconvincingly, so Jess carried on, when Rick sat down.

"Better get Mum to bring us a store full tomorrow - I'm going to phone her. Any orders?"

Rick didn't take it in. He didn't take in the little ones opposite either, or didn't show it. Lotty was nobody, and she sensed he believed it. Her friend Bridget wasn't anybody either.

"Where's your dorm?" Rick asked casually as if he had been a boarder all his life. "What time's lights-out?"

David had forgotten to tell him, perhaps out of embarrassment, for it was in fact nine-thirty, and Rick was not used to going to sleep before eleven.

"Bed at nine. Lights-out at nine-thirty."

Rick dropped his soup spoon. It hit the side of the bowl.

"No way!" he spluttered. "I've got other plans. And so have you two," he said, looking over at Jess. "Library, cloaks. Lots to do."

"Stop going on about cloaks!" said Jess, "Anybody'd think you were a monk or something! Anyway, where did you find those cloaks?"

Lotty was shaking more than ever and trying to say something, but couldn't, so she looked imploringly at Bridget.

"At the back of the stage in the hall! Oh no!" Rick suddenly looked down.

"What's the problem?" asked Tyro.

She looked up. Her question was answered. The general murmur had been broken by the sound of Rick's falling spoon. The man opposite Mr Vespers had turned round. It was Mr Blakemore.

"He's allowed to eat too, isn't he?" said Jess. Mr Blakemore was looking in her direction and gave her a cold stare, which went straight through her, and made her look down. She recognised her mistake. Mr Blakemore smiled duplicitously and continued his conversation with Mr Vespers. The whole room seemed to go cold.

"I'm telling you," said Tyro. "They are definitely up to something! I know they are working against the school. I know it. We have to find out more, and what's more I'm going to start tonight! Remember the first instruction's Initiation; the second, Activation and the third, Control. I'm going to get more active! As for control, who knows?"

Tyro looked up at the table and imagined she saw two monk-like figures sitting at a table in the hall of a medieval Priory. She sensed the sword-crosses on the backs of their habits. The atmosphere around them was dark. Not of the light of goodness and hope. The swords were of death, not for justice and truth.

The little girl Bridget suddenly burst out crying. This got Lotty going too.

Jess leant over and asked them what the matter was.

"Nothing," they said.

Tyro leant over to them, and asked if they could do anything.

The little girl Lotty stared up at Tyro and began to calm down.

"Well," she said, picking up where Tyro had left off, "the food isn't always bad. The other night (after you-know-what happened), the chef gave us a brilliant meal."

"On Mr Rummage's orders," said Bridget. "Secrets!" she

added, nudging Lotty in the ribs as if to keep her quiet and remind her of something.

"Secrets? What secrets?" asked Tyro jokingly. She leant forward over the table as Bridget was scraping the bottom of her yoghurt.

Rick was looking ahead at Mr Vespers and Mr Blakemore, who were in deep conversation.

A burst of laughter came from their direction. Tyro looked up, then down at the younger girls.

They were in class 6R, and had been to the wood on the night of the incident. They were frightened and they knew something that she didn't.

Tyro whispered something to Rick and then to Jess. Both remained impassive, as if in silent agreement.

Mr Vespers rose and spoke briefly. He told everyone to be in the prep room in ten minutes. There was a pause. David put up his hand.

"Yes, David?" asked Mr Vespers. "What is the matter now?"

"What's the matter with him?" whispered Tyro.

"I thought prep was in the library, Sir?" David said.

"It was, but it isn't now, David!" the teacher replied. "Prep will be in the usual two rooms. The library is out of bounds for tonight."

"But, Sir, I wanted some books for homework. Yours, Sir!" David said.

This gave Mr Vespers an opportunity to be condescending. He looked at David and the others. He put on a smile.

"You are excused from working on my homework for tonight, David, and all of you in that class. There will be another time. I don't doubt that you have other work to do. Like revise."

This, coming from another teacher, could have been interpreted as meaning, "Keep quiet, and do your own thing." So David and his friends, having learned that much this year, kept quiet.

"It says on the notice board that prep is to be in the library, and it is signed by Rumbags," Jess whispered.

Mr Vespers and Mr Blakemore had got up and were leaving the room. Mr Vespers stared in the direction of Rick, Tyro and Jess. He stopped short of them, trying to put on a smile.

"What are you three doing here?"

None of them answered.

Mr Vespers thought for a moment and added, "Rick, you must tell me where you've been. I know you like to explore. We wouldn't want you to be making discoveries and keeping them secret, would we? Perhaps you could tell us during prep?"

This was more of an instruction than a request, and carried with it a hollow ring. It also meant that he could not bunk off prep, which he had meant to do.

Rick didn't answer.

"We're boarding for a few days, Sir," Jess said diplomatically, adding, "I'm glad you're in charge of us, Sir!"

Tyro was nearly sick. Flattering Mr Vespers always worked. He bowed in acknowledgement, and turned to Mr Blakemore, said a few words and walked out of the room. Tyro gave Jess a dig in the ribs.

Rick, uncharacteristically, leant over to the little girl Lotty and asked her how much time they had before the beginning of prep. Confirming it was about ten minutes, Rick told Tyro and Jess that he would see them in the prep room, then got up and left with the first group of pupils. He was careful not to draw too much attention to himself by getting too close to Mr Vespers and Mr Blakemore, who were not far ahead.

Where the teachers turned left out of the hall towards the common room, the pupils bore right, along the old corridor, which led back to the main entrance, past the secretary's office via the television room, and another hall.

At this point Rick went ahead and ran up the stairs to the library. He pushed the door to, and went in. He was determined to find the books that Tyro had shown him, but he only had a few minutes, and life would not be worth living if he was caught.

Tyro and Jess went to their classroom to collect their books, in the company of Lotty. Tyro asked her about the night by the bonfire, and little Lotty, in the freedom of the outside, told Tyro and Jess everything, including their sighting of Tom and the two figures.

Tyro and Jess listened intently, with increasing concern, albeit Tom's presence was confirmed news. They thanked Lotty very much and told her not to tell anybody else. They got their books, and returned towards the prep room.

The prep room was beginning to fill up when Tyro and Jess entered. They went to the back row and took out their books. What Lotty had told them made them curious and come what may they were going to discuss it, even if it meant writing notes to each other throughout prep. They were not sure who would be supervising them, but they assumed it would be Vipers.

*

To Rick's surprise, Mr Blakemore had not returned to the library, and he found the book and notebook more quickly than he imagined he would. For once in his life he remembered something to do with school! He ran to the exit, pausing by the open door to look downstairs, to find everything quiet, bar the odd footfall coming from the corridors. These sounded like children's footsteps. He crept down the stairs and back along the corridor, holding the books carefully. He stood by the entrance to Mrs Clicket's study.

Instead of knocking, he pushed the door open and stood there, holding the books behind his back.

Mrs Clicket looked up.

"Yes?"

Mrs Clicket had seen generations of children in her time. There was little she hadn't seen or heard. There was less that she didn't know. She was one of the people who kept the place running and did not get the recognition or reward that they deserved. She saw immediately it was Rick, and put on her slightly formal tone. She loved the children, but did not become too familiar. Rick's story was well known to her. She had never liked him - she thought him distant, if not arrogant - but she liked his aunt even less, and she had heard of the "accident".

"What can I do for you, Rick? The office is closing, so you'd better be quick."

Rick brought the two books out from behind his back, and held them in front of him.

"Photocopy, prep. Project."

"You want to so some photocopying, Rick? Of those books?"

Mrs Clicket looked carefully at the books and could see immediately that they were very old. She understood at once that they were not the sort of books he would need for a project, especially not Rick. Mrs Clicket was privy to many things, and her suspicions were aroused.

She came forward to take the books from his hand, but Rick withdrew them hurriedly and hid them again behind his back. Rick stared at her. Mrs Clicket understood something was very wrong. Should she tell a teacher? Mr Vespers, perhaps, or Mr Rummage, who was still out. She decided to play it another way. She was aware of Mr Rummage's concerns about Mr Vespers.

"Go on, Rick, there's the machine, but hurry. Mr Blakemore would not be pleased. Nor Mr Vespers. I hope you know how to use it."

Rick was quickly at the machine, making copies. He had memorised the page numbers.

"Thanks," he said quietly. "Please don't tell anyone!"

Just as he was about to finish, footsteps could be heard along the corridor. The heavy footsteps of a teacher. The footsteps paused outside Mrs Clicket's door. There was a knock and the door swung open.

Mrs Clicket was already there.

"Good evening, Mr Vespers," she said, as Mr Vespers tried to push his way into the room.

"I'm just locking up!" she said, barring his entry.

Rick stood hidden in the alcove at the back, head and body bent low behind the machine, the books shoved under it and copied pages in his hand.

"I've lost a pupil," Mr Vespers said, smiling testily. "Have you seen Rick?"

"Not a sign, Mr Vespers. If you'll excuse me . . . "

With that Mrs Clicket pushed Mr Vespers back into the corridor, and closed the door.

Mr Vespers was angry, but he had caught sight of a person standing on the other side of the hallway, opening the door to his study, and did not want to make a scene. So he turned and watched Mr Rummage enter his room.

Mr Rummage had had a tiring day and needed a few moments' space before resuming his duties. He did not wish to speak to Mr Vespers, whose shape he had seen as well as recognising his voice, so he began to close the door quietly. Mr Vespers moved back towards the prep room, muttering something under his breath.

A few moments later, Rick emerged out of Mrs Clicket's office. He made his way back up the stairs as quickly as he could, now watched by Mr Rummage, who had seen him as he had turned to close the study door.

Mr Rummage was about to call out to him when Mr Vespers came back into the hall again, and made his way towards the staircase, his pace quickening as he did so.

Mr Vespers caught sight of the library door as it closed, just as Mr Rummage came out of his room. Mr Rummage spoke in a loud, confident voice by way of greeting his dubious colleague.

"Mr Vespers! May I have a word?"

Mr Vespers flinched. He did not want Mr Rummage to know he was after Rick, so he became deferential, knowing how important it was to keep in with him, not only as his employer, but as his unacknowledged enemy. Until he possessed the information he wanted, he had no choice. He could swallow any amount of pride as long as he had not found what he wanted. He was not in a hurry. Soon his Order would even possess Time.

By the time that Mr Rummage had closed the door behind Mr Vespers, Rick was hurrying down the stairs again, the books safe on their respective shelves. The shape of Mr Blakemore, now entering through the main Hall door, forced him to make a hasty retreat back along the corridor. Rick had the copies in his hand.

Mr Blakemore glimpsed a shape but could not identify it. He had work to do of his own and was anxious to get back to it as quickly as possible.

Rick entered the prep room and made his way to the back row to join Tyro and Jess.

"Brought some work?" David called out.

"Sort of!" Rick answered in a friendlier manner than usual. He sat down beside Jess and Tyro.

"We've got something to tell you!" Tyro said.

"I've got something to show you!" Rick replied. He brought out the photocopies from behind him as he sat down. He had no prep paper so Jess passed him a couple of sheets, and a pencil.

At that moment a loud banging against the door revealed an angry Mr Vespers.

In a split second hands were writing across workbooks, book pages were being scanned and turned, pencils and pens sucked, coughs withheld, noses conscientiously wiped.

"Rick, come here! Now!" Mr Vespers screamed. "The rest of you get on with your work. If there's any talking you'll all have detention. Prep is for work, not twiddling your thumbs, David! I'll be back shortly."

This was hardly appropriate for workaholic David who nevertheless looked sheepishly at his open book.

Tyro and Jess were engrossed in their books. Jess was holding a quantity of papers in her shaking hands under the desk, trying not to look at them.

Rick had whispered a few words to her as he got up.

"On no account let him, or anybody, see them."

Mr Vespers gave Rick a dressing down in front of the class.

Rick was determined to remain cool, even if it meant being spoken to like this by a teacher he hated, especially as it was the teacher who was very probably working for the enemy.

"And don't smirk!" Mr Vespers said, after he had told Rick to return to his chair.

"After prep, I expect everyone to be in bed on time tonight. The days are drawing in and we don't want any further disasters, especially with Bonfire Night approaching."

Mr Vespers then stormed out of the room.

Everyone looked at each other, as if to say, "Has he gone crazy?" They all started talking.

Tyro told Rick what Lotty had said. The sound of Tom's name and confirmation that Tom had been seen gave him new determination. Jess handed Rick the copies.

When he showed them to Tyro, her eyes nearly jumped out of her head.

"When did you do them?" asked Tyro.

"A little while ago. Copied them from the library. Books back. No-one knows. Will it help?"

"Of course it will. It means that we can start to understand too, and learn a few things to fight them with. Can you imagine what would have happened if you'd been caught? You'd have been expelled."

"I know!" said Rick. "Except I think Rumbags let me do it! I think Vipers might have seen them."

"What's more," said Tyro, "you've copied something new as well as the pages we saw. It looks like a map - of the mountains like the stars!"

What Rick didn't know was that he had put the books back in the wrong place.

9

Mr Rummage had called Mr Vespers in to see him because he wanted to protect Rick. Rick was trouble, but he was part of the contract of discovery. His tireless energy, fearlessness and devotion to adventure and to his friends impressed him.

He also wanted to check how things were amongst the boarders generally and, as the teacher in charge for the week, Mr Vespers would give him an update. Whilst he happily delegated as many responsibilities as he could, he wanted, in these unusual times, to keep up-to-date. Mr Vespers would be the best person to report anything unusual, as it would prove his loyalty.

Mr Rummage didn't trust his historian colleague. This was not only due to Tyro and Jess's reports. He had already suspected that Vespers and Blakemore were working for somebody else, and decided to draw him into his confidence, to observe his reaction, and to test him further.

He shared with Mr Vespers certain things that he had learnt from his day in Ipswich. In particular that the Stranger had not only volunteered being a member of the Priory, but boasted that the Priory was "close" and would strike again soon; that nothing would stop them, or was capable of stopping them, though he would say nothing about their specific purpose.

Such was the Stranger's arrogance that he assured his questioners that he would escape to lead the next attack, and that his power was already greater than any security could provide. Soon it would be "insurmountable", when "he would be honoured to take personal revenge".

Mr Vespers showed no reaction.

Mr Vespers left Mr Rummage's office feeling confident of his having duped the Headmaster.

Mr Rummage returned to work.

He wanted to make a tour of the school, and to meet with Mr Baxter and Ms Peverell, but Mrs Clicket had left various messages which needed attention. He had been called to London for a meeting the next day with the Ministry. Dr Vale would be there, as well as Mr Brock.

Feeling restless Mr Rummage left his study and went up to the library.

The main reading room felt a little oppressive, and hearing activity from the archives room, he walked on. As he approached the door, he could hear mutterings, a book being slammed down on the table, and angry footsteps moving across the floor. He drew closer. The mirror on the wall showed the figure of Mr Blakemore through the doorway.

Coughing lightly Mr Rummage paused, then entered. Mr Blakemore was sitting at a desk with a book open, taking notes. There was kind of eerie silence, as if some image hung beside him in the shape of Fate, or his shadow.

Mr Rummage coughed again to attract his attention. Mr Blakemore, imagining it was a pupil, turned angrily.

If a man had begun to lose his mind, this was he. He saw Mr Rummage and stared a moment in horror. In the mirror the shape of Mr Blakemore had become the shape of a faceless cloaked figure, visible to Mr Rummage, but not to himself.

Mr Blakemore's anger waned and the figure disappeared. Mr Blakemore's true likeness, or the image of it, returned. This Mr Blakemore would have seen, if he had looked.

"Mr Blakemore, I'm so sorry. I hope I haven't interrupted you. I heard noises and came to see if everything was alright."

Mr Blakemore's transformation was as sudden as its insincerity.

He smiled limply.

Mr Rummage stared him in the eye with a compassionate look that gave no hint of deeper understanding or knowledge. He continued, "How's the research, Mr Blakemore? May I see?"

Mr Blakemore stalled. He did not expect such a direct question at this time of night, in these circumstances.

"I was a bit frustrated because I thought that someone had tampered with, er . . . certain books. They were in the wrong place."

Mr Blakemore pointed to the place from which books had been removed, while closing his notebook and covering it with loose papers.

Mr Rummage was reminded of the words, "The quality of nothing hath not such need to hide itself."

"Perhaps I made a mistake," Mr Blakemore went on.

Mr Rummage's eye returned to the table where other books stood open.

"Nevertheless, we are making progress! I think I have found an important manuscript. The essence of their training. The steps needed to tap the Power."

"And the symbols needed to make them effective?" Mr Rummage enquired.

"Yes, and objects of, shall we say, inspiration, even 'worship'."

Mr Rummage looked at him.

"They include curious depictions of the universe, it seems."

Mr Rummage detected the faintest hint of uncertainty, as if Mr Blakemore had not wanted to reveal so much. He walked over to the book and picked it up. He flicked through the pages.

"You have done well, Mr Blakemore. Let me have the references and your report as soon as you can. Time is running out, for all of us."

Mr Rummage studied Mr Blakemore, whose now more relaxed face spoke of nothing but respect, so inadequate was his art.

Mr Rummage asked Mr Blakemore to join him on a brief tour of the school, which he often took at this time. He would enjoy his company.

"You haven't found the Spearhead yet, then?" Mr Rummage asked.

If Mr Blakemore was put out, he didn't show it.

"We have one or two leads," Mr Blakemore observed, looking carefully into his employer's eyes.

"Leave everything there, nobody will touch anything I assure you. They are still in prep. Unless . . . "

Mr Rummage led Mr Blakemore through the library. He had scored a small tactical victory, an affirmation.

"Unless . . . ? You were about to add something, Mr Rummage?" asked Mr Blakemore, cautiously.

There was no opportunity to answer, had he wished to. As they left the library and went down the stairs, the main door opened and revealed two people removing coats, Mr Baxter and Ms Peverell.

"Mr Baxter! Ms Peverell! Just in time. Come and have a drink in a short while. I have news."

"With pleasure," Mr Baxter said. Ms Peverell nodded.

As Mr Rummage and Mr Blakemore were about to leave the building, Mr Rummage turned.

"Mr Blakemore has, it seems, made an important discovery. You might like to go to the library and look."

Mr Baxter walked up the stairs with Ms Peverell.

Mr Blakemore was led out, trying to hold back his anger.

"I . . . !"

"Do not worry, Mr Blakemore," Mr Rummage said, as they came out into the night air, "there is little that Mr Baxter does not know of these matters. If I were you, I would try to gain his confidence. He might be able to help you."

This was as far from Mr Blakemore's intention as could be imagined and, struggling not to show his feelings, he looked towards the church, which was now lit up. Perhaps the document was hidden there? Beneath its teasing shadows lay the picture which had led him to this place, which had formed part of the curse which he carried. The key document with which his order could blackmail or destroy the church was hidden nearby. He hoped that this most important information was not known by Mr Baxter. He was close to finding it, but this he had not mentioned, even to Mr Vespers.

Mr Rummage and Mr Blakemore met Mr Gruff who had "nothing to report". Mr Grudge and Mr Bellevue were still down by the river. Mr Rummage and Mr Blakemore went on.

"You will remember why I engaged you in this business, or have you forgotten?" Mr Rummage asked.

The night held more fears for Mr Blakemore than Mr Rummage, who seemed to thrive in the cover of darkness, as he was not in its power.

"To find the lost wisdom," Mr Blakemore replied.

"To find a missing piece in the jigsaw, Mr Blakemore. But for the good, not for personal gain, or for power. Not for what you might call 'vaulting ambition'."

"Without ambition there is no progress," Mr Blakemore replied.

"It depends on the basis of the ambition and your definition of progress."

Mr Blakemore would not be drawn further. He asked if he could go back and continue with his work. He felt he was on the point of further discoveries and wanted to maintain the momentum, and do another couple of hours. He did not add that he was anxious that Mr Baxter shouldn't interfere with his papers.

Mr Rummage managed to persuade him to go down with him to the bonfire. He wanted to show Mr Blakemore the place where they would put the Guy.

When they reached the spot Mr Blakemore did not at first look at the stack, but instead into the woods. He saw what appeared to be figures moving through the trees. It was like a sign telling him to prepare.

Mr Rummage sensed Mr Blakemore's curiosity. Mr Rummage had seen them too.

"Just a small exercise. Military. We give them permission from time to time. Be over by morning, and you won't know they've been. The bonfire is taking shape."

Mr Blakemore cast his eye onto the fire, where the sticks and other objects were piled high, ready for burning.

His reaction was instantaneous. His eyes became transfixed in a struggle to avert them, yet trapped by the sight, as if he saw some horrid image beyond them, in a still nascent guise. His body shook, a leer crossed his face, as if he was in scorching pain, perhaps a victim. He panted for breath. Sweat poured from his now strained face, like a trapped child.

Mr Rummage studied Mr Blakemore's reaction. Mr Blakemore now shook from head to foot, terror crossing his eyes, spasms of pain ripping through him.

Mr Rummage could not let him suffer more. He touched his arm, calling gently, trying to distract him, bring him back.

In an instant, the fear had gone, Mr Blakemore turned.

"It should burn well," Mr Rummage said, "as long as the wind is not from the North, in which case the wood will catch too."

Their attention was diverted by two familiar shapes marching over the damp grass, some yards off.

From along the river came Mr Bellevue and Mr Grudge. They seemed to be carrying a set of stakes. They came up to Mr Rummage and soon all four were in conversation.

Shortly afterwards, Mr Blakemore returned alone up the slope towards the school.

Mr Rummage watched Mr Grudge and Mr Bellevue hammering stakes into the ground, that would act as a barrier to straying spectators.

Mr Rummage went on along the river bank, into the dark. His fears had been confirmed. He would have to take further precautions.

After prep, the boarders had about an hour during which they could watch TV, play table tennis, or generally unwind before going up to bed. This was the time when a calm normally enveloped the school, as tired children of all ages merged with night, protected by the ancient walls.

However, there was also the potential for excitement, the end of another day which, if inflamed, added energy to the clamour of expectation: as if play could be heightened in the dreams which many would soon inhabit, where the borders of fact and fiction began to break down. Rumour was born, soon to become myth. The pulse of life generated a consciousness of its own, as if the Hall came alive. Boys (in particular) chased each other and fought battles, or sought out dark out-of-bounds corners. Girls, in separate domains, plotted and spun webs about who was going out with whom, who they fancied. Occasionally their territories crossed, and new worlds were formed.

Some were still children enough to talk of Bonfire Night, and Rick talked about Hallowe'en. He could not contain his need to startle, if not to frighten, those he had in his power. The mystery of his background could be used, as he was learning, to his advantage. He went off and found the cloaks at the back of the stage, which would normally be out-of-bounds were it not for the fact that it was being prepared for the autumn concert by the Head of Music, Mr Piper, who got Rick to help move chairs. Rick thought of finding more underground tunnels, and discovering what amounted to a kind of treasure. For him the darkness was still a game. For Tyro, it had a darker purpose.

Tyro and Jess were thinking how to avoid lights-out. The old Hall beckoned adventure, and now living inside it, they succumbed to its charms. In Jess's case, this included wanting to read all night by the light of a torch, with her head under the covers, only to find that she would fall asleep in the process. Despite her growing adventurousness, she was not going anywhere near tunnels, and staying as close to the hearth as possible, until it was absolutely necessary.

For Tyro the pull was stronger. She was bored, drawn on by an engaging mission, which as yet remained a form of play whose end was unclear, but which she knew she must enact, and which required new horizons. This feeling was born of the curious mix of incidents and dreams which lined her memory, fact-oriented though she was, and still bound by the declining myths of childhood, combined with a new understanding of language.

Tyro thought of her mother alone in the house and felt guilty, and then remembered Dennis was there and felt better, but she still missed home. What had her mother said about Aunt Jane coming to visit them? She had forgotten to bring some important objects, which she could not admit to possessing, and were still part of her personal armoury. It might be better if she forgot them, though she touched the cross-sword about her neck, as if for reassurance. She would have to go home and collect her diary, for she was determined to get that going again, now that she had more to write. And then she remembered Aunt Jane's letter, which she had never opened. She sat up and vowed to find it. It was bound to contain an important message. Letters in stories always do, especially letters from far away aunts who rarely visit. There was also the plan that Mr Rummage had mentioned to them. What could it be? He had mentioned a journey. Mr Baxter had also told her to write down her dreams, but she was frightened to.

Despite their energy, when it came to bedtime there was less fuss than was supposed. It was easy to complain that going to bed at nine was far too early, but when it came to it, the ritual and the newness combined with tiredness to make it seem reasonable after all.

*

Whether the reality of moving about the ancient Hall by night, with shadows everywhere in only unreliable shades of light, creaking floors and empty echoing rooms, had anything to do with it; or whether rumours of ghosts had any influence on their decision to forgo exploration is not easy to say, but it was, surprisingly, with minimal fuss, and maximum curiosity (about trivial things like who actually turned lights out and who woke them up in the morning?) that they made their way shortly after nine, with others, towards their dorms. The word itself seemed old-fashioned, and evocative of sleep. All the stories they had heard from boarders about the special things they could do which mere day pupils could not (like have pillow fights and feasts in the early hours, and hide their worst enemy's clothes in the washroom, and make apple-pie beds - all those things that everyone is far too old for except when they have an opportunity to do them) added to the sense of mystery, and mystery is sometimes helped by old words.

It was not until Matron, Miss Templedean, had seen the newcomers "tucked up", meaning "quietened", in the girls' room (the main dorms were already full), amidst empty beds, soon to be filled by others; and Mr Vespers, who was in charge of the boys, more like a turnkey than a guardian, had done the same, that the Hall became quiet, or as quiet as it ever was. For no old building is without its secret residents, and secretive visitors, who emerge in the shadows and scratch floorboards, and hang like corpses woven into the curtains, rattle pipes and sigh in the empty rooms, as if locked in by the dark and only freed by the moon, against the regular ticking of the old clock.

Somewhere in this enclosed space a figure strode, like the

Fantastical Duke of Dark Corners.

The eloquent movement towards All Saints could not have gone unnoticed by these spirits. They had recently become more active, and soon would be out in force to watch the fire consume old bones. Others, outside in the forest, were on the move, ready to steal the prize. Beneath them all the hum of the underground Chamber purred, and crouched, like a sleeping giant, waiting to pounce. The vast entanglement of tunnels lay like a pulsating brain beneath the surface of the earth. Far below, in the undiscovered country, connections were being made.

The girls were asleep. Rick had begun to snore. At least for one night, a kind spirit has taken charge and allowed all the children peaceful rest, in compensation for the anxiety of day.

*

Having returned indoors, Mr Rummage kept watch for an hour or two: he walked the stairways and halls, checking locks on doors, listening for sounds of movement, before returning to his study to meet Mr Baxter and Ms Peverell. He briefed them on his visit to Ipswich. He confirmed that the Priory were waiting to strike, but that they would not do so without more evidence. Everything hung in the balance. It was now suspected that the Priory, already shadowy, were working for or a cover for someone else, whose intentions were darker still, and whose identity and whereabouts were wholly unknown. The Stranger was believed to belong to both groups, straddling both worlds.

Mr Rummage told them to prepare, to stay alert. Briefings from other sources confirmed that dark forces were gathering elsewhere, and might strike in synchrony. Across the world, the ancient sources of light were doing their upmost to hold the line. The tide was turning. They were safe while the Spearhead was in their hands - at least not in the hands of the enemy. They must find it first, or be destroyed. The battle would begin in earnest soon. The journey undertaken.

*

Later still, Mr Rummage found Mr Vespers and Mr Blakemore working in the library. He felt it best not to appear to be surprised. They knew that Rick had found one of the key books, and had copied it. They realised that Tyro and Jess were part of a larger defensive cell. They were determined to put a stop to their searches, and were devising ways of silencing them, as they had done - or their colleagues had done - Mrs Limpet, Mr Gruff, and, now, God rest her soul, Aunt Patrolia.

*

Rick woke up in the night (he thought he had heard Tom whistling) and Tyro had a curious dream, but neither remembered anything in the morning. Dreams can be like indistinct background music, on the edge of echoes but soothing with familiarity. No amount of searching or conscious recollection can bring them back, any more than the past can be brought back in the present life, once the moment has gone. The night seemed to wipe the slate of their memories clean, or wrapped them up in packaged thoughts, ready for re-opening, at inspection time, later on.

The night owl had swept along the river valley on ghastly wings, twisting, hovering, ducking, as if to evade unseen hands, before plunging deep into the ageless grass. There, talons outstretched, it caught its prey, smothered and crushed it into fragments, regurgitating it in a circle of fur and bone. The lazy grass could not protect the rats against the owl's prying eyes, keepers of the gates between the visible and the unseen, harbingers of wisdom, manipulators of renewal. Nothing could hide from its watchful gaze. What it saw on the

183

edges of darkness it could not speak of, but it kept watch, and had sketched on its ancient memory what others could only glean through symbols.

Beyond lay the Burnchester Arms, across the fields bordered by hedges and ancient scattered trees. The bird passed by, while Dennis sat hidden, waiting. There had been reports. There was movement. Animals were beginning to flee. Unidentified travellers passed with stories of danger from beyond this still safe world, and moved on.

Elsewhere Abby lay in her bed. She thought of Tyro, and then Jack, whose presence seemed to give her the strength to counter growing fear. He felt like one walking beside her. Dennis would return soon, she said to herself. Nevertheless, the doors were locked across the house. Rompy lay by her side.

*

An officer in uniform walked up to the front door of Burnchester Hall and pressed the late bell which rang in Mr Rummage's study. Once inside and settled in a chair, Mr Brock confirmed that the exercise had been successful, that nothing had been seen beyond the habitual creatures of the dark, in the unmoulded, integrated landscape of the Dean Valley that night. No figures, whoever they were, had been identified, no sightings of a child.

Mr Brock left by the same door, followed by Mr Baxter. Yet the figures were everywhere for those who could see.

*

Above, the night vision cameras scanned rhythmically from the tower, through the night. The high observatory looked out onto the dark sky, far into the universe, where there was other movement, monitored deep within.

The sun's first rays broke across the eastern horizon, and sped over the fields and villages. A wave of light flowed into the towns, heralded by singing autumn birds.

The breaking of a new day sweeps away the dark, and brings in a resurrected life.

10

Though she missed home Tyro settled in to boarding readily. She loved the freedom, felt more mature, independent, herself. She could pursue her inner thoughts and face her own personality without having to be answerable to her mother. She was beginning to sense that she had been chosen in some way, but would not have told anybody for fear of ridicule. She began to think beyond school, in dreams and day visions, in images that appeared in her paintings and grew from conversations with friends.

There were no more incidents of the kind that had occurred to class 6R. Tyro had learned more about the events of that evening from Lotty, and gradually pieced together a picture.

Tyro was confused about her fondness for Tom, but she kept this to herself. She was confused by most things now, though her energy was greater than ever. Her determination grew, Jess acting as a counterbalance to her impulsive behaviour.

Tyro thought of her father more. His face came at her when she least expected it. Once or twice she heard his voice. On a single occasion she had gone into the church and asked the image in the painting why he had let her father die. The image had not answered. She asked the image if he really was the son of God. The image in the painting remained silent, but she heard a voice saying, "Thou sayest."

For his part Rick was sometimes angry with Tom. Tom had

never let him down before - they had made a pact - and it had been broken. Something had happened to him against his will, so Rick kept the faith. Tom needed their help, and was fighting in his own way, as he had done in the Domed Chamber. Rick felt that his identity was part of Tom's gift.

Tyro, Jess and Rick's classmates became more important to them, though the rivalry continued between Julia and Tyro. It was as if they were all in a ship together, sailing a troubled ocean, and only together could they find the safety of the shore.

Tyro thought of the boat on the underground stream. She longed to take it and find out where it led. Her thoughts about running away increased. There had been confirmation of a rise in the sea level at Dunemoor. All along the coast, the waters were rising.

Days passed. Then an incident occurred which changed everything. It was just before Bonfire Night.

*

One evening after class, Rick, Tyro and Jess stood at the door to the main teaching block. The guard at the gate looked tired. The sky was overcast, following rain. Most people were indoors.

A few students, hair and trousers drenched, were playing football in the yard with a cabbage which had fallen from a rubbish bin at the back of the kitchens. The leaves were peeling off and it was soggy and heavy. The rain started again.

A meeting was taking place in Mr Rummage's study.

Teachers passed along the corridors carrying books, talking to colleagues, instructing pupils, making sure that the machinery of the school functioned with a consistent beat. One pinned a notice on the board in the hall. The typewriter clicked on Mrs Clicket's desk.

Rick ran into the rain to join the football. John had just

dribbled round David and was about to shoot past a barely recognisable figure inside the goalposts (a couple of crooked sticks leaning against the wall of the main building), when Rick launched a tackle at John's feet, moved away with the cabbage, did a dummy, swung round and kicked the cabbage with an almighty thud at the goalkeeper. John was in hot pursuit. Rick fell backwards onto the hard tarmac into a puddle, clutching his foot. John landed on him on the wet drive.

The cabbage, a little worse for wear, exploded into a spray of flailing leaves, flying in all directions, some torn, others wispy, two piecemeal smack against the common room window. The remaining core caught Harry (the goalie) below the belt, and he, staggering forward, fell on top of the others.

"Goal!" Rick muffled out, beneath them.

"Foul!" cried John.

"Balls!" snarled Harry.

"What a player!"

"Idiot!" howled John.

Tyro and Jess came over to help them up.

A teacher stormed out from the Hall. It was Mr Vespers.

"What the devil do you think you're playing at?" he bellowed. "You're a disgrace, the lot of you! I want you all to report to me in my room, NOW!"

Mr Vespers turned and made for the classrooms.

Rick pretended not to hear.

"Let's get out of here!" he said. "It was my fault anyway! Let's go!"

In an instant they scattered across the yard. John towards the changing rooms, David into the classrooms, Harry towards the main Hall.

Rick, followed by Tyro and Jess, ran towards the church of St Mary Magdalen.

Mr Vespers came out again into the rain. It wasn't just that one or two parents had seen what was going on, albeit mostly from the protection of their cars. It was that one of the cabbage leaves had landed on Mr Rummage's window and he wanted to be seen to be taking action.

Mr Vespers drew himself up to his full height in front of Mr Rummage's study. Mr Rummage appeared at the window, looked out at the scene, and stood for a minute, while speaking to the group behind him.

This was Mr Vespers's opportunity. He had had it in for Rick, Tyro and Jess and this was his chance of taking them out of circulation for a while. Mr Rummage could not deny him.

"Rick! I order you to come back here! Tyro, Jess. All of you! Otherwise you'll all be grounded! For the rest of term! And you won't be allowed to go to Bonfire Night! Is that understood, you despicable children?"

It was of course too late.

Rick, Jess and Tyro were near the church.

The gravestones had a surreal sheen, catching the occasional light from a passing car.

One parent, in his car, watching what was going on, smiled as if reliving a distant memory. The parent, observant by nature and an author, looked at the children. He then turned towards the Hall. Something stirred in his mind, some echo. This was the very same man who, during the summer, had been sitting with his family on the beach at Warblersbay when Dennis had come up to them.

"If you don't come back here! I . . . !" screamed Mr Vespers with astonishing force. He moved across the yard.

Yet he was not unpleased. Mr Vespers did not want to be seen to be overreacting. He was in sight of parents after all, and Mr Rummage. He did not want to let the children get away with it either. So he wore a smile across his face concealing the rage within.

"Got them at last!" he thought, as he watched Tyro, Jess and Rick reach the church. Mr Vespers looked about him. Yes, one or two parents were watching. He wasn't sure whether there was a figure at the window of Mr Rummage's study.

Tyro and Rick had slipped and fallen, adding muddy blotches to their soaking clothes.

"Stupid idiot!" Tyro screamed at Rick.

"You didn't have to come!" Rick shouted.

"I wasn't talking about you! I was referring to Vipers. Still, you are an idiot, Rick."

"I'm soaking!"

"Let's get out of the rain," Jess said.

The three of them ran under the porch. They could hear Mr Vespers's voice. As much as they hated him, he was still a teacher, and they had been foolish. They saw him pause.

Would he come after them? They were too wet and frightened to think of anything other than shelter.

Rick turned the handle and the church door creaked open.

"At least he can't touch us in here," said Jess. "Sacred territory."

Rick had never seen the point of churches.

The three of them entered the cold nave. A musty air met them, as they turned to look back, hiding behind the half-closed door.

To their surprise they saw Mr Vespers had not moved. In the distance, through a window on the first floor of the Hall, they could see another figure.

"Who is that?" pointed Tyro, seeing the shape.

"Looks like Blakemore," said Jess. "Seems to be giving Vipers instructions."

Mr Vespers began to walk back to the main building. He raised his hand to two parents as they drove past him. He re-entered the school. He had regained control.

Standing well inside the nave, the three friends shook their clothes and hair. At first they were a bit nervous. Then they laughed.

"Fancy playing football with a cabbage!" Tyro said.

"It wasn't me. I just joined in!"

"Let's just dry off a minute and then go back," said Jess. "I hope Vipers doesn't punish the others."

"He won't get John or Harry. I don't think he'll bother with David. It's us he's after."

Rick had fallen badly.

He walked forward, his back bent, one arm holding on to it, the other holding an imagined stick before him. He then stood up straight.

The three of them laughed and began to relax. They looked around.

The bare interior of the church was like a drapery of grey, dark pallid shapes seemed cut out of the walls where there should have been light. Lines of silent pews. The chancel arch. Beyond two candles flickered, one on either side of the altar. The church had a strange transforming power.

Rick looked at Jess who was looking up at the ancient wooden roof, which reminded her of storm clouds. She looked disorientated.

"It's only a building built of stone, Jess. A church is no different from anywhere else. Don't believe all that religious stuff. It's a myth. It's only another form of power. That's what Uncle John thinks. He's right."

Jess liked to believe, even if she wasn't sure what it was she believed in. She needed faith of some sort. She was angry.

Rick had never spoken like this before. It had a ring - that's what upset her - an authority almost. His Uncle John was a firm, quiet, unbeliever. Uncle John had seen action. Quiet humble Uncle John had seen terrible things, perhaps done them. In battle. He had fought demons in reality, not in images designed to frighten and suppress. Uncle John, if he prayed at all, prayed in the open air. Uncle John was a good man. He also wore a cross, but Rick hadn't seen it. But Jess needed more.

Rick fell silent.

"What's the matter, Rick?" Jess asked.

Tyro passed the font. It reminded her of a cup, like the cup the Knights of old had always sought, according to her mother - the Grail. The font was for baptism, crossing a threshold, becoming a member of the faith. So her mum had told her. Her mum hadn't yet explained what the Grail was, except that it was a cup with magic powers.

She strayed into the nave. She caught sight of the painting, and walked along the aisle.

Tyro felt a little guilty. She had always run from her mother's entreaties to go to church. It was already part of daily school routine, but to have come here by mistake! Especially in running away! That was strange.

"We ought to go back. Before Vipers comes after us," Tyro muttered, walking on, the painting before her.

They were compelled to look.

The candle flames flickered. Tyro's thoughts strayed. Where had the voice come from that had said, "Thou sayest"?

"What's the matter, Rick?" Jess asked.

Rick did not answer. He looked at Jess, a little coldly, afraid of what she might see. Afraid of what he might find in himself.

Why was he so critical? He longed to see Tom, to go wondering at night in search of something, of treasure, tunnels. This musty old building was oppressing him. How he hated it. He couldn't ignore its power. The picture frightened him. He wanted to get out. He was trapped. He knew that it possessed tunnels, unique ones. Jess tried to touch him, but he pushed her hand away.

Jess felt hurt and left him alone. Rick looked towards Tyro, about to call her back. Jess went up to Tyro and stood beside her.

Then Rick cast his eyes to the floor. What seemed like a tear appeared in Rick's eyes.

Tyro stood in front of the altar, where the painting rested. They had for years come into the church for school prayers, but she had never really looked at the painting before, except on the one occasion when she had tried to avoid the gaze of the figure on the cross, who would not, it seemed, answer her.

They had giggled during prayers, they had slept during readings. They had mouthed the words to the hymns. They had passed notes along the stalls and pews. Yes, she had felt sorry for the figure on the cross. But only because she could feel the pain. Human sympathy. Nothing more. The picture was just a blur. Something with no meaning, except in history books. For her history was not living.

Now the painting held her gaze. She dwelt on the space where the fragment should be. She studied the still peaceful agony of the figure on the cross. She became angry. She wanted her father. She didn't know that the figure on the cross did too, felt abandoned in His hour of need.

Rick moved forward. The tears had gone. He was staring at something near the ground.

The rain fell heavily on the roof. Tyro could feel Jess's breath beside her, and watched Rick ahead of them.

Tyro clasped the object that hung about her neck, ripped it off and threw it to the ground. What was God doing, taking her father away from her like that? She kicked it into the shadows.

She would be burnt as a heretic, yet she believed in something.

"Do you see?" Jess was saying, pointing to the edge of the painting where the missing panel was. The missing panel that was supposed to hold the secret of the whereabouts of the Spearhead. They remembered the debriefings they had had over the summer. They hadn't really understood.

She saw the Spear, broken at the top, nothing but a pole, ineffective, and incomplete.

"Yes, I see," Tyro answered. "Fruit on the ground. The Spearhead is missing. So is the fragment showing where it should be."

"It is the cause of all the trouble," Jess spoke softly.

"Can you believe it has so much power?"

"No," said Rick. "It's only a symbol."

Both Jess and Tyro stood a moment without answering.

"It has to be somewhere," said Rick, moving towards the altar.

Rick moved towards a point in the altar beneath the painting - in fact beneath the place of the missing fragment.

"Come back here!" said Tyro, grabbing Rick by the arm and trying to pull him back. She could now see what he was looking at. She was afraid of what he might do. She was afraid he might invoke the wrong energies. He shouldn't be here. They shouldn't be there.

There seemed to be a gap in the altar stone. Rick suspected that the church had tunnels under it. The church was the one place he hadn't explored at all. But he knew the rumours, and his map told him so.

"It can't be!" Tyro said, releasing her grip, realising what he had seen.

Rick had no choice now, but despite this, the feeling inside the church was not quite right. The feeling inside him was not quite right. He fought it, like he had fought his aunt. His aunt was now dead. For a moment only he almost felt sorry for her, as if, in this cold, damp, empty, inhuman place, he was being reminded of something that he should have known all along. His impatience grew.

He turned and looked at Tyro and Jess.

"Do you see what I see?"

Everywhere there were shadows, but for the candles on the altar. Jess could feel the empty space behind them. Tyro smelled the musty air. She could also feel a growing presence.

"Someone's in here," she said.

Rick was pointing.

"There's a gap in the stone. It looks like an opening," Tyro said.

The three of them looked closely. There was indeed a gap in the altar, as if it had not quite been connected properly. The facing slab and the right hand end-piece were not properly flush, so that a clear gap had appeared, behind which was a shadow.

The three friends stared. They looked at each other. They had completely forgotten Vipers, or that they were in a dark wintry church.

"It could lead us to . . . " Rick began.

It was then that they heard the voice. A soft murmur, a dull incantation.

Jess grabbed Tyro. Rick stood up. They all turned.

Somewhere not far from them. Like a person talking in a dream. The rain had muffled it until now, now that they were closer.

They looked around. They stared into the dark shapes and corners of the chapels on either side of the chancel. The mysterious light. They expected angels to be sleeping, or monks to be praying.

Their minds went back to the events of the summer. They remembered seeing the figures close to the church. They were suddenly petrified. In amongst the myriad shadows of this apparently sacred place, they saw, or thought they saw, figures in the pews, against the pillars, in the very substance of the air. They were losing control. Something else was taking over.

Jess wanted to scream, but found she couldn't. Rick stood ready to confront the demon, for he was sure that that is what it was. Tyro was watchful. None of them was about to run. They could not. Rick was caught between wanting to go back to the altar and finding the source of the voice.

"Oh my . . . !" Jess pointed.

Tyro and Rick followed her pointing hand.

In the side chapel of the north aisle, barely visible amidst the stone, a dark shape knelt in front of the small altar. They could only see the outline with its back towards them. It was barely moving.

They were mesmerised.

On the altar stood a small cross. To one side, the statue of the Virgin Mary with child. The children moved closer, as if drawn. They could now see that the figure wore a priest's habit.

Tyro put her finger to her mouth. She looked at Jess and Rick.

The three of them stood for a moment. Clearly it had not seen them. Then the murmur stopped.

The three of them began to retreat.

The figure rose and turned. It was shaking.

The three friends bent low and moved sideways into one of the pews, trying to avoid the figure's gaze. Desperate not to make a noise. Desperately holding on to one another. They bent low, out of sight.

The figure, now standing upright, seemed to glide slowly along the transept, its head slightly bent forward. Now they could see its face.

"It's the Reverend Sandals!" whispered Tyro.

One of them knocked a Book of Common Prayer from the pew and it fell to the ground.

The friends froze.

The Reverend Sandals turned. To their amazement he hardly seemed to see them. He was in no state to. His face was one of sadness and fear.

But he *had* seen them and was himself taken aback. He needed to compose himself. So he hurried on. When he reached the list of former incumbents on the wall he paused, as he always did, and to the astonishment of the children, made the sign of the cross.

Then he seemed to collect himself, and began to act normally. He walked towards the belfry. He reached the curtain and went behind it.

Tyro, Rick and Jess ran out of the pew and into the aisle.

"How come he didn't say anything?" whispered Tyro.

Jess wanted to hurry away, but Tyro was in no mood to retreat.

She knew that the Reverend Sandals had seen them. She was determined to find out why he was here and in the state he was. She knew he had been weeping. She suspected it was from fear.

She approached the curtain that separated the nave from the tower. Jess tried to pull her back, but failed.

Tyro pulled back the curtain.

"Reverend Sandals . . . Reverend Sandals," she began, assuming her most innocent tone.

Surely he must recognise her.

"Reverend Sandals," Tyro continued, "Are you all right?"

Ahead of them they could see the bellropes. There was a small wooden staircase to the right, leading upwards. The Reverend Sandals was not there.

*

For a moment all three stood bewildered. On the floor beneath the belfry were the remains of some kind of ritual.

A figure appeared above them, at the top of the stairs.

The Reverend Sandals was holding the banisters and trying to smile, but he was shaking. At the same time, he was beckoning them to come up.

Slowly they obeyed, Tyro leading the way, followed by Rick then Jess. Soon they were at the top, and walking across a wooden landing towards an open door, where there was a room.

The room was large and bare, with a desk to one side. Devotional paintings adorned the walls, and there was one tapestry. There was a small altar and a kneeler, and a cross on the wall. There was a silver chalice on the mantelshelf behind it which seemed to shine. It seemed a source of light in itself, though it reflected the light from a single window which overlooked the churchyard, and then the school. From it you could see another window on the second floor of the school.

The Reverend Sandals was at the altar. He turned.

He was near breaking point, the children could see. Even Rick was shocked, as he and Jess joined Tyro and stood in front of their school chaplain, the man trained to guide their souls and fight the forces of the dark.

The Reverend Sandals made the utmost effort to hold his hands out, signifying peace. They were shaking, his eyes were glazed.

"It's all falling apart," he stammered. "What will happen," he went on, as if to himself, "what will happen when all this goes, when the church becomes a ruin, from lack of use? What will happen to us all then? Think about it, children. Without belief, without faith, and the hope that it brings, without the Church, we are doomed." He did not mention power.

Then his eyes focused and he recognised Tyro, Jess and Rick for the first time. He forced a smile. He tried to hide his fear.

The children were too afraid to speak.

The Reverend Sandals looked more closely.

"Tyro, Jess. Yes, and Rick? What, pray, might you be doing here? You are soaking wet. Shouldn't you be in school? Go back at once, before you catch your death. You shouldn't be here, not at this time."

"We were sheltering from the rain," Tyro said.

"If that is all you were escaping from, you are lucky," the Reverend replied. He looked at the altar and made the sign of the cross.

"Is anything the matter, Reverend Sandals?" Tyro asked.

The Reverend Sandals was used to most kinds of suffering, not least his own. He visited the sick of heart, of mind and body. Administered to the dying, comforted the lonely, felt the fury of the unbeliever, who held him responsible for not protecting her dying child. Had felt the fury of the believer who held his God responsible for his dying wife. His faith was being tested to the limits. His strength was leaving him. He was like an empty vessel, a broken chalice.

He was more secure with the directness of a child, knowing that it is children, being largely innocent, who will inherit the earth. He wished he was one again. Tyro's wisdom had always been greater than her years.

He had been trained not to give opinions of his own, to hide his true beliefs, his ambient doubts, except as they reflected the greater glory of the God that he served, but of whose existence he was increasingly in doubt. He had been trained to speak through the gospels. There was no room for personal inquisition, in public. No more than to make himself human, like his flock.

Like much of his flock, starving in spirit though they were, lost and troubled, he could not reconcile his faith with the world as it was, to the myths that he had been led to believe. He still clung to some primitive notion of the child - the Saviour - he had always believed in, finding strength in the children he served on earth. He could not dispel the creeping insurrection of his soul, blackened by uncertainty and tainted with fear. The evidence was becoming less and less convincing. The symbols were breaking up, and the powers of darkness were ready to invade.

He felt it was the beginning of the end. It was as if the remnant reddish wall-paintings that he could envisage around him even in the dark were in fact the stains of the tears of all those who had suffered at the hands of the Church, for suffering the same uncertainty, but with less guile, or training, to repudiate its charms. The guilt of the Church was inescapable, which had caused their sacrifice. A sacrifice which the Church was not prepared to acknowledge.

His church was being visited. He had found signs, signs he did not wish to discuss. The hooded Priory figures - not the cause of the dark rituals - were there in synchrony, for their own purposes, for their own power: searching, gnawing at its fabric, until it would fall, and they would triumph, or triumph through blackmail, and the Church remain, but weaker, if that were possible. It had lived on illusions long enough. What could sustain it now?

Signs of "the other" as he had told Inspector Relish. Of the Dark which could envelop them all. He was afraid that he was too weak to resist.

"No, child. Why do you ask that?"

The Reverend Sandals wore the cloak of innocence more easily than the cloak of faith, but he was used to the eye of God, from whom he could not hide. He knew that Tyro knew that he was lying. He hated himself for it. But he must protect them, above himself. Yet he knew . . . well, no more of that.

"Only, only that we heard crying." Then, as if to distract attention from his pain, Tyro added, "What is this room?"

"Must have been the wind and the rain lashing the roof. Perhaps you substantiated my concerns," he said, changing his tone. "People have been 'using' the church. Perhaps you heard the tears that I shed within."

The three children looked at each other as if the Reverend Sandals had lost his wits.

"This is the priest's room," he continued. "I prefer to call it my cell. It allows me a little space, a retreat. A place to think and pray. We all need a cell."

"I thought a cell was in a prison?"

"Or a group of people working together secretly?"

"That too. That too."

The Reverend Sandals found strength in the children. He wanted to say that he felt like the King of infinite space.

Rick was standing by the chalice, admiring it.

"My own personal Grail," the Reverend Sandals said.

Rick noticed that the chalice carried an inscription. The writing was familiar. It reminded him of the writing from the book he had copied. Tyro noticed it too, and looked at Jess.

"What is the Grail?" Tyro asked.

"The Holy Grail is the Cup into which the blood of Jesus flowed when his side was pierced by the Spear. It is very, very important."

"Does anyone know where it is?"

The Reverend Sandals began walking towards the doorway to the landing.

"It is other things as well," he continued as if he was giving a lesson in class. "The Fount of all wisdom. The Philosopher's Stone. Apart from other things."

"Why is the Spearhead so important?" Jess asked.

The Reverend Sandals paused, and turned. He was now close to the top of the stairway that led down.

"Because it is sacred. It shed the blood of Jesus. Do you not remember the words of Our Lord: 'Do this in remembrance of Me'?"

"But that's bad."

"From the blood, springs our salvation."

The Reverend Sandals was now pointing to the floor below.

"What about the blood of others who have died?" Jess asked.

The Reverend Sandals did not answer.

"Look. The instruments of darkness."

There on the floor a few items, indistinct, lay in a circle.

For the first time, and for a moment only, Tyro, Jess and Rick saw something dark in the shapes. Jess wanted to ask the Reverend Sandals what they were. But she was afraid.

"We'd better go down."

The Reverend Sandals led the way.

"What are you three doing here?" he asked, as he approached the bottom. "Looking for something?"

For a moment there was silence.

"Do you think it really exists, Reverend Sandals?" asked Jess.

"What, my dear?" the Reverend Sandals asked.

"The missing fragment, or the Spearhead. The Grail for that matter." To Jess, as to all of them, these were muddled up as one and the same.

"Of course," the Reverend Sandals said, "it exists. It is the belief that drives us. The image that confirms. Many things exist that relate to the history of the Church. Some are hidden, some are lost. Others are illusions. The picture," he turned to point towards the implacable image behind the altar, glimmering softly in the half-light, "is complicated."

"But if the Grail exists, or the Spearhead, why has no-one found them?"

"Perhaps the belief in it, the possibility of finding it, is what matters."

"Why would anyone want to find a possibility? Why would the Priory?"

The Reverend Sandals was about to answer when Tyro interrupted.

"Reverend Sandals. May we ask you something else?" She was longing to know what he knew. "Why do you make the sign of the cross in front of the list of names on the wall?"

"I was about to say that the journey is perhaps more important than the discovery. Imagine if we found it. Hope, children. That is what matters. Perhaps they don't know where to look."

Tyro was pointing to the list of church incumbents.

"One of my fellow priests suffered a great injustice - for his beliefs, I'm afraid at the hands of the Church. The dark side, shall we say."

Tyro wanted to ask more, but the Reverend Sandals held up his hand.

"Another time," he said.

There was a loud clang. The door of the church shut. Footsteps could be heard.

The Reverend Sandals bent forward. He whispered so that only they could hear. The children seemed shocked by what they heard.

The Reverend Sandals turned. The children turned.

There in front of them stood Mr Vespers.

The Reverend Sandals smiled. His eyes were firm, but his soul shook. Some dark presence faced him, something he dared not fully acknowledge. He must not show his fear. That would be the end. His soul knew when the enemy was at hand, especially in borrowed robes.

"Mr Vespers. An unexpected pleasure. This is not your usual haunt. But you are welcome," he said, lying.

"I was looking for these three," Mr Vespers replied. "The Headmaster wants to see them."

He looked at the three friends, as if he was unable to separate one from the other.

"You have behaved disgracefully. Mr Rummage saw what you did. Saw that you ran from me."

"But we weren't . . . " Rick began. He hated Vipers.

"We were not running away from you, Mr Vespers," Jess said.

"We were seeking shelter from the rain," Tyro said.

"I had asked them to help me," said the Reverend Sandals.

He pulled back the curtain once more to reveal the items on the floor.

"Somebody or something has been despoiling this holy place. I asked them to help me to clear it up."

There, in Tyro's mind, lay the ingredients of the witches' cauldron.

Mr Vespers showed no reaction as the curtain fell again.

"This is a very serious matter, Mr Vespers," the Reverend Sandals continued, seizing his chance, "given the trouble we have had. I think you will agree. But perhaps it is not the children whose help I should seek, but others' . . . "

"On the contrary, Reverend Sandals. If you will allow me. I will make them clear it up. It will give me a chance to think what further punishment to request from Mr Rummage. First they must apologise. Perhaps it will do as well that they pray a while."

The Reverend Sandals could take the hypocrisy no more.

"This is a house of God!" he said, his voice echoing through the church. "You shall seek forgiveness, Mr Vespers! Evil cannot hide here!"

Mr Vespers stared into the Reverend's eyes. Without the presence of the children, he would have succumbed.

The three friends looked at each other, and then at the Reverend Sandals.

Mr Vespers knew how to destroy him. He looked about him.

"I'm surprised at you, Reverend. You who are false. A church whose power arose from blackmail and is forged from myth."

"I believe in a truth that is eternal, as opposed to the power of Darkness that only believes in chaos and itself."

The figure in the painting watched.

"They will catch their death, if the children are out much longer, Mr Vespers. They should go in at once and get dry."

"The work will warm them up, I am sure," said Mr Vespers. "I will take personal charge of the cleaning."

Mr Vespers looked about him. He was in familiar territory. Only he knew the times he had been in this church. He was reminded by the cloaks that hung on the walls. He was thinking something through.

The three friends stood there shivering, wondering how they could escape again. Rick felt that he had missed his chance.

"What do you think, children?" the Reverend Sandals asked, turning to them.

"We are sorry we ran from the school building," Jess began. Tyro gave her a nudge. Rick dug her in the ribs.

"You see, they admit it!" Mr Vespers said.

"We were coming over to the church to research our History homework," Tyro said. She did not want to lie. The Reverend Sandals was more honest than she had thought, and kinder, and he would know about heresy, she thought.

The Reverend Sandals decided to change his approach.

"So be it, Mr Vespers. They are all yours. Children, please do as Mr Vespers says. I am late for my meeting with the Headmaster."

The Reverend Sandals had meant to be in the meeting with the Bishop some time ago. He had to make a difficult choice.

The Reverend Sandals looked into Tyro's eyes. He wanted her to know that he was on their side, that what he was doing was deliberate, a form of test.

Tyro understood.

"But Reverend Sandals, we came to help you," Jess began.

But he had gone.

Mr Vespers looked at the three children.

"You have ten minutes to clear that mess up," he said pointing to the floor. "The Headmaster is too busy to see you now. I shall return with a fit punishment to give you. You will not escape my net again."

Tyro hated him. Rick despised him. Jess clung to a possibility that no longer existed. They did not answer.

It was no use asking where they were to get a broom or something to put the rubbish in. Mr Vespers was pleased that it was they who were cleaning up the desecration.

"You will not be so lucky next time," he said. "If there is one."

Mr Vespers walked out of the church.

They saw the church door shut. Even above the rain, they heard the click of the huge key as it turned in the lock. They were locked in.

I I

Mr Rummage turned towards the group of people who lined his study.

The virus which had haunted him for several months now seemed to be spreading its wings. There was an inevitability to it that belied its power. But without a specific target his own powers were useless. Mr Vespers was beginning to act like Mrs Limpet, as his uncontrolled and exaggerated reaction to the little incident outside revealed. It would not be long before his position would be untenable, by his behaviour only. His probable membership of the Priory, or some such group, made him an added threat.

Pressures on him were growing from outside the school. Major allies had recently taken an active interest, with the ambivalence that that brings. He at the head. Perhaps this was the place to which his life had been driven. "There's a divinity that shapes our ends, rough-hew them how we will." Mr Rummage reflected on Shakespeare's words.

Very soon, maintaining the status quo would not be possible. If an attack came, he might not have the opportunity to counter it, and the results would be catastrophic. The Spearhead was vital of course, but he was no longer sure of its existence, though he would maintain the illusion for as long as it was necessary to flush out the enemy. Illusions can galvanise nations, only truly when they are valid, and not distorted by demonic will. The search adds hope.

He had watched Mr Vespers enter the church, and seen the Reverend Sandals come out. He had seen Mr Vespers return over the drive.

Should he intervene?

*

Having turned on the church lights, Jess tried to persuade them to clear up the remains, but the other two would have none of it. They wanted to escape. The minutes were ticking by.

"I'm not sweeping that stuff! It might be contaminated!" Tyro said.

"I'm heading for the altar," said Rick. "Just think, the Spearhead might be under it, having lain there for hundreds of years. And then we'd be the most powerful people in the world."

Rick started to run and leap, whirling an imaginary sword.

"It's not yours!" Jess protested.

"I'm going upstairs to the cell. I'll join you in a minute. I want to read what was written on that chalice," said Tyro.

"I'll help Rick," said Jess.

As Tyro made her way to the tower again - to the priest's cell - Jess told Rick to be careful.

Rick was already trying to move the end slab on the altar. "You keep an eye on the door, while I open this up."

High above them stood a figure, almost completely still, where the rood walkway would have joined the top of the spiral stairs.

"I'm going to get Tyro," Jess said, turning back towards the tower.

Jess was soon alongside Tyro in the priest's room. They examined the bookcase, which was locked.

"How come we didn't see these before? They're vellum!"

pointed Jess. "Must be very old, and valuable."

Tyro was trying the drawers of the little desk. One was open.

"Look here," said Tyro. The chalice shone not far to her side, in the dark.

"It's a list of priests who have been at this church over the centuries."

"There's something with it," said Tyro.

"Best leave it," said Jess.

Tyro might have taken it and shown it to Mr Rummage, but she decided not to. This would be stealing and they had not been given instructions to steal.

They turned and stared at the walls and tapestries.

"What is this place?" Tyro asked. "I mean, what is a priest's cell?"

"Like his (or her) private quarters. Like the inner sanctum."

"There were no lady priests then!"

"His, then," said Jess firmly before adding, "Actually, I believe there were once lady priests, weren't there?"

"There are now."

"Not in all churches."

"Doesn't feel much like a sanctum to me!" said Tyro, not really knowing what Jess was talking about. The idea of becoming a priest was very far from her mind.

"Those devils on the walls would scare anyone into believing. They look like my worst nightmares."

"Some of the figures have horns and are wearing robes."

"Dark figures in human form." She remembered the empty mirror in the library. "The Priory know we know."

"They need us."

Tyro picked up the chalice and began reading the words inscribed on it.

Jess wrote the latin onto a piece of paper. "Deo Concedente."

"Isn't that the school's motto?"

They heard what sounded like a shout coming from below.

They turned and ran across the landing and down the stairs.

"I've found an opening!" Rick called. His voice echoed through the church.

"Here Tyro, put this on. It'll dry us as well as keep us warm."

Tyro grabbed a cloak and threw it around her. Rick had found three on the altar rail. On their backs were red sword-crosses. Jess put one on and went to turn off the church lights.

"Follow me," said Rick, who was kneeling beside the altar, with a cloak already round him.

The altar drape had been raised and folded back on to the top. The slab of white marble that formed the end-piece had been thrust aside at an angle, so that a gap had appeared, big enough to take a person. The gap led into a dark hole, possibly a tunnel. It was into this that Rick went.

Before the girls could say anything, they heard the click of the door of the church.

"Vipers is coming! Quick!"

"What do we do now?"

"Get out of here!" said Tyro, entering the gap herself.

As far as she was concerned, it would only be a space under the altar table, enough to hide from Mr Vespers for a while. She turned and grabbed Jess and pulled her under the altar too.

Footsteps sounded on the stone floor.

"Who told you to turn on the lights?" Mr Vespers bellowed. Tyro and Jess heaved the slab of the altar to, leaving just enough space to see Mr Vespers striding along the aisle.

Mr Vespers seemed to avoid looking at the painting or at the altar cross. He did not see the figure above him, watching.

Tyro tried to feel her way in the darkness, and whispered to Rick to wait. But Rick was not there. She moved her hands from side to side on the musty floor. The dread of touching something horrible made her careful. The altar could not be a tomb, could it? It might contain relics. She came to a gap. Putting her hand into it, Tyro touched a stair, then another. Swinging herself round she put one foot on the top stair and the other on a step below it. Slowly she backed down. As she entered what felt like a chamber under the altar and beneath the floor, she called to Rick in a low voice, imagining that Mr Vespers might hear them. They could hear the echo of feet along the aisle and Mr Vespers calling. The chamber shook. Jess followed.

"He's right by the altar," whispered Jess, fearful that they might not get out again.

Rick struck a match and lit a candle.

"Where did that come from?" asked Tyro.

"I always carry matches. The candle comes from somewhere else."

"We can't go back!" said Jess.

"Then we'll go down," said Tyro. Rick was already facing an exit from the chamber.

Then something caught his eye. He pointed. The others stared, in the flickering light.

Something was trapped in-between two stone slabs that formed part of the chamber wall. It looked like a tube. Half of it was out, the other hidden. One or two bricks had fallen forward and had revealed what lay behind. Tyro stretched out and took hold of it. To her surprise the whole thing came away.

"What is it?" she said, holding it up to her in the dim light.

Jess was behind her.

"Looks to me like a scroll," said Jess.

"It's certainly very old."

"No time now," said Rick.

Tyro carefully took it and tied it to her. She felt an enormous power coming from it. She struggled to follow Rick, who had gone on.

"Whatever it is, it feels as if it's living. It's spooky."

Jess could feel the strange power too.

Mr Vespers searched the church. His fury increased. The light in his eyes came from another darker place, controlled by another Master than the Divinity that surrounded him. The young people were now in mortal danger. He could not account for his actions if he caught them. And yet his anger was kept in check by a benign force, against which he struggled.

Mr Vespers noticed the altar cloth. He looked at it very carefully. He went over to it. No doubt the wind had blown it out of position.

He leaned over to the cross. The Headmaster would hear about this.

He returned to the main door and locked it from the inside, his confidence growing. He heard a noise coming from the belfry, from behind the curtain. The children were clearing up the mess. How foolish of him not to look there first. Cautiously, he went to the draped curtain and pulled it back.

In front of him stood a tall figure wearing a black cloak, with its back towards him, a clear red sword-cross across its back. The sword-cross shone in the light. It was not one of his own, the cross was uniform. It was of a Templar Knight.

Mr Vespers went up to it, a smile crossing his face, as if in recognition.

"Master, what a pleasant surprise!" he said, half in jest. "I wasn't expecting anyone from your Order yet. Which one of you is it?"

The figure maintained a steely posture, then turned slowly. In doing so it pulled back its hood.

Mr Vespers stood and stared, not knowing how to react.

It was Mr Baxter. His face was severe.

Mr Baxter pointed to the floor.

"Are you responsible for this?" he asked.

*

The film had been been short. It showed beautiful countryside. A village. Mountains. The worn look of summer fields. Sunflowers. Ancients paths amidst ancient pasture.

Farms, ruins, rocks. The scent of herbs and the flight of butterflies.

A red-faced man smiling to camera, holding a map and pointing.

A castle on a hill. Towers. Entrance. A valley. Olive groves and more rocks thrown along a barren slope, leading to a ravine. A jacket lying beside a half-empty bottle. A book. The face in the sunlight. The entrance to a cave, on the wildest of hidden slopes.

Mr Rummage could remember every detail from before when he had been shown the film. It had been part of Mr Baxter and Ms Peverell's report from France.

He remembered wishing he had been there. He had looked at the cave entrance with particular care, and had asked Mr Baxter about it in the minutest detail. Mr Baxter had been inside, but had not got far. The way had been blocked. He said he was sure.

Around the study the small group seemed cocooned from the chill of heavy rain.

"Impossible!" said a voice.

It was the Bishop of Dunemoor, who had followed Mr Baxter's research with great interest, as had others in the Church, here and in Rome.

"I take it this information has not been revealed to anyone else. Will not be revealed," the Bishop added, holding his hands forwards, as if at prayer. "We are susceptible," he added.

"Your colleagues - if that is the right word - in Rome would do anything to stop this coming out. The Priory already claims to be close to finding information that would destroy it.

"With this their power would be supreme. Effectively they would control the whole of Christendom."

"They and their forebears claim they have been doing that for nearly a millennium," said the Bishop, just managing a smile. "The question is whether the myth of secret knowledge is more powerful than the true secret of divinity. Anyway, there is no proof. They would deny it, dismiss it in the strongest terms. People do not want their beliefs further undermined."

Dr Vale asked whether they were any closer to finding the evidence supposedly hidden at Burnchester. Mr Rummage shook his head, but added that he felt they were close. All the signs pointed in that direction. Not least because of increased Priory activity. There was always a correspondence of events at times of great meaning.

The Bishop of Dunemoor had been invited at the request of the Reverend Sandals, who had joined them not long before. The Bishop had been responding to a question from Mr Brock of the Ministry of Defence. How could the Priory possibly blackmail the Church? he had asked. The Church has a history, the Bishop had replied, some of it dark. Its treatment of heresy makes the military look like amateurs, he had said.

"Torture, drawing and quartering, not the fabric of forgiveness. Burning. Pyres for men and women, screaming to death for their beliefs. Beliefs which happened not to correspond to those supported by the powers of the Church. What Catholics and Protestants have done to each other does not need to be given in evidence here. What has been done to others is worse."

"That was a long time ago."

"But blackmail?"

The Bishop did not answer directly. He simply said that the secrets of the Knights Templar - which had given them so much power - had been passed on, down through history, to groups assigned specifically to protect them. Now they wanted to reveal them. The film that they had just seen and the document they were searching for would give them added power. "That is why they must be suppressed or destroyed."

" 'They' meaning the Priory?"

"Yes, or someone working through them. The document should not see the light of day. The location of the film remains above top secret."

"And what exactly is the film of?"

"It is believed to be a tomb. The place is known locally as The Valley of The King," said a voice.

There was silence.

"And the King?"

It was not Mr Brock's place to openly criticise another pillar of the established order, for the military were part of the same crusade, for truth and justice, and power. Mr Brock knew about the need for illusions. He had never forgotten what he had once been told by a leading cleric: that the myth of the Messiah had served them well. Well he knew the myths of his own profession, the cultivation of heroism in opposition to the unruly chaos and cruelties of action. Yet there needed to be some basis for action, some moral and political grounding in which we could believe. Without it there was nothing. Like a church without a congregation, and without symbols. An empty echo. But that core had to be true and just. It had been exactly that in the great cause of the Second World War. Truth stood for all time. Only the imagery changed.

The Bishop was a humane and liberal man, more inclined to read the gospels symbolically than literally, ready to embrace modestly the changes necessary for salvation, according to present day needs, without abandoning the deeper truths beneath the trends in verbal and liturgical doctoring. Privately, this is how he had responded to the abuse of the language of ancient ritual and worship of recent years. It was as if management consultants and PR people were now in charge. What would Jesus have thought? The Bishop smiled inwardly. He had never felt comfortable in his robes. But there was a necessary vanity to humility, which made him feel notionally safe, and gave him some authority over others, if not over himself.

The deepest sadness in him could not reveal what he most believed: that the Church was too weak to be blackmailed. Yet this might also ultimately be its salvation, like the kernel that would not die, and be reborn at the appropriate time, if in different coloured robes. He knew that without symbols, crafted by man with divine inspiration - "according to the Will of God" - there would be no faith, no structures, no ritual; and without these there was nothing. What concerned him most was the extremism that might arise out of chaos and doubt.

"Inspector Relish, please." Mr Rummage said.

Inspector Relish looked up from his notebook. Recent elevation hadn't diminished his appetite for detail. Nor his reliance on his own testimony. Inspector Relish had lost none of his enthusiasm, but his face was a little darker, if only because he was finding it difficult to "git 'em bahstuds". But "git 'em" he would.

"Could you bring us up-to-date on developments from your department? Perhaps you could begin with the undersea search at Dunemoor. And of course the interrogation of the Stranger, and its consequences. Then perhaps I could ask Mr Brock to brief us."

*

Rick, Tyro and Jess continued along the walled tunnel under the church. They were too afraid to go back. They felt that what they had found was very important and were desperate to find a way out.

But going on was horrific. They crawled over old bones. Stony worn skulls came at them in the candlelight, as if gasping for breath. Sarcophagi (like angels' baths) lined the walls. Rick's candle gave them sufficient light to move and to see shadows.

Tyro held the document tight, sensing that her clammy hands might soil its message. How to get it to Mr Rummage? No-one else. How to get out? She thought of Tom. Of flying. She coughed in the musty passageway, as if trying to extract air from its wounds.

The souls of the dead seemed to follow them along the dark, figures watching in shadows, hands clasping at them, waiting to trip them up, anxious to draw them in. Yet there was something moving in the desperation of these souls who, Tyro felt, were as lost as they, and had not yet completed their journey. She thought of the figures over the summer who seemed reluctant to support the Stranger, those who had come from the old fort. It was as if they had not really wanted to help, but had done so despite themselves. Perhaps they needed to be saved or set free.

What was this place under the church, of old bones?

The three children moved on, sweat, not damp, covering their brows. They heard breathing. Was it ahead or behind them?

The candle was burning low. Perhaps it was a figure ready to snatch their trophy. Ready to put an end to their presumption.

Rick put up his hand. The three of them huddled over the just visible light now cupped by Tyro's hand. On one side the wall seemed to have changed.

"Must be the school cellars. There must be a door. And stairs leading upwards," said Jess.

They found an entrance to their right, which led into a cellar room, whilst the main tunnel went on, towards the river.

As they turned the breathing grew louder.

Inside the decayed damp of the cold room, they could just make out a door in the far corner. Rick tried it but it was locked.

Above them appeared to be a gap in the ceiling. There seemed to be a wooden patch there, like a trapdoor. The slightest rays of light filtered through it. They could hear a voice.

The voice of Inspector Relish.

"We're underneath Mr Rummage's study!" whispered Tyro.

"Let's knock on this door." She tried, in vain, to reach it.

Rick dragged over an old tea chest lying in the corner. The three of them stood on it.

"No!" called Tyro. "Listen! Let's listen first. And then knock!"

"Knock before the Thing follows us and drags us off."

Jess thought of Pluto, the God of the Underworld.

But they were mesmerised by what they heard.

*

"Escaped?" called a voice. It was unfamiliar.

"Disappeared might be a better word," said the Inspector. "We held him under the strictest security, twenty-four hour surveillance, armed guard, the best there is. Mr Brock knows the details. He was being treated with the utmost vigilance. But one night he was gone."

"How can that be?" came the voice again. "You are asking us to believe that a man can escape, whilst under the heaviest guard. I don't believe it."

"We had interviewed him for the third day. Mr Rummage was there on the first. I was not able to be present at all of them. I had to be in Southwold, for reasons that I will explain. I had taken the Stranger there the previous day to gauge his reaction to something we had recovered from the bottom of the sea. Something found by Mr Greenshank, the Harbourmaster. But my colleague Inspector Shore, who is very able, and someone in whom I have the greatest confidence, took over. Reading the report of the day's events and having seen the video footage, we learned nothing new, despite his efforts.

"The Stranger's testimony has changed. He had been on holiday in this country for a number of weeks, though he has been visiting for rather longer. Apart from fishing, he has an interest in history, archaeology, and birds. He claims to be from Holland, though our Dutch colleagues have found no record of a Borlick at his address. In fact his address does not exist. He totally denies involvement in the break-ins at Burnchester Hall and the churches over the summer. As for the attack on Mr Gruff (bear in mind Mr Gruff was present) and the death of Mrs Grumble, he simply stared in disbelief. His passport is forged, by the way.

"He admits to owning the Neptune, but now flatly denies any wrongdoing such as obstructing the police, let alone being a member of a group called the Priory, who he claims never to have heard of - despite what he had said earlier. The symbol on the prow of the Neptune is coincidental. He denies everything. Even the testimony of his accomplice he dismissed as mistaken identity. Mr Gruff, whilst at first believing him to be his attacker, changed his view when the Stranger looked at him. Mr Gruff became unsure, and seemed to relapse into a nervous state."

"His accomplice?"

"The man we caught in the Domed Chamber over the summer. The man who was too afraid to give verbal testimony," answered Mr Rummage. "He swears that he is the man we are seeking, though he demanded protection for saying so."

"It is all lies of course. But we have no proof. Forensic have insufficient evidence. Even his fingerprints do not match those on the false coins given to Mr Gatherin in the summer. We were of course due to interview him further, but one night he disappeared. Vanished in front of the camera."

"Can you show us the moment of his disappearance?" asked Mr Rummage.

The Bishop had seen a great deal of the dark side in the world, and remained impassive. To him nothing was impossible. Dr Bartok observed as a psychologist, Mr Brock as a military man having to deal with the reality.

"Of course. If you will give me a moment, while I change the tape," Inspector Relish said.

Jess wanted to break through the trapdoor, but Tyro held her back.

"Let's hear them out! They've never told us the whole story. This may be our only chance. I wish we could see that film. I only half believe it," said Tyro.

Jess expected to see a figure emerge from the darkness. She wanted to scream, but nothing would come out.

Rick was doing his best to peer through the crack in the floor. He was beginning to pick bits of wood out of the wooden trapdoor, to give them more light.

As they listened, the horrors of the summer came back to them, as if the tunnel was a conduit for the past, and the words above them its inspiration. What they had discovered in the library, and the strange activities of Mr Vespers and Mr Blakemore, as well as the document which Tyro held, became enmeshed with it. Time seemed to have stopped. Present, past, and future seemed to be crawling all over them, like the mist from the sea. But unlike the summer each of them faced the situation in a different way. They wanted to engage in the story, they didn't just want to react to events. They were longing to break into the room and show them their discovery, but they might break the spell.

*

There was complete silence as the group watched the footage which showed the Stranger's disappearance. Inspector Relish played it over and over again. There were gasps of incomprehension as, in front of the camera's eyes, the figure that they had begun to know so well, yet knew not at all, melted before them. If they had not seen it they would not have believed it.

"The tape has been examined by all our experts. They have no explanation."

The sight of something beyond their understanding was both riveting and unnerving. They were being introduced to a new dimension of the world. One they would rather not have known. For some of the audience, memories were evoked of the Dark Master - though they had been unconscious then - like the presence of a darkness that seemed to arise from deep within, which they could not identify. As if some presence was knocking at the door of their minds waiting to be released, so that it could play havoc with their minds. It was above all against this that the group needed vigilance, and against which the greatest battles would be fought.

Mr Brock's update brought them back to earth. He started with the current security situation with military understatement, the cool aplomb that comes with objectification even of tragedy. He explained the situation at the school and beyond. His people had not had any further signs of activity or presence within the school grounds. The presence of security teams, albeit discreet, may have contributed to the Priory's caution. Yet the Priory's options were limited and they would have to strike soon.

There had been intelligence reports of activity at other sites, and his department was on a general state of alert, though details remained strictly under wraps. Doonwreath had confirmed recent contact.

American observers confirmed activity at various sites across the continent. Colleagues elsewhere in Europe and in Russia, China and Australia were beginning to see signs of similar disturbances, though their focus on ancient sites was less intense, if only because they were more dispersed.

Nothing could be fixed on any particular group. The activity did not seem coordinated, and the perpetrators obscure, which was of double concern. There had been sporadic acts of violence, but no other deaths.

Mr Brock had requested personnel to take up permanent station under Burnchester Hall, below level two. Though most of its instrumentation was automatic, this was a precaution, in case of further intrusion. Burnchester was a sensitive observation point and played an important role in co-ordinating Doonwreath's work. Yet Mr Brock was not privy to all that Mr Rummage knew.

They had been requested, Mr Rummage said, to continue mapping the tunnels and repair what could be rebuilt. The site's power was still unpredictable. Why not capitalise on a security situation and do a bit of research at the same time? As for imminent threats, nothing could be specified for certain. There was however a significant moment due on or around Bonfire Night, according to his research.

"The Priory must continue to believe that they can breach our defences. Only then can we establish their identity and aims," Mr Rummage concluded.

Dr Vale was curious to learn that activity was global, and not merely tied in with a specific tradition of the West.

No-one had mentioned the Spearhead.

*

A figure was making its way through the dark towards Tyro, Jess and Rick.

Though Tyro had heard something behind them, she could not tear herself away from what she was hearing.

The new voice was that of Dr Bartok.

Dr Bartok had treated Mr Gruff after the attack in the old boathouse. Mr Gruff's face was vivid in her mind, and with it came memories of that evening. Memories of Tom, and again of flight. This time the flight seemed more like a dream than a reality. Dr Bartok was talking about a thing he called the Dream Notation Chamber, and his research into dream language, and its ability to foresee. Dr Bartok had also treated Mrs Limpet, the Biology teacher who had locked Tyro in the experiment room, the teacher who had sliced a rat's head from its body, while its teeth remained embedded in her hand. The teacher who had spoken of multiple identities. Who had lost control of her senses.

Dr Bartok said that the ability to elicit, describe and interpret dreams gave us insights into the unknown, not just concerning the dreamer. Some dreams, he said, related to worlds we had not yet experienced, but glimpsed, including perhaps the obscure world they were beginning to confront. Perhaps even other worlds, other civilisations. If we could understand the language which was beginning to emerge in dreams we might be able to tell many things.

"We cannot be sure, of course," Dr Bartok said, "because we are dealing with numinous symbols. But as with any language, we are seeking to identify patterns, and recurring images. Some of these images we feel sure relate only to the individual, the life and concerns of the individual, the things that lie beneath his or her conscious mind, or have been symbolised for him, occasionally erupting into a dream form, as if to present the owner, who does not recognise them as his own, with a picture image of the myth that should be explored, that would help him on his journey.

"Other dream images seem to be common to many people, even peoples, and therefore have wider meaning. Images that occur everywhere in the world. The purpose of the Dream Notation Chamber is, as the title suggests, to reveal and describe. That is our first task. The machine merely records what it sees in the mind of the individual, and projects it onto a big globe, like a screen in the shape of the world, or the sky. It allows us to share the private activity within. Only much later can we begin to interpret. That is the second task, which we are just beginning."

"Why is this so important?" asked the Inspector.

"If we could interpret the images correctly, we might have access to knowledge that is currently hidden. That may have been lost, but is there for those who wish to seek. That may tell us things we need to know. Mr Rummage knows from his work in intelligence that, despite his love of facts, it is also insight, the ability to see beyond the moment, beneath the surface, to intuit knowledge that the enemy thinks is hidden, and may be hidden from itself (the enemy, that is), that gives him the edge. It may even allow us to glimpse the future. It may lead us to find the images that will act as powerful symbols for our new age and unite us all.

"That knowledge would be the source of great power. Used for evil, we would be destroyed. For good, we might be saved. Allied to symbols is the energy that creates them. What is it? Where does it come from? There are a few who interpret dreams, with true insight. My experiments show that new images are being thrown out. Images that may enhance our future beliefs. I believe there are people who can interpret the language, or begin to. Some of them may be present here today."

"Isn't this playing at God?"

"Or God playing with man?"

"Perceiving God, perhaps. And now of course, other things have made this ability more important. Other threats. Other signs which the dreams may help us to explore, and fight against."

"Please explain," said Mr Rummage.

*

It happened quickly. Before Dr Bartok could continue, there was a muffled scream and a hammering on what seemed to be the door. Mr Rummage ran and opened it, but found Lotty and Bridget lingering in the corridor, soaking from the rain.

There was another scream, and more hammering.

"Not there!" came Inspector Relish's voice, "from that direction!"

The Inspector hurried to the corner of the room, in front of the window, followed by Mr Rummage.

The sounds grew louder. Everyone was now standing.

Mr Rummage looked at the floor, just in time to see the old wooden cover burst upwards into the room and with it the screams of frightened voices, and hands reaching upwards for help.

Jess came out first. Behind her Tyro and Rick tried to follow.

Mr Rummage pulled Jess's hands, whilst pushing away the boards with his feet. "Grab the others!"

Tyro and Rick were struggling to get through the hole in the floor. Behind them in the shadows, just visible, a hooded figure was trying to clutch at their legs and drag them back down. The children kicked furiously. The figure which had crept up on them, silently, held firm until it knew it would be pulled up too, and let go. He stared at the people looking down. The figure had seen the parchment. He had seen Tyro carrying it.

With a piercing glare strong enough to destroy the most ancient curse the figure looked at Mr Rummage and at each of the faces, who tried to avert their eyes.

"I will return! That girl has taken what is ours!" He pointed to the parchment which Tyro held.

"We will pursue her and those two with her, and anyone else who gets in our way, until we have what we seek. That is the Master's will. Our Order cannot be destroyed! We are invincible because we have conquered death! You will all pay the price!"

The Bishop held out his cross.

With that the figure let out a huge hollow laugh, a demonic empty rattle that seemed to shake the room.

In a moment it was gone, into the shadows, into the tunnel, which way nobody could see.

The children were safe, all three sitting on the floor, shaking. Jess was crying her eyes out, Rick and Tyro trying to comfort her. Tyro could not forget the stare that had seemed to pierce her soul like the point of a spear.

"I'm going after it!" shouted Inspector Relish.

He leapt into the empty space, taking a torch out of his pocket as he went.

Dr Bartok followed, though he was not as agile as he would have wished.

Mr Brock was on his phone instructing his men to guard all known exits to the tunnels in the area, particularly those close to the river. He also called in a team in support.

Tyro held out the document which had survived intact. Now that Jess was safe, she turned to Mr Rummage, and handed it to him.

"We found it under the altar, Mr Rummage," was all she could say before she went back to her friend, her hand trembling with excitement as much as fear.

Mr Rummage glanced at it. Mr Rummage, the keeper of the ancient library of the school, knew its significance immediately.

He passed it to Mr Baxter, who had come in some minutes earlier. The Bishop was standing beside him, the Reverend Sandals with him. Dr Vale was close by.

"For your eyes only, Mr Baxter, though it will be of interest to the Bishop, and Reverend Sandals," Mr Rummage said. "Whether we should allow them to see it is another matter." He looked at the two priests. "You wanted evidence."

Mr Rummage went to his desk and called the staffroom to alert his colleagues and then Mr Granger, Mr Grudge and Mr Gruff. He asked them to come to his office immediately. He called Matron to come and see Jess, who was now sobbing again.

Mr Baxter moved to the side of the room with Dr Vale, carrying the document. He had managed to separate from the Bishop and the Reverend Sandals, to their evident annoyance. Dr Vale was nodding.

Mr Rummage went over to Jess and bent down.

"Jess, are you OK? You are safe, I promise you. No-one will get you now."

Jess looked up at the Headmaster. Suddenly she saw a person who was on her side, not the authority figure who could make or break her.

Mr Rummage got up, and looked at each person in turn, wondering whether anyone had seen anything through the window or had heard the screams. The two children outside undoubtedly would have.

"Gentlemen," he said. "You now know first hand something of what we are dealing with. I would ask you to wait here for a little while until the situation is clearer."

The Bishop was about to protest, but Mr Rummage assured him that he would soon be able to leave. It was not that that concerned him. He wanted the document. Mr Rummage ignored his request.

Mr Rummage made for the door. As he did so, Mr Baxter approached and whispered to him.

"It looks genuine," he said in a low voice, holding the parchment close to him.

Before opening the door, Mr Rummage turned. "I shall be back as soon as possible. We have not finished the business of the meeting, despite the interruption. I would like Tyro, Jess and Rick to stay here. It goes without saying that everything we have witnessed remains confidential. We do not want panic. This may be just the beginning."

Mr Rummage had named Rick, but he had gone. Nobody had noticed him leap back into the tunnel after Inspector Relish and Dr Bartok. Tyro had wanted to go too, but could not leave Jess, and she wanted to know what it was that had been found. She saw with growing curiosity the Bishop now sitting as he unfolded the parchment that Mr Baxter had passed to him, on the understanding that he would hand it back immediately.

"It's OK, Jess, we're safe," Tyro said, turning to her old friend.

Jess looked up at her.

"Rick's gone! I haven't the strength to follow. Let's pray for him."

"There are others with him," Tyro said.

Mr Rummage opened the door.

There in front of him stood Mr Vespers. Under no circumstances did he want Mr Vespers to see the document, so he stepped outside and closed it behind him.

Mr Baxter had met Mr Vespers not long ago in the church and had already briefed Mr Rummage. Mr Vespers had caught sight of Tyro in the Headmaster's study, and tried to contain his rage. He caught a glimpse of the Bishop beside the Reverend Sandals.

Mr Rummage pre-empted him.

"Mr Vespers, this is not a good moment."

12

The discovery of the document made an immediate impact. The Bishop claimed it as the church's property and demanded to take it with him. Mr Rummage offered to make a copy. He could not allow the original out of the Hall until it had been inspected by others and then it would only go to the securest vault, probably in Cambridge.

Above all, the break-in from the cellars was a sign of how close the enemy was.

Lotty and Bridget, who had seen through the open door of the study, passed on what they had seen, or imagined, to their friends. Rumours began to spread.

Someone had seen Jess crying. Vipers had gone too far.

He had been in a fight with Mr Baxter. Rick had disappeared, a figure had been seen.

What was to be done? What would happen?

Whispers, like the wind in the leaves, cannot be stopped at will. Like the wind in the trees whispers have a habit of signifying some other force.

With the excitement of Bonfire Night stalking them, Mr Rummage tried to scotch the rumours by asking staff to go round the school and dispel them in the strongest terms.

Mr Rummage asked Mr Brock to take immediate steps to strengthen security at the Hall and send other teams into the tunnels. Inspector Relish, Dr Bartok and Rick must be found.

No stone must be unturned. The place must be searched up and down, whatever it took.

He tried to contact Dennis, for a report on any possible incursions into his security measures. He called Mr Veech. He wanted him present so that a full record could be kept, but not yet to go public. The scoop to come would keep him waiting. The governors must be informed.

Parents must not know of the evening's events, for the moment. He needed to delay until he had assessed the significance of these developments. The school's remaining open was on a knife-edge.

Mr Rummage asked his secretary to come in, and spoke with her quietly. Mrs Clicket took the document and left the room. Moments later she returned and gave Mr Rummage a sealed envelope, which he gave to the Bishop with a few whispered words.

Mr Rummage was clear of the threat that Mr Vespers posed, but he wanted to keep him onside as far as possible. He needed him to lead to bigger players, not least the figure in the tunnel, who he suspected to be the Stranger. The enemy were ruthless and would become more so as they got closer to their prey. But he must wait until he knew more.

The Bishop left with the Reverend Sandals. Before he did so he blessed the room and went to the opening in the ground and made a sign of the cross. As he went to his car he was observed by Mr Vespers.

The Bishop was thinking he would wait until he had studied the document at his leisure before contacting colleagues in Rome.

For his part, Mr Baxter was relieved. The consequences for security were enormous, the threats immediately increased, but he was pleased to have found an important piece in the jigsaw.

His mission was not to destroy but to help the process of change that had begun long before the existence of such documents were suspected to exist. The Church was crumbling anyway. This was only confirmation of what many had deduced in other ways. This was not the Middle Ages, fortunately, nor the seventeenth century, when he might well have been excommunicated or burnt as a heretic, the heresy in this case of seeking the truth. Even if the document should fall into the wrong hands, there would no doubt be other pieces of evidence, now that the drip was turning into a flood.

*

Mr Gruff was not his normal self. The attack which he had suffered in the summer had left scars, though he had insisted on returning to work thinking he had made a full recovery. He carried out his duties in a way that made him feel he was important to the community, still. He had been afraid that retirement would have left him empty (he had neither family, apart from his sister in Margate, nor interests, to support him). He needed the sense of belonging despite the effects on his memory of that atrocious night.

Over the months since the incident he had become sure of who his attackers were and why he had been chosen. It was not just that he was the keeper of keys, and therefore had access to the school and to the library and perhaps therefore to knowledge about the Spearhead, which was so crucial.

He was regarded as a traitor, and they had come to pay him back.

Before he had come to the school he had associated with a fringe religious group whose persuasion he had found attractive, but whose true motives were very far from the ones nominally espoused. They had given him the sense of importance that he needed. He gratefully adopted beliefs which appeared to offer solutions to the problem of life: of identity, of purpose and role. The aim, he was assured, was to restore to power those of the true path, meaning of course initiates and the leaders of the group concerned.

He had stumbled into a sect - not so far from the Priory - who would restore the heir to his proper throne, and re-establish the true Church.

For this to happen, proof of the heredity of the Grand Master was needed. The proof had been kept secret for hundreds of years, had indeed once been under the control of the sect itself, but had been lost in their earlier dissolution and in their attempts to protect the evidence.

The document found at the Church of St Mary Magdalen was a crucial element in that evidence, as were the missing fragment of the picture and the Spearhead of Destiny. There were other pieces, but none so important.

What the Priory didn't know was that there was other information of greater potency which would dwarf their claims, and make their designs seem trivial. Only a very few people knew of this, across the globe.

Mr Gruff had sworn absolute secrecy and devotion to his masters.

However, shortly before he was to be fully initiated and become a true follower, some inner strength, perhaps prompted by the intervention of a higher voice, had raised doubts and he soon abandoned the false path and fled incognito to another life.

He had found a home at Burnchester. But he was a traitor to his former masters, now his sworn enemies, and they were not in the habit of being rejected, without reprisal.

It was for this reason that the attack had been so savage.

Mr Rummage was aware of Mr Gruff's past and that his presence might bring the enemy into the open, but he did not expect such violence.

In regaining some degree of health and with the help of Mr Grudge, he wanted even more to help Mr Rummage. But his judgement and his health remained impaired, leading to a simple error which left the gates open to the tide. He casually mentioned to Mr Vespers that the Bishop had left with a "freshly sealed package".

*

Tyro and Jess's friends wanted to hear every detail. The break-in under the altar left them nervous; the description of the desecration disgusted; the return of a figure frightened. They scrutinised the behaviour of Reverend Sandals and Vipers. The class felt it had become one.

Teachers' attempts to dampen speculation failed dismally.

More and more children were being drawn in, giving them a sense of purpose which left them feeling like heroes of a new campaign. Who would be next? When would the next break-in be?

Rick's disappearance made everyone anxious, but such was their optimism that he would be found (as he had only recently been) that his absence was passed over as merely temporary, especially as he was not alone.

Julia hated Tyro and Jess the more for their continued glory.

As if to curry favour she gave Tyro and Jess some information about her father's work which should have remained confidential. Julia had seen a paper on his desk at home, which seemed to have been written during his time at Cambridge. Tyro became less trusting of Julia than before, but could not deny her interest in what she had discovered.

During supper, ze chef, who occasionally appeared at the side door, glanced in the direction of his old friends. Mrs Moffat, who was staying late and was one of the staff present, spent much of the meal talking with Ms Peverell, in subdued tones.

To compensate for their mood, paper hats were given out. Prep was suspended. There were competitions after supper.

Mr Rummage and Mr Baxter knew the momentous significance of the document found that evening. Mr

Rummage had given instructions for the original to be locked away in the safest vaults of the school where the most secret and important papers were kept. All those who had come into contact with it sensed its power.

Mr Vespers walked about with a scowl on his face that would have made Caliban look like an angel. He was angry, dangerous and losing control.

*

Tyro and Jess went to bed exhausted. Popularity and the glare of attention were not much compensation for the dangers that they all faced. Inevitably they were still worried about Rick.

Hearing no news of him, after supper they had told Ms Peverell and Mrs Moffat that they wanted to go in search. Mr Rummage had prevented them.

Should they try and follow, without permission?

"I'd like to," Tyro whispered across the dormitory that night, to Jess, who slept in the bed next to her, "but I've got a feeling it's best not to. I don't know why."

"Of course I know why you want to, Tyro," Jess said.

Tyro was thinking Tom would guide the three in the tunnels, or at least be present when he was needed. She thought that Tom would help Rick, more than he would have helped anybody.

Tyro rolled over and fell asleep before she could say goodnight. Jess stared up at the ceiling for a few moments, trying to catch any sound that might be coming from outside - even though they were on the third floor.

*

Mr Rummage remained up late into the night. He walked along the perimeter of the school grounds with Mr Baxter. In the quiet of the darkness, the two men were able to exchange news and confidences without fear of being overheard in the whispering corridors of Burnchester Hall.

As they walked along the river Dean they could see that the water had risen substantially, especially close to the site of the bonfire, and was now unusually high. Beyond was the belt of trees where the children had been so frightened and where Tom had last been seen. They could see pools of water spreading into the wood.

"Mr Vespers and Mr Blakemore know that we know," Mr Rummage said, "but they have no choice but to proceed."

Along the far river bank a shape was gliding through the air. The white owl was quartering the long meadow grass. As it reached a point opposite them, it turned and dived to the ground out of sight.

"I take it the document is genuine?" asked Mr Rummage, knowing that Mr Baxter had looked through it, before locking it away for safe keeping.

"It is one of the missing pieces. It only confirms what we already know. It will add to the Church's fears. That is why they will want to suppress it. As for blackmail, I don't think they have enough power to warrant it; though their enemies, notably the Priory and those behind them, think they have."

"Do you think we should have lent a copy to the Bishop?"

"It will not be as much of a revelation as we think."

"And the Spearhead?"

Even in the darkness, Mr Rummage could see a glint in Mr Baxter's eyes.

"And what about Doonwreath. What is the news from there?"

"Doonwreath continues to scan the four corners - rather the infinite corners of the universe - as far as it can. No further signals, though the conjunctions, I am told, are close to being perfect."

"Must bring back memories," said Mr Baxter warmly. Mr

Rummage, in a past life, had been an astrophysicist, and worked on deep space.

"Neither the document that we have found nor the Spearhead that they believe exists is their greatest threat. They do not recognise the inescapable truth."

"Nor do their enemies."

Mr Rummage was silent and they continued to walk for a few minutes.

There was a crackling sound. They both stopped dead still. Someone was in the woods. They stared into the empty space trying to catch a moving shadow.

"Who's there?"

There was only the sound of the two men breathing, and the thud of pumping hearts.

Both men went forward.

Beyond them in a moment, a moment only, they caught the shape of figures in the trees, no more than the breath of wind. These were not threatening shapes, rather souls, wandering, as is their right, over ground that they knew well.

"I sometimes wonder," Mr Rummage said, feeling the slight chill of a passing shadow, "if these are not old soldiers returning to old haunts."

"How lucky we live in our own age, and not the age of Galileo."

"I fear for the Bishop."

"I fear for us all."

*

Tyro dreamt of being at home again. It was summer and the birds were in full song. Biscuit was lying on the gravelly drive asleep in the sun. She was looking out of the window with music playing in the background.

Below, in the distance, two people were walking on the lawn towards the pond which formed the garden boundary. Rompy had his bottom in the air and his head below ground. Occasionally his bottom would wiggle and his legs push and his body began to disappear too. His head would come up for air. Bits of dirt would fly up behind him (she could imagine the sound of his smothered grunt in the earth).

One of the figures was her mother. The other she felt sure was her father. He had a familiar gait, though she sensed that it could not be him. And yet she didn't think it could be anybody else. She did not want him to turn round, in case it wasn't him. She remained comforted in the knowledge that it might be.

She opened the window and called out.

"Mum, Dad! What are you up to?"

Suddenly nobody was there. Only Biscuit asleep on the gravelly drive.

There was a thudding noise, a regular heavy beat from beyond the horizon. It was, no doubt, the army firing range that could be heard from time to time. It made her jump.

"Tyro! Come down! You've got a letter!"

Tyro ran out of her room and down the stairs. There was nobody there. Her mother had gone to work.

From the kitchen window she saw Rompy gallop over to Bill, who was carrying a rake.

There was a letter on the table. She knew the writing immediately. It was from Aunt Jane.

She picked up the letter, opened it and read. Her face was transfixed, a face of terror and confusion, furrowed with tears of disbelief. She looked up and saw her father in front of her.

Her body shook, the dream dissolved and her eyes opened with a distant glare. Jess stood beside her. The letter of her dream lay unopened in the box beneath her bed, as it had done for many, many months. She had always been afraid to open it, in case she could not bear the pain of what it said.

"What is it, Jess? What's the problem?"

Jess simply looked at her and pointed over her shoulder to the window.

"People," she whispered. "In the distance. I couldn't sleep. I thought you should know."

Tyro crawled out from under the bedclothes, threw on a crumpled dressing gown and hurried with Jess over to the window.

Tyro strained her eyes.

"Mr Rummage and Mr Baxter. Probably just checking the grounds. What time is it?"

"Beyond them, beyond the bonfire, in the trees."

"You're right!"

The figures were gone.

Tyro felt for the pendant that she had hung about her neck. She felt ashamed. She would go in search of it in the church.

"Ghosts," she said. "Unhappy souls."

"Soldiers who paid the ultimate price?"

"What are they trying to tell us?"

"Something about what they had learned. Their ability, perhaps, to move over time and place."

To her own surprise she said this without emotion. She was no longer afraid.

"Did you know," said Jess, "that close to the bonfire is an old burial ground. According to Mr Baxter."

Bonfire Night was only a few days away.

*

At breakfast the following morning, Tyro and Jess were amazed to see a muddy looking figure eating porridge.

"Rick!" Jess called. "Where have you been?"

Tyro was reminded of the time he had led Rompy into school on a piece of string, at the beginning of their adventures.

"On a ramble," Rick said. "There's lots to tell you."

Within moments Jess and Tyro were sitting opposite him, with a mug of tea and two slices of toast each. Others from their class had drifted in and soon the table was full, squashed towards Rick. They were delighted to see him back safe and sound.

There was no point in being secretive any more. They were pretty much in the same boat now.

Others besides Tyro and Jess had seen the figures in the grounds. No longer were such things a source of terror.

"We saw Strangelblood - at least we think it was Strangelblood. Nobody seems to have seen him before," Rick said.

"How do you know it was him, then?" David asked.

"We were on his land. He was behaving as if he owned the place. And he's up to something. Something big. What we saw suggests that he and the Stranger are in competition. In fact deadly enemies."

"Enemies?"

Rick was about to start his story when Mr Vespers entered. He made a point of ignoring Rick altogether. He was looking his most treacherous.

The slurping, munching, sipping and whispering soon gave way to panic about the morning's lessons and the homework they hadn't done. Julia suddenly leant over the end of the table and said loud enough for everybody to hear.

"Anybody who has not done the Maths can borrow mine."

Everybody turned.

"What's got into you?"

"Roberts is away. Apparently he's ill. Had an accident I heard and he had to go to hospital. According to my Dad."

Tyro and Jess said nothing.

"We don't have Maths anyway. Remember?"

"Oh, Heavens! We've got a field trip today. To Dunemoor. Mrs Moffat is taking us!"

Seeing Rick had made everybody forget that they were going out and that they had to get ready. They were to take a pencil and notebook, their Biology notebook of course, and warm clothing. A packed lunch would be provided.

Rick told his story as they walked along to Mrs Moffat's class. It was very similar to Inspector Relish's.

*

Inspector Relish had reported to Mr Rummage at about five that morning. Rick had been an invaluable guide. He had taken them along a maze of old tunnels, in various states of repair, as if he had lived in them all his life. Dr Bartok followed in the rear, mumbling much of the way about the tunnels of the mind. He wasn't exactly a hindrance, but found it difficult to keep up.

His praise for Rick was unstinting.

Mr Rummage couldn't help but feel a certain pride, but told him to summarise, as time was limited.

The figure which had followed the three young people had been too swift for Inspector Relish, Dr Bartok and Rick, and they soon lost sight of it.

After about twenty minutes or more underground - having dropped deep into the earth before rising again - they came out into the base of an old shelter on the edge of a wood. Looking about them they could see little, though in front of them open land declined towards a lake. Beyond that a mansion stood on a hill, in the darkness. Inspector Relish suspected it was the residence of Mr Strangelblood. The wood they had come out in adjoined the river Dean, and was Mr Pinchet's territory.

Inspector Relish could just make out the shape of a man emerge from the house. He seemed larger than most men. The shape moved to the side of the building and was lost in the dead ground, behind some bushes close to one of the wings.

Inspector Relish decided to investigate and asked Rick and Dr Bartok to follow him closely. They hugged the edge of the wood until they reached a set of outbuildings some distance from the house. One of the buildings contained evidence of people having recently been held captive, though the door was now open. They followed the buildings round until they came to an open courtyard.

It was here that a hand grabbed the Inspector about the neck and dragged him back into the trees. Rick and Dr Bartok tried to respond, but they saw Dennis's face.

Dennis relaxed his hands and put a finger up to his mouth, whispering "apologies" to the Inspector, who regained his balance.

From their hidden position the four of them saw two men gesticulating aggressively, standing in the middle of what looked like some kind of temple.

One of them was the Stranger - the figure they had chased in the tunnels. The same who had disappeared from his cell. The other he assumed was Strangelblood. It was the same shape Inspector Relish had seen a few minutes earlier.

"Never step foot on this land of mine again!" Strangelblood growled. "You, with Pinchet's connivance, have betrayed me by coming here against my wishes. You have decided to go your own way. You have ignored my instructions. If you think you can win this battle alone, you are wrong!"

"For the last time," the Stranger shouted back in reply, "it is time to pass the fight to someone younger. A younger man who has been brought up in the arts of which you once were Master!"

"Once!" The older man seemed to grow in stature. He took out a dagger from the sheath behind his back and launched forward at the Stranger.

The Stranger was too quick for him and stepped aside.

Mr Strangelblood steadied, his face red with fury, but without a mark of sweat on it. In an instant he was calm, back in control.

"You are no longer my son. Never return. Leave the area before you are overcome by my forces. The Priory are nothing

- nothing but pawns. Ever since you disobeyed me, you have been doomed. You will be thwarted in your search. I suggest you abandon all hopes of finding what we seek. Remember I can invoke powers that are absolute. I have the capacity to draw upon the oldest powers that Darkness can offer. Hear you not the words: 'In the beginning there was only me.' "

Before the larger man had time to turn, the Stranger, now seeming himself to have grown, spat at the feet of the older man. The older man looked up. They stared into each other's eyes, with an intensity which would shake the world.

"King of The World indeed!" said the older man, and burst into a fit of demonic laughter.

Beyond them stood a small figure, glowing in the night, reminding them of something. It was like the figure of Tom.

Mr Strangelblood walked past the figure without turning. The Stranger, as before, seemed struck by its silent intensity. That they knew each other was clear.

It was the only thing which caused the Stranger pain.

There was only one other force which Mr Strangelblood feared. It was neither this nor the power of Good, which he felt destined to overthrow. It was something older than all of them. Something that stalked the universe, and appeared when it was decreed.

13

Mr Rummage had invited all the parents to attend Bonfire Night with as much enthusiasm as seemed proper.

There might be safety in numbers, but numbers in close proximity also meant vulnerability.

A wrong judgement could lead to horrendous, perhaps irrevocable, consequences. If he got it right, nobody would know until long after events, by which time neither he nor they would probably be there to see it. He was not looking for gratitude. As long as his family and close friends and colleagues gave him support, he would find the additional strength he needed from elsewhere, through his energies and the alignment of the higher forces that he was powerless to understand, but acknowledged nonetheless, and could occasionally invoke.

He thought of the Ring of Loth, of the silent stone that he had found, of the unstable power which he helped channel to destroy the emerging Dark.

*

Mr Rummage did not frequently visit the church of St Mary Magdalen. It had become a background source of comfort and energy for him, part of his own landscape, one of the givens in his life. He would look at the painting and reflect on how it had become what it was. On the sacrifices that gave it meaning. Of the particular depiction which allowed it to be human, and Divine. Of the symbols which gave access to the infinite.

He would sometimes go along, often with Jenny, and sit in the church and engage in an ancient act of communion, rich in ambiguity and uncertainty, rarely ineffective. It was one of a number of places where his mind could regenerate and where he could find strength and peace, though its specific value was also unique. In the evolution of our devotional needs, what would be next? What symbols, what structures, what authority and liturgies would sufficiently unify us to continue our everlasting journey towards the light?

Mr Rummage loved the painting, in so far as it represented supreme human skill, the expression of ancient craft, and a source of hidden revelation and meaning, but he knew, as all those who looked closely and reflected knew, that it was an image painted by an artist, perhaps a group. He wondered what had happened to the Daughter of God. The darkened Virgin Mary stood unambiguously next to the painting, as if to remind him of the default.

Why had this separation been made, in the symbols and in the story, which had the power to instill great passion, ignorance, and blind idolatry, as well as humility and insight? Perhaps the Order of The Magdalene, if it existed, were intent on redressing this imbalance. If only it could become manifest. Perhaps it was shadowing the Priory and would emerge in the feminine in another guise.

What really drew him there was the thought and the knowledge that before the Church, other traditions had flourished, and something different would arise out of the ashes of this, should it ever become nothing but a heap of rubble.

Mr Rummage hoped the Church's evolution would be progressive, and that it would continue to pay due homage and respect to its history, whilst including other traditions and faiths, and unite rather than destroy. It was the search for this principle which drove him on: in the school, the country, and beyond. Not for domination but for respect of complex diversity and needs. Of the plurality by which only we become One.

Mr Rummage consulted Mr Baxter. They decided on a change of strategy and agreed with Mrs Moffat to proceed with their plan earlier than had been intended.

*

In this interim period, the period before Bonfire Night, Tyro's moods swung from excitement to disbelief that she and her friends had a special place in events.

Mr Rummage brought Tyro, Jess and Rick together one evening shortly after the discovery of the document, under another pretext, to brief them about what might happen and their future role.

"As you have shared many experiences, and have been drawn into mysteries that are a long way from being fully understood, much less solved, I wanted you to be as prepared as possible for the coming time."

It was very rare for Mr Rummage to sound so cautious. He looked into their eyes, and tried to convince each personally of the importance of his message.

Rick normally couldn't sit still. Today he did. Tyro and Jess listened carefully.

"Events in the summer, about which we have already spoken, were only the beginning. Your amazing discovery of the document and the reappearance of the Stranger, with other conjunctions which I cannot explain now, make another 'attack' inevitable. I do not just mean an attack on an individual, horrid and possible though that is, I mean a major event which may threaten our very existence."

Mr Rummage looked closely at the three children.

"The fact is that if there is another attack by the figures - the Priory if that is who they are - in the coming days or weeks, we may not have the strength to repel them. They are missing several important elements that they seek: the document is one; the fragment which is now hidden (and perhaps not genuine) is another; and of course the Spearhead, which has not yet been revealed. Any of these would greatly add to their power."

"Why then are they stronger than us?" Tyro asked.

"I'm not saying that they are stronger - we intend to make them feel that they have the upper hand, but it is likely that the source of their darkest power, what they call the Dark Master, may reappear, may already have reappeared, in another guise. Our own defences, this time, may not be so effective.

"In principle they should be but we never know until the moment we are called. In practice there may be something else, beyond their control or ours, which may determine the outcome of any conflict. Something that we have no control over at all. Nobody does."

"You mean, Sir, that there is a power even greater than ours or theirs, even greater than the power of the Spearhead?"

"Undoubtedly more powerful than their power or ours, to date anyway. Greater than the additional power invoked by the Spearhead I do not know. But I think that is possible. Be that as it may, we still have the advantage. Burnchester is very potent and there are a few of us who know enough to draw down enormous force. Besides, whatever this great source of power is, it may be on our side."

"Like you did from the Island, Sir?"

"Nothing of that magnitude can come from man or woman alone."

Mr Rummage paused.

"I want you to be prepared for a journey. I hope to give you more information in the coming days. You will receive some basic instructions about where to go and what to do, in these letters."

Mr Rummage gave them each a sealed envelope. On each was a seal with an ornate design, of ancient origin. He also gave each of them a small packet, sealed with the same seal.

"Take the envelope and the packet and hide them. I want you to prepare a bag. Make sure nobody sees it. Take enough clothing for a few days. Mr Baxter will give you a compass and a map. My wife Jenny will give you food. When these are ready, be prepared for immediate departure. You may have to flee at a moment's notice. I hope to inform your parents but it may not be possible until after you have left. I shall inform them of the possibility. In fact they already know a good deal more than you realise. Just like your father did, Tyro."

Tyro jumped at the mention of her father.

"My father? What's Dad got to do with it?" Tears welled up in her eyes.

"A great deal. He was a very important man. One day it will be explained, do not worry. Make sure you read that letter of your aunt's. I feel sure she would appreciate it. I am sure you would too."

Mr Rummage put up his hand as Tyro tried to speak.

"You know you have been chosen. It wasn't just what happened in the summer that proved it. There is other evidence too, not least what you have done since. One day, I will explain as much as I can. Follow the instructions in the letter to the detail. The journey will be difficult. You may sometimes travel alone. But you will not be. Remember, there are others involved, though your part is the most important."

The children wanted to ask so many questions. But Mr Rummage went on.

"If we succeed, the future will be very good and there will be great joy and celebration. If we fail . . . well, I must not dwell on that."

There was a pause. The bell rang for supper.

"Now go. I wish you good luck. You have an important role, as does Tom."

Mention of Tom made them start. They got up to leave and went up to Mr Rummage and shook his hand.

The telephone rang. Mr Rummage picked up the receiver.

It was Inspector Relish. The Bishop had been attacked. He was not likely to survive the journey to hospital.

*

Jenny decided she must take a more active lead in helping with Burnchester affairs. Seeing the effect events were having on her husband, she became at times a spokesperson for him. Jenny knew her strengths and decided to use the principles of music. She assumed that conversation followed similar patterns to composition and orchestration, each component counterbalancing the other in tonal connection until some resolution could be found. Parents who were angry or frustrated were like the troubled notes of a discordant sound, which nonetheless contained the elements which if better orchestrated could be transformed into revelatory expression.

Jenny's school knew the rumours about Burnchester. The Head there followed them with interest, taking some precautions to protect it, not without a degree of ambiguous superiority, of vindication of the modern against the traditional.

Friends from both schools talked, exchanged news, in a competitive spirit.

However, beneath the superficial differences, teachers, parents, and governors of the new school were kept informed via the unofficial vine that connects people and protects them from surprise or ignorance and the threat of dictatorship.

Some of the pupils began to wander into Burnchester, and wait for their friends, even though most now were boarding and the security guards at the gates warned them off. There were so many entrances and exits however, that these intrusions were often successful.

The very crisis, which events had become, had a galvanising effect. So it was that rivals became close allies, for the time being at any rate.

*

The exceptions were Mr Vespers and Mr Blakemore who remained isolated. Their inability to disguise their intention in the face of shrewder observers forced them into a role which would, it was hoped, flush out the source of the forces of which they were only the front.

Mr Rummage had nevertheless tried to tell colleagues to be wary of casting judgements without proof. He told colleagues that they should be treated with respect, and just as any other colleagues, until - and only until - there was evidence to do otherwise, and that the evidence could be proven. He knew of course that this was something of a lie, and it pained him to go through the motions of such process, but he had to ensure, to the best of his ability, that they felt assured of their place in the story.

*

"I have an announcement to make," Mrs Moffat said. There was a moment's silence followed by a groan from a familiar source.

Before the groan could become too loud, Mrs Moffat went on.

"I have been asked by the Headmaster to take you on an outing, though a 'downing' would be a better description."

Cheers from the class.

"But you have to be well-behaved and serious," Mrs Moffat went on, "because this is not an ordinary outing like our recent visit to Dunemoor, and there is an important purpose."

This slightly dampened the tone. "Purpose" sounded too much like work.

There was a knock at the classroom door, and the handle moved. The door opened and Mr Rummage entered. He stood quietly by the door.

Mr Rummage spoke as if on cue.

"It's time you learned a little bit more about the history of the school," he said. "Mrs Moffat has agreed to show you - initiate you into might be a better description - a place of great age, incalculable importance and . . . power. There will be no games, no talking. Regard it as the first step in something you might need later on. We all might need. Circumstances may make it necessary. Anyone misbehaving will be answerable to me."

Then he added, in a softer voice, "It has a bearing on recent events."

The class was now completely silent. He had never referred to "events" to any class.

"Take this opportunity. Not many people have it. Watch, listen, learn. And be careful! You will feel the pull of enormous power. Do not fight it, otherwise you will be taken in."

The adrenalin kicked in. "Events" could only mean "mysteries".

Their excitement was palpable, as if they were about to witness something hidden. No longer would it only be Tyro, Jess and Rick. They too would begin to see for themselves what they had only heard secondhand.

Tyro felt a strange distance from Mr Rummage's announcement, not only because Mr Rummage had already spoken to her, Jess and Rick about their coming role.

It was that she felt destined to be one step ahead, as if she were the herald, the pathfinder along a journey that others would have to take, the consequences of which they could not know or avoid. And that would lead to further isolation.

She began to feel afraid and wanted to cry. She longed for her mother and father.

She was still only a young girl, though her body often made her feel older. She longed to be in her room at home, surrounded by her toys from childhood, with the box beneath the bed, which she drew out in times of loss. She would have to survive without them. She had not even opened the letter from Aunt Jane. Why not? Even Mr Rummage had mentioned it to her! She would do so immediately after school! She felt terrible.

Tyro looked at Jess and wiped away a tear. Jess thought it was a tear of joy. Tyro would have to survive like so many others. She must be strong. She had friends to help her, but her strength must come from within. She could not escape her anger. So many people had suffered, it seemed, for no reason at all. How could there be a God? What was this Spearhead that carried so much power? Nothing but an illusion, she felt sure. She had not found the small cross-sword that she had cast down in the dark nave of the church.

Out of the depths of her mind's eye, a vision came to her. She saw the painting in the church, and saw that the paint was running down the surface and onto the floor. It left a sea of colours below an empty frame. She saw the church break into a heap of stone and rubble. A ruin, visible only from the future. What she could not see was anything to replace it. The land was laid waste, as if waiting for the restoration of the King.

There was no sign of the school, of people, of civilisation in any form, perhaps not even of life.

*

Mr Rummage looked at each student in the class. He looked at Mrs Moffat, nodded slightly, turned, and left the room.

There are very few people in the world who can make a pact with others without speaking. One of them was Mr Rummage.

Unless you were in competition, you could only agree to engage with him, and be on his side.

The class began to chatter, like the first murmurings after a broken spell. Mrs Moffat intervened in time.

"You heard the Headmaster," Mrs Moffat said. "Anyone who misbehaves will answer to him. Now," her voice lightened but remained firm, "take out a pen and notebook and prepare yourselves."

There was a rattling of pencil cases and a shuffling of papers and books, then silence.

Mr Baxter had entered the room. He stood at the back of the class, hands behind his back. None of the pupils had seen him.

"Please come up to the front of the class, one row at a time. Mr Baxter is here to help us."

As the front row moved forward, everyone turned and saw him.

There was a murmur of approval.

Within a short time the class was filing into the preparation room, helped by Mr Baxter. Inside Mrs Moffat stood at the closed door which led to the tunnels, through which Tyro and Jess had descended over the summer, before events had taken over, and their memories turned to dreams.

One by one each pupil walked into the room. Mrs Moffat ticked each name off against a list, as if to double-check their existence, in case anyone might become something else down there before their return. The whole class soon stood in preternatural light, breathing more quickly. Waiting. Mr Baxter stood by the class door.

Their anxiety grew. There was no going back now. The room had that unmentionable odour of death, the empty cages evoked images of dissected animals, though Mrs Moffat never used such techniques.

Everyone knew that Tyro had been shut in here. Everyone, even Julia, could feel the pull of the dark from behind the closed door and the terror that Tyro must have felt.

In one collective moment they all recognised something of what she had suffered.

Tyro could feel their empathy. She hated being singled out. Her friends looked at her, which made it worse.

Tyro didn't feel special and yet fate had somehow decreed otherwise. It was something she must accept, humbly, otherwise she would be answerable, well . . . to whom? God? Yet He had not apparently protected her father, so He didn't care. She hated herself for doubting, just as she hated the need to believe, troubled in mind and spirit but unable or unwilling to find refuge - where she could not say.

She felt, in vain, for the cross-sword that she had discarded.

Tyro thought of Rompy, her lovely dog. She remembered the day that Rompy had walked in the field at the back of her house, and followed a scent. When it had gone, he followed another, just as her mind sometimes led her along paths that were short, and misguided, but which would also bring her back onto the right path if only she allowed herself to relax and let her mind go free. It was this that was most like flying.

It was in this moment, while everyone waited for Mrs Moffat to open the tunnel door, that Tyro was struck by an idea.

It was to do with the cages in which the animals waited or were kept before being sacrificed. Looking at them carefully, she seemed to see, in their emptiness, beyond people's bodies ahead of her, their bodies trapped, yet their spirits free, living but unattached, in pain, and yet seeking peace, searching and yet at rest.

She remembered the figures, the different figures of their adventures: those who had been reluctant to intervene when the Stranger had sought their help; those who blindly followed him as if they were part of his own body; and yet others she had seen when she, Jess and Rick had had a picnic, and which nobody else had seen. And the figures she had seen from her dormitory window. She thought of the animals again.

And then she knew. The figures who had followed and haunted them, the figures of the darkness who had so savagely attacked Mr Gruff, were like the spirits of the animals which had been sacrificed, come back to life. Out of control, manipulated, perhaps half-alive. Troubled, seeking rest, seeking the peace that they had not found on this earth. Perhaps, just like the animals, they too had been sacrificed. They had died, been killed before their time. They wanted to come back, and would follow anyone who could make them believe that they could. Some, no doubt, were evil and were doomed, but others - most - were lost, and needed a guide to bring them into the light of day. She was confused. Something lay in this depiction, as yet unformed.

It was the Master Writer who felt that his judgements of people made in childhood were almost always confirmed in adulthood. Tyro sensed that what she saw in people was mostly right, and that frightened her because it allowed her to see beneath their masks.

People were defenceless without them.

Tyro's reverie and the hushed silence were broken when Mrs Moffat reached the tunnel door. Mrs Moffat took the handle and turned.

The door opened. There was total silence as she and Mr Baxter led them down the steps into the dark.

*

Mr Rummage stood in the field next to Mr Bellevue and Mr Granger. They were looking up at the great pile of bonfire. Mr Rummage liked to look at it before it was set alight. It always amazed him that whatever shapes were thrown on to it, once the foundation had been formed the whole compacted into a conical shape.

The techniques for building the fire required that a channel be open to the centre of the base. The base was formed by paper covered with small dry sticks and then oily sacks. This core was loosely packed to allow enough air in to light it without difficulty, the air along the channel supplemented by smaller amounts from the spaces between the rest of the structure.

The central core (like a mini dome) was overlaid with a stronger structure of sticks, onto which the main body of the fire could be placed. More and more pieces were thrown on, without specific method, though its final shape was determined by the base.

Because the core was protected it could be lit at any time, given the right spark. Its effectiveness depended on there being enough air to allow it to light, but its being sufficiently close to the sticks for the flames to catch, though not so close as to be smothered.

To protect the core from any seepage of water from rain or defrosting twigs, it was lightly covered with a plastic sheet, which also acted as a stimulus to the flames.

In this way, once the core was alight, even the dampest superstructure would eventually catch fire.

Such preparation of the bonfire was essential. The whole school, parents and other visitors would be there to observe the spectacle of fire and the fireworks. There could not be any mistakes.

The bonfire stood about seven metres high and as many wide at the base. It had been positioned on this same spot since the days of the Cheesepeake Lumsdens, close to the trees by the river.

Mr Rummage looked at the two men.

"Best ever. Thanks."

Then his face changed from one of delight and gratitude, to questioning and deep concern. He saw the water level of the river Dean.

"Gentlemen," he said. "I've never seen the water level so high. Is it not too close to the bonfire?"

Mr Granger saw that the river had broken its banks close to the base and at other places in the woods and onto the playing fields. It had risen since he had last seen it. It was still, apparently, rising.

Mr Granger and Mr Bellevue looked at each other. The thought of having to move the entire pile filled them with dread, but they could see it would be necessary.

It would have to be moved up the hill away from the river and the trees. It would have to be placed on the rise that formed an ancient burial mound.

As he walked back Mr Rummage's thoughts turned to the Bishop. He felt the deepest sorrow.

He feared what the impact of the news of his passing would be.

14

The day of the bonfire arrived. From the first glimpses of light Mr Granger was down on the field putting up the rope fencing.

Mr Bellevue was setting up the fireworks.

M le Petit, in his flamboyant chef's mantle, was overseeing the positioning of the trestle tables for the food and drinks.

The weather seemed to be in a mood of uncertainty, but was dry. The river however had risen further, the after-effects, no doubt, of the rains that had fallen for the last few days.

On the coast, the tide was expected to be a record high.

*

"Doesn't it look strange?" said Tyro to Jess, as they looked out from their dormitory window. Neither she nor Jess had forgotten the meeting with Mr Rummage which had changed everything, though they had barely mentioned it again, thinking it might precipitate their departure.

"The bonfire is in the wrong place."

"Looks pretty much the same to me."

"Come on, you two!" came a call from the doorway, "you won't get any breakfast!"

"Something is going to happen, I know it. If anything happens to me, Jess, will you come after me?"

Jess looked at her old friend almost as a rebuke.

"It's just that, after our visit to the Chamber the other day, memories came back to me like nightmares of darkness."

She paused a moment. "We never did know what really happened down there before the flight."

"Come on," said Jess, leading her friend out of the dorm. "Let's get some food in us. It's going to be a long day. You never know, we might go on a journey together."

"I shall miss this place."

In assembly, Mr Rummage was upbeat. He told the children to enjoy themselves, though anyone having a water fight after the fireworks would have to help clear up the following morning. This was a tradition and a price worth paying as it involved missing lessons.

Mr Rummage reminded them that parents and guests were to have their food first. Children had a tendency to grab at food whenever it appeared. Could we show some manners? Everyone was to be on their best behaviour.

Mr Rummage emphasised that children were to stay within the limits clearly set out by the markers around the playing fields, and to report at regular intervals during the evening to their parents or teachers.

He stressed that the security guards were there to keep an eye on things - especially bad behaviour - wished them all a good day and a pleasurable evening. The only teachers not present were Mr Vespers and Mr Blakemore.

Security had been stepped up, and uniformed officers were even now being escorted across the grounds of the school, to cover every entry.

After assembly the recovered Mr Roberts was in a subdued mood, and gave them a test.

Ms Peverell read a story from one of her gothic tales, and asked the class to do a drawing of what they imagined.

She left an illustration open on the table. It showed a wild hilly landscape, covered in rocks and stunted trees. There was a castle high on a mountain in the distance. A track could be seen in the foreground below, which soon became lost in the wooded ravine along which it seemed to go. There was a bird, probably an eagle, in the sky. It was a livid colour, like the sunset, and its head was turned upward. Beyond were turbulent storm clouds, suggesting a gale. The storm portrayed a livid energy, ready to take the eagle, according to the whim of the Gods, for it did not have the power to steer its own course, as its struggling majesty showed, in its natural dominion of the air.

The eagle seemed to be making wings towards the castle on the mountain. The dark forest in the picture seemed more inviting than the wild sky.

The eagle might be carrying a message, someone said.

"What message?" asked another.

"A warning," came a third.

"Of what?" asked a fourth.

Such was the artist's skill that hidden between the trees on the ground, close to the edge of the forest, beneath the leaves, there seemed to be the shapes of animals, watching and waiting.

The path suggested, from the sections visible between the overhanging branches, that there must be people walking along it, though they could not be seen.

This idea got the class most animated. The thought that they too might be there, in the safety of the partially obscured track, making their way to a castle in the distance, inspired them. They imagined carrying packs, and food and tents, like hiking. They imagined songs, and marching (there was a humming in the class).

They could not have seen the bridge that crossed the ravine ahead, but they could imagine it as observers of their own myth, there in a hollow beyond the middle ground, and beyond which the foothills rose steadily.

Tyro thought that the castle was a ruin.

She noticed that the landscape continued beyond the castle in the distance above the horizon, where there were obscure breaks in the red cloud, hinting at either the sky or the sea. It was not possible to know.

"What's it called, the picture?" someone asked.

"The castle," came a reply.

"The sick eagle," said Tyro.

"Why sick?" asked Ms Peverell.

"Since when do eagles fly upside down?"

"It's flying loop the loop."

There was laughter.

Ms Peverell had obscured the title at the bottom of the page, and asked each pupil to invent one of their own.

Whilst they thought, Ms Peverell gave a commentary on the picture and how they might adapt it for their own drawings. It was not her style to interfere too much at this stage with the creative processes of the students, and something else was on her mind.

When she ended her narrative, there was a rare stillness in the class which made her feel gratified, as if some ancient process had been at work within each of them while they drew on the page. One illusion inspiring another, in concrete form, out of the substance below.

Rick said that the sky in the painting resembled the sky lit up by a fire, and the talk switched to the bonfire.

Someone said that the picture was still, yet moving, like a fire.

Tyro asked if Ms Peverell thought anything might happen, which put her on her guard.

"Concentrate on the painting, Tyro. There's not much we can do about it if it does."

Ms Peverell hadn't meant to be like that.

"I don't really think so," she added.

The question had broken the ice. The answer needed more explanation. The talk turned to the "goings-on" in the school.

Art was so often the place where you could find refuge, discuss anything, try anything, play and yet work at the same time: fail, enjoy, be. Ms Peverell never disclosed confidences. She was sympathetic and kind. She guided their energies to a higher goal. Besides, art dealt in the real, and they felt safe talking about danger here.

Like the skipper of a boat at sea, Ms Peverell changed tack, to go with the change in conditions, not as a soft option, simply to make best use of the power at her disposal.

She tried to talk through their anxieties which were deeper than they realised.

Ms Peverell faced their fears head-on. From the Domed Chamber and its power, to the figures and the school's hidden secrets, she managed to return to the picture as a parallel depiction of a journey into the unknown, with threats from the dark, but with a goal above them, guiding them on.

There was darkness perhaps, but the end would be alright.

"After all, we'd all like to live in a castle, wouldn't we?" she asked.

"Not as a slave," somebody answered.

"Especially not in a ruined one."

"Look," Ms Peverell said, "even if something does happen, which I don't think it will, there is the whole school full of you ready for a fight, and there is all that security. Don't let your imaginations carry you away. Like the eagle. It has a place, but isn't in everything."

"Perhaps the castle is us," said Tyro.

The bell went.

Everybody got up to rush out of class.

Before they could, Ms Peverell stopped them and told them off.

*

During break Tyro went with Jess to Mrs Clicket's office to

call her mum. She wanted to check that she was coming, and if so could she bring some balloons and a pair of jeans. Abby said she would but was in a hurry, "so see you later." She asked Tyro if she had seen Dennis anywhere, but Tyro hadn't.

In the hall there were a number of people who Tyro took to be parents, and there were teachers coming in and out of the common room.

Through the windows, she could see one or two people walking along the river bank, probably Mr Gruff and Mr Grudge.

Tyro could sense something else. Sensitives who see beyond the moment, or the deeper meaning, into that other realm, or those other realms to which they are drawn, suffer alone.

The two girls walked off in the direction of the next class. It was Mr Vespers's lesson next, and there would be trouble if they had forgotten their homework.

The class, to their astonishment, was reading silently. Tyro and Jess looked towards the front and saw a teacher with his back to them, so they hurried to their desks hoping that they would not be noticed.

They were somewhat surprised at the speed with which everyone had settled.

When the teacher had finished writing on the board he turned and faced them.

It was not who they thought. It was Dennis!

"Mr Vespers is not able to be here today."

The class heaved a huge sigh of relief. There was desktop rattling from the football supporting brigade as Dennis began to speak.

"I have been given this question for you to do. As you can see, I am only standing in for Mr Vespers. Please use your books. You may start."

"Where is Mr Vespers?" Tyro asked.

Inspector Relish stood high on Folly Hill. He scanned the valley with binoculars, and then to his left and right, though his view was blocked by Mr Strangelblood's woods. What he, Dr Bartok and Rick had witnessed a few nights ago had caused him great alarm.

The meeting of Mr Strangelblood and the Stranger added a new dimension to the situation. There were now at least two strands to the potential enemy, one that he had known, the second which was new. Mr Strangelblood, though secretive in his private life, was also a public figure, which made the situation more difficult. The encounter changed his thinking. The missing element in the chain of command might be this very neighbour. Mr Strangelblood had links around the world to people in high places. Including Rome.

To make things worse, Inspector Relish did not wholly trust what he had heard and witnessed. Despite their differences, the Stranger and Mr Strangelblood might decide to work together in the short-term.

His effort to get a full profile on Mr Strangelblood had proved useless. Perhaps he had given the authorities no cause beyond the occasional association with doubtful characters. He would seek higher authority. The Stranger's "reappearance" was never far from his mind.

The little that Inspector Relish knew only added to the mystery. He knew that Mr Strangelblood had long had an interest in science and was a sponsor of a secret initiative to develop ways of taking people into deep space, and most particularly for colonisation.

According to Dennis, the part which interested him most was the issue of selection. How should people be chosen, for what must be one of the greatest challenges for humankind, and perhaps its greatest opportunity for survival? There was growing concern about the planet's capacity to self-regulate, and protect itself from the excesses of its people.

What concerned Dennis most was Mr Strangelblood's preoccupation with what he called "dark energy".

Watching him was going to prove difficult, such was his own art of concealment and the sophistication of his electronic and other protection, as well as the protection he was afforded, perhaps in a grudging degree, by virtue of his financial status alone, and the influence that this bought.

Dennis believed Mr Strangelblood was interested in the Knights Templar. He had also contacted Dr Bartok, via an intermediary, about his research into the Dream Notation Chamber.

Inspector Relish had been horrified to find the dungeons which had been so recently occupied.

Was Mr Strangelblood waiting for the right moment to act out his part, or put his art into practice?

*

Security at the school had been increased dramatically, though most of it would not have been seen. The security teams themselves had not been told the true purpose of their presence. They had been on many covert exercises before. It was not for them to question. It was presented as a defensive measure. It was to test their initiative in the event of the unknown, the sort of unpredictable event for which we can never prepare, despite our best efforts.

"What are the chances of an attack, Sarge?" someone had asked.

"Better than Wyemarket Wanderers winning the Cup," came the reply.

Nevertheless the seriousness of their exercise was revealed in the extent of the hardware that they carried: night vision binoculars, high sensor listening devices, heavy calibre combat rifles, stun grenades, stun gasses, masks, and other classified methods for taking out enemies. What they could not guard against were other realms.

These security personnel were in constant touch with the observation tower, which acted as the eyes of the old building, though the command centre was underground. They were professional, a little sceptical and mostly bored.

*

School was over. Surrounded by the veil of darkness, children dispersed hurriedly to put on their home clothes.

Tyro, Jess and Rick had prepared their special packs in the event of instructions from Mr Rummage. It all seemed far-fetched, now that the evening was upon them.

At tea the noise levels rose to a crescendo before Mrs Moffat came in to quieten things down. After it, the children left to meet parents and wander out into the dark.

Tyro met up with Abby and they had a few minutes talk outside the main building, and then in the children's common room. Abby sensed Tyro's unease, but Tyro was silent about her own fear. Yet she felt almost at breaking point. Memories of the summer certainly played a part. The hidden mysteries around them, part concealed by default, part by design, added to the furnace of her own soul. She wanted so much to tell her mum about her possible journey, but did not know how to, perhaps because she was unsure about what her mum would say, and yet finally she did, and it came out in tears.

Abby was shocked. Tyro spoke in garbled messages and images, a series of unconnected worries about dreams, rumours around the school, almost premonitions, that added up to a vulnerability she had not seen in her daughter before. It was the very vulnerability that allowed the forces bent on power to attempt to exploit wherever they can.

Brave as Tyro was, the images beckoned yet warned simultaneously. It was only due to the goodness of those around her, of her mother, of Jess, helped by the memory of her father, combined with a sense of some greater power watching over her, that she managed to show the brightness of her personality at all.

Tyro was trembling. Abby held her tightly and took her into a quiet area.

Abby tried to be upbeat and positive. She did her utmost to quieten Tyro down, with the help of Rompy, whose soothing touch and inbuilt enthusiasm for anything - especially rabbits - could not but put a smile back on her face.

Abby determined that Tyro should come back home that night. She concentrated on the news from home and the evening ahead, telling her to stay close to her.

Tyro calmed and smiled, as if she had forgotten what had gone before; as if she only needed to let go of her pent-up anxiety to dismiss it altogether.

Jess appeared, then Rick, then others from her class. Tyro rushed off, without a moment to say goodbye, let alone for a kiss, leaving Abby in that slightly desolate frame of mind that so often befalls parents left adrift by children moving on, in the moment or in greater Time. As we all do when something "other" forces us upon a journey, asking us to bid farewell to those we love.

Joined by friends, the mood brightened. The lights of cars along the drive, the sound of welcomes and loud hellos claimed something back from the night. The gathering of people, here to celebrate an evening of joviality and friendship and spectacle, soon dispelled all doubts. Dennis showed his face, and there was Inspector Relish amidst the crowds now filtering towards the parterre where M Le Petit had set his stall, and was tasting the concoction he had made (from "'ze finest 'erbs especiallee imported from Franze") liberally enough to be sure it could be counted on to raise the spirits.

Mr Rummage and other teachers were serving. Jenny was talking to parents in front of the food stall and guided each of them to a grilled sausage and a roll covered and coloured by a ubiquitous red gunge that called itself tomato sauce.

The evening was going to be unforgettable. A new mood emerged.

Children mingled with parents, one or two in fancy dress (against the Headmaster's instructions), even in cloaks (a worse crime), ready to unburden them of food, like friendly scavengers; some with bags bulging with what might have been drunken balloons; interchangeable, like humanity in general, part of the larger story, of which we are only the smallest fragment in nothing but a moment in space.

Amidst these groups moving like a tide on the sea, now at the ebb, now moving toward the shore, some appear destined, for reasons that are beyond our ability to understand, whilst all have a place, an important place, if only we recognised it, and valued humility as much as will.

Below them, towards the river, which was still rising, one or two torch lights are stirring, around the huge shadowy shape of the bonfire, perched in its new position. A few children stand along the rope fence watching, some walking, others running with sparklers.

Guards stand discreetly at marked spots at the edges of the domain. All is being observed from the observation tower.

The fire will soon be lit.

15

Mr Rummage's voice rose over the landscape.

"The fireworks will begin in ten minutes. Please make your way to the bonfire. There will be further refreshments, so carry your cups with you! Here's to you all. To us all!"

Mr Rummage raised his cup and made a point of sipping.

"To us all! To Burnchester Hall!"

When the cheers subsided, he continued.

"Just before the fun starts, I have something to add. It is your support that makes these occasions memorable. We are very grateful to you all for coming." He paused.

"Enjoy the evening, and please let me know immediately if you have anything unusual to report."

There was another cheer from the people gathered close to the tables under the light, and a whistling from the children. A few were preparing for the water fight, out of sight. No doubt others were roaming the grounds, enjoying the cover of the dark.

Tyro, Jess and Rick were wearing the cloaks that Rick had found.

"Where did you get them from?" Jess asked.

"Don't ask!" Rick answered.

Now the tide of people moves towards the bonfire which has been lit.

People line the rope barrier. Others are closer to the river.

The noise of children is everywhere, intermingled with the sounds of the wind amidst the trees.

Tyro, Jess and Rick are with John. John has already hurled two water-filled balloons at Julia and Jane, who retaliate. The fun has started.

Rick and John run off in pursuit of two boys from another class.

Before Tyro can launch an attack, a teacher has come up to them and told them to stop. It is Mr Roberts. He hopes things won't get out of hand.

Over the trees beyond the river, a soft light touches the cloud.

Down river, beyond the boundary of the school, a white owl is hunting along the grassy verges, watching for movement in the grass.

Other animals, which are on Mr Strangelblood's land, are active. A badger roots in the leaves at the base of an oak, deer amble on the far side of the wood, rabbits are spread across the banks and verges, ever watchful for the fox.

Mr Pinchet creeps about on the far bank, carrying a gun. He is not the man he was. The animals are no longer afraid of him, but suddenly they are alert for something else.

There is an air about the evening, which the animals can sense. They are on their guard. They stand still, move into shadows, sniff the air, run into burrows. Something has entered their domain.

The flames cut deep into the sides of the pile. The wood hisses and sizzles. The flames leap above the top of the still standing cone where the Guy sits, its straw body wrapped in old clothes. Its head is proud, though its face is hidden. Its fate is sealed. Too late now. It is but an old doll, yet it seems to want to come to life.

Abby stands beside Dennis, who has been walking the perimeter of the school. He asks if she has seen Tyro and Jess. No, she hasn't. She has her hands out to see if there is any warmth from the fire. There is, but there is cold at her back.

"Is anything the matter?"

Dennis doesn't answer. He looks about him.

"Pretty impressive," Abby says. "Do you remember how, at home, as children, we used to have our own bonfire? How lucky we were."

Dennis is troubled and Abby can sense it.

"Something is in the air. I can feel it," Dennis says.

"They would be foolish to try anything tonight. There are too many people about. Don't spoil the evening."

"They will try anything, in desperation," Dennis says.

Tyro comes up to them, says "hello," and moves on.

The familiar presence of her mother is enough. She is laughing with Jess, yet beneath the facade, she is worried. She stands opposite the fire.

The flames are licking the Guy and its hair is caught, a roar goes up.

"Serves him right!" someone says.

The figure dances in ritual pain as a ball of fire, raggedy and shaking, bits flying off it in the wind. These are carried high and far. The fire is bursting from the centre and generates a powerful heat. The faces along the rope, even at some distance, feel its warmth and look for each other's faces in the reflected light.

Mr Bellevue and Mr Granger move beside the barely visible stands on which the fireworks are placed. One carries a torch, the other a taper.

Tyro watches the broken branches twist in agony, and then break in dissolution into ashes. The irregular spitting of the undried wood adds a solemn beat to the light and heat. It is as if some serpent lies at its centre, waiting to rise to drown the flames in blood.

Tyro can now hear cries. She can see the outlines of people burning, screaming for help in the agony of their breathless final time. Burning people for their beliefs. She feels angry beyond her capacity to understand. She wants to scream. She wants to enter the fire and save them. People who did not follow the rules.

Tyro wants to bathe their fading hearts. She holds Jess as tears well up in her eyes. Heretics from every faith, minorities, lunatics, witches, the despised.

A silent, hidden figure watches the same flames and thinks of his predecessors, trapped in a burning castle, high on the hills of southern France, struggling to save the secrets of his order.

A huge roar goes up. The first fireworks flare. Tyro smiles through her tears at the colours filling the sky. Rick has gone off. Typical Rick. Abby, now with John and Clare, waves at her daughter. Lines of faces stare at coloured forms spreading across the night, symphonies of light, a joy to all who see. They are like souls gliding.

The bonfire is at its peak. Tyro hears the screams again, and thinks of all the others who have perished at the hands of demented human will. The barbarism and inhumanity of what we do to those we do not understand. How can there be a God?

Only plurality, allied with humility and strength, can save us from the torment of fascism in all its forms.

Abby thinks of her husband Jack, who fought for these principles, whilst maintaining his own beliefs. We all need guiding light.

The tree of many fruits, high on the hill of paradise.

*

Figures begin to move across the dark landscape, out of the forest, along the river, hooded and cloaked. These can not be detected by the security apparatus, and are invisible to most people, but they are there.

Some are solitary, others are in small groups (comrades,

perhaps, seeking retribution for the sins they did not commit). One group wears red sword-crosses on their backs, ready to bribe others with the promise of a return to life, in return for their help in creating the terror that they plan to instill.

The Stranger is ever watchful.

The fireworks paint the moving sky, symbols of an orchestrated energy, prescribed and passing. They dance colours, explode, shower, mingle across the night.

Mr Bellevue and Mr Granger strive for a crescendo of light. The younger children stare, the older children pretend not to, before returning to their own world where freedom meets mythologies which give them meaning.

Rick is prowling with water for his chosen target. Tyro and Jess walk away from the main crowd to avoid attack.

Parents watch over their children with occasional glances, looking up at the fiery lights, in memory.

Mr Rummage is making his way towards the bonfire. Jenny is with him. For a few private moments, they walk alone towards the ember glow.

Mr Baxter is nowhere to be seen.

Mr Rummage is concerned that the burial mound on which the bonfire stands has been disturbed.

"You can't disturb the dead," Jenny says.

The fireworks grow more impressive. The master artificers have worked miracles.

A pulsating explosion defies the night. The rocket's head splits into smaller phalanxes, and breaks into cascades of fire.

From the mingled shapes Mr Rummage can detect a sentient energy, like a chthonic entity, precursor of temporate life.

The screeches from other fiery sprays augment the thunder overhead.

Even in the dark, the overshadowing arch of cloud is felt.

The fire, beyond all the rules of nature, seems to grow. At the fireworks' peak, a storm drowns the noise of laughing children. Lightning flashes seems to devour everything in their path.

Mr Rummage looks around him. He detects movement along the far river bank, like an extension of the storm. This is not the movement of personnel he knows. He takes Jenny's hand.

In that moment they both know.

"It's happening," he says. "We must act quickly, whilst people are unaware. Before it is too late."

Mr Rummage hurries up the hill away from the crowds.

He has seen something in the embers of the fire which has horrified him. He barely dares speak its name. It looks like a burning cross, marred with blood.

He prays that he is wrong.

He contacts Dennis and asks him to go to the church. Dennis knows by the tone of his voice not to question why. Dennis does not know where Inspector Relish is. Mr Baxter has not been seen either.

Laughter rises above the children. M Le Petit's delicious scent of wine, sprinkled with herbs, pervades the senses.

More and more people arrive back through the rain, amidst the growing thunder.

Out of nowhere, a slow steady murmur invades the air. At first no-one notices, so dominant are the sounds of the fireworks and storm. The fire continues to spit against the rain, deceiving the murmuring voices.

Now there are shouts as children race across the dark field.

"You . . . !" comes a voice as it receives a dowsing.

Parents and children watch the last rocket leap like a released spirit, an Ariel, into the tormented sky. High it goes, and higher. There is an explosion. People stand expectantly, then turn to each other, empty but exhalting, and begin to make their way back towards the stand.

Dennis has run back from the church through the rain, his face tense with fear.

He joins Abby beside the fire. Something moves in the trees behind them. The fire is so powerful, surely nothing can cross its domain.

"We must find Tyro and take her home."

Tyro appears behind them, and clutches her mother's coat, as a young child might do. She ducks to avoid the water-filled balloon hurtling in their direction. It hits Abby on the legs and splashes all over her, just as Tyro moves away to avoid it, and runs on into the night. Tyro calls, "sorry, Mum!" out of the darkness.

Abby calls out. Then she shouts, desperately.

"Tyro! Tyro!"

Parents look towards her.

"It's alright, she's here," says one. There she is again. Running with her friend whilst trying to splash a third, then climbing up the hill to the cold tap ready to throw more.

Abby watches Tyro closely, while Dennis goes to Mr Rummage.

The dark murmur increases. Along the far bank of the river, unseen by the milling crowds, a line of dark figures wait.

Other figures have come from the Church of St Mary Magdalen and stand in line round the back of the school, to cut people off. Others wait in the trees close to Mr Gruff's house.

High on Folly Hill a figure in a black cloak stands watching, untroubled by the patrol guards who have been overcome with pitiless disdain. Beside one of them Mr Pinchet lies lifeless. There is no possibility of further treachery now. Mr Pinchet released the prisoners on Mr Strangelblood's land. They have escaped.

Figures appear on top of the church tower. Not one is visible to the camera as it swings in search like an all-seeing eye which sees nothing.

Mr Rummage runs into his office and dials the emergency number.

Mr Brock waits at a Military HQ some distance away, for

reports from other sites, though none are as eminent as this. Mr Brock watches the coast around Dunemoor, close to where the Neptune was last seen. There has been nothing. He knows that no military weapon can counter the force. He answers coolly. His reaction is immediate.

The crowds have moved up the hill.

Mr Rummage calls Mr Baxter, but there is no reply. He tries Inspector Relish. He cannot reach Dennis either. He will have to act alone.

Mr Rummage hurries from his office up the stairs to the library. He goes to the manuscript room. There are still some papers on the tables. If he is not mistaken he senses something in the room, but he has no time to check.

He calls out, but there is no reply. He opens the door that leads downwards to the tunnels and fixes it open as best he can. It might offer one escape route. He runs down the stairs to the marbled area where the lifts stop. He picks up the phone next to the lift dials and calls. From far below comes a voice. He speaks only one word: "Initiate."

He runs up the stairs again and out of the room. Instead of turning back downstairs he runs to the third floor.

At the end of the corridor he comes to a fire exit. He goes out onto the roof where he walks along the parapet past the gabling. To his right he can see the helicopter landing site. At the side of this stands a small rectangular box with a keyhole at its side. He moves swiftly to the box, takes one of the two keys from his pocket. He places it in the hole and turns.

Beams of light explode from the darkness. The whole area is lit, including the pad, highlighted by a red circle. The rest of the rooftop and the observation tower sparkle in the rain. He moves to the edge of the roof, deliberately making himself visible.

People's faces turn with the light. They gasp. There are shrieks of wonder from the children, who imagine that this is all part of the show, and Mr Rummage the star.

Mr Rummage can see out over the nightscape. He stops directly in the line of the brilliant beam which lights up the oldest and most beautiful part of the Hall.

He looks down and faces the crowd, now closing together.

Mr Rummage can see shapes moving along the river. Some have crossed the river and wait in line along the near bank. Others stand at the end of the playing fields, and yet more have come round the eastern part of the Hall towards the main entrance. He knows that there will be others.

He must not cause panic. He wants to channel the untapped energy of parents, staff and children, untrained and unaware, to counter the force that surrounds them. The military, for all its bravado, will be useless.

He looks for Mr Baxter. He wants to tell Tyro, Jess and Rick to prepare. He has given them some idea of what they might be expected to do. He knows that success or failure is on a knife-edge.

Mr Rummage has never been so afraid in his life.

The figures will not target everybody, at least not at first. Most people will be of no interest to them, but people will panic, those who can see. There are some ready to do everything in their power to take the enemy on. He knows that the children for the most part will be safe. Except Tyro, Jess and Rick.

The crowd below begins to feel uneasy.

"Ladies and gentlemen," Mr Rummage begins. "The evening is not drawing to a close. It is just beginning."

There is silence. Then there is a murmur.

Children continue to chase each other across the grass, throwing water, and returning to refill. Others hide in the changing rooms, where a second front has opened up between different groups. A few stragglers and adventurers are hidden in the school and in the grounds. The fun is endless.

Tyro and Rick and Jess have now secured their cloaks.

"We have unexpected visitors . . . " Mr Rummage says.

There is a curious cheer.

But this time, it is not directed towards Mr Rummage. Just as he has begun to speak, something else has distracted their attention.

Coming around the far corner of the Hall, just where the Headmaster's study faces the field below, a group of multi-coloured figures make an entrance, and they are dancing. They all wear cloaks, and have hoods over their heads, and they are singing a joyful song, whilst moving to their own rhythm.

At the centre of the circle that they form another figure, wearing a long low robe and holding a staff (it looks like the base of a spear), seems to be dancing too, yet with occasional waves of its baton orchestrates the group around him.

What is clear to everybody is that these figures wear on the back of their cloaks a clear red cross.

People begin to laugh, to clap, a few even to join in the singing. Some are bemused, one or two even try to flee though it is impossible.

Children are enthralled, coming alongside the group and trying to join the dance.

The figures in the background remain still, watching.

Tyro, Jess and Rick are now close to the dancing troupe.

Above, the sound of a helicopter fights against the thrust of thunder.

Mr Rummage tries to speak above the noise.

"We do not have much time," he says.

Mr Rummage knows who the lead dancer is. A quick look in the direction of Ms Peverell confirms it.

"This has been the best bonfire yet. You have all been marvellous. Thank you for coming. Thanks to Mr Gruff, Mr Grudge and Mr Bellevue for all their work, and everybody else involved."

The audience are watching and listening. Now they clap to the rhythm, and move to the beat.

Mr Rummage turns up the volume on his speaker.

"Unfortunately it is not all good news. I want you all to listen very carefully. Listen now."

Mr Rummage pulls from his pocket a firework which he places on the ledge of the roof. He lights the fuse. Within moments a huge cascade of light rises and adorns the sky, coloured lights tumbling to the ground, like a miraculous flare. In the corner of the dome of light a helicopter can be seen approaching.

People turn and look around and up. Some can now see the shadowy figures in the background, who begin to stir. The golden candle is out.

Mr Rummage throws a banger in the air. There is a ferocious explosion.

Everyone is still, though the dancers still dance, and the rhythm becomes more sombre.

The helicopter lands on the pad behind.

Mr Rummage speaks, as the softest music begins to pervade the air. It seems to come from within or below the house and yet has captivated people outside.

The rain falls heavily, the drenched people in their cups and the glowing fire on the ancient burial mound offset the thunder, the dark figures and the dancers. Mr Rummage is inspired.

The music is like a distant chorus to his devastating words.

As he speaks, Mr Rummage watches the dancing figures, who have reached a point below the main crowd, and are now spread in a thin line along the edge of the path which separates them from the field, the river and the fire.

Children continue to run, though some have begun to tire and have come closer to M Le Petit's tables, rejoining their parents.

One or two of the more adventurous remain in the open. Mr Rummage has seen them.

The haunting figures have moved forward. Some are just on the far side of the fire, which still spits flames.

Parents who now see the figures watch in horror, mesmerised.

"You there!" Mr Rummage bellows. "Come closer or you will not hear! Children, come here, now! Before you are taken!"

His voice is controlled.

"Our celebration is over. You are free to leave, if you can, though your way may be blocked."

People listen, as at a play.

"The time has come. I need your help and support once more this night, in ways that you cannot have imagined. I would not be saying this - I speak with the utmost seriousness - unless it were vital. I am sorry I did not know, could not know this might happen, but I would ask you to follow my instructions carefully, and those of my staff. Above all stick together, and make sure you bring your children with you. Call them now. Call them now! Take them into the hall. I will give you instructions there. Above all, do not go back towards the river. Under no circumstances separate from your families and friends. We must stick together. Under no circumstances approach the fire."

There is silence. The mood has changed like the passing cloud, from sunshine into night. The chatter and the laughter, the calls and cheers are nothing now. Few understand what Mr Rummage is saying, though his tone is clear. There are shouts from one, and screams from another, but the group soon rally and move to get their children.

As they disperse over the field, Mr Rummage continues to speak, with the thunder in the distance, and the rain beating down, and above all the fire, low but seemingly solid, reaching its ember stage. He watches this carefully.

"The worst has happened. The rumours which you have heard so much about, and some of you have been privy to, have been fulfilled. I repeat. I am speaking to you now with the utmost seriousness, though you will understand why I am saying these things as if in celebration, with the music playing."

He tries to lighten his tone, as if to distract other ears.

"We have been surrounded by figures who are dangerous. Some of you may have seen them, many will not. They are there. They are from another time. We have a few moments only to gather our children up, and make our way into the main school. They will only harm you if you try to stop them. The army will do what it can. It is me they are after. The time is now."

Some people treat what is happening as part of the evening's entertainment, despite Mr Rummage's words and tone. Then there is a sudden melee of noise as their reaction sets in. They look about them. Some can see figures moving above the grass, in a long line. Then the line stops. One or two parents try to attack them, but they get nowhere. They are repulsed without effort.

There is pandemonium. The parents grab their children and try to make their way into the hall, others hurrying round to the front of the school where their cars are parked, seeking escape. Teachers have dispersed to get the straggling children inside, though not all of them can be persuaded, or found, amidst the shouts and tears.

The parents, now under escort, follow the security guards into the hall where they had a meeting not long ago. Some head for the Domed Chamber.

The only ones not to move are the dancing troupe who stand in a line still facing outwards into the darkness and the haunting shapes not far away.

The dark silent figures now stand within a hundred metres of the main building, a small distance from M Le Petit's stalls. There are many more in the darkness. Many more in the woods, over the dark landscape.

One of the figures steps forward.

It is the Stranger.

16

"You are surrounded. You cannot escape. Give us what we seek and you will be released. Otherwise, I cannot be held responsible for what happens to you - or your children."

The figure of the Stranger spoke in the darkness, some metres from the embers of the fire. It seemed to grow with the light behind it as did the obscure shadow it cast over the ground. The other figures remained still. For those who could see, there were endless rows now, and others were arriving. They seemed to be coming from all directions, from the Iron Age fort and Mr Strangelblood's land, from the eastern fringes of the school, from the direction of the sea, and from the wooded area near to the church.

Though terrified and bewildered, the need to save their children focused parents like nothing else could. Could their energies be focused on the enemy?

Mr Rummage watched from his position above.

A few parents and teachers ran to the edge of the diminished territory that they could still claim was the school's, seeking children who might be lost. There were many places where they might hide - the changing rooms, the teaching block, the wooded hedge that lined the playing fields. The selfsame in which Rick and Tom's tunnel entrance lay.

Hurriedly the children were gathered. At first they thought it was a game, and ignored all pleas from parents and teachers alike, then argued and struggled. They didn't want their fun to end, tired though they were. There was crying as well as exhausted gratitude from those who had been saved from another drenching. There was bewilderment and fear. The parents and teachers tried to console them.

The only people who were missing were Tyro, Jess and Rick.

Tyro was concentrating, trying to focus, watching the figures from a first floor window, seeking inner help. Her destiny was ahead of her. Jess was beside her urging her to find her mother and tell her she was safe. Rick was agitated. He wanted to get out there and do something.

"Jess, we must prepare," said Tyro calmly. "For our journey. Whether it is together or not I do not know. We have to get our things."

They could hear the sounds of people below, their names being called. Abby came running up the stairs to find the three of them, and threw her arms around them.

"What are you doing? We've been calling you. I'm so glad you're safe. Come down."

Below, children, parents and teachers were continuing to make their way into the dining hall which overlooked the open field where the figures still stood. M Le Petit had abandoned his refreshments outside and went into the kitchens to prepare some hot soup. While he was there he put in an SOS call to Mr Gatherin at the Burnchester Arms.

Teachers searched dormitories and found Matron carrying as many towels as she could for the children.

The military commander who had arrived by helicopter took over from Mr Rummage and asked everyone to go inside, and await instructions. This gave Mr Rummage a few moments.

Parents could go to their cars, only if they were parked within sight of the main entrance.

If they tried to leave, the commander continued, they would do so at their own risk. They still had an opportunity to flee under their own steam, though the window would not be open long.

Abby leant over to Dennis, and together they decided they would make an exit now, with Tyro, Jess and Rick beside them. First however, they wanted information.

Mr Rummage had come downstairs and was on the phone to security. Parents were at his door.

He called Doonwreath. He called colleagues elsewhere who were protectors of such sites as his. He also called Mr Veech. He wanted this out. The guards on duty could not be reached or were not answering. This must not become known. He would ask the commander to send for reinforcements from barracks nearby. The situation must not be allowed to get out of control.

In his study were Dennis and Inspector Relish.

Mr Rummage finished his calls and was about to speak to them, when there was an eruption from the hall, like a huge scream and the sound of feet stamping the ground. Parents immediately ran to see what the trouble was.

Mr Rummage and his colleagues rushed out and made their way to the hall, only to see people in broken rows pushing and shoving towards the window which overlooked the meadow and the fire. There was a murmuring of shock and awe. Mr Rummage ran to the side door, which looked out into the night.

In the hall the children held their hands to their faces, as if they were being shielded from a blinding light. And yet they could not be shielded from this intense energy.

The Stranger stood outside not far from the window. The security guards who had tried to intervene had made no impact.

The Stranger's appearance so close to the building, separated only by a shield of glass, made people scream out.

Some tried to make their way to the side exit, in order to challenge him, but Mr Rummage stopped them. He bellowed above the chaos of noise through a loud-hailer, warning them that their attempted intervention might mean the death of themselves and their children. The parents were restrained against their will. One or two remained close by, ready to go out and confront the figure. Most returned inside the hall, and prepared to collect their children and partners, and try to leave while they could.

The collective energy of the people inside the building was overwhelming - even the Stranger and the figures could sense the strength of the potential that they faced, though they also knew its incoherence - a mixture of excitement, anger and fear, and heightened by the danger of uncertainty. It was like a huge iron spring about to snap. It needed focus and control. It needed a master guide.

Mr Rummage wanted to lead them in a counter-attack. But he could not do so with so much confusion. He could not do so in this state of uncertainty. He could try alone, and with Jenny, but the forces were too great for them and he could not imagine persuading any of the people to go underground. Not yet. He could not initiate them, without some induction. He needed something else, some unifying image that would give them hope and aim. Mr Rummage needed a sign.

Some of the crowd moved back through the hall, with their children, and on through the building towards the main exit before fleeing into the night to find their cars.

One or two managed to escape before a powerful force seemed to prevent them, a force that effectively trapped them all. It was as though a curtain had descended in front of them. Impenetrable, invisible, final.

*

All along the edges of the school, the security teams positioned to intercept the figures had been brushed aside, completely unable to stop them.

The huge chain of dark figures, led by those with sword-crosses on their backs, chanted a mesmerising refrain from the depths of history and the earth. Behind and all around them, as if in answer to the sound, as some manifestation of their intent, there arose from the ground, in a vast circle around the whole school, equidistant from where the fire burned, a huge wall of energy. Gradually it arose like an ice sheet, moving upward, above the height of people, trees, buildings, the Hall, one gigantic pinnacle, like the head of a huge rocket. It was translucent and threw off a pale gleam, and formed an impenetrable veil between the space it encircled and the world beyond, obscuring the beauty of the night, and the world, now unreachable. Higher and higher it grew like a cone of darkness against the freedom that they sought.

Most people were transfixed, as if they could not escape their destiny, and the only recourse was to observe its creation. Some fought against it, others struggled to find a gap in the wall. Children watched, awed by the sight, as the Stranger stood in the light of the dying fire, while the huge, monumental Dome of pale light stretched above them. Soon the entire school and the space around it, including the church and the buildings, were encased. From afar it might have seemed like an unearthly Cathedral spire, beyond which lay the stars and the rain, and infinity.

Mr Rummage knew that there was only one place from which he could start to dismantle this wall of energy, and that was the Domed Chamber.

As the astral dome became complete, the awe of the many turned into panic, a panic of shouting in the struggle to flee in the realisation that they could do nothing. It was clear that nobody could escape. Several had tried in vain and had returned badly dazed, in some cases unconscious on the heavy drenched ground.

The Stranger, obsessed with his own power, and his own presumed immortality, was oblivious to the dome.

Mr Rummage moved towards the secret entrance to the Chamber below.

The figures had moved closer, forming lines like knives wedged in the flesh of a sacrificial head.

The fire was a heap of burning ash, like an upturned crucible of molten light, casting the Stranger's shadow.

Bursts of steam blew upwards from the embers.

From that mist a shape seemed to appear. It was a monstrous figure of unknown horror. A power that grew with the incantation that beckoned it, like a serpent twisting from the ashen branches it had consumed, licking the wounds of the victims it had betrayed, it had fed upon to become itself. One who would be manifest. One who would rule. One whose eternal task was to seek to overthrow the Light and regain the throne and glory that was lost. The Stranger watched.

Desperate to take shape, to recast its shadow in material form, it struggled and twisted into a near becoming. But another force had begun to work against it. The energy wrought within the conical shape above it, multiplying the power of its disciples in death into an anvil of despair, was not enough to give it shape. It lacked the ultimate power it needed.

It needed the very power of its earlier victor, in order to take shape. It could not yet be reborn, it could not become the thing it wanted to be. People instinctively cast out their own dark energy on to it, denying it strength. The mental battle raged until it began to fade, drawing gasps from the crowd.

As quickly as it had come, the primordial evil collapsed into itself, and became nothing. The fury of its failure, the jealousy with which it beheld its earthly servant the Stranger, would have driven a stake through the largest heart, except this one, which has no blood, and feels nothing but cold in the depths of its unrivalled shame. It would seek vengeance by other means, and wreak havoc instead with souls, stealing the breath of life from those it could tempt with false rewards.

People continued to cast their own darkness out, whilst

covering their eyes, so as not to contact those that would drain them of life and force them into the abyss, turning them, gorgon-like, into silent effigies for eternity, servants to the Dark Master, whose hordes of sordid wealth were only equal to the vile glory of its acquisition, in the Halls below.

People cried in fear, gripped by terror; children clung to their parents at the sight of this archetypal ghast, whose darkest dreams had been close to fulfilment, but could not yet be.

Mr Rummage, drained and tormented in the Chamber below, knew that this was a temporary respite, a mere precursor to the next encounter.

At the very moment when the Dark Master had become extinguished, at the very point between death and life, it seemed, something else had taken the evil presence's place.

There, in the middle of the circle, calm, still, untouched by the fury of the flames, perhaps created from it, stood the figure of a child.

Where there had been horror and petrified fear, there were cries of wonder and joy.

"Look!"

At first people thought it was an illusion, created from the mirage of the steam, and made obscure by the darkness of the night. Then there was pointing and shouting.

The Stranger stared in fury, in the direction of the dying embers of the fire.

The other figures beyond, some of his own servants, stood transfixed, no longer able to move forward.

The Stranger faced the child.

The child was one that they knew. He seemed to have come out of the fire, or walked through it from the other side. It was as if he had grown out of the final flames.

In that moment, Mr Rummage acted.

Tyro, who had stood and watched entranced, suddenly screamed and ran forward, breaking away from Abby and

Dennis, and stood apart facing Tom, for it was he, with the Stranger to her left, between them. Jess and Rick joined her.

"Tom!" Tyro screamed, trying to attract his still gaze.

"Tom!" Rick called.

Jess came forward too and called.

Tom watched the Stranger. He did not need to look about him. He knew he was surrounded. So he whistled. It was a whistle that three young people knew well.

The Stranger could not move, but to raise his arm and curse aloud.

"Get thee hence! Vanish from my sight!"

Figures tried to move forward and seize the boy, but could not.

The figures cowed. The Stranger was furious.

Other figures, without the sword-crosses on their backs, seemed to hold back voluntarily, their allegiance clearly not guaranteed. The Stranger ordered them to advance, but they would not.

So in a controlled moment of rage, the Stranger focused his eyes on the night, looking for the figure who had dissolved into the pit, willing to conjure it back to life for the power that he needed to vanquish. But his powers were inexact, and it became diffused.

At that moment the dancers, dressed in theatrical cloaks of the same design as those they strove to parody and confuse, began to dance, orchestrated by the figure in the middle, who held a baton like a wand.

Tom whistled in time to the music.

The music was entrancing. Something magical was taking place that all could see. Other people began to join in, and formed a chorus. The huge dome above them like a cathedral.

A glow shone in the air, lighting the Church of St Mary Magdalen, then the entire enclosed space within the unearthly energy Dome. High in the celestial spheres, brilliant lights flickered.

Every figure bowed and froze, people were transfixed. Nothing moved, nothing could move. The Stranger was unable even, it seems, to breathe. The stillness was like the moment before an eclipse, so intense and profound the silence, the waiting, for the peace to come.

A robed Figure in white seemed silently to emerge from near the door of the church. It crossed the graves, crumpled and thin and splattered in blood, like undried paint running from the canvas on the altar, an image of the eternal, come down from its artistic space. The crown of thorns had been cast aside. A fragile human cast in the role of the divine. The light was intense, and all revealing.

The Face captured a supremely agonised smile of peace, offering hope on the thorns of sacrifice. The robed Figure stood a moment so that all could see, and all could recognise. The Figure held its hand against the left hand side of its body, near its heart. Where the spear had entered its side, the hand came away, revealing the cut, where the blood dripped. There for a moment a cup could be seen, capturing some of the falling drops.

In its hand the Figure held something. It seemed to have taken a small object from its body, as if it had been lodged there. The Figure seemed relieved as if a pain had passed, like a thorn removed after long years of hidden suffering. Like the burden of eternity.

The Figure saw the child and moved towards it. Nothing moved. Nothing could move. It held out Its hand to Tom, who lifted his to greet it. Tom seemed to take the thing the Figure held.

Tom looked up.

The Figure seemed to speak. The Figure raised its hand and blessed the boy, and then the people and the figures before him.

Some figures stood in shame.

In that moment no power on earth, or sky, no power at all

could move. The legions of the lost or damned stood entranced, even the Stranger averted his eyes, as if to deny the love he might receive for his return.

The Figure then disappeared into the night. It seemed to rise into the air and melt away.

Inside the church the canvas was bare, except for one lost piece. Now the image of the fallen Spearhead lay at the base of the blank frame, as if from it might spring new life.

On the top rim of the wooden frame sat a white dove, bleeding.

People began to awake from what had seemed a dream.

The Stranger saw what the child held.

Tom stood at the edge of the fire's base, a stillness on his face, passing all understanding. He looked again for Rick and Tyro and Jess, and saw them not far off, to the left of the Stranger.

He walked forward. In that same moment, what he held was now in the domain of the normal world. For a moment, there seemed to be an incision in his left side, through his jersey, caked in dry blood. Tyro, Jess and Rick saw it. Then it was gone.

"Rick. Get ready. Tyro, prepare. And Jess. Just as Mr Rummage said. I will follow if I can. I do not know what is in store for me. For any of us."

Rick tried to come forward and take the hand of his friend, for he had seen what he held. But the heat from the fire was too much for him to bear. He held out an arm, but could not reach him. The object in Tom's hand was small and bright. It gave off an energy of great purity.

Tyro and Jess saw the object.

The dancing figures had drawn close to Tyro, as she stepped forward. Jess and others from their class moved up.

The torment of Tom became their tears of compassion.

Some of the parents now filed out of the hall and stood behind the children. They could not have come forward had they wished. They knew a deeper act was being played out, something they could not touch, only observe. It was as if they were observing something from the collective imagination of them all, had it not been for the treacherous sight of the Stranger watching Tom, ready to strike and steal what he held.

Mr Rummage, back from the Domed Chamber, understood.

Mr Rummage led some people once again below ground, whilst the situation was in stalemate above. Some parents, unable to comprehend, confused, dazed and tired, took their children to their cars, hoping to drive through the energy field that stood between them and the world beyond; beyond the barrier like a huge arcane cave. Their path was blocked.

Tyro moved towards the fire, sweat pouring from her forehead. She saw what Tom held and went to touch his hand and the object that he held. In her mind, suddenly, came an image: like the image she had just seen, of the sad, noble figure in the painting, whose meaning she had failed to grasp yet whose presence she could not deny. She thought of her father. She knew that the journey was about to begin and that she had to take the object that Tom held, before the Stranger could wrench it from him, and plunge them into despair. In Tom's hand was what appeared to be a small oval shape. Older than time, yet of time, and dormant in its grave sunken beneath the floor of history and chance, ready to serve those who could make its true worth come alive.

Tom looked at Tyro.

The Stranger began to move.

"Remember what I said, Tyro!"

Tyro was close to Tom, Rick only a few inches back, Jess behind both, and the parents were struggling to come forward.

Tyro felt about her neck for the cross-sword which she had discarded. She looked at Tom, approached him again, reached out and touched his outheld hand.

The Stranger saw this too and continued forward. Parents tried to approach, ready to defend to the death if necessary what they beheld, though they knew not what it was. The dancing figures started to mingle with the dark Priory figures who had joined the Stranger.

The Master Dancer held his wand high. So they became confused, and the players became part of the illusion, and for a short time destroyed their continuity, as the figures looked about them and, thinking they had been instructed to dance, began to move to the music that sailed about them like a ship. Jenny had caught the sound and was leading it from a flute that she held as she walked towards them, like a feminine Pan.

Beyond them all, in the obscure region around the perimeter of the school, but also of antiquity and greater time, three figures robed in white walked in solemn step: a trinity whose laws none can transgress, none can revoke, to whom even the ancient Gods paid homage. Of all the powers that exist anywhere, those of Darkness were most afraid of these, for their law is absolute and without redress. Over these none can prevail.

Neither the power of the ancient Chamber nor of the stones of Loth could compete with these. Nor could the power of the Stranger, not even the ancient evil of the Dark Master.

The powers of light and love and truth were not afraid, for they would be given new form, robed in glorious garments standing upon the threshold of eternity.

People awoke from their trance, as in the Dream. Tom spoke again to Tyro.

"Remember what I said."

The Stranger waited for the right moment. He would try to ensnare them all.

Rick went up to Tom and hugged him. They seemed to laugh together.

Tom whispered, "We will meet again."

The Stranger's closest circle, two of whose faces were now visible, with swords hanging like broken crucifixes on their backs, watched every movement, about to strike. Tyro and

Rick and Jess had seen Vespers and Blakemore. Darkened shadows of iniquity.

They had not seen the three figures in white.

Parents now emerged and surrounded the figures. They started shouting at them demanding to know what they thought they were doing, going up to them and throwing punches if they could. Some of the figures stood still. Others merely lifted an arm, and the humans were thrown to the ground. Children were running and making for their friends, and scurrying in and out of the motion of bodies, adding to the strange encounter. The wall of the huge dark lit dome hung above and over them.

The military commander had called for reinforcements and had been told that they were on their way. They would meet the unworldly barrier to the school from all sides: outside the main gates, along the perimeters of the grounds, touching some of the land on the other side of the river, on Mr Strangelblood's land, and be able to do nothing. No amount of armour nor weaponry could break this opaque wall, like the wall between the enclosed mind and the mind that is free to seek the infinite and go on journeys unknown to man. It was this freedom above all others that the Stranger and the Dark Master wanted to destroy.

They wanted homage, not independent thought. Not the ability to fly.

*

Mr Rummage was in the Domed Chamber. He had taken with him a few whose energy he required. He began the ritual of self-erasure, and prepared his imagination, creator and created, for the sake of those he had to help, according to His will.

Others stood in the empty church and prayed in front of the mysterious painting, now an empty frame, but for the fragment carrying the Spearhead.

Though the central image was lost, those who knelt in front of it imagined it still.

The painting, whose smile of infinite sadness could not have failed to touch the most hardened heart, had been so imprinted on the mind that the empty frame hosted it still. The hope of everlasting life.

Nearby, Tom moved forward.

The Stranger and the Priory were close to the children. There would be no mistake this time. There would be no second chance.

They knew what they had seen.

"I order you to give up what you hold!" called the Stranger. "Take them all!"

The Stranger struck first, lunging at Tom. At the same moment Tom swung round. The Stranger grabbed Tom's hand and was about to take the object, when Tyro seemed to rise above the ground and took it from his hand. The other members of the Priory lunged forward at her, but Rick and Jess blocked their way, and they too seemed to lift above the ground. More figures circled them. They were many rows deep and the children could not now move except into their hands.

Behind, where the bonfire had stood, a vast empty space appeared in the ground. The ashes flew into the air and tumbled into the abyss. Down and down the hole grew larger, infinitely dark, infinitely deep, the glowing ash sinking to the core.

Tom was being taken. Rick, Jess and Tyro were trying to help him, but he told them to flee. The figures could not do him any further harm. He laughed as they held him, though they and the Stranger could only get so close. Something held them back, the power that the child had over them still held sway.

Tyro, Rick and Jess would not leave Tom. Tyro held the object out in front of her, to ward off the demonic figures, not knowing what she held. The power was enormous, and they all fell back, leaving the four exposed. Many parents tried to intervene but they could not. They could not touch them.

A white dove landed on the grass and became the Figure from the painting.

On His side a deep cut, spewing blood. The Image held its hand high, a flash of blinding light reached out to the object that Tyro held, and illuminated it above the night. "With this object my blood was further spilt. It contains the thing you seek, which will lead you to our Father. My time is coming to an end. My time is nearly past. But do not mourn. Take this in remembrance of me."

The three children tried to run, but their path was blocked, until the dancing figures created a path and protected them as they raced across the ground. Abby and Dennis screamed at Tyro to come back, John and Clare did the same to Jess, and yes, the figure of a gentle man, recently held hostage by Mr Strangelblood, none other than Rick's Uncle John, tried to call, though his voice was hoarse. He hobbled forward.

"Rick!" he cried. "It's your uncle."

Another voice called out to them to "git 'em bahstuds!", running like a demon over the ground attacking figures furiously with a golden sword.

On and on the children moved, gaining from the Priory who in pursuit had fanned out, moving over the ground as if on air, and overtaking them on wings.

Soon the children reached the wall and they could go no further.

They would have to find some other way. Their power was not strong enough for this.

17

Tyro, Jess and Rick turned and faced the hooded figures. Tyro held out the sacred object, and for a while the figures cowered.

Parents and teachers created a human wall around the young people. Amongst these were Inspector Relish and Dennis, with Clare, Abby, John and Uncle John close behind.

Tyro remembered Tom's instruction. She also remembered the power of incantation that they had all begun to learn in the Domed Chamber on their visit with Mrs Moffat. They had made several other trips into that dark region. Drawing from the energy flow from those about them, the three children focused on the figures beyond them, and seemed to hold them there for enough time for them to decide. The figures fought the human wall, trying to break through, as yet in vain.

The three young people looked from one to another, as if seeking a solution. Then an idea came to them.

The dancing figures had turned the corner of the main building and again began deliberately to mingle with the Priory group. The leader, dressed in the robes of a magus, stood alone and moved his wand, trying to break the spell. The fighting stopped in the confusion, neither side wishing to hurt their own.

Thunder crackled above, streaks of fiery lightning descended over the valley, lighting the whole domain for a moment, revealing the people and figures under the Dome's massive height. All about them seemed to be chanting, as if the energy in the air provided music too.

The children decided to separate. Rick would go one way with Jess, Tyro would go alone. Tyro felt that the figures would not believe that she, carrying the sacred object, would do so. There was no time for a proper farewell. They hugged each other and parted.

The Priory tried to smash their way through the wall, with increasing violence. Blood flowed from the heads of John and Abby, others lay on the ground, trampled amidst the battle.

As he broke through towards the two young people, the Stranger became suspicious. He felt no energy from them. He turned towards the single figure, now some distance away.

Tyro moved swiftly, shadowed by her bleeding mother. Mr Baxter was now at her side, along with Dennis, who was fighting off two Priory members whilst trying to keep them off Abby. He felt nothing but bone through their cloaks.

They knew that they could not protect Tyro much longer, though they fought as long as they could.

As she moved on, Tyro felt a strange sensation. She sensed the energy of the sacred object coming to her aid. Yet it was as if it was within her, like her dream taking shape through her mind's eye in the world. It was the voice of her father calling to her, and the soft sadness of her mother's tears that she could see in front of her, like tears of blood, as she struggled to keep up.

"God bless you, darling!" Abby cried.

"Mum! Mum!" Tyro screamed, seeing the agony of her mother falling to the ground. Dennis bent beside her to help her.

"Go, Tyro! We will be alright! Go! Go now! Make for home!" Abby fell to the ground.

The swarm of figures descended on them.

Tyro saw the Stranger. She could not wait, or she would be captured too.

She was terrified. She wished she could fly again, though she felt too old. There were different ways to fly, Tom had said. She wanted to kill the Stranger.

"Why am I so weak? Why are we all so weak in the face of darkness?" she screamed aloud as she made towards the energy wall in front of her, her body slowing.

The Stranger and other figures were closing.

"We have her now!" he cried.

*

Mr Rummage was back on the parapet, struggling to focus the energy to curb the Stranger's power.

He could do nothing about the wall. The wall that had been created - from where or how he did not know - to keep the Priory in, would also prevent him from leaving. Thus they would all be prisoners.

Tyro prayed as she stumbled to the wall. She held the object out in front of her.

She felt a gap, a hole, an invisible space through which she could wriggle.

There was no time to delay. She slipped through without a word, even to wave goodbye.

The Stranger reached the place, but was locked in. He turned in fury at his crew and ordered them to break through.

Abby, now on her feet, and Dennis came up to a point nearby. They watched Tyro through the translucent shield drift out beyond it into the fresh air, her cloak trailing behind her, tears in their eyes, unable to help. "God's speed," Abby whispered.

The Stranger rushed upon Dennis and thrust him aside, Dennis struggling to hold him. Dennis pulled back the figure's hooded head and stared into the face, swearing revenge. Dennis held a piece of cloak which made the Stranger more angry. Strong though he was, and trained enough to quell certain forces, he was no match, though he did not give in easily. Dennis fought and fought like a caged lion trying to block the figure's path, to trip it, to hold it back, and down. To obscure its view, to keep it from the path it sought.

Tyro had gained a little more time, though the Stranger knew he could not follow by this route. He would have to go another way.

*

Passing between the two domains, Tyro came out on the other side into the fresh night air. The air was still and, though autumnal, spring-like in its fragrance. The moon was clearly visible and full. The school behind her at the end of the long drive, opaque behind the veil. The softness of the air made her pause. Her tiredness conspired against her freedom. She waited for a moment hoping that Jess and Rick would come, or her mother who she could see trying to face down the Stranger, with Dennis and now Inspector Relish. But they were nowhere to be seen.

She took off her cloak and shoved it into the pack that she carried. She decided that she must make for the sea, through the wood at the back of Mr Gruff's house, if necessary going via one of the tunnels if she could find the entrance. This would give her cover from pursuit. Going home would be a mistake, she felt sure.

She ran and ran, soon obscure in the trees close to Mr Gruff's house. She ran towards the river, but decided not to go to the river's edge, rather to keep above it, along the hedge that skirted the field. She put the object in her pocket. It seemed weightless now. It was more like a companion than a burden. Still she missed the cross-sword about her neck.

Tyro knew that there would not be many minutes before she was followed. She assumed they would be upon her soon. She looked about her as she ran, fearful of the shadows in the trees.

Yet it seemed that all the figures were now trapped in the dome. Perhaps in this new world of hers, adjacent to the world of fear from which she had come, there were no shadows.

She came to Shelter Field. She did not know of any tunnel entrance nearby. She continued past the brightly lit Burnchester Arms, from which noise and joviality spilled out into the night, as if the revellers were ignorant of the horrendous events nearby. She wondered that Mr Gatherin had not heard. She did not dare go in, fearing to draw attention to herself, knowing that the Stranger had once been there and might yet have peopled it with spies.

She thought that she was being followed. She hoped it might be Jess or Rick playing a trick on her, so she called out.

She wanted to go home, turn north and run over the fields, and curl up beside Biscuit and fall asleep, while listening to music. Even washing-up and homework seemed like bliss. But something about the thought of the old house, large and empty, made her afraid. It was a risk she dared not take.

She thought of Biscuit lying on the bed, and of the adventures she and Biscuit had had, when she was little, as she wandered over the lawn, a little girl, playing, living out the stories that her father had told her. She thought of Rompy. She felt sure he would like to come too, wherever she was going. No amount of adventure would be enough for him. He didn't know fear. He had that happy ability to go anywhere and make the most of it, even if he put himself in danger from keepers who might not be so sympathetic to his wanderings, danger from cars who might not see him, danger from getting lost, wandering far from home.

She could go back and hide up close to the school. There were many people ready to help, who would come to her aid, as long as she stayed nearby. Perhaps she should go back inside with the others. What did it matter if the Priory got hold of the object that she held, as long as she was safe and she could be with her friends and her family? She longed for Jess and Rick. And Tom. She had seen him again and he had given her hope. The other two would find her, she had no doubt. The three had agreed a plan to meet. They were bound to come.

Then she remembered the Dark Master, and the Stranger. She remembered their own imprisonment. She knew that the object - whatever it was - must not fall into their hands. She thought of throwing it into the sea.

Tyro thought of Mr Rummage's plan. She determined to get some distance from the school, and then phone her mother, or Dennis, to see if there was any change, if they could meet. But of course they were trapped too.

Tyro did not want to be stopped by the military or the police, until she had decided what to do with the object. She was afraid what they might do with it. She wanted to make sure it was put in a place where it could not be found or destroyed. She did not know where this might be. She continued to run. Then she turned to see if the huge dome of energy was visible. She had not seen it fully until now.

There it was in the near distance, like a huge pointed cone - quite like a large spearhead - against the dark sky, a curious filter of light, from which little escaped. She could see the glimmer of reflections in the walls. The sight of the dome gave her some reassurance. At least it was not a dream, at least she was still sane. But she was wet and tired and dirty, and she had no food. The shape seemed like a large spacecraft ready to launch into the night sky.

She realised after some minutes that she was not alone. When she passed on the far side of the Burnchester Arms, she felt eyes were watching her, but she could not tell whose. Even in the open fields, and along the lanes that she ran, she sensed that others were with her. She must not show fear.

She continued to walk over the fields. The night was still, the stars high and clear, the moon full. This was the freshness of the countryside that she adored. She took a deep breath of the clear air.

She wondered if she would fly again. Where would she fly to? To her Aunt Jane perhaps, or to the beach where they had gone in the summer, or to the town of Wyemarket, and to the cafés or shops there, where she was known. There were plenty of people there or in her village who would take her in, but she dared not risk it. Besides, she couldn't fly. She tried a little jump. It was no good. Perhaps she never had.

Tyro looked about her. Though she was much older now and she carried an object of great power and beauty, she felt a lightness in her feet. Perhaps her body was trying to compensate for a lack of food, and pretend to her that there was nothing to worry about. Perhaps the lack of food made her lighter. But that didn't work either. She was very tired. She knew she could sleep, but she did not dare to stop.

She started to skip and run at the same time. She felt like a child again, skipping along in the still night. She tried it again, and this time her skip seemed longer. She seemed to hang a little in the air and glide downwards gently before touching down again.

Again she skipped. This time she hovered above the ground for several seconds while the grass passed under her feet, and then she descended and touched down. She could not believe her senses. She felt guilty. She stopped. Looked around. Faced forward. Ran a little. Skipped. There it was again. The floating step - whoops, she nearly fell over backwards - that carried her along for several metres above the earth completely weightless, before giving up and depositing her on the ground. Not quite as before, more like a private show, an experiment to give herself confidence.

This time she slid and fell backwards onto the grass. She was not used to it. She was not concentrating. She was upset, and even wetter now. But there was no doubt about it. She had been flying.

Tyro lay on her back and looked up at the stars.

If she could fly again, what use would it be? What use were

dreams without people? What use was flying without a destination? It was all very well having fun, but she was older now. Think what her mother would say. And her father. Where was he? Up there too. Perhaps she could reach him by flying, if he was in Heaven, assuming there was one. She didn't believe there was.

Dreams were nothing without people.

She was a few metres from a small road that led the back way to Greenfield, which she had travelled on with Jess and Rick, over the summer. If she went right she would head towards the sea, if straight on she would pass Rick's house, and the churchyard where she and Jess had lost the Stranger, and escaped into the tunnel that led back to the school. She thought again about the boat on the underground stream. Perhaps the boat would carry her to the place she needed to go. She saw herself swimming in the South of France, and going under, searching the depths. She saw the octopus. She thought of Warblersbay, with its cautious simplicity, and Dunemoor's ruins beneath the sea. Should she go there?

What she needed most was the warmth of home. What larks!

There was no going back. She could not tell how far or where it would lead, and what adventures would befall her, but she sensed a growing strength which made her who she was. She forgot that shadows might follow her, and try to take her on a journey of their own, and rob her of the gift that she possessed, and the power that she held. She dismissed her dreams of flight. There was no need for either in her new world. She thought of the castle in the picture and of the sick eagle. Ever onward, ever upward, the journey hidden and obscure.

The evening of fireworks came to her mind, and waterfights, and running around the glorious fields, with the rain pouring, and people mingling on the tired grass. She remembered the motley crew of dancers, and was reminded of her English lesson and the witches, of which she had been one. Mr Baxter and Ms Peverell. They would be there too. What was Mr Baxter thinking, bringing the dancers, confusing everybody? And Mr Rummage on the roof of the school? Who were those coming to the sacrifice?

The illusion had been shattered by the arrival of the dark figures, like souls, and the screams of children, and the bewilderment of parents. Mr Rummage had disappeared. Where had he gone? She wondered about the huge force field which shut people in and out. There it was! Look! She remembered the Image from the painting.

She wondered what would happen when the news broke. People from all around would come to look, and to lend a hand to set people free. But what use would they be? They could not get in. Nor could those inside get out. Would those inside be trapped for eternity, in constant battle or in a constant standoff, fighting illusions, for a piece of history that had gone missing?

She hadn't even looked at the object properly. It was so simple, just an oval shape. Hardly a Spearhead. Not the Spearhead. Surely not *the* Spearhead.

She walked back in the direction of Greenfield. There beside the road was a little hut, where someone probably kept their garden tools. No, she would not go there, she would walk on, she would head for home after all, and on the way find the ditch at the end of the field, the ditch she had walked along as a child and hidden in, in the roots of trees, until her mother and father became frantic and came in search. So she trudged over the damp meadow behind the church of Greenfield.

She walked for over half an hour. She was too tired to go on. She lay down, shivering, barely able to stand.

The eyes were all about her. Watching.

She lay down beneath the roots of an old tree, the selfsame that had held her young shape many years before. She was asleep, in a cup of leaves. She might have been in the forest of Arden.

The eyes watched, then moved forward. Others stood close by. They came up to her, sniffed and retreated a little way. Just enough to keep a safe distance. Just enough to keep an eye on her. They were aware of the terrible events in the school, just as they were aware of Mr Pinchet's vermin control, but could not do anything about it, try as they might from time to time. Sentient beings know when something is wrong.

The forces of good are not always visible, sometimes they hold back. There are many worlds, always awake to those who seek or see. The forces of the other side are not always visible either, but they generate a different atmosphere. And this was not theirs. Besides, tempestuous storms generate a level of alert which necessitates higher understanding of the forces from the skies - we will not say Heaven, though it may be quite like it.

*

In the distance, inside the wall of energy, there was a stand-off. Mr Rummage had returned to take charge. He had done what he could in the Domed Chamber. He had activated the energy sources below, to try to counter the dark powers. But this time his skill was unequal. Perhaps the absence of the object that Tyro had been given left him a little vulnerable. Otherwise he might have had the upper hand. But the Priory figures could do little more without the same object. They were angry and some tried to lash out at the parents, who held their children tight. But the Stranger held them back. It was Tyro that he and they were after now, and Jess and Rick. They would lead him to the Spearhead. Yet they were trapped inside the dome. They must find a way to follow. Otherwise they would take Mr Rummage.

Most parents and children had returned inside the school. Some had tried to escape, in vain.

Though in disarray, the figures were not in retreat. An

argument had arisen between figures of different orders and groups, and it was this which prevented a potential disaster, the taking of hostages or worse. Mr Rummage knew that though the barrier to the outside held them in as much as others out, including the figures, he also knew that they could escape by a subterranean route, into the darkest recesses of the hidden tunnels below, into unknown territory, and they might take some people with them. They would also try to follow Tyro.

Mr Rummage had asked the military to block all exits as far as they could, and seal off the escape routes they might take. By doing so, however, he might also block off his own, should he need it, and the escape of others. He would have to use his secret way.

Mr Rummage's proximity to the figures allowed him to watch them. Mr Baxter went so far as to ask them about themselves, a level of curiosity which led to outrage, and a fight between Mr Baxter, Dennis and two of the figures.

Being understood was not something that the enemy wanted. Part of this lay in the need for anonymity. Part of the illusion of its potency lay in the fear it evoked in other people's ignorance. To become integrated into the whole was not in the interests of the demonic. It wanted the territory for itself, not to be recognised and have its power diffused, except on its own terms, with total control over others.

Mr Rummage knew that by keeping the figures in, Tyro would have some time to make her escape.

Rick and Jess were desperate to join Tyro. They would have to go below ground. Rick had his map. They were ready.

*

Tyro's face was still. Her body relaxed. She had hidden the object inside a pocket and wrapped it in a handkerchief. She was asleep.

305

Not far along the ditch, deep down, in the realm of an ancient root, a door opened.

Tyro dreamed. In her dream, she rose high into the air. She was flying. At first she was excited, because she could remember the feeling well, and was glad to recapture it. She was alone, but it did not matter, for it was day, and she was now above her own house, in summer, some years before. Her father was in the garden digging. He loved to dig. He always said that this was the way to travel. If you want to explore the universe he said, look down, as well as up.

"What are you digging for, Dad?" Tyro asked.

"What does anybody dig for, Ty?" her father replied. "One day you will dig for yourself, and the answers will come one by one. Worms, old bones, tunnels. The stars. You might even find the head of an arrow, gold. A Spearhead even."

To her father of course, she was standing next to him. So he handed her the spade and asked her to have a go. But to her, she was in the sky, watching. So she refused.

"How can you reach the stars by digging, Dad?"

Then her father had gone and she was higher than she wanted to be and became afraid. The familiar sights of home and the places that she knew well and could identify were only a fragment in the bigger story, now lost pieces in the jigsaw of time and place, and memory. Everything joined invisibly by a Hand larger than anybody's on earth. Above and below. The old alchemists knew.

She could see the countryside around, her mind was spinning as clouds appeared. She was lost and afraid, trying to steady herself, crying, "Why me?" She longed for her mum, and Rompy and Biscuit and Jess and an end to this sad search - which had only just begun - because it only brought trouble and difficulties, and she wanted peace and calm and simplicity and a home life, just like a cat. And a mother and father.

Tyro travelled higher and saw the oceans (was that a whale?) and the countries' shores, and the curve of the earth, turning, as she rose, into a globe of mixed colours in a vaster firmament of light and dark, brilliant and alive.

She went higher still, much faster than any object known to humankind, many hundreds, thousands, hundreds of thousands of millions of billions of trillions of infinite moments above the earth in the empty kingdom of infinite space, full of silence and surprises like nothing on this earth, yet unable to be reached without it. Here, too, eyes watched. Not the same genus, but belonging to some other life form which had grown like our own, apparently from nothing, but conjoined with these by mysteries and travel and interconnections of which we were afraid or would deny. One day they would meet.

This would make a wonderful essay for school (Tyro thought), now travelling at the speed of eternity ready to land for sandwiches and tea on the nearest moon, if they would have her. And would there be figures here too, and people wanting what other people had, always putting themselves above others, and not listening or loving, or being anything other than rather selfish, but human all the same?

Perhaps there was no evil up here, it was just part of the parody of happiness on earth, a futile place missing the point of its purpose. Isn't that what the Spearhead might provide? A galvanising symbol?

And there below, in the infinitesimal small, she could see the places of worship. These places came and went, and changed shape and sometimes positions, and spread and contracted, like the impulse of a heart, or an invading army. People could be seen inside them, and outside them, and away from them. Some were broken and bare, others new, often close to each other, many built from the ruins of the old. Only the impulse was ever present, the energy, the drawing down of the spirit into symbols by which the great Invisible only can be seen.

She tried to imagine the Church of All Saints next to her house, and then she saw it, and the church of St Mary Magdalen, and she saw the Face in the picture, an image on

307

canvas, nothing more, an image drawn down by the divine in man, inspired by God. What image would be next? What images would supplant those we know now, what would the future Domes contain? The Face in the picture remained static. "Thou sayest," a voice had replied. The canvas was blank. The Figure had gone.

There, three figures robed in white, more ancient still.

Tyro could see into the observation tower of the school.

The next moment she was at home again. Her mother was calling from downstairs, telling her to get ready for school. She turned over and fell asleep.

Dancing shapes. Music. Animals came and went. Some standing sentinel.

From the open door came a figure. Its feet were long, its toes like twigs with spiky turned up ends. Its legs thick and trunk-like, its body straight, its arms like the branches of a wavy tree. It had hair sticking out on its head and long hair down the sides of its face. It seemed to belong to the earth, or the forest, it being a sort of browny-green. It wasn't clear whether the figure wore a robe, or whether there was just a mass of wavy hair tumbling down its body.

The figure was sprightly and walked towards the sleeping girl.

In his hand he held some dried leaves. Perhaps they were herbs.

He stood by the girl, beneath the moon.

The first light of dawn was creeping over the horizon. He looked at the girl without any expression and threw leaves over her, as if to keep her warm. He bent his head, as if listening, and straightened it again.

He seemed satisfied. He put his hand in her pocket and took out the object, which shone in the night. He opened it. He looked inside. He shut it again, and placed it back in her pocket. He turned and went back to the open door, entered, closed it, and was not seen again.

Tyro awoke and felt something close by her. At first she jumped. Then the warm thing started to lick her, and she could feel a tail smacking against her legs.

"Rompy! What are you doing here?"

She tried to give Rompy a hug, but he was trying to drag her over the open ground, as if to show her something.

Putting her hands up to her eyes, Tyro got up. She would shortly be back on the road to Greenfield, and be able to have breakfast at home. She seemed dazed, as if she had forgotten where she was.

It was hot and dry in the heat of the sun. She became confused. She was nowhere near the ditch where she had fallen asleep. She remembered the ditch now, and the night's events were coming back to her. She looked about her for clues. The dome. The field. Where were they? There was nothing.

She started to cry. Rompy was ahead of her, with his back to her, his tail wagging.

She tried to phone her mum. It rang and rang, but there was no answer, just her mum's voice asking her to leave a message.

She could feel the wind through her hair, which she wanted to brush. Her clothes were dry, which surprised her, and so was the land. Hadn't they had a huge storm? Shouldn't it be covered in puddles from the torrent of the previous night? The ground was a bit sandy too.

She moved towards Rompy and stood next to him. She reached down and gave him a pat, thanking him for coming to find her. He had come a long way on his own.

Rompy would be trouble to look after. She could fend for herself - if she had to - but fending for a dog might not be so easy. Still, she couldn't take him back, especially as she didn't know where she was. She thought of Rick and Jess. The object. Where was it? She checked her pockets. It was still there.

She stood staring ahead. There in front of her, and below her, was the sea, waves beating in the brilliant sun against the stony shore. To her left was a village skyline she recognised. She was determined to go and find some breakfast. To her right in the distance she could see the cliffs.

She remembered the summer. Everything became familiar.

Tyro looked back at the place where she had woken from, a shallow beneath a patch of heather.

"Come on Rompy, we'll go and find some food."

Rompy led the way onto the beach, which she could follow left towards the village.

Crunch crunch went her feet on the stone.

*

There was a sudden cry.

Out at sea was a small boat, not much more than a dinghy. Two people were trying to stand up, but having to sit down with the movement of the waves. Hands were waving furiously. Tyro looked towards the boat as carefully as she could, but didn't recognise the shapes.

It was only when Rompy's name was called and he raced into the water and swam out towards them that Tyro knew.

She threw her pack into the air. She raced into the water until it was up to her waist, and then up to her neck and soon she was having to swim, though the boat had got a little closer. She began to choke in her excitement, as two pairs of hands tried to grab hold of her and eventually hauled her in. Rompy was already there.

Tyro rolled onto the bottom of the boat. A pair of arms were thrown around her in a big, wet hug. The arms belonged to Jess.

Tyro righted herself.

"Jess! Rick! What . . . Oh no! My pack. I've left it on the shore!"

"It's OK, we'll go back for it," said Rick, "we've got to get some food anyway, stock up. Prepare. Rumbags was right. We're on our own now. We haven't much time."

They looked at each other and laughed.

"Prepare! I want some food now! Let's go and have breakfast in the village. What day of the week is it?" asked Tyro, "Rick, Jess! What are you doing here? How did you get here? Is Mum alright? What happened? And the boat? Is this the boat from the tunnel?"

"The others are still enclosed in the wall. We only just managed to escape. We think three of the Priory did too. We were followed."

Jess looked towards the cliff-tops, as the boat came closer to the shore. Close enough for Rick to jump overboard and wade to the beach and collect Tyro's bag.

The tide was coming in and the wind was getting up off the sea.

Rick threw the bag to Tyro who was now sitting upright. He pushed the boat round and climbed aboard again. Tyro went up to him and gave him a hug.

"Thanks, Rick,"

"I presume you've still got it," said Jess.

"I've no idea what to do with it. I was going to throw it into the sea."

"Not very sensible. Rumbags gave us further instructions. He got them to us just in time. The object is very important. It might save us all. We must on no account let anybody take it."

Rick let out the mainsheet until it caught the breeze.

"Let's go and get that food," he said.

Tyro raised her eyes and looked at Jess. Beyond, she saw a figure on the cliff-tops. There seemed to be smoke rising in the far distance.

"Thanks for being here. I didn't fancy being on my own."

"I remembered what you said."

"Thanks, Jess. You're a real friend."

"I can't say I'm looking forward to it."

"We have no choice."

"We'll be alright, together."

Tyro joined Rick at the tiller and the two of them steered the boat out to sea, as Jess took the jib sheet. The boat, however, seemed to be powered by its own force. The three of them looked at each other, and laughed.

The boat took them into the little harbour, where they could stock up and have breakfast.

As they approached the harbour wall, Tyro recognised the Harbourmaster's hut.

They were surprised to see the Harbourmaster carrying a large bulging bag.

"Instructions from Dennis and Mrs Wander to give you this," Mr Greenshank said. "Everything you need. A radio in case you need to call the coastguard. Food for days. Sleeping bags, torches, wet weather gear. There's some sort of instrument in the bag too, with instructions. Suggest you get going. It seems that figures have escaped."

Mr Greenshank made a point of handing the bag to Tyro and bending down, just as they were about to tie the boat up.

"Thank you Mr Greenshank, but we wanted to have breakfast," Tyro said, trying not to sound offhand.

Mr Greenshank looked about him and then at the three young people.

He didn't need to say anything. They had already seen. Two figures were at the far end of the harbour, asking questions. They knew who they were.

"Head north. Your mother and Dennis and the others will follow if they can."

"Is it safe?"

Seeing the difficulty they were having getting the boat out, Mr Greenshank jumped aboard and took the tiller. As he did so he told them to duck down.

In minutes they were heading out to sea again.

"Are they alright, Mum and Dad?" Jess asked nervously, speaking for all of them.

"They are all still trapped inside the school. The place is surrounded. Police, military everywhere. Haven't you seen the aircraft overhead? It'll be all over the news by now. Nobody can get in or get out. There have been incidents elsewhere too. It's spreading."

As the boat reached the harbour mouth, Mr Greenshank handed Tyro the tiller and leapt across to some rocks at the base of the pier, nearly slipping into the sea.

"By the way," Mr Greenshank shouted above the breeze. "If you see strange lights, do not be afraid. Good luck!"

They had sailed too far to hear any more. They waved goodbye.

There were a few minutes silence. The need to make headway forced them to concentrate.

"This is it," said Tyro aloud. "The beginning of the journey."

She was looking into the watery depths, wondering if the octopus had come.

Also available: The Mysterious Burnchester Hall

Books can be ordered from any bookshop
email: burnchesterdome@yahoo.co.uk